FOREVER FILTHY

DIRTY TEMPTATION SERIES
BOOK 2

SAMANTHA BARRETT

First Edition.

Cover Art by LM Designs

Formatting by Jaye Pratt

Editing by Elizabeth Gardner

*You like to be fucked with the lights off?
What about being fucked in the woods in broad daylight by
masked men who have been hunting you?
Turn the page, stroke that clit and get ready to get wet.*

CHAPTER ONE

Vivian

"Lordess, we must leave now to make it to the opening in time." I lift my gaze from the stack of books scattered around my desk and sigh. At the rate I'm going I will never pass any of my college classes!

"Okay, David." I say as I grab my purse, pull my dress down, fluff my hair, and deem myself ready. Given that I am only nineteen and still have not graduated from college has some of the members of The Brotherhood unhappy about me becoming their lordess. I weeded out a lot of the assholes that voiced their loyalty to Thomas Valerian, the previous lord that ordered my father and Ezekiel's dad to be killed.

A lot of people think I was handed this role, they have no idea the amount of struggles I faced in order to claim my birthright.

"You also have a meeting with Brodie Holmes regarding the new expansion to the high school," he reminds me as we walk outside. I nod and pull out my phone to make sure I have my notes handy. I spend the car ride to the opening going over my notes and making sure I have all the key points highlighted and ready to go. Brodie is the best contractor in the county and he is one of the few people in this town that can't be bought. He won't proceed with the expansion unless I can prove to him that this will benefit the community.

For the past year, I have spent all of my time trying to right the wrongs of the lords before me, including both mine and Ezekiel's fathers. I know my brother and his best friend think that the light shined out of our dad's asses but the truth is, they were just as hungry for money as Thomas. My twin brother always held a candle to my father's memory and thought he was a God. All his efforts to keep me from ever leading the Haven Saint's was for nothing. Vox has no idea our father and Ezekiel's were just as bad as Thomas.

Just thinking about my brother has a sharp pain making itself known in my chest, every time I think about him or my best friend Nova, nostalgia always hits me like a bitch. The lies and secrets are what tore us apart. Well, his secrets and my lies, or maybe it was the other way around? Who the fuck knows but for a solid year I have been on my own. I won't allow my mother to visit me, the backlash I received when I took over the Saint's still holds a bitter taste in my mouth so the further away from me she is, the better.

"Lordess, we are arriving now." I nod and slip my mask into place, as I said before, I am nineteen so it's not ideal for me to be seen as the face of a multi-billion-dollar operation.

"David, tonight needs to go off without a hitch. This is the first big night for me as the Lordess of the Haven Saint's and I can't afford you fucking it up by calling me *lordess*."

He cringes and nods. "Are you sure this is the way you want to do things?" I can hear the uncertainty in his voice and I get it, I really do but right now with the stigma and the blowback from Thomas's shady dealings, I have no other choice but to be in the background and watch from a distance. Tonight is the first night that we will have all the big players and the big names under one roof. Only the members in The Brotherhood of Hollow Hills know I am the lordess, as far as all our *partners* around the world know, David is the L, of the Saint's. I want to sit back and watch tonight and see who can be trusted and who doesn't think with their cock!

"Yes, I want to judge them. A lot of these men will think it unwise that a woman is the leader of a brotherhood and I want to hear their unfiltered thoughts. I want to see them and watch how they move, interact and deal with the women tonight."

"I understand, Lord—Vivian." I smile and shoot him a wink.

"Now you're getting it, Davey-boy," I coo, earning a stern look from my right-hand man. I never thought David and I would become as close as we have and even I have to admit, I wouldn't have gotten this far without him. He was an unlikely ally and someone I thought would rise against me. In the time I spent gathering intel and finding weak spots in The Brotherhood for Nikoa Tempest—Ezekiel's estranged uncle—I thought David to be loyal to only Thomas. Turns out I was wrong and I have never been happier about that.

I glance out the window and smile at the sight of *Lividica*. The hotel is a front, what's behind the glitz and glam of the hotel is where the real money is. I needed to make a statement when I first took over and knew instantly this would be the way to not only please the members of the Haven Saints but it would also create more jobs for the locals. As much as the men detest the fact that they are being led by a woman, they couldn't help but be overjoyed by Lividica's grand opening. Not only did I win brownie points for this opening but the fact

I have made them all swear to keep my status as lordess a secret seemed to go over way too well. "There was another letter," David says so casually before he climbs out of the car, I force myself to remain calm and get my game face on. David extends his hand inside the car.

I place my hand in his and allow him to help me out of the car. I'm instantly blinded by the flash of cameras and fight the urge to lift my arm to cover my eyes and hide. David places his hand on my lower back and I stiffen without meaning to. I keep a fake ass smile on my face and allow him to lead me inside the hotel. This place is awe-inspiring from the outside but upon entering, the opulence is next level. The inside is decorated in red, black and gold. The furniture is sleek, and the waitresses and waiters are dressed in the finest uniforms but this is just a front for what is behind those big red doors. Guests can book rooms and spend as long as they like here, but unless they are members of Lividica they cannot enter these doors.

David stands in the lobby and makes small talk with a few people while I observe everyone. I take in the crowd as we all wait for one of the hostesses to announce that we can enter. Pride simmers inside me, I made all of this possible. I brought this dream to life. Those old fucks may not want me here but I also won't allow them to push me out. I originally wanted to shut the Saints down and say fuck you to The Brotherhood that cost me my father but when I looked deeper into their records and actually listened to the stories some of the members told me about my father, I learned he wasn't the man we thought he was.

"This here is my date, Emily." At the mention of my fake name, I push away those thoughts and turn my attention to the two men David is speaking with and smile politely. It grates on my nerves when their gazes immediately drop to my tits and the older man with the receding hairline smirks. David clears his throat pulling their gazes back to him. "Emily, meet Drew Anders and Ford Booth." I smile and nod. "They are owners of Anders Booth Construction." It hits me then, these men are the ones that Thomas used to build his condos and homes for his real estate business, they are crooked and pay whoever they need to so they can cut through the red tape and sell shitty homes to good people.

"We were just telling David here how perplexed we are that our services weren't called upon to build this place," Drew, the older man, says. I force a smile and wait for David to answer, I need to see how he does under pressure.

"Your services are always needed but for this particular project we went with the company that the architect we hired recommended to bring this masterpiece to life. They did extraordinary things, don't you think?" David doesn't wait for their reply, he leads me over to another group of men who introduce themselves as the councilmen. These men at least have the decency to try and be discreet about their ogling of my tits. The way they speak about me like I'm not here is fucking disgusting.

This just cements it for me, I plan to steer The Brotherhood away from these crooked fucks by taking us in a direction where we can all make money and not rip people off in the process. Lividica was built to win over the brothers but it was also built to help the people of our community. I want to do shit like this, not rip people off just to line my own pockets. Unlike the lords before me, I don't see people as a way to make a quick buck. I think that if I can form the right bonds with certain people we will all be able to work together and help each other build something fucking epic.

A waiter comes into the lobby and takes all the hotel guests to the next level where the ballroom is so they can enjoy a live show and free meal courtesy of Lividica while the *others* stay down here, these are the men who are involved in all things to do with The Brotherhood and we cannot allow the general public to be around when we discuss business. Once the guests file out there are only roughly forty or so people left in the lobby.

A hush falls over the room when the lights dim and the windows and large glass doors that allow the press to see inside turn black to block out their view. The big red doors open and nerves begin to take flight inside me as I watch the reactions of everyone in the room, the men look excited and almost eager while the minimal women who are here look bored. I designed this place to captivate not only the men but the women as well.

A gorgeous brunette appears in the doorway wearing a sexy red lace lingerie set that has the men clearing their throats and reaching up to loosen their ties. Her eyes are alight and the blood-red lipstick she wears enhances her full lips.

"Welcome to Lividica where the seven deadly sins are welcomed and all kinks are praised and embraced by different women *and* men." Her sultry voice echoes around the lobby sending tingles down my spine. I look at the women who now seem intrigued and ready for what lays beyond these doors. The possibilities of what this place can offer are endless.

CHAPTER TWO

Vivian

Everyone follows the hostess while David and I hang back, when the lobby is finally empty he turns to me with a triumphant look that sends pride swirling inside me.

"I doubted you." His words have me reeling back but I remain silent. "I thought you were crazy for wanting to open this place, I never thought a palace like Lividica belonged in Hollow Hills but it turns out, I was wrong. Judging by the looks on the guy's faces who don't even know what awaits them inside there, they will all want a Lividica in their hometowns."

"And the women?" I press.

He smirks and nods. "Stephanie Jones, Jimmy's wife is one of the hardest women to ever get to crack a smile or even hold her interest for more than a second but tonight, when those doors opened, I never saw the smile fall once on her face and she was one of the first people to follow our hostess."

I search his eyes trying to detect any lies but I see nothing but the truth. "Do you think The Brotherhood will be pleased?"

He nods eagerly. "Yes, I think you have certainly won most of them over with this venture."

"Most?"

His face falls. "Lor–Vivian, you have to understand that these men are hard-headed. No matter what you do, some of them will never be okay with a woman leading them. They see women as an accessory and nothing more." I clench my fists at my sides and bite down on the inside of my cheek to keep my retort inside, these fuckers still think women are to be seen and not heard. Well newsflash for these cocksuckers, I'm the boss and they had better get used to being beneath me.

I allow David to lead me through the doors, and the two guards who man the entrance pull them closed after we enter. The walls are covered in silk drapes, and the color theme in here is the same as out front but somehow, it seems different. It feels... darker and more sinister. I smile at each of the girls as we pass them, they all wear different types of lingerie and some have even dressed for role play, school girls, teachers, nuns, you name it and Lividica has it. Most of the men are already seated around the tables in the main lounge room with girls in their laps.

I see the wives or dates of these pigs standing off to the side. David follows my gaze, then gives me a gentle nudge. I take a deep breath then lock eyes with Tatum Lawson, the manager I hired to run all things Lividica. She nods then steps out from behind the bar, unlike the other women who work here Tate dresses in a pair of black slacks and a white blouse. The girl is effortlessly beautiful, her long blonde hair is out and curled, her makeup is minimal but enough to make her blue eyes pop. The men all turn their attention to the blonde goddess. Unlike me,

Tate doesn't falter under the pressure of their gazes, she lifts her chin and shows them she is not someone to be fucked with.

"Ladies, why don't you allow Andre to show you to the *women's* den where all fantasies and desires are met and brought to life in a single night? Allow them to give you the gift of something unholy." The ladies cheeks all tinge pink and some even shake their heads and wave away the offer but it's their eyes and the intrigue in them that give them away. Their curiosity is peaked, they want the fantasy Tate has promised. They all want to be worshiped by a man who will ensure they are pleased and will make it their life mission to make sure they come before they do.

When a woman shoots her husband a look asking for guidance, he waves her away, unbothered by the fact she is about to be brought into a separate room that is filled with men dressed for *them*. Unlike men, women will have a separate entrance into here. Women are more discreet with their desires and wants so I wanted to make sure that we not only catered to the carnal needs of the men but also to the women. I want them to frequent Lividica and tell other women about it, unlike men. You can guarantee that women will talk and spread the word discreetly if they are satisfied.

Tate motions for Andre, who is dressed in a suit, to lead the ladies down another corridor and into their section where their husbands can't get to them. The only people with keys to that back half are Tate and Andre, not even I have a key to that room with me tonight. It not only protects the men who work for me but, if a husband were to discover his wife's affair, also protects the identities of the men and women who visit.

Before the night can carry on and the men take the girls off into the rooms allocated to each girl, David steps forward and nods for Tate to silence the music and brighten the lights.

Grumbles sound out around the room but quickly stop when David clears his throat and draws all eyes to him.

"This better be good, I have a hot piece of ass here ready to suck my cock," a ruddy red-haired man with a pot belly shouts out. I keep the disgust from splaying across my face at the sight of the front of his pants tenting. The brunette at beside him smiles up at him and pats his chest sexily. Every woman in this room is here of their own free will and knows they can quit or stop any sexual act at any time. My employee's safety is the most important thing to me above all else and I will not allow any of them to be harmed or treated poorly, all for a buck.

"Before the evening's festivities can continue, I believe we all have some business to discuss." A few rounds of grumbles and boos go around the room but David holds up a hand silencing them all. "If there is no business then there is no pleasure." The girls instantly stand from the men's laps, the others pull away and move toward Tate who now stands at the back of the room with four guards who are hired to man this section of the hotel only. We have a roster of twenty guards, four in here and four in the ladies section, they change out every six hours with two men always manning the red doors at the front. When the red-haired man from earlier tries to reach for the girl who is at his side, Tate smacks his hand away and glares.

"You may be some big shot out there but in here, I'm the fucking boss," she snarls, the man turns a shade of red as his anger rises. "You make one wrong move and I will throw your fucking ass out of here and sever your membership." Her threat meets its mark when the man growls in her face and then waves his hand as if dismissing a dog. I shoot Tate a discreet look that I hope conveys my thanks for her handling that situation, but I can see much like myself she wants to smack that asshole.

"Now, let us establish the rules," David says. "Your

membership covers the cost of admission but not the fee of the girls. Each of them charges their own fee, which is to be paid before anyone is getting a happy ending." The firm tone he uses is shocking, I've never heard David sound so... dominate. "If any of the girls hit the red buzzer in the room, you will be removed immediately and your membership will be revoked. Before any of you start voicing your disgruntlement, remember that you all have signed NDA's. If any of you break those terms then you will be hunted and let me assure each of you, my brothers are not the forgiving type and will make sure that the price of your error will cost you your life." Many of them turn solemn and some of the playfulness has left them as David's words sink in. "Ladies, would you excuse us for a moment?" All the girls nod their heads and Tate leads them to the back where the locker rooms are.

"Let us get this discussion done before my wife comes back and ruins my fun with that fine piece of ass." Disgust rolls through me at the councilman's comment, what he doesn't realize is his wife would have forgotten all about him and his piggish ways the moment she entered the other section.

"With the new leadership of the Haven Saints, I know there have been some... worries—"

"With you now leading, there are no issues but when we heard a bitch wanted to be lordess..." The man lets his sentence trail off while the others laugh, some remain silent and say nothing. But I know this man, this is Clive Bruce. He is the district attorney and as dirty as they fucking come. From my understanding he is the very man who made evidence disappear in the Alexander Denver case that may have proven his innocence. Thanks to Clive, we will never know if Alex was ever innocent.

David doesn't falter in his response. "Edmund Tempest

decreed nearly twenty-one years ago that a woman would lead the Saints and as one of the founding members, I would have thought you would have supported our previous lords declaration, Clive." The man himself turns a shade of red as he narrows his eyes on David.

"I respected Edmund and Virgil but both of them were weak, Thomas at least had the balls to do what needed to be done."

Fuck this!

"My name isn't Emily," I announce. The men look at me with irritated looks.

"No one cares, fuck off in the back with the rest of the whores," Clarence Howard calls out—he's trying to run for senate.

"You'll pay for that comment!" David snaps.

Before anyone else can cut in, I push on. "My name is Vivian Tempest and I am the Lordess of the Haven Saints." Their faces all wear varying looks of shock, outrage and downright hatred. "Tonight was a test, a test most of you failed. I wanted to see how each of you conducted yourselves without knowing who I am. You all disappointed me except for a mere few."

"You can't test us—"

I cut Clive off before the asshole can continue. "Yes the fuck I can and I just did. Now sit your ass down and listen closely because I will not repeat myself, Mr. Bruce." He shoots me a scathing look but does as he's told. I run my gaze over all of them, noting how some of them stare at me with respect while others look at me like I am a blow fly they want to squash. "You may not like the title I wear but that's too fucking bad. I didn't fuck my way to the top or get handed this role. I fought for it and won as most of the Saints would agree given how I claimed my position on the night of the Saints Ball a year ago. This brotherhood was meant to empower the communities and help our families establish ourselves, but over the past two decades all The Brotherhood has done is take from innocent people to line their own pockets. That shit stops now!"

CHAPTER THREE

Ezekiel

Three weeks later...

I haven't seen Hayze or Archer since we were banished. I've wanted to reach out to them and try to explain what happened but always lost the nerve. I don't think they would even take my calls if I tried but it's not like either of them has reached out to me. Vox refuses to speak to me whenever my sister calls. Even after suffering through the loss of my brothers and *her*, I'm still grateful to know that Taylor didn't die and is in fact alive and well. She just has a different name now. Her story isn't mine to tell, I'm just so fucking glad she had the strength to escape the hell she was put in and find us without meaning to.

I shift and wince in pain, nearly a year later and my hip is still fucking causing me pain. Even after Vivi betrayed and banished all of us and our families from Hollow Hills, I still chose to be blooded in for her. As her husband, she had the choice to take the beating from the Saints that all new lords—or in her case lordess—go through or give the honor to me. I took it without her having to ask because I would rather die than ever allow those cunts to touch a single hair on her fucking perfect head.

It took me a long time to recover from being blooded in for her but once I did I spent my days tracking my boys. I found out they had applied to college and are going to play ball for some elite rich preppy school, Crestview Heights University or better known as CHU. They have one of the best teams in the country and I know Vox and my sister have applied there as well.

I don't think any of them know that we are all going to end up in the same place.

I didn't choose CHU to play ball, I chose to go there so I can bring the Filthy Few back together. Which is why I arrived at CHU a week early to catch Hayze and Archer off guard. Nova is the only one who knows about all of us coming here together, she's nervous about how Vox will react to seeing me and the guys but it's time he learned that Vivian is mine—*ours*.

The only reason I haven't killed him for touching my sister is because I know he fucking loves her. He proved that by saving her and risking everything we had worked for just to prove that he loved her.

Nova is so madly in love with Vox nothing else in the world seems to matter except for him. Living next door to my sister and ex best friend for the past year has been tense. Vox refuses to come to dinners with our moms or even look at my house when he goes out. I know him, and I know he thinks I betrayed him by marrying Vivian. I didn't marry her because of the reasons he thinks I did.

I'm pulled from my thoughts when I see Hayze and Archer stumbling toward the dorms with a few guys and girls trailing after them. Fuck, my boys have changed a lot in a year, we had never gone more than a day without speaking or seeing each other. We may be a foursome but Vox and I were always closer and the same goes for these two idiots. I step out of the car and move around the front to lean on the hood. The second Archer tenses I know he can feel my eyes on him. Hayze spots me and instantly sobers. They say something to their group before they storm across the lot toward me. Before they can come at me, I lift my shirt slightly so they can see the gun in my waistband which forces them to a stop. Both their faces morph into masks of anger.

"You want to come here after months of silence and bring a fucking piece with you?" Hayze scoffs in disgust. "Take the beating like a man, you little bitch."

I raise a brow at my friend and purse my lips. "I'm not here to fight," I say.

"Then why the fuck did you come here, you backstabbing fuck?" The venom in Arch's tone has guilt gnawing inside me.

"Because we need to talk."

"I got nothing to say to you," Hayze spits out, then moves to leave but I stop him with my words.

"Vox and Nova will be here next week." That has them both looking at me with judgment in their eyes.

"Ah, so because he's fucking *your* sister he forgives you, nice." I push off the hood of my car and step into Hayze.

"Talk about my sister like that again and I'll put a bullet between your eyes," I warn.

"Fuck off, Ezekiel, we got nothing to say to you. Go back to your best friend and *wife*." He spits the word wife like it burns his tongue. I can see Archer's hurt over this and thinks I betrayed him but I didn't.

"I had to do it."

"Why?" Hayze roars.

"Since when the fuck did you fall for Vi?" I clap back.

"Long before you and Archer, dumbass, but I respected her too much to act on my feelings, unlike you fuckers."

I shake my head. "I never fucked Vivian, Hayze." He reels back clearly surprised by my answer and I dart my gaze to Archer who is looking everywhere but at us. "But, clearly Archer did," I snarl.

His brown eyes burn with anger as he glares at me. "Yeah, I did. I touched her and I don't fucking regret it because she wasn't just some chick to warm my fucking bed. I was prepared to go against Vox for her."

"Well, why didn't you?" I fire back.

He scrubs a hand down his face. "Because I got scared of how much I felt for her," he admits bitterly. We're all silent for a while as we digest everything.

"Why are you here?" Hayze asks, sounding tired.

"I want her." They both snort.

"You fucking have her, dumbass, the ring you still fucking wear shows you own her! We lost, so fuck off and leave us alone," Archer snaps.

"I didn't win shit! She stood there and watched as I got my ass beat and didn't even look like she cared. I want her out of there and back with us but I need your help." Both of them share a look before turning back to me.

"What the fuck do you need us for?" Hayze grits out.

"I had a friend hack her system and decline all her college applications *except* for CHU." Both their eyes widen as I smile smugly.

"You did what?" Archer rasps out.

"She still has to graduate college before she can fully lead the Saints. Vivian is going to be touring CHU," I tell them.

"I know that look," Hayze mutters.

"What look?" I snap.

"The one you have right now, fuck face. It's your *I have a plan* look." I grin but neither Hayze nor Archer smiles. Arch seems to be too lost in his own head to even fathom what is happening around him. "Archer and I are done with this shit, even if she does come here..." Hayze clamps his mouth closed and drops his gaze to the ground, unable to finish.

"She will come here, I made sure of that when I—"

I snap my mouth shut when Archer pushes into me, getting right in my face. "*We* don't know her. If we fucking did then she wouldn't have married your fucking ass," he roars. Guilt churns inside me at the sight of pain etched into his features. I had no idea Archer felt this strongly about Vivian. I always knew he was soft for her and that there was a spark or whatever the fuck you want to call it, but I guess I just chalked that shit up to her being the one none of us could have and you know the old saying, you always want what you can't have.

"It's not what you idiots think," I grit out, then shove Archer back. He tries to come at me again but Hayze darts his arm out, stopping him.

"You came here to do what, Ez? Rub it in that you got the girl, then fucked it up so you came crawling back?"

I shake my head. "You have it all wrong, Draven. I married her to save her fucking life and all of yours!" I snarl.

"No, you may have saved her life but you fucking ruined ours and you ruined our brotherhood for the sake of you wanting to be the fucking hero. I hope it was worth it, asshole," Archer spits then stalks off. Hayze stares after him for a second, then sighs and scrubs a hand down his face.

"Why are you really here, Ezekiel?"

I meet Hayze's gaze and I hate that I can see so much apprehension in his eyes. Never before has he ever looked at me like this and I fucking hate it. Archer may be right, I think I really did break us and I don't know how to fix it.

"I meant what I said. I want her, Hayze."

"Since when?" he shouts.

"Since always! I was just never obvious about it like Archer who followed her around like a love sick puppy."

"If you want him to forgive you, then you need to give her up." I balk at him.

"What?" I grit out.

Hayze shakes his head and then glances in the direction Archer stalked off. "He's in love with her, Ezekiel. He has been for years. Him finding out the way he did that you married her nearly fucking broke him. He was ready to go against Vox and take every broken bone he would have given him just so he could date his sister. Can you say you would do the same for her?"

CHAPTER FOUR

Vivian

"Are you sure you will be okay with running things?" I ask Tate who waves me off as she wipes down the bar. My nerves are frayed. Three weeks ago we opened Lividica and the opening night was a hit, the partners were put in their place and some were kicked the fuck out. I got what I needed from that night.

"You'll be gone for a couple of weeks. I can survive without you breathing down my neck. Go check out the campus." I purse my lips, hating that I am lying to her but the truth is, I don't know who I can trust right now. I've been getting letters every week. At first they were harmless but then suddenly they shifted, they became more sinister. I have a feeling I know who it is but I can't be certain. I mean, I did ruin a few lives a year ago, so I guess you could take your pick.

"It doesn't matter if I fall in love with the place, it's not like I could actually go there."

Tate's brows furrow as she looks at me. "Why not? I mean

no offense but you reek of money so it's not like you couldn't afford an Ivy League school."

I snort at her observation. Sometimes I wish I had someone to talk to aside from David about all of this shit but I have no one. Taking the crown meant losing everyone I cared about. I justified my actions from that night by telling myself I was doing it to save them all, there is no way Thomas Valerian and his evil prick of a son Nexus would have let my brother and his friends live if Nexus married Nova. I wish I could talk to Tate about all of this but she has no idea who I really am, she just thinks I am a trust fund brat who opened a sex club.

"Yeah, I guess you're right. I gotta go but I'll call you later and check in." She's already turned away and waving at me over her shoulder before I finish speaking. I fucking love her attitude and how she gives zero fucks about what people think. I climb off my stool and head out of the back of Lividica and meet David in the lobby. He's talking with the manager of the hotel so I hang back and pull out my phone. I sigh at the sight of unopened messages from my brother. I have plenty from Hayze and Ezekiel as well as Nova but not one has come from Archer. He hasn't tried to call, text, or even come back to Hollow Hills since I banished them. I have no right to feel hurt over this, but it doesn't stop the feeling from sneaking up on me.

I clutch my phone and close my eyes as I try to breathe through the pain in my chest. I never meant to hurt Archer when I agreed to marry Ezekiel. Marrying Ez was a strategic move, having his last name gave me the power I needed to set them all free but what I didn't expect was for them all to act like butt hurt bitches and turn their backs on me. I guess I deserved their anger but all they had to do was fucking fight! The only one who actually did was my brother. Fuck those three assholes, they never lifted a fucking finger to try and stop me or show me I meant a goddamn fucking thing to them.

Turns out, they are just like every other gutless motherfucking mommy's boys who never want to show their feelings because they think it makes them look weak. Real men can express themselves and be open and honest about their feelings.

BY THE TIME we reach the CHU campus I am exhausted, my back is aching and my neck is stiff as fuck from the long drive. I haven't had a break since I took over the Saints. Everyone, including David, thinks I am here to tour the campus since all my other applications were declined. At first I was hurt and pissed off until I did some deeper research into the school and its board members and was shocked at what I had learned about the five youngest members who actually own half the school.

When my driver hands me my bags, I thank him and wave him away when he tries to carry them for me. I may be the lordess but I haven't forgotten where I came from. I didn't grow up getting my ass wiped for me, we were taught to stand on our own two feet. I make my way across the grass and head toward the dorms. A ball of excitement takes life inside me. I've always dreamed about going to college and all the experiences I would have with my brother and the guys. Growing up we would talk about college and what we would get up to, there was never a question if we would all go to the same school, it was just a given.

I push all thoughts of the past away as I drag my luggage behind me and input the code on the panel next to the door that was sent to me by the dean. At this late hour I expected everyone to be in bed but I was wrong. I smile at a few girls who look like they are dressed for a night on the town. Happiness fills me when they smile back and wave. One even hands me a flier as I pass by. After a couple of wrong turns and a trip to the wrong floor I finally find my room. I push the door open and sigh in relief when I drop my bags. I look around the room and a pang of longing hits me right in the chest. This is what I have dreamed about for years and I gave it all up to try and protect their innocence and my soul. I drop down onto the edge of the unmade bed that I'm assuming is mine and huff in annoyance.

I should have been here!

I shake away the bitter thought and look across the room to see my roommate's side is practically untouched. There are bags and a few textbooks but nothing personal. Her bed isn't even made and has me questioning if she is a late arrival like me or does she just not stay here? I look down at the flier in my hand and read over it. There is a campus bonfire tonight on the beach. I pull my phone out and plug the address into the GPS and smile when I see it's only a short walk away.

You aren't a college student, Vivian!

Sadness envelopes me, it's Friday night. I should stay in and read over the new contracts David emailed me on the drive over. I know the expansion of the high school and opening our own college is important for all future members of the Saints but this is a college party.

"I could go for an hour?" I say aloud, nibbling on my lip while debating my options. It doesn't take much convincing, I decide to go over the contracts in the morning and enjoy my first night. I may never get another chance to experience something like this, lord knows I would never have been allowed to go if my brother and the guys were here. I was only allowed out if one or all of them were with me but not tonight. Tonight I am going solo. I mean for fuck's sake, I own a sex club now and I'm not the same naive little girl I was a year ago. I know the world isn't filled with kind people. I also have my can of pepper spray in my purse so I'll be fine.

I CAN'T WIPE the smile from my face as my sandal-covered feet sink into the sand. My hair gets caught in the wind and smacks me in the face, some of the strands getting caught in my lip gloss but I pull them away and tuck them behind my ear. I make my way toward the crowded bonfire and can't help but stare at the guys and girls as they dance around to the music with red solo cups in their hands. The girls look so carefree and happy, the guys seem relaxed without a worry in the world.

I envy them.

I can't remember a time when I didn't feel worried or stressed about the future. Unlike everyone at this party, our futures weren't guaranteed. We had to fight, claw our way out of the corner our father's backed us into until I took matters into my own hands.

"Hey, why the long face, beautiful?" I snap my head up and lock eyes with a guy who has one of the warmest smiles I have ever seen. I drink him in and swallow audibly. He's shirtless and wears a pair of ripped jean shorts that hang low on his hips. When he chuckles I lift my gaze back to him. He runs a hand through his black hair and pushes it back from his forehead, his blue eyes filled with wonder as he stares down at me. "You must be new here."

"H-how..." I clear my throat and try again. "What makes you say that?"

The sexy smirk that touches his lips has my heart rate picking up. "I would remember seeing you around campus." I feel the blush coating my cheeks and duck my head for a moment before pulling on my big girl panties and facing him again.

"That obvious, huh?"

He shrugs. "Kind of, yeah." Both of us laugh at that. "Can I get you a drink?" I must hesitate too long because he quickly adds. "We don't do kegs here, all drinks are sealed and any left lying around are tossed." His words put my worries at ease and I find myself nodding and following after him. He grabs me a wine cooler and hands it over. Sure enough, it's sealed. He and I stand side by side as we people watch. The cheer squad run through a routine while everyone watches. I can't put my finger on it but something about this place seems different to Hollow Hills.

"Do you go to school here...?" I don't know his name so I let my sentence trail off. He smiles down at me and extends his hand.

"My name is Matthew but my friends and family call me Dawson."

I cock my head to the side. "Why do they call you Dawson?"

He smiles sheepishly and rubs the back of his neck. "It's a long story but the gist of it is, my dad wasn't around when I was born so I demanded everyone call me by my last name so I could be closer to my old man I guess."

I reach out and touch his forearm. "I'm sorry."

He smiles and shakes his head. "Don't be, my dad's one of the greatest guys I know."

"So, he's around now?"

He nods. "Yeah, he has been since he found me and my mom when I was four." I don't know why but I get the feeling he is uncomfortable talking about his family so I change the subject.

"I'm Vivian."

"A pretty name for a pretty girl." For the second time tonight I blush. "Got a last name?"

I open my mouth to say *Hatchett* but then realize, that is no longer my name. "Tempest. My name is Vivian Tempest."

"Your name suits you, you definitely seem like a temptress." I can't help the laughter that bubbles out of me.

"Oh, that was real smooth, Romeo." Dawson shoots me a wink.

"So, CHU, huh?" he says, changing the subject. Sorrow unfurls inside me. Dawson seems like a great guy but he's also a stranger and would never understand the dynamics of my life.

"I'm actually just here for a meeting with the board." His brows jump to his hairline, his eyes suddenly turn accusing and I take a step back. "Is everything okay?" I ask.

He shakes his head and the look vanishes. "Yeah, I guess I'm just so used to everyone knowing who I am and who my family is."

"What do you mean?" I press.

"Everyone at this party has tried to kiss my ass so they could get in my good graces so I could put in a good word with the board so they won't get kicked out for failing their classes."

I frown up at him. "Why would they want to kiss your ass?"

He sighs and scrubs a hand down his face. "My father and four uncles own half the school and sit on the board of CHU." Surprise ripples through me, I replay his words a few times until they sink in.

"I swear, I had no idea who you were. I only came tonight because I was handed a flier when I arrived..." Feeling suddenly out of place, I try to flee but he grips my wrist, halting my escape.

"I'm sorry, I didn't mean to accuse you of anything, it's just hard... you never know who is real and genuine anymore—"

"Or just using you because of what your last name is?" Surprise flickers through his gaze.

"Yeah," he breathes out.

"I get it, back home I never really had any friends because they always wanted what my last name could get them or just to get close to me so they could fuck my brother and his three best friends. Well, everyone except one. Nova never cared about my last name or my brother and his friends." Longing hits me hard and I gasp for air at the mention of Nova. I miss her so much. "I have to go," I rush to say and yank my hand free of his hold. I ignore him calling out for me to come back as I run back to the dorms.

This was a stupid idea coming here. I run along the beach, choosing to go the long way around so I wouldn't bump into anyone along the footpath. I don't know why I ran but I just had to get out of there, it was too much thinking about... *them.* I thought I was past this point where just the thought of them would bring me to my knees. I guess I was wrong.

I stop running and bend over, placing my hands on my knees as I try to drag in a lungful of air. I tense when I get an eerie sense that I am being watched. I slowly push up and discreetly look around. Trees line the bank on one side, on the other is nothing but open ocean. What I didn't take into account when I ran off was that it's pitch black out here except for the lighting of the moon. I wrap my arms around myself when a cold shiver works its way down my spine. I take a deep breath and try to reason with myself that I'm just envisioning this feeling of being watched because of the letters, but then I see a shadow emerge from the trees.

CHAPTER FIVE

Fuck!

My breathing quickly turns ragged as the figure comes closer, forcing me to take a step back, I dart my gaze to the left and my eyes widen when I see another figure. Fear grips me in its clutches. I turn to run back the way I came, but there is another person standing there. I've never been in a situation like this before, I was never alone. I always had my brother or one of the guys with me but now I'm here on my own... trapped.

I peer over my shoulder and curse under my breath. Unless I plan on swimming away from these three, I have nowhere to go. They all move in sync and come toward me. With no other option I force myself to stand tall. I am Vivian Tempest, Lordess of the Haven Saints and I will bow to no one. The closer they get I can see they are dressed in all black, but when the one directly in front of me steps into the glow of the moon everything inside me stills at the sight of the mask. I dart my gaze to the other two and the sight of both of them wearing those masks has anger spiking to life inside me.

How fucking dare they!

I clench my hands into fists at my sides as they all creep in closer, forming a semicircle around me. Thanks to their clothing and masks I can see nothing but their eyes. I don't need to see more than that. I know those three sets of eyes all too fucking well. Those eyes all looked at me with betrayal and heartache the last time I saw them, these bastards made their choice.

"I'll give the three of you traitors five seconds to turn and walk away or I'll have you hunted by The Brotherhood." I'm proud of how my voice doesn't waiver. I run my gaze over them and force myself to remember that they left me. They chose my brother and refused to fight. I know I have no right to feel the way I do but they hurt me. Left Horn—Hayze Draven, steps forward, forcing me to take a step back which has him halting his movements.

"We aren't in Hollow Hills anymore, Vivi baby," he says.

"Don't fucking call me that!" I snap.

"You can't banish us from here, Vivian." I cut my gaze to the Right Horn—-Ezekiel Tempest, my husband and glare at the bastard.

"Fuck you," I grit out.

"Are you offering?" I turn and face No Horns—Archer Malik, the boy who broke my heart.

"Oh, look you can speak!" I snarl. Archer steps forward but Ezekiel snaps his arm out, halting his movements.

"You banished us, we never turned our backs on you, Vivian." I scoff and shoot Ezekiel a scathing look. Out of the three of them he has always been the one to never spare my feelings and always call me out on my shit. I may not have ever had a relationship with Hayze and Ezekiel but a part of me has always felt so connected to them.

"You turned your back on me the minute you allowed me to think my brother had murdered you." Ez sucks in a sharp breath at my admission.

"And what about us?" Archer pushes. I run my gaze over the three of them. They wear these masks to conceal their identities and used the Filthy Few as a way to garner intel on the Saints but somewhere along the way they lost humanity to these masks. They thought I had no idea about the Saints or the Filthy Few. I allowed them to believe that since it made them feel better thinking they were protecting me, but I watched them change every time they put those masks on. They stopped being the four guys I cared about most in the world and they became... monsters who gave zero fucks about the people they hurt as long as they got the information they needed.

"There stopped being an us when you chose to leave me behind and run after my twin," I answer without remorse. "I have no idea how the three of you found me or why you are even here, but you will stay the fuck away from me. I don't need you or want any of you in my life." I don't wait for a response as I turn and attempt to flee, but Hayze cuts in front of me and blocks my path. "Move!" I snap.

"I can't." The anguish is clear in his tone but I can't find it within myself to give a damn. Where was this compassion when my world was falling apart? They all left me, every single fucking one of them—Vox included.

I crane my neck and meet his gaze. Unlike Archer and Ezekiel, who can shut down their emotions in a second, Hayze has never been able to do that. He likes to think he can be unreadable but the truth is he can't. He wears his heart on his sleeve and that is one of his best qualities and the reason he had so many girls falling to their knees for him. I mean, the fact he is six foot three with a killer body, tattoos on his arms, back and ribs with striking green eyes and brown hair you just want to run your fingers through also helps.

"Then let me take an idea from your playbook," I snarl, step around him and stalk off back toward the way I came. I try to keep my pace even so they don't see how rattled I am after seeing them. When I hear them running after me, I bite back the growl that wants to break free and stop me in my tracks as I wait for them to cage me in. Where was this persistence before?

This time when the three of them stand in front of me with their masks resting on the tops of their heads, I wasn't prepared to see their faces. Ezekiel's blond hair seems longer, his gray-blue eyes are filled with pain. Unlike the others, his ink is hidden beneath his clothes. I look at Archer next and the sight of his features pulled taut in anger just fuels my own. His brown eyes burn with rage as he stares at me, his black hair is slicked flat against his head. Unlike the other two, his ink is everywhere for all to see, wearing his tats like armor.

"Grow the fuck up, Vivian," Archer snaps. I reel back in shock. "You think we had a choice? We did what we did to save your ungrateful ass and look at where that got us! You wound up shitting on me and marrying my best friend!" The pain is entwined with anger, I hear it in his voice but this mother-fucker is tripping if he thinks I will stand here and take the bullshit he is spitting at me.

"I shit on you?!" I scream. I don't give him a chance to respond. Hayze and Ez back up a step, leaving me and Archer facing off against each other. "You son of a bitch, you shit on me long before that asshole and you know it."

"How?" he bites back.

"You took my fucking virginity and then acted like it never fucking happened just so you wouldn't have to face my broth-er's wrath!" Hayze and Ezekiel both swing their gazes to

Archer, I can see their anger wafting off them in waves. "Do you have any idea what that did to me? You fucked me then snuck out of my room. The next morning, I tried to talk to you but you avoided me only to text and tell me it was a mistake and should never have happened."

"You dumb fuck!" Hayze snaps at his best friend.

"I'm gonna break your fucking jaw," Ez spits.

Archer throws his hands in the air. "Oh, so you flirting with my two best friends was your way of paying me back? Oh, no, that's right, your form of payback was changing your fucking last name to match his!" he roars. I stumble back a step. Ez darts an arm out, wrapping it around my waist. Fire instantly burns through me at his touch, but I don't get a chance to think on it too much because Archer is right there shoving him away from me. "You may be married to her but you don't fucking touch her!"

Ezekiel pushes forward and gets right in Archer's face. Hayze drags me back and anchors me in front of him. His warmth instantly seeps into me and I'm powerless to stop myself from inhaling his intoxicating scent. Ezekiel grips the front of Archer's hoodie and presses his forehead against his.

"She's my wife, you need to deal with that shit, Arch. I won't say sorry for marrying her—"

"It never should have been you!" Archer snaps.

"It had to be me, brother," Ez whispers. I hear the hint of regret in his tone and that shit hurts. I pull free of Hayze's hold and don't spare any of them a look or even utter a word as I stalk off again. This time I don't stop when I feel the three of them trailing after me. I keep my head down the entire walk back to the dorms. I want to scream at them to fuck off and stop following me, but I know from years of experience with them that they won't listen to me. All my shouting will do is invite them to talk to me more and that is the last thing I want. When

I round the corner and spot the dorm building up ahead I almost sigh out loud.

As we draw closer I notice a couple coming from the opposite direction. I envy how loved up they look in the shadows. He has his arm around her as she huddles into his side, laughing at something he said. They step into the light at the same time as we do and then everything freezes as the guy and I lock eyes. My breathing hitches, my heart skips a beat and I suddenly feel like I'm five years old again under the pressure of his gaze. Shock is plastered across his face, his mouth is slightly ajar at the sight of me.

"Vi?" I tear my gaze from him and look at the girl who is staring at me like she has seen a ghost. I can't even force a smile as I turn back to the guy at her side. When I feel the three behind come in closer that's what seems to snap everyone out of their haze.

"What the fuck are you three doing here?" Vox snarls. Nova dropping her gaze to the ground and has me cocking my head to the side. The instant she lifts her head and locks eyes with someone behind me—I'm betting it's her brother—I know without a doubt that this wasn't some coincidence, they set us up.

I take a couple steps away from them to keep them all in my line of sight as I speak to Ezekiel. "Did you really think this was a good idea, setting everyone up to be in the same place?"

The dick doesn't even look ashamed about his actions. I look to Archer and Hayze next and at least both of them don't look guilty so I think we all have Ezekiel—the snake—Tempest to thank for this little reunion. We may be outside but I feel like I'm trapped between my past and my future. I closed the door to this part of my life. I moved on from the five of them and claimed my place as the lordess. None of them thought I was strong enough to lead... well, Nova did in a sense but I saw the doubt in her eyes on the Night Of The Saints when I set them all free. Even though they betrayed me I gave them the gift of their freedom. What a fucking fool, right?

"Yes. None of you would have agreed to this if I hadn't arranged it," he answers without missing a beat. Vox growls and attempts to close in on Ez but Nova steps in front of him, placing her hands on his chest, halting his movements. I never thought I would see the day where a girl had any type of control over my brother but here we are.

"Vox, he's my brother," Nova pleads as she looks up at him.

Vox drops his gaze to Nova. "And that is the only reason I haven't fucking snapped his neck for what he did to my sister, witch." The other three say nothing. I shoot them a look, waiting for one of them to say something, any fucking thing to show they have changed but as usual, Vox's word is law and they always submit to my brother. My phone vibrates in my pocket. I pull it out to see it's David calling. I say nothing to the others as I answer the call and head for the dorms. They shout for me to come back but I don't listen, I bring the phone to my ear as I punch in the code and stalk inside.

"David, I'm assuming something went wrong since you are calling me this late?" I say it as a way of greeting.

"Lordess." His tone is low and he sounds stressed.

"What happened?" My tone is firm. I quicken my pace to get to my room quicker so I'm not having this conversation out in the open.

"Your *Bird*—" That's what we have been calling the fucker that leaves me letters, it seemed fitting since the bastard always manages to escape our grasp and flies away before he can be caught. "Upped his game, I think this trip to CHU may need to be cut short."

"Why? What happened?" I grit out as I push my bedroom door open and sigh in relief that my roommate isn't here. I lock the door before making my way over to the empty desk and dropping into the chair.

"You aren't properly protected there. At least if you are here we can have around the clock guards tracking your movements." The slight hysteria in his voice is putting me on edge.

"David, what the fuck happened?" I grit out.

"Lordess, a package was delivered to your home address."

He's stalling. "David, tell me what the fuck was in the package now and stop putting it off. I'm tired and—"

"The DA's head was in the box, Lordess. We believe the person behind these letters is Alexander Denver." My breath stalls, my vision turns hazy and I turn ice cold. David and I had assumed the letters were coming from an unhappy member of The Brotherhood, someone who just wanted to scare me into stepping down but this... this is terrifying.

"H-how could it be him?" I stutter out.

"Even behind prison bars, Alexander Denver is still known to run things in the outside world. He has a partner, or so the rumors go, but no one knows who it is."

"Why the fuck is The Butcher coming after me?" The tremble in my voice shows my fear. I swallow a couple of times to try and control my erratic heartbeat and calm myself but I can't. I never thought sending Alexander that letter telling him that Nexus was the one that killed his sister would result in this happening!

"I don't know, but I am working on it, Lordess, and so are the other members."

"Those bastards would be loving this, they want me gone just as much as The Butcher clearly does," I force out.

David sighs. "You would be surprised how most of them have changed their tune since you opened Lividica. A lot of them are singing your praise, Lordess, they have even noted that their wives are happier." That brings a smile to my face, a lot of the men think their wives are using the *free spa* at the hotel but Tate, David and I know better. As soon as their husbands disappear through that red door, they are rounding the corner to the other entrance to visit the ladies only side. After another five minutes, I agree to cut my trip short and return to Hollow Hills in four days.

I have a meeting with the board of CHU that I can't miss.

CHAPTER SIX

Archer

Seeing her again after so long has my head all fucked up. Vivian has always had that type of hold over me, all she had to do was enter a room and I would lose all train of thought. She became my sole focus.

Then she went and fucked me over.

She married Ezekiel, my best fucking friend. I used to dream of the day she would become *Vivian Malik*. Thanks to her need for power and revenge, she went and blew my fucking dream out of the water. She isn't mine anymore—she's *his*.

"You fuckers are going to stay away from my sister." Vox sneers as he glares at each of us. Nova turns her back to Vox and faces us with a pleading look in her eyes. I don't get it, even after all the fucked up shit he did to her—*We* did to her—she still stands here defending him, loving him and wanting him by her side.

I had that.

"What Vox is trying to say is—"

Hayze cuts Nova off before she can finish. "You don't have a fucking say in what we do, asshole."

Vox scoffs and rolls his eyes like the condescending prick he is. "When it concerns my sister, I have every fucking say…" He lets his sentence trail off as he studies the three of us. When his eyes narrow and his lip lifts in a snarl, it hits me. When I look over at Ez, his mask is resting on the top of his head and poking out from under the hood of his jacket. "You motherfuckers hunted my sister, didn't you?" It's posed as a question but none of us answer.

Nova snorts, drawing our attention to her. "*A favor asked is a debt owed.*" She snickers as she recites the line of the Filthy Few. We were once a brotherhood of our own until… everything went to shit. All our hard work, the pain and suffering we went through was for fucking nothing. The whole point of the Filthy Few was to find the proof we needed to get rid of Thomas and Nexus but our cause changed and became about protecting Vivian so she would never have to be blooded in. Before Nova showed up we knew Thomas was trying to find a way for Vivi to marry his cunt of a son to secure his place as the Lord of the Haven Saints.

"Why the fuck are you three going after my sister and forcing her to ask a favor?" The cold tone of Vox's voice pulls me from my thoughts.

"We're not," Ez answers.

"Bullshit! Why the fuck are you bringing out the masks?" Vox has a hero complex right now and its starting to grate on every one of my fucking nerves.

"Because the Filthy Few isn't just about you, dick, it's about all of us and if we want to push her to ask a favor we will. As I recall, you managed to force Ezekiel's sister to do the same thing," I taunt but instantly feel like an asshole when Nova drops her gaze to the ground. Vox wraps his arm around her waist and pulls her flush against him as he shoots me a look I know all too well, he wants to break my face.

Bring it on.

I don't have to hide now, he knows how I feel about his twin and I'm done hiding that shit. It's time he realizes he doesn't call the fucking shots around here anymore.

"Both of you shut the fuck up!" Hayze snaps, I turn to my brother and scowl. "Don't fucking look at me like that, Archer!" He doesn't give me a chance to respond before continuing. "Ez set us all up, can't change that shit now, can we? I'm gonna be straight with you all, I want Vivian." My jaw unhinges, Ezekiel looks just as shocked but it's Vox who holds my attention. He doesn't seem... surprised, nor does Nova. She just smiles proudly which is fucking weird. "I get it, you want to break our jaws then go ahead because I'm done playing this game where I act like I don't notice her. I stepped back because I know Archer is in love with her." I don't get a chance to interject before he is pushing on. "I was okay as long as she was happy but then Ezekiel went and married her and fucked shit up."

"What's your point?"

"My point, Vox, is that I'm not backing down this time. I'm telling you this because of the friendship we once shared and that's it." Hayze steps forward only stopping an inch away from Nova, sandwiching her between them both. "Try and stand in my way or put a stop to this, I'll break *your* nose and forget all about you once being my brother." Hayze brushes past them without a backward glance.

"My sister's the reason the three of you fled," Vox mutters.

"No. We left because once again you and Ezekiel thought we were nothing but sheep the two of you fuckers could lead. He may have blindsided you with the whole marrying Vivi and shit, but everything else was on the both of you. As far as I'm concerned the both of you are dead to me. You got the girl and the ending you wanted but was it worth the price of your twin, best friends and The Brotherhood we created?" I don't stick around for his answer, I chase after Hayze and catch up to him at the back of the dorms. He ignores me when I call out to him, so I run in front of him and block his path. Anger is burning in his green eyes, his chest is rising and falling in quick pants, his fists clenching at his sides. Out of the four of us, Ez and Vox were always tighter with each other than us but the same can be said for me and Hayze. We're all brothers but even siblings have favorites. I know Hayze like I know myself, which is why I know he needs to be the one to speak first. If I do it, we will end up throwing hands and that's not what either of us needs right now.

It takes him a minute to regulate his breathing, eventually sighing and scrubbing a hand down his face and that's all I need to know we aren't going to fight.

"Why didn't you tell me how you felt about Vi?" I say barely above a whisper. In truth, I'm scared of his answer because much like him, I would rather see him happy with the girl and watch from the sidelines than break my best friend's heart by finally getting the girl I've always wanted.

Hayze tugs on the strands of his hair and begins to pace around in front of me. Out of the four of us, he is the more approachable and easy going except when it comes to his feelings, he hates talking about how he feels and always closes everyone out. The only person I have ever seen with the power to get him to open up is the girl that apparently both of us want and it would seem Ez wants her too, which makes this whole situation so fucked up!

"How the fuck was I supposed to tell you?" he growls.

My lungs deflate as I shove my hands in my pants pockets and rock back on my heels. "I don't know, H."

He stops pacing and faces me, the pained look in his eyes shreds my chest open. "The night of Darion's party, we went to celebrate after we won the championship game."

I frown. "What about the party?"

"That was the night I knew I first wanted her." My brows nearly hit my fucking hairline.

"That was years ago!"

He nods. "That was freshman year."

"I know!" I snap.

"But even before then, I knew I liked her, I just didn't realize how much until that night. When she showed up with Vox, I couldn't take my eyes off her."

"Why didn't you fucking say anything?" I shout.

"Because you were fucking looking at her the same way!" he roars. Understanding dawns on me, I remember that night because it was the first time I had even busted a move on Vivi that I couldn't pass off as an accidental touch or something like that. That night, I kissed her.

"You pulled back because of me," I mutter.

He throws his hands in the air. "Yes. I was good with it, I swear, but then..." He doesn't need to finish, I already know what he is going to say.

"Ezekiel went and married her and made her fair game." A whoosh of air escapes him as he nods.

"Yeah," he whispers. I run my gaze over my best friend and hate myself for not seeing the signs earlier. For years he hid his feelings, but now, I see them clear as day. He's hung up on Vivian and it's scaring the shit out of him. Not only that, I know it's weighing on him that he's still just as pissed with her as I am but it's the unknown that would be killing him.

Does she feel the same way about him as he does her?

A pit forms in my stomach, a part of me always knew he was different with her but being the selfish bastard I am, I chose to block it out and not see what was right in front of me. For years he stood back and watched me fuck up with Vivian. Every time I hurt her, it was him that would sit with her, cuddle her on the couch and watch her favorite movie to cheer her up.

What the fuck are we going to do now?

CHAPTER SEVEN

Vivian

It's a beautiful Saturday morning and as much as I want to hide out in my dorm room to avoid running into my brother or the others, I don't want to waste what little time I have here. I force my ass out of bed to shower and change into one of my bathing suits. I throw a shirt over the top—it's so long it stops just above my knees. I refuse to acknowledge the fact that this shirt is one I stole from Ezekiel last year. I used to steal all of their shirts. I love sleeping in them, just to have their scent wrapped around me as I drifted off, as it always made me feel safe.

I grab my towel and Kindle, then head for the door. Just as I lock it behind me, my phone rings. I frown when I see who is calling but answer the call.

"Drew, how can I help you on a Saturday?" I say. Drew and his friend Ford own Anders and Booth Construction, they are the ones handling the expansion of the high school and building the college since I couldn't get Brodie to agree until recently.

"Vivian, I don't have good news." My stomach sinks as I choose to take the stairs instead of the elevator.

"What happened?" I ask, praying that it isn't something major that will delay the expansion further. It's already costing us more than I had hoped thanks to the constant problems we are running into. I swear, I never had this many problems when I had commissioned the contractors for Lividica. The rebuild on that went smooth. I hadn't worried about a single thing and now I am starting to wonder if I should have just rehired the same team from that build for this one. David urged me to use members of The Brotherhood so it didn't look like I was trying to ice out their businesses but honestly, I was worried they would purposely fuck up jobs just to get at me and make me look incompetent. Every month we have a meeting and each time more than half a dozen of the brothers make complaints about how I have done this or that and its starting to piss me right off!

"One of the new guys found asbestos in the roof, all construction has to be halted until we can fix that problem." I'm grinding my teeth so fucking hard I may actually break them!

"Drew, this is the fifth hold up we have had—"

"I can't help these problems, I wasn't the one who built the school so you need to blame those assholes." His tone is grating on my nerves, I hate how he and Ford speak to me like I'm stupid. "We're doing the best we can and working overtime, my crew is busting their ass."

"Yes, yes, I know." I take a deep breath and try to compose myself as I exit the building and head for the beach. "I'll have David source a crew—"

"We know some guys—"

"No!" I cut in as each time he has suggested a crew, they

have taken longer than needed to fix the problem, which is why I'm starting to think him and his partner are just fucking with me now. "I'll have a crew of my own brought in and since your crew is clearly tired and under the pump I will be bringing on a new crew to help with the workload."

"Hell no! Ford and I work alone and—-"

"You either do as I'm telling you or I fire your company and bring in a whole other crew that I'm sure won't run into the amount of problems you have. I'll have David send you the details." I end the call without waiting for a response. "Fucking males always thinking women are stupid," I growl out.

"Well, that's not fair to the rest of us good males who think women are amazing." I snap my head up to see Dawson standing a few feet away with a warm smile on his face and a volleyball clutched between his hands. I can't stop the smile from spreading across my face.

"Sorry, I just got... work problems."

He purses his lips and nods. "What's your plans for the day?" Before I can answer my phone rings, cutting off my reply. I sigh when I see it's David. I hold my finger up and shoot him an apologetic look as I answer the call.

"Drew called you, didn't he?" I say as I bring the phone to my ear.

His answering sigh gives me the answer before he voices it. "Yes, he isn't happy."

I turn my back to Dawson as I answer him. "I don't give a shit, he has been playing us David—"

"I know, but we need to keep the brothers happy."

"Why?"

"The night of the Saints." I grind my teeth, he has been mentioning that for months now. I have a backup plan. If they try to vote me out they will all lose!

"They vote me out, then they will lose everything. Fix this, David. I want this matter handled before I get home."

"There's been another delivery from our bird." I still instantly. "A letter was delivered."

"What did it say?"

"I didn't open it."

"Why not?"

"It states on the back that you are to be the one to open it when you *return*."

I gasp, fear trickles down my spine. "He knows where I am," I breathe out.

"Yes, I have sent six men to you. You need to return with them—"

"No. I'll leave tomorrow afternoon and not a minute earlier." Before he can argue I end the call, then take a few deep breaths and try to calm my nerves. It takes longer than I want to admit but feeling a presence behind me leaves me no choice. I turn and crane my neck back to see Dawson studying me with a look of concern. He takes one look at me and then nods.

"Come on, you look like you need some fun." A humorless chuckle escapes me.

"Yeah, I could use some fun." He smiles, grabs my hand and leads me toward the beach. He doesn't press me for what soured my mood, he talks about mundane shit and I find myself appreciating him for trying to take my mind off things without prying. When we reach the beach, I see a few students playing volleyball. Dawson tries to lead me toward them but I plant my feet.

"What's wrong?" he asks.

I nibble on my lip trying to figure out a way to tell him that I don't want to be around people right now. "She just wants to hang out with her bestie. Don't worry, she'll totally watch you from here though." Dawson frowns for a second but when I shoot him a small smile he nods and releases my hand, then runs off to join his friends. "He seems... nice." I ignore her, this was my beach day to hang out by myself and of course she had to turn up.

I scoff and go about laying my towel out, then rid myself of my shirt and lay down on my stomach. I watch Nova, from the corner of my eye, mimic my move, neither of us saying anything as we watch Dawson and his friends play. A memory hits me then of the day we all ditched school after Nova beat up Nicole and we spent the whole day laughing and playing around, even had a bonfire that night.

"You thinking about the last time we were at the beach together?"

I exhale and nod. "Yeah."

"That was one of the best days I have ever had, Vi." I hate that there is this divide between her and me. She was my best friend before she was Vox's. Nova isn't like any of the other girls I know, she never tried to use me to get closer to my brother or the guys. She wanted to be my friend because of who I am. "I miss you," she whispers.

I slam my eyes closed as guilt churns inside me. "I miss you too," I whisper.

"Then why have you been avoiding my calls and texts?" The hurt is clear in her tone.

"Because I know who you share a bed with," I answer bitterly.

"Vivian, I would never tell him anything. I love your brother so fucking much to the point I can't even put it into words, but you're my best friend... my only friend." The reminder of what she lost has me turning to face her. Tears fill her eyes but don't fall. She tries to smile but it doesn't reach her eyes.

"How's my mom?" I ask, changing the subject.

Nova smiles and this time it does reach her eyes. "She's amazing. Mom, Olivia and Jane have been hanging out so much. They've opened two new floral shops and they all seem... happy... ish."

"Ish?" I push.

Nova's eyes soften. "Jane misses you, Vivian. Every week she asks me if I have heard from you and it breaks my heart every time I have to tell her I haven't."

I inhale sharply. "It's better for her this way."

"What way? She is hurting, Vivian. She thinks you chose The Brotherhood over your family just like your—" She clamps her mouth closed and I narrow my eyes.

"Like my father and Ezekiel's?" Her brows draw in. "Yeah, I know all about what my father and Edmund used to get up to. Virgil Hatchett wasn't a saint like my brother painted him out to be, nor was Edmund. Sorry, Nova, but your dad was a piece of shit just like mine." She reels back like I slapped her.

"Edmund and Virgil were trying to save you all from joining the Saints."

I scoff and laugh but it's a bitter sound. Nova frowns as she stares at me. "Is that what he told you?" I don't give her a chance to answer. "He was wrong, Nova. Our father's weren't heroes. They were power hungry bastards and only cared about getting richer. The Saints are thirsty for power and will stop at nothing to get it."

"Then why are you leading them?" The confusion is clear in her tone and on her face.

'Because I'm smart. I know their weaknesses and how they work. I just needed time to fix all the wrongs. They think they just have to survive another couple of months until Night Of The Saints where they can vote me out, but if they do, it will be their downfall." She studies me for a solid minute before her eyes widen and she gasps.

"Holy fuck," she breathes out. I smile darkly and shoot her a wink. "You're fucking them over from the inside."

I tilt my head side to side. "I refuse to confirm or deny your claim."

"Why?"

"Because my father and yours tried to take our lives from us and so did the Saints. I won't let them win. They will all go down. I told you a year ago that there is nothing worse than a woman's scorn and I meant it. They will all burn in fucking hell for what they did!"

"Vivi, I say this with love, but you are a bad bitch and I am in awe of you."

I snort. "Cut that shit out."

"I mean it. You sacrificed your family for this and you gave up... your guys."

There it is, the elephant in the room.

"They aren't my anything, Nova."

She pins me with a deadpan look. "Girl, I've known for a lot longer than you think that there is something there between you and the three of them."

I shake my head, denying her claim. "There is nothing between me and them. At one time, maybe I thought there was something with each of them, but they all made a choice... so none of them are worthy of me or my time. Plus, it's not like I could have all three."

"Says who?"

I balk at her. "Uh, society?"

She waves me away. "Fuck normal, who says you can't have your cake and eat it too?"

"Vivian?" I snap my head toward Dawson, grateful for his timing. "Come on, we need two more players, please." I nibble on my lip and turn to Nova who shrugs and stands. I follow her lead and join them. Dawson introduces us to everyone and they all smile welcomingly, which puts some of my anxiety at ease. It's hard getting used to the fact people here don't know me or my last name, it's fucking wicked to be honest. I just wish I didn't have to leave this place to finish what I started.

CHAPTER EIGHT

Hayze

Archer and I decided to take our minds off everything and spend the day at the beach. He and I are joking around when we spot Vox. Instantly my mood sours at the sight of him. When he finally looks up from his phone and sees us standing here he freezes.

"Great," Archer mutters. I follow his line of sight to the other side of the beach entrance to see Ezekiel making his way toward us. His steps falter when he looks up but he doesn't stop coming this way.

"What the hell are you two doing here?" I snap.

Vox glares at Ezekiel who comes to a stop beside him. "Unlike you fuckers, I came to meet my girl," he snarls. Ez shoots him a scathing look.

"Well, isn't that funny since my sister texted me to meet her here as well." Arch and I share a look and then I tilt my head back and groan.

"Fucking Nova," I snarl.

"Watch your fucking mouth!" Vox growls.

I shoot the fucker the bird as Archer answers him. "Looks like set ups run in the family because she texted us to meet her here as well." Vox and Ezekiel both look confused at his answer but the sound of laughter draws my attention further down the beach. The sight before me instantly has my blood boiling and my feet moving on their own accord. I hear the others following after me but don't pay them any mind. The sight of some cunt hugging Vivian has me seeing red.

It doesn't help that she is wearing a teal, two piece bathing suit and the bottoms are up her fucking ass, showing off the swell of her perfect cheeks. My pace slows when she pulls out of his embrace and I see the smile on her face. Nova rushes up to her and throws her arms around her friend.

"We won!" Nova shouts as she pulls back and high fives the fucker that was hugging Vivi. Archer comes to a stop on my right, Vox and Ezekiel stand on my left as we all watch the girls from the sidelines. It's as if a string is tethered from Vox to Nova because suddenly she spins around and locks eyes with him. Her whole body relaxes and a smile stretches across her face. She shoots Vivian a sheepish look. Vivi follows her line of sight and unlike Nova, her body locks up and the smile vanishes from her face at the sight of us.

Vivian turns back to Nova and we can tell Vi is pissed by the way she is throwing her hands around and glaring at her friend who tries to look sorry but fails. Then suddenly Vivian is tearing away from Nova and marching toward us. Vox, the cocksucker, chuckles at the sight of his twin red faced and angry. I can't stop my gaze from dropping. Her tits bounce up and down as she stomps toward us and my mouth waters. My hands itch to reach out and cup those perfect tits in my hands and pinch those nipples until she is squirming beneath me and begging me to sink my cock into her.

"What the fuck are you all doing here?" she snaps and pulls me from my thoughts.

"My sister invited me," Ezekiel replies without missing a beat.

"The witch wants me here," Vox says.

Vivian turns her gaze to me and Archer. "Nova set us up," Arch answers. Vi turns back expectantly and I throw caution to the fucking wind, I'm done playing games.

"I'm here for you." Her mouth parts on a silent gasp. I feel the three guys staring at me but I don't take my gaze off the girl in front of me. Taking it a step further I push forward until my bare chest brushes against her and she has to crane her neck back to meet my gaze. "This time, Vivi baby, when you run, *I'm chasing you.*"

She opens and closes her mouth a couple of times but no words come out. "You guys want to play?" I dart my gaze over her to the fucker who needs me to break his hands and narrow my eyes.

"Yeah, we're in. Four of us against you all, but you touch my girl or sister again and I'll snap your fucking arms," Vox warns. Vivian growls and the rest of us chuckle. The three guys make their way over but I don't move. I bend down until my lips brush the shell of her ear, loving the way she shivers.

"Want to make a bet, Vivi baby?"

"W-what kind?' she stutters out. I fight the smirk from breaking free. She was doing so well acting all tough and unbothered until she felt my flesh against hers.

"We win, you spend the night with me."

She sucks in a sharp inhale. "No." She tries to pull back but I wrap my arm around her waist anchoring her to me. I flick my gaze to Archer and Ezekiel staring right at us, expecting to see anger in their eyes but all I see is... acceptance?

"Scared of a little wager, baby?"

"No." She tries to break free but it's futile and we both know it.

"Then name your terms."

"We win, you leave me the fuck alone and never come near me again."

I tsk and drop my voice lower into a husky purr. "And if *we* win?"

"What do you want?"

"You spend the night with the three of us."

"I'm not fucking any of you."

I chuckle and relish in the way a shiver runs down her spine. "I never said anything about fucking, just dinner."

She takes a second to answer. "Just dinner?" I pull back and smile down at her.

"And if you're a good girl we might eat you for dessert." I shoot her a wink and leave her standing there with her mouth ajar as I make my way toward the guys. I've never wanted to win a game so fucking much in life!

"What was that about?" Ezekiel asks as I pass by him to head to the other side of the court.

"A little bet," I answer with a wicked smile as I turn to face Nova and her team. Vivian looks flushed.

"What bet?" Archer hedges.

I shoot him and Ezekiel a wicked look. "Better win this game boys so we can spend the night with Vivi baby." Both their eyes widen.

"The fuck does that mean, asshole?" I roll my eyes and turn to face Vox who looks like he is two seconds away from breaking shit.

"It means, you need to back the fuck up and accept what

this is. We all have our problems with each other, but Vivian has nothing to do with that. Stay the fuck in your lane, Vox. You are not getting in the middle of this." He stalks toward me and doesn't stop until we are chest to chest. I can hear Nova shouting for us to cut it out, but we both ignore her. Ezekiel and Archer dart forward, ready to intervene if one of us throws a punch.

"She's my sister," he snarls.

"Your point?" I taunt.

"Either play the game or get the hell off the court." At the sound of *my* girl's voice I step back and wink at her asshole brother.

"Sure thing, Vivi baby," I call out, never taking my eyes off her twin who stands there turning red and grinding his teeth.

The tension between the four of us is suffocating but I refuse to crack under the pressure of it or even acknowledge it. Vox on the other hand, it seems like he wants nothing more than to have it out with the three of us.

"Nova, want to serve, babe?" Vox snaps his head toward the other side of the court so fast I swear I hear his neck crack. Without permission laughter bubbles out of me. That fucker must have a death wish, first he touches Vivian and now he calls Nova babe. Vox's upper lip twitches as he watches Nova take the ball from the cunt, moves to the back, then he turns to us with a bloodthirsty look in his eyes.

"I want a truce until we slaughter this cunt." I can't help but laugh at the fucker, Vox doesn't take well to anyone looking at Nova let alone someone calling her *babe*. Ezekiel and Archer are both smiling and shaking their heads. "I'm serious, we take them down then go back to hating each other, deal?"

"Only if you agree not to interfere tonight when we win." He grits his teeth at Archer's request.

"Fine! Now, can we teach this cunt a lesson?" he snarls.

"Game–fucking––on," Ez says.

"Let's fuck shit up," I add.

And we do, we slaughter these little punks in the first round. Dawson and his friend are sweating as they try to keep up with us but years of football has us conditioned for endurance. Ezekiel and Archer may have been kicked from the team, but they never stopped training and because of that Arch made the CHU team with me and I have a sinking suspicion the new QB coach told us about, is none other than Vox-fucking-Hatchett. Nova is panting but can't stop smiling, clearly her and Vox are having a silent conversation with their eyes. I turn to Vivian next, she seems angry... I wonder why? I chuckle to myself at the sight of her all red faced and pissed off at the world. When she looks at me I purse my lips and send her an air kiss. Her nostrils flare, Archer and Ezekiel both laugh and somehow I know without having to look at them that they are thinking the same thing as I am. My laughter dies off when a wicked look enters her eyes. She straightens from her hunched position and turns her back to us to face Dawson, giving us the perfect view of her ass. I bite my lip to keep from groaning.

"Hey Dawson?" she sings songs.

"Yeah?" he answers.

"What are you doing later?" My body turns rigid, both Ez and Archer stand to their full height.

Dawson frowns and takes in the sight of her, then suddenly the dumbfounded look on his face is replaced with one of pure enjoyment. "Taking you out?" he answers.

"You want a broken fucking jaw, asshole?" Ezekiel snaps. Dawson snaps his head toward us. I push forward so I'm standing between Arch and Ez with only the net separating us from him.

"Not really but what am I supposed to say when a beautiful

single girl asks me what I'm doing later?" The little cunt has a death wish for real.

"Who the fuck said she was single?" Archer snaps.

"I am!" Vivian shouts as she shoots us three a look of pure malice.

Ez snorts and I know he's about to drop *the* bomb. "Hey, Dawson?" The dumbass faces Ez with a frown. "If you're planning to take *my wife* out for dinner, the least you could do is ask me first." Vivian's mouth pops open, Nova chokes on her own spit, then Dawson and his friend share a loaded look before turning back to Vivian for an explanation. Vox uses their moment of distraction to move forward and throw his arm around Ezekiel's shoulders like they are still close.

"I think what my brother-in-law is trying to say is that my sister and my girl aren't available tonight." The humor in Vox's tone has Vivian's face reddening.

"Fuck off, Vox. Take your ass and your three asshole friend's asses the fuck home." The second she turns her back to us I lose the battle. I duck under the net and head for her. Dawson darts in my path to try to stop me.

"You try to stop me from getting to her and I'll snap your fucking neck, pretty boy. Don't get involved because she doesn't need your weak ass to save her." I shove the fucker out of the way and ignore Vivian's threats as I bend down and lift her ass off the ground and fling her over my shoulder. I look at my boys next and wag my brows.

"Later, Nova," I call out as I stalk off ignoring Vivian punching my back and spewing threats.

"You hurt her and I'll kill the three of you, then piss on your fucking graves!" Vox shouts. I wave at him over my shoulder with my free hand. I can't stop myself from smiling, winning never felt so fucking good!

CHAPTER NINE

Vivian

I pound my fists against his bare back and even dig my nails into his flesh but he doesn't miss a step or even falter when I draw blood. I lift my head when I hear the other two laughing. I shoot both of them a look that promises to slit their throats in their sleep.

"I fucking hate you three!" I force out through clenched teeth.

Archer pouts. "Don't be like that, baby, a bet's a bet."

"It was best of three, assholes! You fuckers cheated!" I scream.

"You broke the rules when you tried to fuck with us and get that cunt to ask you out." My nostrils flare as I glare at Ezekiel.

"I hate you the most," I spit out. The bastard just shrugs. "Fucking put me down, Hayze!" I kick my legs and continue pounding my fists against his back. I'm so fucking embarrassed, I can hear people laughing and calling out for their friends to look. Never in my life have these idiots ever manhandled me like this before!

"Of course," Hayze says and I sigh in relief, happy that he is finally listening until the bastard slides me down his front, causing my breath to hitch. He keeps his hands on my waist and pushes me back until I'm flush against... a car. I look around and notice we are in the parking lot. I turn back to him and frown. The frown vanishes when he plasters his body flush against mine. Ezekiel and Archer cage me on each side. I dart my gaze between the three of them wondering what the fuck is going on. Ezekiel just flexed his big dick energy not five minutes ago, outing me as his wife and Archer pretty much tried to piss on me to mark his territory, and yet here they stand with smirks on their faces while their friend is plastered against me.

"You owe us dinner," Archer rasps out. I shake my head trying to come up with a reply but their close proximity is short circuiting my brain. I came to CHU with a plan and the instant these three barged back into my life my carefully crafted plan is long forgotten.

"I... uh... I—" My mumbling is cut off when Hayze grips the back of my neck, forcing me onto my tiptoes. I attempt to fight but then he shocks the fuck out of me and robs me of air when he seals his lips to mine. Instant fucking sparks! My mind quiets and my body relaxes into him. I grip his arms to keep me steady. He forces his tongue inside my mouth and the second I taste him, I moan without consent. Our tongues are a tangled mess, everything around us begins to fade as I get lost in him.

In this kiss.

When I hear a groan from my left, reality crashes into me. I snap my eyes open and turn my head to the side, gasping for air. Hayze finally releases me and steps back giving me space. I can't look at any of them.

I just kissed Hayze Draven!

Not only did I kiss him, I did it in front of the boy who took my virginity and my fucking husband!

"Get in the car, Vi," Ezekiel rasps out. I keep my head down and do as he says without argument, I'm too stunned and confused and... hot... really fucking hot to argue. I climb in the back and nibble on my lip. Ezekiel climbs in beside me and I huddle closer against the door as Archer and Hayze get in the front. I don't ask where we are going when they pull out of the lot. I don't even look up the entire drive. I'm too fucking confused and angry, I'm pissed at them but more than that, I'm angry at myself for allowing them to get inside my head again. Out of the three of them, I never expected Hayze to be the one to make the first move. I know there is unfinished business between the four of us but I never realized Hayze... liked me. I mean there were signs but I didn't allow myself to read too much into them.

As the car slowly comes to a stop, I lift my head and peer out the window. It's a small cottage style beach house with white shutters and all to boot. The guys all climb out of the car but I don't move, the house may be cute and all but I am not playing their games. I have too much weighing on me already and I don't need to add their mind-fuck games to the list. I see Archer reach for the door handle and quickly push the lock. He may not be able to see me through the tint but I sure as fuck can see him, and the look on his face is priceless.

"You really think a locked door is going to stop me?" he taunts from outside. I scoff and scoot forward and lean through the middle to hit the central locking on the driver's side and shoot Hayze and Ezekiel the middle finger through the wind-shield. Put that in your fucking pipe and smoke it, assholes! I flop back into my seat and wait for them to give up and go inside, the second they do I am making a run for it.

"Vivi, baby, you get one chance to do this the easy way or we resort to more... *pleasurable methods.*" The humor in Hayze's tone just grinds on my nerves. How can he act so unbothered by what just happened? No one knows about me and Archer, that shit has been kept a secret for years because I know Vox will murder him if he found out, but then Hayze gave zero fucks when he slung me over his shoulder in front of my brother—who I might add did nothing to stop him! Then to top it the fuck off, he kissed me, out in the open where Vox could have seen!

"Fuck you!" I scream, then cross my arms over my chest.

"You were warned," Archer teases. I sit here smugly, knowing they won't smash a car window to get inside—the smugness evaporates within a fraction of a second when the car beeps and all the locks disengage. I'm too slow, the door is yanked open before I can hit the lock again. Archer reaches for me, I kick out and relish in the sound of his grunt as I scramble to get to the other side, but he grabs my ankle and drags me toward me. I scream and kick to get free. He yanks me down the leather seats until my ass teeters on the edge and he is standing between my open legs. I sit up and attempt to smack him across the face but he grips my wrist halting my attack. "And here I thought you would put up more of a fight."

"Go fuck yourself, Archer." I sneer.

"Your bratty attitude is starting to piss me off, baby."

My eyes widen in indignation. "Good, then leave me the fuck alone, asshole."

"You were free for twelve fucking months. You came back to us not the other way around, Vivian." His words smack into me like an avalanche. I hate to admit it but they fucking sting like a bitch. Whatever Archer sees in my eyes has him dropping my wrist and stepping back. He doesn't ask as he grabs my hand and yanks me out of the car. He drags me toward the house and I hear the other two following after us. When we enter the house I expected to find it messy since they clearly live here but surprisingly, it's clean and has a real homey type feeling to it. He bypasses the modest kitchen and rounds a corner to a living room with the most stunning view of the ocean. I don't protest when he shoves me into one of the seats, I just sit here and stare out at the water.

Oh what it must feel like to be the ocean and be free to do as you please.

"We need to talk." Ezekiel's words drag me out of my thoughts and smack me back into reality. I release a long exhale and cross my arms over my chest. I don't miss the way the three of them drop their eyes to my tits.

I scoff and glare at the bastards. "You want to talk, then stop looking at my tits!" I snap. The three of them ignore me and continue to stare so I choose to be a real bitch and yank the small triangles to the side exposing my tits to them. "Take a good look, boys, they're tits and every girl has em!" The three idiots groan and don't even attempt to look away. I fix my top and let out a huff of annoyance.

"Well, that was distracting," Hayze says but the husky tone of his voice indicates he enjoyed the show more than he is letting on.

"Why the fuck am I here?" I bite out. The three of them just stand there and stare at me like I am the final piece to their unsolvable puzzle. I realize then that I left my phone and my stuff at the beach. "One of you better go get my shit from the beach!"

"Nova grabbed your things, she'll drop them off at your dorm," Archer says in a bored tone that pisses me off.

"Well, could you assholes at least get me a shirt or something so you can stop checking me out?"

"Now, why the fuck would we do that?" I gape at Ezekiel.

"Uh, because it's my body and I don't want you looking at it," I defend.

"The marriage license you and I both signed says I can look and touch whenever the fuck I want." I choke on fucking air! Hayze and Archer both mumble beneath their breath but my focus is rooted on Ezekiel.

"That's not what that means." My retort is weak and we all know it.

He shrugs. "Don't give a fuck. You can try to rationalize what's happening all you want, Vivi, but it doesn't change the fact that we are here and *we* all need to talk."

"Talk about what, Ezekiel?" I scream as I climb to my feet and get right in his face—well, chest but who the fuck cares! "You faked your death and didn't tell me, then those two assholes took off and left me a fucking note, a fucking note! None of you thought to call or text, you just left me behind." Ezekiel's eyes fill with guilt but I'm not done. "Do you have any idea what watching you die was like?" He opens his mouth but I push on. "It fucking killed me!" I scream and I hate that tears begin to fall down my cheeks. "I wanted to lean on Hayze and Archer to help me, but then they left. I was on my own and grieving the loss of not only my brother but the three of you! So, now tell me what the fuck we have to talk about because from where I'm standing, I don't think anything you three say will change my mind and make me want to stay."

"I'm in love with you." I stumble back a step and lose my balance, falling onto the seat I just vacated. I stare up at Archer with wide eyes and my mouth open. I search his gaze and I see nothing but the truth.

He means it.

I shake my head trying to deny his claim. "It's true, Vivian," he implores.

When he takes a step forward I raise my hand halting his

movements. "No," I whisper and bat away my tears, my chest is on fire and my mind is reeling. He finally said the words I longed to hear from him for years. "You don't get to say that to me, not now. Not after everything you put me through."

"I'm so sorry." When he reaches for me I smack his hands away. Hayze pushes him back and warns him not to try that shit again.

"You fucked me, then left me. You acted like I didn't exist. Stopped replying to my texts and when I would enter a room, you would leave. It took me years to come to terms with the fact you just wanted to be the one to fuck the infamous Vox Hatchett's sister."

His face pales. "That wasn't why I did it!" he roars.

"Everyone calm down," Ezekiel shouts. "How about we all take a minute to calm the hell down and maybe just cook some food then we can... talk."

I sigh dejectedly. "I have nothing to say," I admit quietly.

"Well, then you can listen because clearly we all have a lot to say and you aren't leaving here until everything that needs to be said is said," Ez answers.

"What is your hope out of this little pow wow?" I snark.

"For you to realize that the three of us clearly have feelings for you, Vivian, and none of us are willing to let you walk away."

Well, fuck! That was not what I expected to come out of my husband's mouth!

CHAPTER TEN

Ezekiel

I stand in the kitchen chopping up some vegetables for the stir fry while the others shower. After my declaration Vivian didn't argue any further. She accepted the shirt Hayze offered her and stormed off to the bathroom. Archer wasn't happy about me showing up at their house yesterday with my bags but fuck him, that's what family does and I refuse to live somewhere else if we are going to make this shit work. The three of us need to have a conversation and now seems like the perfect time as the both of them enter the kitchen fresh out of the shower and only in a pair of shorts each. Clearly they are hoping the sight of their ink and abs will have Vivi falling into bed with them.

"Want a hand?" Hayze offers.

"Nah, man, but we should talk before Vivi gets out of the shower." Both of them share a loaded look then sigh. "Just sit your asses down." They both grumble but do as I say and each pull out a stool at the breakfast bench across from me and sit their asses down. I can see both of them are feeling as awkward as I am but this conversation needs to be had so I break the ice. "She wants all of us but she just won't admit it." Both of them stare at me like I've lost my mind. "Hear me out—"

"She will never go for that, we just need to let her choose," Archer says but I can hear the tension in his voice.

"Okay, so say she chooses Hayze, you gonna be good knowing your best friend is fucking the girl you are in love with right next door to you?" Arch's face morphs into a picture of rage. "Exactly, not only would it eat you alive it would ruin your friendship."

"Like the one we have with you?" Hayze snarks, earning a scowl from me.

"You need to let go of the fact I married her! I did what I had to do," I defend.

"No, you did what you thought would help secure your place in her life. Don't pretend like that decision was about her, it was about you and what you wanted."

I drop the knife and throw my hands in the air. "I'm not gonna say sorry because I'm not. Should I have told you? Maybe, but I can't change that now, can I? So suck it the fuck up and move on because I'm not backing off. She may have my name but I'm not deluded enough to think she doesn't want either of you. Now, how about you two idiots come to terms with that because tonight, we are going to show her what it would be like to choose *all* of us."

"Say what now?" Hayze rasps out.

"Tonight, we are going to show her with our actions what she means to each of us. If either of you have any reservation about sharing, now is the fucking time to speak." I admit, the thought of ever sharing a woman never occurred to me until Vivian. Knowing that these two feel as strongly about her as I do, makes the decision easy for me. These two idiots are my brothers, we may fight sometimes but what siblings don't?

"What if she doesn't want that?" Archer asks.

I shrug. "We don't give her a chance to doubt us. We show her that we are united and that she doesn't need to make a choice because we are all choosing her and she needs to do the same by choosing us."

"She is fucking pissed as hell at us, Ez. We all left her and cut her out because we thought we knew best." I deflate a little at Hayze's admission.

"I know. We just need to try to make up for our mistakes and pray to fucking Lucifer she forgives our dumbasses and prove to her we will never put our relationship with Vox before her again."

A throat clearing has us all swinging our gaze to the entrance to see Vivian standing there in one of Hayze's shirts. "Yeah, proving that shit to me is going to take a lot longer than one evening." The bite in her tone isn't missed but I choose to ignore her snide comment and ask.

"You hungry?"

She rolls her eyes but there is no heat to it. "Yeah, I could eat."

"Have a seat." I flick my gaze to the stool between Hayze and Archer. She nibbles on her bottom lip which has me gripping the edge of the counter to keep from going to her and pulling it free. It takes her a solid minute before she finally resigns herself to her fate and makes her way over to the stool. She is careful not to brush against either of them as she sits down and rests her elbows on the counter. I run my gaze over her, loving the sight of her wet hair loose and her face free of makeup but it's also the shirt she wears that adds to her sex appeal. I never thought seeing my girl in another man's clothes would turn me on, but I was wrong.

"Can we get this conversation over with? I need to get back to my dorm. I have shit to do and an empire to run." The reminder of what she is in charge of has me gritting my teeth. She should never have put herself in a position where she was forced to lead the Saints. The reminder of them has me biting back a growl, those cunts took their time beating me as I got blooded in for her. Vivian stood there and watched without an ounce of emotion on her face, she looked so fucking callous and devoid of a fucking soul. She was the perfect picture of the true leader of The Brotherhood, her father would have been proud of the stone-faced woman she was.

It occurs to me only now as I look at her, did she not care about me being blooded in because she doesn't feel the same way I do?

"No." I frown and meet her hardened glare.

"What?" I ask.

"You said that shit out loud," Hayze answers for Vivian, sounding uncomfortable. I cringe but don't comment because I need to know the answer. Does she feel the same way I do or am I just wishing for something that will never happen?

Vivian's face blanks of all emotion, she looks untouchable like nothing we say or do could penetrate the armor that she surrounds herself with.

"I saw you die once before," she says this like we are discussing the fucking weather! "Seeing you die again just felt like a movie on repeat." She shrugs her fucking shoulders like what she just said didn't just destroy something inside of me. I stare at her for a moment utterly perplexed and astounded, she didn't care...

She doesn't feel the same...

"You can bullshit them, Vivian, but you can't lie to me." I turn to Archer who is glaring at Vivi. The girl refuses to pay him any attention and keeps looking around the kitchen like she finds it so interesting. Archer snaps his arm out and grips the back of her neck forcing a hiss past her lips as he turns her to face him. The hateful look in her eyes could peel the skin off any man.

"Fuck off!" she spits out.

Archer isn't one to be deterred, he leans in close enough, just leaving a sliver of space between their faces as he speaks. "You forget, *I* am the one who taught you how to lie and not show an ounce of emotion. If you meant what you just said, you wouldn't have had to mask your reaction." My brows shoot up as I study them.

Vivian makes a bold move, she turns her whole body toward Archer, he opens his legs wider so hers can slip in between his. She places her hands flat against the tops of his thighs, when she bites down on her bottom lip and bats her lashes at him, he changes. Gone is the anger and the need for control, she switched the roles on him so quickly he didn't have a chance to prepare himself and now he is nothing but putty in her deadly hands.

I cut a glance to Hayze who is watching them both with rapt attention, it's like he doesn't even realize it but he's shifting closer to her effectively placing her between the both of them. Vivi on the other hand registers what is happening and fights not to tense as she keeps Archer in her clutches.

"What hurts more, baby, the fact you think you know me and want to take credit for what you think you taught me or is it that you now know I don't need you to run a fucking empire in a man's world?" Her words have Arch whipping around but she doesn't stop, she stands. Hayze mimics her move but her sights are set on Archer, she stands between his legs and drapes her arms over his shoulders and leans in until her lips ghost over his. "It's not nice when the person you want most fucks with your feelings is it, Archy baby?" I fight not to smile, Vivian has definitely changed and fuck me if it's not for the better, because the show she is putting on now has my cock rock fucking hard and dying to sink inside her.

Archer's nostrils flare, then in a swift move he is on his feet and has her pressed up against the breakfast bench with her back to me and him right in her face. Hayze darts his eyes to me. I give a subtle shake of my head telling him to let this play out.

"You want to act like a heartless bitch then go for it, Vivian, because you and I both know you feel more than you are willing to admit."

"I don't feel anything for you bastards," she grits out.

Archer laughs but there is no humor to it. He grabs her waist in one hand then uses the other to grip her hair and tug her head back so he can look her in the eyes. "Oh, baby, I taught you how to lie better than that."

"No—"

Arch cuts her off. "Shut the fuck up." Instantly her body turns rigid. "Good girl." Hayze must see the same thing I do, when a shiver travels down her spine we both lean in closer. I hate to admit it but Archer may be the only one who knows what she likes in the bedroom but outside of it, Hayze and I know her better than him. Archer leans in and seals his lips to hers. I watch as if I am in a trance. Her body melts into him, wrapping her arms around his neck pulling him closer. Hayze groans. As if she just remembered that they aren't alone in the room, shoves Archer back and then whirls around to face me and Hayze. Archer glues himself to her back and ignores her warning to fuck off when he pushes her hair to one side and begins kissing her neck.

Vivian's eyes are wide as she looks between me and Hayze as Archer continues to lick a trail along her neck in time with his hand skating down her stomach. Her throat bobs up and down, her eyes are wide with worry but I can see the need in the depths of those blue eyes. She is trying to reason with herself that what's happening is wrong and not normal but when have we ever been fucking normal?

Normal is boring!

When Archer's hand slips under the shirt she wears, she gasps and tries to pull free but he secures her to him with his other arm banded around her waist. "Archer!" she rasps out.

"They want you like I do. Now do me a favor and take what we are about to give you," he mutters against her neck. Her mouth parts on a silent gasp and both Hayze and I groan knowing Archer has just stroked her pussy. "For someone who hates us, you seem to be soaked for the monsters that ruined your life, baby."

"S-stop," she stutters out as her eyes roll backward.

Archer rests his chin on her shoulder and looks directly at Hayze. "Get on your knees and taste her." Vivian's mouth parts as if to argue but the moment Hayze knocks the stool out of his way and drops to his knees before her she clamps it shut.

Hayze grips the hem of her shirt and lifts it, exposing her perfect pink pussy with Archer's finger inside it. He slowly withdraws his digit and brings it to her lips, smearing her own wetness across them, then he darts his gaze to me. "Kiss her while Hayze eats her pussy." Normally, I'm the one who is giving the orders but it seems that role has shifted when it comes to giving our girl what she wants. I abandon the vegetables I was meant to be chopping and stalk around the counter. Archer peels the shirt off exposing her to us. She wears nothing beneath the shirt and fuck her body is a masterpiece. Her tits are perfect, big enough to fill my hands and perky, her nipples are pebbled to hardened peaks begging for me to take them in my mouth.

"Eat her cunt," I growl as I step forward and watch as

Hayze lifts one of her legs and flings it over his shoulder exposing her to him. "Put that pussy on his sideburns, baby." She cuts a glance to me for a second, the lustful look in her eyes has me cupping myself through my pants. The three of us watch as Hayze leans forward and swipes his tongue through her slick folds.

"Fuck!" she cries out. I step forward and cup her face between my hands, forcing her to look at me. I need her to see me, not Archer or Hayze, me! The instant I see recognition in her eyes, I lean down and swipe my tongue across her lips tasting her. I groan, fuck she taste so good. Before I get a chance to savor more of her taste, she cries out again. I seal my mouth to hers and swallow her moans.

This situation is like none I have ever been in before. Hayze is on his knees eating her out, I'm kissing her, while Archer is behind her. Her tongue tangles with mine and I moan. I open my eyes and watch as she skims her fingers through Hayze's hair then slings her other arm around my neck, holding me in place. I peer over her shoulder to see Archer pushing his pants down. I've seen his, Vox and Hayze's cock's enough over the years that it doesn't shock me to see it again. He runs a hand down her back then grabs her ass and squeezes. She moans into my mouth and pulls me in closer as he kneads the globes of her ass.

"I'm gonna fuck you now, baby," Archer rasps out. She breaks our kiss and turns to look at him over her shoulder. I'm sure she wants to protest and tell him to fuck off but Hayze is too good at keeping her distracted so she nods. I bend down and capture a nipple in my mouth as Archer begins to slide inside her, I can feel the instant he does it. Her body arches forward and she digs her fingers into the back of my hair and tugs on the strands.

"Oh fuck, Archer, it's too much," she cries.

"Just wait till you have the three of us in every fucking hole." The image Archer's words paint has my cock twitching painfully in my pants. "Fuck, baby, I missed this pussy."

"Archer, I need you to move, I'm gonna come," she pleads.

I release her nipple with a wet pop and stare down at Hayze. He sucks her clit into his mouth as Archer begins to fuck her. The sight of her naked and being ravished by my best friends is an image I thought would anger me, but instead all it has done is turn me the fuck on. I rid myself of my shirt and love the way her gaze immediately swings to me as she drinks in the sight of my naked flesh. Her eyes trail down my body and watch as I push my pants down my legs and kick them to the side. Her eyes are wide and glued to my pierced cock.

CHAPTER ELEVEN

Vivian

What the fuck is happening right now?

Fuck, I can feel my orgasm building and it's been such a long time since I have felt this way. Hayze laps at my pussy like he can't get enough of me. Archer is sliding in and out of me with ease thanks to how fucking wet I am. The sight of Ezekiel before me stroking his cock has my mouth watering.

I need to taste him.

Fuck it, I've already crossed a line with these three so I may as well take fucking control and embrace this moment before it's over. I have no idea what is happening right now but I'm too wound up to question it. I push Hayze away, then step forward, forcing Archer out of me. Neither of them say anything as I step toward Ezekiel. Unlike Archer and Hayze, Ezekiel won't bend to my will. He's the one who always forces me out of my comfort zone which is why I know if I told him to come to me and let me suck his cock, he would have refused.

I hold his gaze as I slowly lower to my knees. I can feel the other two's gazes on me, watching to see what I will do. I tentatively reach out and grip him in my hand. I can see the bead of pre cum on the tip and my mouth waters, needing to know what he tastes like. I have only ever done this with one person and the thought of that person watching me do this turns me on. I swipe my tongue across his head and love the sound he makes.

"Suck his cock, Vivi baby." I do as Hayze instructs and wrap my lips around Ezekiel while still holding his stare. His eyes have darkened and I love the way his face contorts the further I take him into my mouth.

"Fuck yeah, baby." He praises me when I pull back and do it again. When I spy Hayze out of the corner of my eye, I smirk around Ez's dick at the sight of him standing at my side with his own cock out. Shit, they are all huge! I know women always say it's hard to find a man with girth and length but it so happens I have three men standing around me with both. I reach out and smack Hayze's hand away and replace it with my own. His head falls back and a groan tumbles free from his lips. I spy Archer on my other side and instantly release Ez from my mouth, Archer knows what I want and lines himself up with my mouth. Unlike Ezekiel he doesn't go slow. His fingers tangle in my hair and then he is fucking my face forcing me to gag around his length.

I can't explain how fucking empowering this moment is. I switch from sucking Archer off to sucking Hayze off while stroking the other two with my hands. I may be the one on my knees but I know I am the one with the power and it is fucking exhilarating. These three guys could pick any girl they wanted to fuck, yet the three of them are standing before me. I'm still so angry and hurt but my body has taken control and all I can think of is the release I know they can give me.

Fuck, I need it!

Hayze rips free and groans, I stare up at him spit trickling down my chin while still stroking the others. Ez yanks on my hair and forces his cock into my mouth making me gag around him.

"I need to fuck her." Hayze's voice is a husky plea and I want to grant his wish but I can't do anything aside from gag and try to breathe as Ez thrusts in and out of my mouth. Unlike most girls, I discovered after the first time I had sex that I don't like sweet and slow. I like to be fucked and ravaged until I am begging for him to stop. Archer is the next to pull free and I want to pout but I can't.

"Get the lube, she's getting all three of us," Archer barks. I feel myself gush and know without a doubt that my arousal is coating my inner thighs. Hayze stalks off and returns a minute later. Ezekiel pulls back and I slump forward gasping for air. An arm bands around my hunched form and lifts me. It's Hayze. Archer leads us into the living room and pushes the small table out of the middle and nods for Hayze to put me down.

The moment he puts me on my feet I suddenly feel... awkward and unsure until Hayze lays down on the rug and reaches up to me, I take his hand and allow him to pull me down on top of him. I go to reach for his cock but he stops me with his words.

"If you don't want this, say the word and it all stops, Vivi baby." I smile down at Hayze, he's always been the caring one out of the four of them. Rather than use words I lean down and capture his lips in a kiss that I hope portrays that I'm okay. I'm too scared to use my words in case my anger takes control and I ruin this moment. I can go back to blaming them tomorrow but for tonight, I need this.

I reach between our bodies and line his cock up with my

pussy. I slowly sink down onto him hissing. Fuck, he's big. Hayze breaks the kiss and stares up at me then cups my tits, twirling my nipples between his fingers. I throw my head back and moan as I bounce up and down on him.

"You think you can take us as well?" I turn my head to the side to watch Ezekiel squirting lube on his dick, my body turns hot instantly and suddenly it's not about what I can handle but what I need from each of them, and right now I need them all filling me and taking away my power. I need them to put me at their mercy and force me to submit control to them.

"Yes," I breathe out. Ez shifts so he's behind me and gently pushes me down until I'm flat against Hayze's chest, to distract me from the feeling of Ez rubbing lube on my forbidden hole, Hayze kisses me. I melt into him and kiss him back. When Ezekiel slowly begins to breach my ass with his thumb I tense.

"Just relax, baby, try not to fight it or it will hurt." I breathe through the sting and try to listen to what he is saying but I can bet my life on the fact that Ezekiel hasn't ever had some guys dick in his ass, so his advice doesn't really mean shit right now. Hayze pushes a hand between us and slowly circles my clit, drawing a long moan from me. My body takes on a mind of its own and I start thrusting down on him, I gasp when Ez matches my pace and then pain bleeds into pleasure. Fuck, I feel so full. I keep my thrusts slow and love how good this feels. I break my kiss with Hayze and look up to see Archer standing above me, I sit back and open my mouth, instantly his cock fills my mouth and I moan at the taste of him.

I whimper when Ezekiel pulls his thumb out but it's quickly replaced by his dick and I tense, fear begins to take a hold of me. I know for a fact his dick is a *lot* bigger than his thumb! Archer strokes my cheeks and smiles encouragingly.

"You can take us, baby, I know you can. I swear, you will feel so good." I nod and brace myself.

"Hayze, fuck her and play with her clit," Ez barks. Hayze does as he is told and thrusts inside me causing a strangled cry from me. I clamp down on him when he pinches my clit between his fingers. Ezekiel starts to push forward and I choke on Archer when a searing pain rips through me, tears instantly threaten to spill.

"Breathe through it, baby, and focus on what I'm doing and sucking Arch's dick," Hayze advises but it is a lot easier said than done. I try to block out the pain and focus on the feeling of my orgasm building but each time I feel him pushing inside me it's like my orgasm comes to a standstill. It feels like hours later before Ezekiel is finally balls deep inside my ass, he groans and I cry out in pain and pleasure, but then suddenly my focus is on Archer when his fingers tangle in my hair and his movements become erratic. He's going to come.

"Fuck her, I need to see it before I come," Arch orders, like slaves to their own needs, both Hayze and Ezekiel obey. It takes them a second to find a rhythm and it takes me a moment longer to forget about the pain and then suddenly there is nothing but pleasure. I find myself pushing back against Ezekiel and slamming down on Hayze needing more from them both as I chase my high. "Fuck, baby, you've never looked more beautiful," Archer growls. "Suck it harder, baby, I'm going to come and I want you to swallow every fucking drop of me. I need to be inside you like they are." The dominance in which he says this has me wanting it as well. I hollow my cheeks and bob up and down faster as I continue to fuck the other two.

I feel Archer swell a moment before he's throwing his head back and roaring out his release, then my mouth fills with warm liquid. I swallow around his cock and try as hard as I can to not let a drop escape but I can feel some trickling down the corner of my mouth. Archer pulls out, swipes his thumb across my mouth then pushes his cum covered thumb back inside. I hold his gaze as I suck it clean and swirl my tongue around the digit loving the groan that escapes him. Ezekiel gripping my hips and slamming inside me has me releasing Archer so I can scream.

"Holy fuck!" I scream out when he does it again.

"I want to watch her come all over your dick, brother," Archer says as he drops down onto the sofa across from us. I feel powerful with him watching me fuck his friends. I push back against Ezekiel until my back is flush against his chest and tilt my head back. He takes the hint and bends down to kiss me. Hayze tweaks my nipples and I know I'm done for in a matter of seconds. They both must recognize the way my body turns stiff because their pace increases and their thrusts grow harder and faster. It's like they are racing to the finish line to see who can get me to come first.

The moment my orgasm hits, lava floods my veins and everything around me becomes white noise as a tidal wave of pleasure like I have never felt before rips through me. I scream so fucking loud my throat turns hoarse, my vision is blurry as the two of them continue to fuck me, chasing their own release. Hayze is the first to come with my name on his lips. Ezekiel is three thrusts behind but unlike Hayze who roared out his release, Ezekiel bites down on my shoulder, drawing a pained cry from me that quickly turns to pleasure when he reaches around and pinches my clit forcing another round of after-shocks to tear through me.

Utterly spent and exhausted, I flop forward onto Hayze and close my eyes, fucking exhausted. His arms come around me and hold me close. I feel safe and cocooned in his embrace. That was the hottest moment of my life and I can't stop the tired smile from stretching across my lips as I give into the exhaustion and allow it to pull me under. I just hope I'm not plagued by nightmares like every other night.

CHAPTER TWELVE

Hayze

We've all been sitting around on the sofas, waiting for Vivian to wake up. When she passed out in my hold earlier, I fucking panicked until Ez told me we just exhausted the fuck out of her. His words did ease some of my worries but not all of them so I refused to let her go. I've been sitting on the sofa for who the fuck knows how long, it's dark out now and she still hasn't woken. I can't seem to keep my hands off her. Her naked body is pressed against my own with a throw blanket covering us both. Her hair is a tangled mess but she has never looked more beautiful to me then she does now. Archer got a cloth and cleaned her up earlier but I didn't miss the way he looked at her like his life had meaning again.

When we got to CHU, I saw some of the old Archer, the guy who loved to play ball and train until he couldn't stand, but there was always something missing. I didn't realize until earlier that it wasn't a something it was a *someone*. I look over at the two of them to find both their gazes laser focused on Vivian. The only lighting is from the fire Ez lit earlier, the stars and the moon offer some lighting but not much. None of us have said much since... well since we all fucked her. I can feel the tension in the room and the last thing I want is for her to wake up and regret it but I also don't want her waking and feeling this tension so I decide to break it.

"I'm not sorry." My voice sounds gruff from hours of no use.

"What?" Arch asks.

I exhale and look between him and Ezekiel as I speak, I need them to see how serious I am. "I don't regret what happened earlier and I don't want it to be a one-time thing." My heart begins to pound inside my chest as nerves work their way through me. I'm fucking worried that both of them are going to deny me and want her to choose between the three of us—I can't lose her. For years I have stood back and watched her from a distance and always been there when she needed me. I'm done being the guy in the friendzone, today showed me I have a shot with her and I am grabbing that chance with both fucking hands and not letting go without a fight.

"That's up to her," Ezekiel says quietly.

"I'm not walking away again," Archer admits.

"Then what do we do because I am not letting her go. I stood back before but not anymore, not after..." I clamp my mouth closed not wanting to finish my thought.

"You've tasted her?" Archer pushes, earning a growl from me. "Fucked her?" My upper lip lifts in a snarl. "Felt her come all over your cock—"

"Shut the fuck up, asshole!" I snap then cringe when Vivian stirs in my arms. Both of them lean forward and watch her with rapt attention. I take in the looks on their faces and see that none of us will let her go without a fight but the biggest question is, will she choose us all?

"The choice is hers to make. If she wants us all, then we need to figure out a way to make this work." Ezekiel's tone is stern.

"How?" I ask.

He shrugs. "For one, we need to make sure everyone is good with sharing her. Second, there will be times she just fucks one of us, will we be good with that? Third—" He drapes his arms over the tops of his thighs and hangs his head as he exhales loudly. "Her brother will come for all of us. None of us are innocent now and Vox isn't stupid, he's going to find out what happened here tonight and be out for blood."

A pang of guilt hits me. I love Vox, he's my brother. I know we haven't spoken in a year but a bond like the one the four of us share isn't one that just goes away, it's a bond that lasts a lifetime. The things we have done together, the things we have seen, would be enough to make any man weep but not us. We had each other to lean on and help us survive the nightmares we each faced after the first kills. Over time, it became easier and we grew numb to the gore and the prospect of death. We killed to try and gain our freedom but it wasn't just for us, we did what we did to get Vivian free of The Brotherhood and it appears all we did was drive her toward them. Now she leads the very men who wanted to see her married to a monster.

"Let him come, I'm ready to meet my maker if that's what it takes to show him she isn't just some girl to me," I answer without hesitation.

"Agreed," Archer replies.

"Now, we just need her to decide what she wants," Ezekiel breathes out.

"Why couldn't you have asked me what I wanted years

ago?" she whispers. I drop my gaze to her and smile, but the hurt look in her eyes has it vanishing.

"Would you have realized you wanted more than just Archer?" I push. She nibbles the corner of her mouth and frowns. I reach out and smooth the lines from her forehead, loving the way she melts at the feeling of my touch. "He was the center of your world," I whisper, her brows pull in. "All you saw was him until…"

"Until he broke my heart," she says quietly. I look at Archer and feel bad for my brother as he drops his gaze to the floor, clearly riddled with guilt.

"If he didn't do that, you would never have noticed there were two other guys who were crazy about you." She lolls her head to the side to look at Ezekiel. The usually grumpy fucker cracks a sad smile but I can see the pain he is trying to hide. She slowly turns back to face me.

"It doesn't change the fact you all chose my brother and left me." The hurt that laces her words has my chest splitting open. I grip her waist and position her so she is straddling my lap. The blanket falls around her, exposing her naked back to the guys and her tits to me. I'm powerless to stop my eyes from falling to take in the sight of them.

When she clears her throat, I flick my gaze back to her and wink. She doesn't try to cover herself which I am grateful for because now that I have seen what lies beneath the clothes she wears, I never want to see her body covered again.

"What's it gonna take for you to realize that we did what we did to save you from a fate we feared was worse than death? We tried to spare you from being blooded in, which you clearly found a way around. But, did it ever occur to you that becoming the lordess paints a target on your back?"

"I didn't need saving. When are you all going to realize that? If you had all trusted me you would see I am doing exactly what you four could never do." She tries to push off of me and fear grips me. I feel like if I let her escape my hold she will flee and we will never get her back, so I wrap my arms around her waist and kiss her. She fights me and tries to break free but I overpower her. I prod her lips, seeking entrance but she keeps them closed so I cheat. I thrust upward and the instant she feels my cock glide against her pussy she gasps. I use her moment of distraction to gain entry. When my tongue swipes hers she slackens in my hold and the fight drains from her.

When she grinds against me I break the kiss and bite down on the tender flesh of her neck, loving the way she throws her head back and cries out, "Hayze." Hearing her moan my name has the mask wearing monster inside me rearing its head.

"I need to fuck you, Vivi baby," I mutter against her skin.

"Do it." I grip her waist and lift, turning her to face the others. It's as if she forgot they were here because she stills in my hold.

"Throw your legs over mine." She does what she is told on autopilot. I situate her so the guys will get the best view of her. "Put my cock inside you."

"But—"

Ezekiel cuts her off. "Do as he says!" She jerks in my hold and fumbles between us as she lifts up then shakily grips my cock and lines it up with her entrance. She drops her chin to her chest and I'm not having that. I reach around and grip her throat, forcing her head up.

"I want you to look at them as you sink down on my cock, baby." I hear her sharp intake of breath and can already feel her wetness coating the tip of my dick. I smirk when I see Arch and Ez pushing their pants down and freeing their cocks. The sight of them stroking themselves has her growing bold. She slowly sinks down and I groan loving the way her pussy pulses and clenches the fuck out of me.

"Oh, fuck," she moans once I'm fully sheathed inside her.

"Tell them how good my cock feels inside you," I demand as I thrust inside her, pulling a sharp cry from her lips.

"Hayze!" she breathes out.

"Tell them!" I roar.

She jerks her head and faces them. "He feels so good," she rushes to say so I reward that and fuck her, loving the way she tries to take control but she will learn I call the shots, not her.

"Open your legs wider so they can see how well you are taking my cock." She does as I ask and opens herself wide. Both the guys groan and stroke themselves faster at the sight of my cock disappearing in and out of her. "Look at them, baby." She does as I say then moans. "Do you like watching them while I fuck you?"

I expect her to ignore my question but she surprises me when she answers, "Yes. I love them watching me." Her answer seems to please the guys as well, I can see them strangling their cocks trying not to come, they want to come at the same time as her.

"Look at them, baby, they want to come with you," I growl as I slam inside her, loving the cry that tears from her. "They're sitting there wishing they were me, they want to be the ones inside this pussy."

"Oh fuck!" she grits out as she meets my thrust. I can feel the walls of her pussy clamping down and I know she is moments away from shattering but I'm not done.

"They want to feel you clamping down on their dick when you come. Look at them, baby." She does. Both of them look strained and ready to come steal her from me, but the both of them won't risk her getting scared by the three of us fucking her again. "You want to feel their cocks inside this perfect little cunt?" I whisper in her ear as I begin to circle her clit.

"Oh fuck, yes." Her answer surprises me.

"Not tonight, this dirty little cunt belongs to me," I growl.

"Hayze, I'm so close," she whines as she bounces up and down on my dick.

"Ezekiel, come eat her pussy, brother." Vivian gasps when Ezekiel stands and comes toward us. When he slowly drops to his knees her whole body begins to turn a shade of red. "Keep your eyes on Archer, baby. I want him to see what we're doing to you." She lifts her head and stares at Archer who stares at her with a hunger I have never seen before. The second Ezekiel swipes her clit she leans forward and screams. "She won't last," I grit out as I pound into her. I can feel my own orgasm cresting and I won't be able to hold off. "Fuck, Ez, I'm gonna come, I need you to make her come once I do." When she slams down on me again I lose it, my hold on her hips turns bruising as I roar her name as I shoot jets of cum inside her pussy. I've barely finished coming when Ez rips her off my dick and drops her down onto the couch beside me. He forces himself between her legs, then slams inside her. Her back arches off the couch as a scream filled with primal need tears free.

"Fuck yes, baby, I won't last. I need you to come," Ez growls.

"Just like that, please don't stop," she begs as Ezekiel fucks her like a ravaged man. Four thrusts later Vivian is screaming so loud our neighbors would be sure to hear. Ez follows her over the cliff a second later. I smirk at the sight of him dropping his weight on top of her. I jolt in surprise when Archer appears and pulls Ezekiel's off her. Vivian stares up at him with wide eyes. Arch smirks down at her but it's dark and sinister.

"Get up." She does as he asks but her legs are shaky. "Bend over and rest your hands on Hayze's thighs." I laugh at the fucker but Vivian just stands there unsure so I soothe her worries with my words.

"It's okay, Vivi baby, he wants me to watch you come on his cock for teasing him." Archer winks at me and smiles. Vivian does as he asks and rests her hands on my thighs but refuses to look into my eyes. I grip her chin and lift her head, forcing her to meet my stare. "I want to watch you." Her mouth parts in a silent gasp. Archer slides up behind her and lines himself up, then slams into her without warning. She cries out and jolts forward but he keeps her positioned where he wants. Ezekiel shifts and sits beside me. Vivian takes it upon herself to shift so one of her hands is on his leg and the other on mine. Archer growls his approval behind her.

"You like that?" Ez asks.

Her eyes are glassy, her cheeks are flushed and this is a sight I would kill to see on her daily. She looks well fucked and ready to pass out again.

"Yes, fuck, this is so fucking good. All your cocks are fucking perfect," she says.

"You gonna come, baby?" Archer rasps out, sweat beading his brow and I know he's ready to blow but I don't want to leave our girl hanging so I play nice and reach out, so I can play her clit. She jerks and cries out.

"Oh fuck, keep fucking me like that while he plays with my pussy." Her words have me grinning like a fool.

"Fuck yes, take my dick, baby. I want you to come all over it. You gonna be a good girl and come for me, baby?" Archer presses.

"Yes, I'm coming!" she cries out. Archer continues slamming inside her relentlessly until Ez and I are forced to keep her up until he finally comes. Vivian flops into our arms when Archer finally pulls out and drops to his ass on the rug, panting. I glare at Ezekiel when he pulls her into his embrace. The fucker just smirks and tells me to get a cloth. I do as he says only because our Vivi baby just took a triple cream pie. By the time I return with a warm cloth she has passed out in Ez's hold. I look at Archer who is fast asleep on the rug. I creep closer but freeze when I hear a whisper.

"I've loved you from the moment I met you, I'm sorry I was a coward and didn't tell you. After I thought Taylor died, I was too scared to love freely in case another girl broke my heart but unlike my sister, you have the power to rip the damn thing right out of my chest."

Well, shit! The emotionless fuck does have a heart. I guess none of us realized he gave it away a long time ago...

CHAPTER THIRTEEN

Vivian

I slowly blink my eyes open and just lay here staring up at the ceiling. The sun hasn't even risen yet but I'm wide awake and know I need to get out of here and get my head back in the game. I slowly sit up and try to be as quiet as I can. I look around and can't help but smile at the sight of Archer slumped in the single seater. I look to the other side and my heart melts at the sight of Hayze curled up on the sofa with a smile on his face even as he sleeps. I drop my gaze to the ground and my whole body tenses at the sight of Ezekiel sleeping on the floor beside the sofa I passed out on. But it's not the sight of him on the ground, it's the gun resting beside him that has my breath hitching.

Ezekiel Tempest has always been the one with his guard up, much like my twin. Ez doesn't smile freely like Hayze. Archer may be wound tight but even he can let loose and relax. Last night was the first time I have ever seen Ez so unguarded and not walled off. He let me see the real him, they all did and that makes leaving them so much fucking harder. I slowly stand and tip toe over Ezekiel. I snatch one of their discarded shirts off the floor and snag Archer's shorts as well. I quickly pull them on and tie the pants to keep them from falling down. My hair is a tangled mess so I just pile it on top of my head and rock the messy bun look.

As I make my way toward the front door, I pause just to take one last look at them. The three of them are such polar opposites but yet somehow, they have forged a bond that will surpass the test of time. They are brothers in every sense of the word. I never thought any of them would ever bat an eye at me, they are gods amongst us but yet, the three of them want *me!*

I had all three of them inside me!

I can still feel the ghost of their cocks. I'm sore but in the most delicious way. I give myself a minute to dream about what it would be like to wake up to the three of them every morning. I know it's not conventional but fuck, I want that life. I sigh, then turn and flee. I need to finish what I started back home so I can have a chance at discovering if this is something that we could really have or was it a one-time deal?

I quietly open the door and close it behind me, smiling when I don't hear them coming after me. I turn around and the smile instantly vanishes from my face at the sight of my brother leaning against his favorite car. That Hellcat and his Challenger Demon were the loves of his life until he met Nova. I dart my gaze around, trying to find an escape but grit my teeth because I know even if I tried to run he would catch me.

"Don't run," he pleads. I swing my gaze back to him and study my twin, he looks the same but different. He stands there with two coffee cups in his signature dark wash jeans, Converse and plain black tee. His hair is a tousled mess and his eyes are bloodshot, he clearly didn't sleep last night.

"How long have you been here?" I ask as I slowly make my way toward him. His eyes instantly trail down my body, the tight set of his jaw tells me he doesn't like the sight of me in his friends clothes but tough fucking luck.

"Long enough," he clips out and hands me a cup. I eye it warily, he rolls his eyes. "It's a caramel latte with two sugars, full cream and extra chocolate on the top." I roll my lips over my teeth to keep from smiling. Vox has always hated how I take my coffee but the fact he stills remembers my order warms my heart. "Come on, I'll drive you back to the dorms." I open my mouth to protest but he holds a hand up, stopping me. "You gave those three a chance, the least you can do is give me one as well."

My brows raise. "I didn't give them shit, they kidnapped me!"

He pins me with a deadpan look, then scoffs. "Yeah and you look so distraught about that," he mocks then climbs inside the car. I growl and stomp my bare foot.

"Fucking asshole," I mutter as I round the car and climb in beside him. He doesn't start the car, he just sits there gripping the wheel and staring out the windshield. I can tell he is warring within himself about something. I remain silent and wait.

"I need you to answer me honestly."

"Ask me what you want, Vox," I say tiredly as I lean back in my seat and sip my coffee. I swallow the moan that threatens to escape me at the sweet taste.

"Do I need to go in that house and beat the shit out of my three best friends?" I choke on my coffee and pound a fist against my chest as I try to breathe. My brother just sits there and doesn't move a muscle. When I get myself under control, I turn and glare at him.

"What the fuck?" I snap.

He slowly turns his head toward me but doesn't release the wheel from his death grip, his eyes burning with anger. I can tell it is taking everything inside him not to break into that house and murder his friends.

"I'm not fucking stupid, Vivian, and even if I was, the hickey on your neck is a dead fucking giveaway about what you and... they did." He shudders in disgust.

"*Them?*" I push.

His eyes narrow. "They aren't as slick as they fucking think. Nova may have put it together before I did but I know they all have... intentions with you."

"*Intentions?*" The humor is clear in my voice.

"Don't be a brat, do I need to murder them or not?"

Tears prick the backs of my eyes, even after a year apart my brother is still willing to fight for me and that means more than he knows. I shake my head. "No."

"Then why are you doing the walk of shame at five in the morning?"

I balk at my twin. "I am not."

His face blanks. "Ah, bullshit!" he mocks.

"Start the fucking car, Vox," I huff out.

"The second I start this bitch they are going to wake up and come running out here, you ready for them to chase you?" His question floors me for a second.

"Why do you sound so happy about that?"

He exhales loudly and his shoulders deflate. "Because they finally found their balls." I snort but bite down on my tongue so I don't blurt something crass out. Vox's gaze is fierce as he stares at me. "They didn't come to me for permission or even ask if they could date you, they *told* me. They didn't give me an option to fight them on this. *They* are choosing you over me, Vivian." My jaw slackens and my brows draw in. "Now, I'm going to ask you again, sister, are you ready for them to chase?"

"I—I..." I clamp my mouth closed, unsure how to answer that.

"I can only hold them off for so long, Vivi. Those three won't let you walk away now... after..." Disgust is clear in his features. "Look, just make sure you are ready for this because the Filthy Few broke up a year ago and now suddenly you wind up here and those three revived it to capture you. Don't think they are above playing dirty because they aren't."

I mull over his words for a while and I'm grateful for the fact he doesn't rush me or push me to make my mind up.

"I have to go home today." Vox shakes his head, clearly not happy with my answer but he doesn't argue. They may not know it but I am doing this for all of us. Vox was right, the second he starts the car and begins to pull out of the driveway I see the front door fly open in the side mirror. Archer, Hayze and Ezekiel all stand there staring after us with varying looks of shock, confusion and sadness and it pains me to be the cause of that reaction.

"What are you really doing at the Saints?" Vox's question startles me.

"What I'm supposed to do," I answer in a clipped tone.

"I call bullshit. You didn't seriously think I wouldn't be keeping tabs on you, did you?" I grind my teeth.

"Stay out of it, Vox. I mean it."

"Stay out of what exactly?"

"Nice try, douchebag. I mean it, you need to stay the fuck away from Hollow Hills."

He glances at me for a second before focusing back on the road. "I would say you have a week tops before those three come after you, Vivian. Wrap up whatever it is and be ready because I doubt I will be able to throw my weight around with them this time."

I shift in my seat to face him. "You're okay... with this...

with me and them?" His eyes close for a second as he inhales sharply.

"You want my honest answer?"

"Yes!"

"No, I'm not okay with it." I deflate and drop my gaze to my lap. "But, I've lost you once already and I won't risk that happening again." I lift my gaze back to him to find him looking directly at me. "When they come back to Hollow Hills to take you, I'll be with them. I'll help them and deal with whatever this thing is as long as it means I get my sister back." His words shouldn't inspire hope inside me but they do. I wish I could confide in my brother but I can't risk it not with so much uncertainty inside The Brotherhood.

Vox pulls into the parking lot outside my dorm and I sigh at the sight of six men stationed outside the building. Vox gruffs at the sight of them but remains silent. When he kills the engine, I don't get out, we just sit here silently for a while drinking our coffees. When students begin to appear I know my time is up, I have to let go of my brother once more and finish this thing.

"Thank you," I whisper as I reach for the door handle.

"Vivian?" I peer back at him over my shoulder, the worry lines that mar his face kills me. I never meant to hurt him.

"Yeah?"

"I'll always have your back. I walked away a year ago because I knew it's what you wanted—needed. But, I can see it in your eyes..."

"See what?" I push.

"The fear. You're terrified and it's taking everything inside me to not keep you here. I need you to tell me you're going to be okay. I need to know you will be okay because I can't... I can't fucking lose you, Vivi." The anguish in his voice is what breaks me. I shift and lean over the console to wrap my arms around him. He holds me close and tight like he doesn't want to let go.

"I'm okay, I got this," I whisper as I pull back and force a smile for his benefit, then climb out of the car but his words have me pausing for a second.

"From the womb to the tomb, sister." I don't respond or look back as I make my way toward my building. The guards all nod at me but say nothing about the state I'm in.

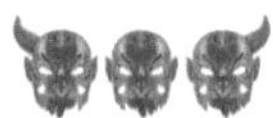

I STAND OUTSIDE THE BOARDROOM, waiting for them to call me in. Nerves thrum through me, it took me months to uncover the truth and now that the finish line is in sight I can't help but feel like everything is going to blow up in my face. When I finally checked my phone earlier, I had numerous missed calls from David. Another letter and box. I'm fucking scared to find out what's in the box after the last one.

I need to find out who the fuck is behind these letters. I have three suspects.

Thomas.

Nexus.

The Butcher.

Call me crazy, but I would rather it be one of the first two. They are familiar and reachable but Alexander isn't. Everyone has heard the rumors. He claims to be innocent of the crime he was accused of and hey, he might be, but he sure as fuck was no saint. He was the head of one of the deadliest crews in the nation and since his arrest, the Denver Kings have essentially vanished. I'm pulled from my thoughts when the double doors open and a man wearing a pair of plain jeans and jumper appears. I gasp, I recognize him! His blond hair styled roguishly and his blue eyes shine with warmth.

"Mrs. Tempest?" It still shocks me to be addressed as *Mrs. Tempest*. I stand and smile as I make my way toward him with my hand outstretched, he wraps his larger one around mine.

"Call me Vivian, please," I say with a smile.

"Nice to meet you. I'm Crue Hastings," he says with a nod and releases my hand as he leads me inside. Crue Hasting was drafted into the NFL and had an amazing fucking career in the league. I pause in the entryway when I spot Dawson sitting there beside a mirror image of himself—his father. Including Crue and Dawson there are only six people in the room and I was led to believe there were more members of the board. Each of them stands from their seats and makes their way toward me with their hands outstretched. I recognize another two of them, Corvin Williams and Saint Morgan, both of them were in the NFL as well.

They're all dressed in plain clothes which makes me feel overdressed in my pants suit.

"Darius Lockhart," the first guy says as I shake his hand. The next one is Saint and I swoon. I had a crush on him years ago. I beam when Corvin Williams shakes my hand.

"My brother is a huge fan," I blurt. Corvin smiles and ducks his head in thanks. The next to step up is Dawson's father, Beckett Dawson. After the introductions are made, Crue leads me around the table and pulls a seat out for me. I look at Dawson feeling nervous but he shoots me a reassuring smile. Crue rounds the table to join the others. The six of them sit at one end of the oval table. I sit alone at the other end.

Saint reaches for the folder in front of him and opens it. He hands the others a piece of paper each, then focuses on me.

"Mrs. Tempest—"

I cut him off. "Vivian, please."

He nods. "Vivian, I must give you credit, you are very persistent." I fight not to smile.

"Our wife is the reason we are taking this meeting." I gape at Crue then dart my gaze between him and Saint, he said *their wife.*

"Katie was impressed with the way you hacked her system." I bite my lip and smile sheepishly at Beckett.

"I would be lying if I said I was sorry," I admit, which has all of them chuckling.

"Impressing our wives isn't an easy feat, Vivian. The fact you managed to impress all four of them means they see something in you we don't." My confidence waivers at Corvin's decree. "We're all curious about why it was so important you met with us specifically."

"What makes you think it was you five I wanted to meet with and not the board?" I retort.

"You may be able to hack Katie's system but she is better and counter hacked you without you even knowing. My wife doesn't like it when another woman snoops around my background and tries to force her way into a meeting with me and her brother. You have ten minutes to explain yourself or this meeting is over and you will never get another chance," Darius bites out. I look to my only friend in the room. Dawson nods for me to continue so I take a deep breath and do just that. I put my bad bitch hat on and channel all the big dick energy I have —if I can take the three alpha males like I did last night, I can take these guys.

"Okay, can I be frank?" I ask.

"Fuck formalities, Vivian. Give it to them straight or they will get bored and stop listening," Dawson says. I nod my thanks.

"Okay. I know that you five are the owners of BCD'S—"

"That isn't a secret." Saint cuts in to add.

"But it was at the start. The three of you managed to funnel from your investment in the stock market into a small startup that led to you owning a multi-billion dollar resort franchise."

"Your point?" Darius clips out.

"My point is that I need to know how you did that."

They all share a loaded look before Beckett eyes me and the scrutiny with which he assesses me has me fighting not to fidget. "Why would we tell you that?" he asks.

"The only reason I am disclosing this information is because I received the signed NDA from Alexa Williams a week ago."

"Nothing you say will leave this room regardless of an NDA," Corvin tacks on.

"Upon my investigation I found that some of you faced a similar problem as I currently do. I have a... company that I need to funnel money from without my... partners knowing and put it into a company under my name." I cringe at how vague that sounds but I can't give them more details than I already have. I have the basics down but I need to funnel the rest out so there is nothing left and the accounting team will know if I drain all the accounts.

They remain silent for a long moment studying me, then they begin speaking in hushed tones while I sit here trying to strain my hearing but still can't manage to work out what they are saying. When they break apart, they all face me with serious looks.

"I can see here upon Katie's investigation into you that your twin brother and his three friends transferred here." I grind my teeth and force myself to nod, I don't want to involve any of them in this. Corvin smirks then continues. "You get your brother and his three friends to agree to finish out their schooling here at CHU and bring our team to the championship four years in a row. You have a deal." I balk at him.

"We also need Ezekiel Tempest, who I am assuming is your husband, to join the team as our star wide receiver," Crue adds.

"How do you know how they play?" I ask.

"We don't just take any transfers onto our team at CHU. Hours of tapes have been watched before we select. Coach may be the face of the team but make no mistake, Vivian, the five of us are the ones who give the final nod on who joins and the fact my son thinks your brother is good enough to take over his place as starting QB, that means something." I swing my gaze to Dawson, I had no idea he even played football let alone that he is the fucking quarterback!

I open my mouth but no words come out, I can't promise them anything. I want to lie and say yes to it all but if all of this turns to shit, then I can't guarantee that the guys will do anything to help me.

"I can't promise you that," I admit quietly, feeling utterly defeated. "I want to sit here and lie and tell you that they will do as I say but I can't."

"Why not?" Saint asks.

I shrug. "Because one day I hope to attend CHU as a student and lying to the owners doesn't seem like the best way to start. Thank you all for your time," I say as I stand.

"Wait." I still half way out of my chair and look at Darius. "Sit down." I do as he says. "The fact you didn't bullshit us is the reason we will help. If you had agreed to our terms we would never have given the information you needed."

I gape at him. "Are you serious?" I rasp out.

"Yes. Now, get your phone out and start recording." I do as Crue says and sit back and listen while they explain everything. This is one of the final pieces I needed! I suddenly feel like I might actually be able to pull this shit off.

CHAPTER FOURTEEN

Vivian

By the time I walk out of the meeting the sun is setting and my mind is reeling with all the new information I have gathered. The fact they even offered me a scholarship in computer science under the guidance of Saint and Crue's wife Katie has blown my mind. I can start next year and I am beyond fucking excited for the first time in a year, I can see the light at the end of a really dark tunnel. My car is idling at the curb so I slip into the back seat. My guards packed up my bags for me so I wouldn't have to return to the dorms and risk bumping into one of the guys.

I spend the long drive home catching up on emails and returning calls, the Saints are clearly happy with the opening of Lividica. Tate sent me an email updating me on the profits we have made since opening night and I can admit the figure has far exceeded my expectations. I'm considering opening a few more clubs just like it around the country. I open my next email and still, then pull my phone out and dial David.

"Lordess," he answers on the second ring.

"Why am I looking at an email from the warden of Alexander Denver's prison?"

"I don't know." He answers.

"I need you to do some digging, he could be the one behind the letters and the packages—"

"It was another head," he blurts out. I gasp and try to remain conscious as I breathe through the nausea.

"W-who was it?" I stutter.

"I think it would be better to discuss this when you get back—"

"Who the fuck was it, David!" I scream.

"Kelly Valerian." A sob tears out of me. I end the call and nearly drop my phone twice as I dial Nova. My heart is in my throat as I wait for her to answer, it rings for so long I begin to think she isn't going to answer but then she does.

"Vivian." It's not Nova, it's my brother and he sounds murderous.

"Vox, I have to tell you something."

"Vi, I am going to ask you this once and I'm not fucking around. Do you know who took Nova's mother?"

Tears spill down my cheeks. "No," I whisper.

"But you know something?" he pushes.

"Hmmm," I mutter.

"Vi, my girl is breaking apart hunting for her mom. Olivia and mom called her after I dropped you off and we flew back to Washington to find her house trashed and her missing. Ezekiel, Hayze and Archer are on their way here to help us track down the fucker and bring Kelly home so—"

"She's dead." My declaration is met with silence. I pull my

phone away from my ear to check the call didn't get disconnected.

"Hold on," he grits out then I hear movement and a door closing before he speaks again. "Lock down those emotions Vivian and tell me how you know."

I inhale and swipe my tears away and lock my pain away as I compose myself. "A package was delivered to me this morning, David just let me know that the box contained Kelly Valerian's head."

"Fuccccckk!" he roars. I can picture him ripping at his hair and pacing as he tries to think about his next move. "Why you?"

"What?"

"Why the fuck would you be sent her head?" I can feel his anger through the phone and my heart aches for him, I know this loss is going to shatter Nova. She went through hell trying to get her mom back when Thomas held her captive and now this.

"I don't know, Vox, but I plan to find out," I vow.

"How the fuck do I tell her, Vi?" he asks brokenly. Vox has always been my pillar of strength, he was my rock growing up and always protected me as best he could and it seems now is the time to repay him.

"You hold her through this. You make sure she knows she always has you by her side and she isn't alone in this. I know you don't like it, but you need to let Ezekiel comfort her as well. He is her only family left. She knows Olivia is there but its Ezekiel she will cling to and you need to let her."

"I can't break her heart."

"I'm so sorry, Vox." I mean it, I wish there was another way for this to play out. "What do you need from me?"

"Remove the banishment, Vivian. She is going to want blood and I won't deny her."

"A favor asked is a debt owed," I volley back.

"Grant me this favor sister and the Filthy Few will be in your debt."

"I'll see what I can do but in the meantime, all I can offer is a ceasefire until the culprit is caught. I'll have The Brotherhood track down who the fuck is behind this, you have my word."

"Vivian?"

"Yeah?"

"Tomorrow, when I call you make sure you answer my fucking call because I know you are keeping shit from me and I want answers, real answers."

My lungs deflate. "I can't promise you anything. Tell Nova I'm sorry." Then I end the call. My hand itches to call my own mom and tell her I love her, but I can't put her at risk. Whoever is behind this is clearly watching me and I have already put my brother and the guys in danger by being around them while I was at CHU. I get so lost in my own thoughts, I don't realize we have arrived at my house until the driver opens the door for me. I gather my purse and climb out, then stare at my large home.

It's stunning and everything I thought I would ever want in a home, but what I didn't bank on was how lonely it would feel to live here on my own. There is no warmth inside its walls. I don't have friends, so other than David and the guards, no one ever visits me. I suck in a large breath, then stalk inside. I lock down all my emotions and head into the dining room where I can hear voices.

"I want men stationed around the house, someone is targeting the lordess and our main focus is her safety. Am I clear?" David's devotion to my wellbeing means a lot, he has been a rock for me through this whole thing. When I enter the room, everyone turns to me. I nod hello and David quickly dismisses them but the second I spot the pink cardboard box at the end of the table, I stop breathing. I can see that blood has seeped through it. I move toward it on shaky legs, noticing a pink ribbon on the floor near it. This sick fuck wrapped up the head of my best friend's mom like it was a fucking gift!

I reach out to push the lid off but David grips my wrist. "I need to see," I say quietly.

"Lordess, it's not a sight you want to see. It will haunt you." I turn to David and whatever he sees in my eyes has him sighing and dropping his hold on my wrist. "As you wish," he says, then steps back. I gather all my courage and push the lid off the box. The sight instantly robs me of air and I start hyperventilating. Kelly's head sits there, perched on a bed of roses, her skin pale white with a strange purple hue to it. The smell is overwhelming. I fight not to gag. When I look into her eyes, tears cascade down my cheeks. The look of utter fear in her soulless eyes will be what keeps me awake at night.

"Where are the letters?"

"I placed them on your desk," David answers.

"Get the men to take Kelly to the morgue and preserve her as best they can until I decide what to do with her." I leave the room and swipe away my tears, now is not the time for me to break and give into my girlish emotions. I'm the fucking leader of a brotherhood filled with ruthless men and they can't see me as weak. I find the two sealed letters on my desk. I drop my purse to the floor, then sit down behind my desk. I stare at the letters for so long my vision turns hazy. "Woman up, Vivian!" I chastise myself.

I reach for the first letter and tear it open.

Masks may hide the truth.
They may keep you hidden but I see beneath yours.

Oh, what a sight it is.
You tried to steal from me and for that you will
be taught a lesson.
You shouldn't have left because now you left them
all behind.
I hope you enjoy my gift, he shouldn't have tried
to rise against me then he would have lived.

What the fuck?

I read over the letter again trying to make sense of his cryptic words but I come up blank. Clearly he is talking about the DA but what did Clive Bruce know that I didn't? I reach for the next one and tear it open, not giving myself a chance to back out.

Roses are red, my demons are fed.
Violets are blue, so just let this stew.
Wonder is a privilege that she will see, for
treachery is dead.
In her eyes I saw the red, the haze of fear
kept the demons fed.
Oh, what a sight it was to see her begging and
pleading.
Keep me waiting and you shall see, you are fond
of riddles now let us see.
Come find me and this will end.
Watch who you trust, for they are my men.

His fucking poem sends a shiver of fear down my spine and I suddenly feel cold to the bone. This sick fuck is loving killing and butchering the people—wait, butchering!

Alexander Denver!

I reach into my purse and pull my laptop out. I click on the email from the warden and agree to be added to his visitor list. If this sick cunt thinks I am scared of him, then he will learn really fast that I am not someone who can be intimidated. I won't allow him to hurt another person. I didn't know Clive well but his blood is still on my hands.

"Lordess?" I look up from the letters and motion David in.

"What is it?"

"Word has spread about the DA's murder, The Brotherhood wants answers."

I grit my teeth. "They will have answers as soon as I get them," I snap.

"With the Night Of The Saints fast approaching, I fear we will need to appease them and keep them on our side."

"I need the banishment lifted from my brother and the others." His eyes widen and an emotion I can't read flickers through his eyes, but it vanishes just as quickly as it appeared.

"You can't lift a banishment, once it is decreed there is no going back. It's a life sentence."

Fuck!

"Okay, I need to make a call," I say, dismissing him. Once he closes the door behind him, I dial Vox's number and he answers on the third ring.

"Yeah?"

"I can't lift the banishment, if you return to Hollow Hills you have to return as your alter ego." I cringe when I hear Nova gut wrenching screams in the background.

"Okay. We'll be there tomorrow, I have to go." He ends the call and I feel like a piece of shit, my best friend is breaking apart and here I am still trying to play catch up with the cunt that killed her mother. Tomorrow I will look Kelly's killer in the eye and make sure he knows his days are numbered. Being the lordess means I have the power and connections to have someone taken out, even if they are rotting in a fucking prison!

CHAPTER FIFTEEN

Archer

The moment Vox called and told us he needed us, we didn't ask questions, just packed our bags and got on the first flight back home. Hayze thought we should drive but flying is quicker and right now, we just need to get back to Washington. As we pull up in front of Nova's house an eerie feeling settles over me, something feels... off.

"Something's wrong," Ez grits out then launches out of the rental car with Hayze and I chasing after him. He doesn't knock, he just throws the door open and is immediately met by the sound of Nova screaming. We all run into the living room to find her on her knees sobbing while Vox kneels behind, holding her. I look to the opposite side of the room to see Jane and Olivia standing there with tears trailing down their own cheeks. I spot Mary behind them and frown when my mom walks around the corner. The second our moms spot us, they all race over and wrap their arms around us and cry. Hayze, Ez and I share a look of confusion as we hold our moms.

"Bring her back!" Nova screams, the pain in her voice shreds me. Nova isn't the type of girl to cry over nothing, so to see her this distraught means something really bad happened, which is when I notice we are missing someone.

Kelly.

"Ma?" I say quietly. Mom pulls back and stares up at me with worry in her eyes. "Where's Kelly?"

Her bottom lip trembles. "Someone murdered her," she chokes out, at her confession Ez's face blanks of everything as he gently pushes his mom and steps around her to go to Nova. Vox snaps his head up and stares at Ezekiel with a pleading look.

"Help her," he begs. Ez nods and Vox reluctantly releases his hold on Nova and scoots back while Ez kneels down in front of his sister. He gently grasps her face between his hands and forces her tear-stained head up to meet his gaze. The stoic look on his face and the way he is able to control his own emotions while his little sister is breaking in his hands staggers me.

"A favor asked is a debt owed, sister." Nova's mouth parts on a gasp.

"Ezekiel!" Vox roars.

Ez cuts his gaze to Vox. "Shut the fuck up, she needs this. She needs a purpose and we will grant her that wish." He drops his gaze back to Nova. "A favor asked is a debt owed," he says again.

Nova looks at Ez with a broken look in her eyes, the same look she had the night she lost her best friend, Waylen. "She's gone," she chokes out. "She made me go to college, she promised she would be fine and that I didn't have to worry about her. She fucking promised!" she screams. Olivia begins to cry quietly beside me so I shift my mom to one side and wrap my other arm around her. I know this must be hard for her, all she wants to do is comfort Nova as any mother would, but she also knows Nova only saw Kelly as her mom, and for her to try and comfort her now would be dishonoring Kelly.

"Ask the favor," Ezekiel snaps.

"Can you bring her back?" Nova screams in anger. "Can the Filthy-fucking-Few grant me that?"

"No. But we can grant you the vengeance you want, I swear it. On my life, I will not rest until I deliver the son of a bitch to you. Ask the favor, Nova, and you will have the Filthy Few at your beck and call until we take the life of the cunt that took your mom from you."

"I want them all to pay. I want Nexus to die for taking Waylen from me and I want whoever..." She breaks down again but Ez doesn't push her, he just waits for her to find the courage to finish asking what she wants. "I want whoever took my mom from me to suffer. I want them to pay for what they took from me, can you give me that?" The resolution in Ezekiel's eyes astounds me, he has always been the only one out of the four of us to be able to shut down his emotions and focus.

"Given who you are to me and to Vox, a second favor will be granted. You have our word, we will deliver them to you." Ez looks to Vox and nods for him to come forward. This time when Vox reaches for Nova she leaps into his arms and straddles his lap, then buries her face in his neck as she cries. I've never seen Vox so out of his depth but still so in control, it's an odd combination but one that brings a smile to my face. He's changing and it's all thanks to the girl he has in his arms, who loves him more than anything.

I hope my girl can love me like that.

I push that thought away as Ez approaches us. "We need to

make a call." The order is clear and one I am happy to obey given the situation. I release my mom and his and follow him out of the room. He leads us up the stairs to a guest room. Hayze closes the door and moves to stand by the window, keeping his back to us.

"What if she doesn't answer?" Hayze asks. I look at Ez who just shakes his head. We're all thinking the same thing but Hayze was the only one with the balls to ask it. After being woken by the sound of Vox's car and seeing him driving away with our girl, the three of us have been in a sour mood wondering if we fucked up. Did we push her too far? Does she regret what happened? All these types of questions have been plaguing the three of us all day.

"I have this feeling, I can't explain it—"

I cut Ez off. "But you feel like somehow Vivian is at the center of all of this?" He eyes me with surprise, then nods stiffly.

"Yeah, exactly," he mutters.

"If she is, then she won't tell us. We need her to come to us and not to ask a favor. I want her to come to us because she *needs* us." I study Hayze for a long moment and take in his disheveled appearance. He looks like shit and has barely spoken to me all day.

"You know her and you also know she would rather chew off her fucking left tit than admit she needs help. Was her going behind our backs and performing a hostile takeover of the Saints not enough proof for you?" I shoot Ezekiel a warning look, her takeover is still a soft spot for Hayze and me. I know Ez says marrying her was for her protection but there is still that seed of doubt in the back of our minds.

"If we push too hard, she will run and as much as I fucking want her, I also won't force her into *this*." Hayze motioned between the three of us.

"She seemed to enjoy the three of us just fucking fine," I add. When the door opens and we see Vox standing there looking utterly helpless and lost, the whole mood in the room changes.

"Vivian is trying to lift our banishment." The words that tumble out of Vox's mouth are not the ones I expected to hear.

"Why exactly would she be doing that?" I ask.

"Kelly Valerian's head was delivered to my sister earlier today. That is why she is trying to lift it because she knows I am going back there and no fucking banishment will stop me. Whoever the fuck thought they could come for *my* witch and break her heart is going to fucking learn what happens when you hurt what is mine!" His words play on a loop. Vi was sent Kelly's head! A fucking head for Christ's sake! The venom in Vox's tone is enough for me to know he isn't kidding, he's about to put that mask on and wreak havoc on Hollow Hills until he finds out who the fuck hurt his girl.

"Fuck, does Nova know?" Ez growls.

Vox scrubs a hand down his face and shakes his head. "No."

"What does she think happened to her mom?" Hayze pushes.

"She thought her mom was taken again but then my sister called and I had to tell her that her mom... was murdered. She doesn't know how, just that she's gone and that's the fucking way it will stay, am I clear?" The three of us all agree without argument, if we can spare her the pain of knowing the details then so be it.

"What the fuck are we going to do? If this insane fucker is sending my girl the head of her best friend's mom, then we need to get to her." I swing my gaze to Hayze in surprise. Ez and Vox are both staring at him as well, but he doesn't fold under the pressure, instead he stalks and pushes between me and Ezekiel to stand before Vox. "I'm gonna say this one last time because that look on your face is pissing me off." Vox looks like he wants to break Hayze's jaw. "She's your sister but she is *ours*! Deal with that shit because it ain't changing. I respected your boundaries for years but not anymore. I love her, Vox, and there is nothing you can do or say that will keep me away from Vivian."

Pride swells inside me, I couldn't be any more proud of my best friend for finally going after what he wants.

"Same goes for me," Ez adds. "You're my brother, Vox, and I will go to hell for you but not before I get the chance to really love your sister. I know I fucked up by marrying her behind your back, but given the chance to redo it, I wouldn't change it because knowing she has my name is everything I could have wished for and more."

Vox says nothing, just turns his head toward me as if waiting for me to declare my intentions for his sister. I should have done this years ago but I guess it's better late than never.

"I'm surprised you never realized earlier what she meant to me. I've been in love with her for years, Vox. I was just too much of a chickenshit to admit it earlier but not anymore. If you can't accept how we all feel, then that's something we'll all live with but you have to know that we will all choose her. Over and over again until our dying days."

He runs his gaze over the three of us, the intensity in his eyes would have most guys crumbling and pleading for his forgiveness but not us. We're all prepared to sacrifice our friendship with our own brother for her and he has to know that the choice wasn't easy for any of us to make but she is worth losing everything for. Vox's phone pings with a message, he pulls it out of his pocket and instantly glares at the screen.

"Pack your shit and make sure you have your masks," he grits out.

"What happened?" Ez asks.

Vox slowly lifts his gaze then turns his phone toward us so we can read the message.

VIVIAN

> Don't come, I can't lift the banishment. I know what I have to do to end this.

Anger courses through my veins like a wildfire, when is she going to fucking learn that we are stronger together.

"We leave first thing in the morning. If you aren't in the car when it's time, then I'm leaving your asses behind," Vox snaps before storming out of the room and slamming the door closed. The three of us stand here silently for a beat until Hayze speaks.

"Is it wrong that I'm getting turned on at the thought of hunting our Vivi baby?" I snort out a laugh while Ez just shakes his head and pats him on the shoulder.

"Not at all, my friend, but this time when we catch our pretty little mouse, she is going to get punished for running. It's time she learns that we aren't quitters and her place is by our sides and in our beds and not leading the fucking Saints."

Well fuck, I couldn't agree with Ez more and the thought of her splayed out in front of us, ready and waiting to take our cocks again has me growing hard. Yeah, she is definitely getting fucked hard for the stunt she's pulled. I pull my phone from my pocket and unlock it. The guys are all staring at the screen as I type out a message.

ME

> You may be an angel seeking chaos but we are the devils seeking refuge inside you. Run as fast as you can, little mouse, because we're coming for you.

I don't expect a reply but when I see the three little dots

appear almost instantly I wait with bated breath for her reply. I feel the guys anxious energy as well.

VIVI

I was a fallen angel when the three of you left me a year ago, now I'm a phoenix ready to rise from the fucking ashes but it won't be with you by my side.

"Add me to the fucking chat!" Ez clips out. I do as he says and add both him and Hayze to the thread.

EZ

We'll be at your side and your back protecting you from every angle.

VIVI

The only thing I need protection from is you three.

HAYZE

So you admit that we are a foursome?

ME

facepalm emoji What those idiots are trying to say is we have your back.

VIVI

Why?

EZ

Because we love you.

HAYZE

Because you mean everything to us.

ME

You are our everything, Vivian, did we not show you that?

VIVI

Oh, so that wasn't a one-time deal?

HAYZE

Not if you don't want it to be…

VIVI

So… I get all three?

ME

yes!

VIVI

Really?

EZ

Yes! You get the three of us.

VIVI

So, I get to fuck the three of you whenever I want and you only get to fuck me?

ME

yes!

HAYZE

Of course!

EZ

We don't want anyone else.

VIVI

Yeah, I think I'll pass but thanks for fucking my brains out. I can still feel the ghost of your cocks in every one of my holes. Xxx

VIVIAN HAS LEFT THE CHAT

"Fuck!" Ez bites out.

"Now I need a cold fucking shower!" Hayze snarls.

"She is going to fucking pay for that stunt!" I vow.

"So, this is for real, we're all going after her?" Hayze asks.

"Yeah, man. We're all going for her and we aren't leaving that fucking town until she is with us," I answer.

"I want the fucking Saints burned to the ground before we

leave. I know those cunts are somehow linked to whatever happened to Kelly."

I nod in agreement. "Yeah, someone is trying to rise against Vivian and we need to take the cunt out."

Tonight we rest, tomorrow we go hunting for our little mouse.

CHAPTER SIXTEEN

Vivian

I woke this morning with a renewed sense of determination flowing through my veins. David tried to talk me out of this meeting today but I rebuked his worries. If this asshole thinks he can hurt the people I care about, then I need to look him in the eyes and show him I'm not afraid. I'll take him down before he can try to take another person I love. My heart is aching for Nova and the loss she has suffered but I can't allow my emotions to take control right now. I need to keep a level head. After this meeting I have to head to Lividica and speak to Tatum and revise some of her ideas. I also want a client list of who has been frequenting the girls in case I need leverage.

I swore I would never stoop that low to extort anyone but I'm left with no other option now. I have four weeks before the Night Of The Saints and I need to fix everything before then. The construction on the high school has finally started going ahead since I sent the new crew over to help out. Drew and

Ford haven't called once this morning with another unexpected hurdle, all the excuses they gave me previously seem to have vanished. I knew those assholes were taking me for a ride. I also have a meeting with The Brotherhood tonight. According to David there is a lot of unrest amongst the ranks.

When fucking isn't there!

As the car comes to a stop outside the prison, I give myself a moment to get my game face on. The last thing I need is for Alexander to see through my armor and see the scared little girl I am hiding beneath the boss bitch mask I am wearing. Arnold opens the door for me and I step out, then brush my jacket down and smirk to myself. I chose to wear an all-white pants suit sans the shirt underneath so the swell of my breasts can be seen. I'm guessing showing him the girls will keep him distracted enough from seeing beneath my mask. I walk briskly toward the entrance and sign in. Given my status and who I am, I'm afforded more leeway than most.

A guard leads me down a long corridor. The coloring inside here is dim and depressing. It's a beautiful day outside but in here, it's cold and miserable. It feels like it's designed that way to keep these prisoners from feeling any semblance of happiness while they are locked up. The guard opens a door and motions for me to enter, the room bare except for a small table and two matching chairs.

"The prisoner will be here in a moment, Mrs. Tempest. Please, have a seat." I nod my head in thanks and choose to remain standing. I lean against the far wall and cross my arms over my chest to disguise the shaking in my hands. I may look the part but the truth is I am fucking terrified. This man was named The Butcher for a reason, I've seen the pictures of his victims. The name is fitting. He stumped many people with his surgical cuts and how clean he dismembered the bodies of his victims.

My train of thought is interrupted when the door on the other side of the room unlocks. My breath lodges in my throat when it's pushed open. Two guards step through the threshold with Alexander behind them followed by two more guards. I avert my gaze, not ready to lay eyes upon him just yet. The guards secure his handcuffs to the metal hooks on the table, his ankles are cuffed to the horse shoe bolts in the ground next.

"When you're finished, call out, we'll be just outside the door," one of the guards say as the four of them leave. The sound of the door clicking shut behind them has fear skyrocketing inside me. I thought I was brave enough to do this but it seems I was just a timid little girl trying to play boss bitch. I try to keep my composure but I still don't have the strength to actually look at him. Even with all the press surrounding his arrest, not a single picture of him was leaked, he had no social media presence.

He was a ghost.

"You came all this way, the least you could do is look at me." His voice is raspy and deep, the sound alone sends a shiver down my spine.

We'll be at your side and your back protecting you from every angle.

Ezekiel's words from last night play through my mind and give me the courage I need to make it through this. I slowly turn my head to look at the notorious killer. The instant I lock eyes with him I gasp.

He is not what I was expecting!

The news said he was hideous, old and deranged. I expected to see an old balding man with a potbelly and sweat stains, not *this*! Alexander Denver is... fucking gorgeous!

The orange jumpsuit does nothing to diminish his beauty. His hair is shoulder length, it's brown with streaks of blond through it. It's clear he must be lifting weights in his yard time.

His brown eyes are the lightest shade of brown I have ever seen. Tattoos cover the tops of his hands and his neck, I can see some ink cover the tops of his chest thanks to the top buttons on his jumpsuit being left undone. I can tell he is tall even from him sitting. Those handcuffs don't look strong enough to hold him if he wanted to break free and snap my neck. Alexander runs his gaze over me and to my utter surprise his eyes never once linger on my tits, he keeps them focused on my face which shouldn't impress me but it does.

"I won't hurt you." The sincerity in his voice shouldn't settle my nerves but it somehow does.

"I know who you are," I find myself blurting out.

His features grow taut. "And who exactly is that?" God, the growl in his voice is fucking alluring, he wouldn't even need to kidnap his victims he would just need to speak and they would follow him like the call of a siren.

"I've seen the pictures."

"And I'm sure there are many images of you on the internet but none of them really show who you truly are, do they?" His reply stumps me. "Did you come all this way to judge me and tell me what you *think* you know or was there another reason?"

I uncross my arms and let them dangle uselessly at my sides as I search his eyes. When I don't see any ill intent, I slowly make my way toward the table and slowly lower into the vacant chair, never once taking my eyes off him. His eyes, God, they hold so much fucking pain and it robs me of breath. How can a convicted murderer have such a painfilled look in his eyes?

"Did you do it?" I ask.

"Do what?" His face is impassive and it makes me incredibly hard to fucking read.

"Did you kill Kelly Valerian?" I grit out through clenched teeth. His brows draw in and form a deep V. His eyes skate between my own trying to read me but he won't see shit.

"Isn't she the step mother of the bastard who murdered my sister?"

"Yes."

Alexander scoffs and shakes his head as he leans back in his chair, well as far as his restraints will let him. "You've read all the articles online and clearly seen the news. How many bodies did they find?"

I gape at him. "They found over thirty!" I shout.

"Exactly!" he snaps back, causing me to shrink back slightly. "And were any of those fucking bodies women?"

I open my mouth but snap it closed. I try to recall everything I have read and seen in his file. My eyes widen and my jaw unhinges when the answer hits me. "You never touched a woman."

He flicks his hands in a *duh* gesture. "You may think I'm an animal but even I have a code, and hurting women and children isn't something I do. I punish the guilty, not the innocent." I sit here and let his words sink in slowly. He has never hurt a woman which means, my key suspect—my only suspect—isn't a suspect at all. "Why did you send me that letter, Vivian?"

I shake my head to clear my thoughts and focus back on him. "Huh?"

"You told me who killed my sister, why?"

I dart my tongue to moisten my lips, unlike Ez, Arch or Hayze he doesn't follow the movement just keeps his eyes on mine. "Because he deserves to pay for what he did to her. She wasn't the only one he hurt—" I clamp my mouth closed when his eyes darken and his fists clenched on top of the table. His nostrils flare and his breathing turns shallow as he tries to control his anger. My body takes on a mind of its own, I reach out without thought and place my hand atop of his. Instantly he stops shaking and his eyes slowly return to their normal color. When I attempt to remove my hand, he twists his own quickly and traps my hand in his. My eyes widen in panic and my breathing now mirrors his from a second ago. Fear has me gripped in its clutches.

"I will never hurt you, Vivian, you have my word." Call me fucking crazy but I believe him. When he smiles it's small and doesn't reach his eyes but I slowly begin to relax and stop fighting to get my hand free. I let him hold it. His hands are calloused and rough and it feels strange having my hand held by a serial killer. I know the guys have done *things* but I have never seen what they have done with my own eyes like I have with Alex.

Alex?

Since when did we get comfortable enough to start giving each other pet names?

"Nexus hurt more girls, your sister was just the one who sadly didn't get away." His breath stutters for a moment. "I'm so sorry for what he did to her. None of us had any idea until last year what a real fucking piece of shit he is."

"He was never on my radar when I began my search, my sister never hung out with rich preppy boys. Elanor wasn't like most sixteen-year-old girls, she was weird and loved books." The smile that stretches across his face is filled with love and pain. "She would get so angry when I would annoy her while she was reading. I still remember the last book she didn't get a chance to finish reading."

"What was it?" I ask quietly.

"*Beautiful Liar* by Jerry Pratt or something like that. It was a mafia book about a girl and three guys. Ellie loved those types of books and it used to drive me insane when she would tell me that she would never just end up with one guy, she wanted three like the girls in her books." I feel my cheeks begin to heat, much like his sister. I too have read my fair share of reverse harem books and I envied those girls in the stories. I was never brave enough to ever dream about the three guys I wanted most to ever love me and find a way to make a relationship between the four of us work but somehow... they found a way. "What Ellie failed to see was that my two best friends wanted to be two guys in her harem."

I gasp and my jaw unhinges. "Your best friends?" He nods. "And you didn't murder them?"

He scoffs and shakes his head. "Vatican and Pope would have given their life for her and loved her like no other. They would have cherished my sister and treated her like a queen. It would have been an honor for me to watch them love her."

"Wow," I breathe out.

"I assume your brother didn't take it well when his best friends confessed to loving you?"

My brows hit my hairline. "How do you know that?"

He rolls his eyes. "I may be a caged dog but that doesn't mean my pack isn't still out there."

"You don't seem like a dog."

"I'm not, I'm the alpha." The conviction in which he says that sends a shiver down my spine. I don't doubt him. I can tell from the way he holds himself and naturally commands attention without trying that he would be an imposing force against any man.

"How old are you?" I blurt without thinking, then smile sheepishly. He laughs and the sound is melodic and strange, seeing a man that looks like him laugh brings a real smile to my own face. He releases my hand and relaxes into his chair so I do the same.

"So, we're asking personal questions now?"

I purse my lips and shrug. "I guess so."

"I'm twenty-six."

"I assume you already know how old I am?"

"Nineteen, you have a twin brother who is a few minutes

older than you. You have a budding relationship with three of his best friends, his girlfriend is your best friend who is—sorry was—was the stepsister of the cunt that took my sister from me."

"Should I be worried you know so much about me?"

He shrugs. "Depends, do you have anything to be worried about?" he counters.

"More than I want to admit," I say bitterly.

"Want to know something?"

I nod. "Sure."

"Ever since you sent me that letter I've had my pack tracking you and garnering every piece of information they could. Turns out you have more skeletons in your closet than a graveyard."

I chortle. "Nice reference."

"I try my best to please."

"What skeletons are you referring to?" I press.

"For starters, you are the lordess of a brotherhood that is planning to kill you." I gasp.

"What?"

"You may think I'm a monster, Vivian, but I can assure you that what they have planned for you is much worse than what I have done. If I was you, I would do my best to finish... I guess we shall call it a hostile takeover and get out."

I swallow audibly and stare at him with wide eyes. "How do you know about *that*?" I hiss.

"Lividica?" I stare at him with my jaw practically in my lap. "I know a lot. Halo managed to find a lot of things about you, *Mrs. Tempest*."

"Who the hell is Halo?"

"Halo is my hacker, he can find anything out about anyone. People think they don't leave a trace behind but they're wrong. You just have to be smart enough to look in the right places and he does. I'm not saying this to scare you, I'm telling you this because..." He clamps his mouth closed and turns away from me, it takes a second for me to realize what he was going to say.

"I remind you of Elanor," I whisper, he growls and grinds his teeth.

Slowly he turns back to face me and the guilt ridden look in his eyes robs me of air. "I couldn't save my sister, but I have a chance to help you and I am offering you my help if you want it."

"What's the debt?" I ask on instinct.

His brows pull in. "There isn't one. I have nothing but time in here, helping you would keep my mind active instead of focusing on my retrial."

"Your what?"

His face turns serious. "Do you know why I am serving three life sentences?"

"For the murders?"

"Yes, but do you know which ones?" I shake my head, I didn't exactly focus on that part of his conviction. "I was convicted for the murders of three girls."

"But... but you don't hurt women." I sound like an idiot but I can't find it within myself to care.

"No, I don't. Someone went through great lengths to frame me and I have a feeling I know who the fuck it was and that cunt will pay for this."

"Who was it?"

His eyes turn murderous. "Thomas Valerian."

I reel back. "He didn't know what Nexus—"

"If you really believe that cunt didn't know what his son did, then you are deluded. There is nothing Thomas doesn't know, he was never on my radar. I had no idea why I was being arrested that day. My lawyer proved I was nowhere near where those girls were murdered but the judge still ruled against me and it wasn't until I got your letter that we started digging into Nexus and his family. Turns out, Judge Garfield is a dear friend of Thomas."

"Oh my God, they set you up!"

"Oh, they did more than that. The girls that were murdered were butchered but not by me. Any witnesses suddenly disappeared, those girls' families are nowhere to be found now. I am serving three life sentences because that cunts' son murdered my sister and this is his way of keeping me silent."

"Let me help you," I blurt out without thought. Alexander jerks in surprise but I can't find it within myself to take back my offer, so I push on. "Help me find the person who killed my best friend's mom and sent me letters and I will help you get out."

"How are you going to do that?"

"You said you know about the Saints. If that is true, then you know we have lawyers, judges and... well, we did have a DA but his head was delivered to me as well."

"Fuck, Clive Bruce?"

I nod. "Yeah, did you know him?"

"I actually did. He was trying to help me. I just met with him a couple of weeks ago." I study him for a moment trying to piece everything together. I was led to believe that Clive was the one who put Alex behind bars and made evidence disappear.

"Clive offered you a deal, didn't he?"

Alex smiles. "You are very perceptive."

"Don't patronize me, I get enough of that from my brother."

"Don't be hard on your brother, it's his job to keep you safe."

"Don't avoid my question."

"Yes. Clive offered me a deal."

"What deal?" I push.

"That's a conversation for another time."

I huff out my annoyance. "Whatever."

"Vivian?"

"What?"

He turns somber and his eyes take on a furlong look. "If you are serious about helping me get out of here, then I will help you but just so you know, I would have helped you regardless."

"Why? You don't know me and yet here you are offering to help me track a killer."

"Because I would have given anything for someone to have helped my sister that night. I meant it when I told you that I'm not the monster you think I am. What you have read about me isn't everything you think it to be. My only stipulation for helping you is that no one touches Nexus Valerian. I have plans for that cunt that make dying in hell seem like a daydream."

CHAPTER SEVENTEEN

Ezekiel

"She is fucking kidding right?" Vox snarls from beside me. I turn and glare at the asshole, the mask covering my face dulls the effect of my glare but he can still sense it. "Don't fucking look at me like that, you were thinking the same thing." I grind my teeth hating that the fucker is right. She has been sent a severed head and only has two guards patrolling her house.

"What's the plan?" Archer asks from behind one of the trees he and Hayze are hiding behind.

"You want to take out her men or walk through the door?" I ask them. I can tell from the look in their eyes that this is the time to teach our girl a lesson. I smirk from behind my mask and pull my hood up as best I can, thanks to the horns on these things it makes it hard. Archer is the only one with no horns so he doesn't face this issue.

Vox turns to us, clearly ready to start barking orders like he always has but not today and not when it concerns her. The three of us split off to surround her house. It's nice and tucked away from the main road but she made a huge fucking mistake by not having more men stationed around the place. I leave Hayze and Archer to take care of the two guards while I head for the power box around the back side of the house. It takes me four seconds to find the breaker I need. The second I pull it, the power cuts out and the house is bathed in darkness. I remain still and calm as I give my eyes a chance to adjust to the darkness before I slink around the back.

I try two windows and happy to say both are locked but when I twist the handle on the side door and it opens. I make a mental note to punish her for this error! I inch inside, careful to keep my steps light as I creep through her house. At the sound of her voice I freeze against the wall that separates the kitchen from the living room where I can make out her figure pacing furiously.

"No, David, I don't know what happened, the power just cut out." She pauses for a moment listening to his reply. "No, don't worry I'm sure Sean and Carter will sort the problem shortly." I look around to see if the others have made it inside but I can't see them. "Yes, I met with Tatum earlier and we went over the figures. Look, I'll fill you in about the details when I see you later. I'll be leaving here in a few hours for the meeting." I wait for her to end the call before I creep in closer ready to strike but then she whirls around so fast and faces me I freeze. "There are only three people on earth that can make the hairs on the back of my neck stand up and have my skin heating by just being in the same room. Did you really think I wouldn't know it was you guys that cut my power?"

To say I am surprised is a fucking understatement. I catch movement over her shoulder and as if to prove her own point, she spins around and comes face to face with no horns aka Archer and left horn aka Hayze. I watch as her body begins to relax and without thought I press forward and plaster myself against her back. I wait for her to push me away but instead she melts into me. I wrap my arms around her waist and anchor her to me.

"What are you guys doing here?" she asks breathlessly. Hayze and Archer push forward until they are just out of touching distance, I can tell from how stiff they are that they are demonstrating some severe self-control by not giving into their need and touching her.

"We're here to bring you back with us, you don't belong here anymore, Vivi baby," Hayze says gently.

She sighs and shakes her head. When she tries to pull free I tighten my hold. Vivian tilts her head back and looks up at me. "Till death do us part will come a lot sooner if you don't release me." The laughter that bursts out of me is without consent, but it brings a smile to her face so I can't be mad. I reluctantly release her and she instantly moves to Hayze, lays her hand flat on his chest and cranes her neck back to meet his stare. "I can't leave."

"Yes, the fuck, you can!" Archer snaps. She turns her head toward him and reaches out with her free hand to grab his.

"No, I can't. I need you three to trust me and understand that I have this all under control—"

"How is my girlfriend's mom being murdered, you keeping shit under control?" She whirls away from the three of us to face her brother who is standing at the base of the stairs. We push in closer and stand behind her, showing Vox we are on her side and he better watch his fucking tone before we put him in check.

"I didn't know anything was going to happen to Kelly, I swear, Vox." At her admission Vox rips the mask off and storms forward. Before he can reach her, I dart in front and place a hand against his chest keeping him back.

"Come at her like a raging dick again and I'll fucking put you on your ass," I grit out.

He smacks my hand away and gets right up in my face. "You need to remember, she is *my* fucking sister, asshole."

I push forward until my mask digs into his forehead. "And you need to remember I fucking out rank you where she is concerned. She's *my* wife, asshole!" Vox shoves me backward. I try to catch myself but I'm too late, I fall into Vivian but luckily the guys catch her before she can hit the floor. Guided purely by my anger, I rush forward and tackle Vox. We land on the small table in the living room, smashing it to pieces beneath our weight.

"You stop them and you fix the fucking lights!" I hear Vivi scream just as her brother's fist connects with my mask and sends it flying across the room. This has been a long time coming and I know Hayze and Archer won't stop it, so I fight and punch him in the face and I feel the skin on my knuckles split thanks to his fucking mask. Vox has been holding back and trying to focus on Nova to keep his mind off what's been happening between us and Vivian, but without Nova here, there is nothing to tame the fucking monster.

"Baby, you have to let this play out." I hear one of the guys say as Vox and I continue to trade punch for punch and roll around the floor, breaking shit. I grunt when the fucker lands a good punch to my ribs. I throw my legs over his and use all my weight to roll him onto his back and jab him twice in the ribs for payback.

"That all you got, you fucking pussy?" he roars. I grip the bottom of his mask and rip it off, tossing it to the side. I don't stop there, I throw a right hook and manage to clip his jaw before he bucks his hips and tosses me off. The lights flicker on and we both sit there panting and covered in sweat, I can tell from the look in his eyes this is far from over and I'm not about to back down either.

"I got a lot more, you dumb fuck!" I snap back.

"You're fucking weak, Ez," he taunts.

"I wasn't weak when I walked the fucking line for her!" I roar. I hear Vivian gasp but I don't take my gaze off her brother. "You want to fight it out and try to act like you're the top dog, then come on, motherfucker, because I'll take it all but I will *never* walk away from her."

"You can't have her! None of you can."

"For fuck sake, Vox, no one is taking your sister away! Your fear of losing another loved one is killing her!" I scream. Vox jerks back and stares at me with wide eyes. "She isn't your father, she will never leave you but if you keep trying to control her life, you will push her away. The three of us have been in love with her for years but always held back because we knew how you would react. I love you and you will always be my brother but you need to let her go, Vox. She won't abandon you like your father did." I see the exact moment my crushing words hit their mark. I wasn't trying to hurt him intentionally, I would never want to break him emotionally but he has to realize that him smothering her and trying to hide Vivian from the world is what led us to this moment. She blocked us all out when she made a move to claim the Saints as her own. She banished us from ever stepping foot in our hometown because he forced us to choose.

"He's right," Archer mutters, drawing our gazes up to him. He stands there with his mask firmly in place and his hands stuffed in his pockets but it's the look in his eyes that has both of us remaining where we are. I cut a glance to Hayze to see him standing firmly at Vivi's side like a protector. Arch reaches up and tears his mask off, then clasps it between his hands, staring down at it with a strange mixture of remorse and anger. "When we started wearing these things, I thought it would be a way for us all to grow closer. A part of me even hoped it would help you focus on something other than your sister so you wouldn't know I was... falling in love with her." Vivian gasps and stares at Archer in surprise. "I have loved her for years, Vox. Fuck, I wanted to tell you so many times but every time I gathered the courage to do it, you would remind us how her and your mom were all you had and you would never allow anyone to take them from you."

"So what? You thought you would fuck my sister behind my back?" Vox grits out. I slowly push to my feet and move toward him, he glares up at me when I offer him my hand. The fucker knocks it away and climbs to his feet on his own. "I know how the three of you dicks get off, not once have you ever kept a girl—"

"Because none of them were *her!*" Hayze roars. It's still strange hearing him discuss his feelings and being so open about it, the fact he actually is starting just goes to show how much Vivian does mean to him and cements my decision that we are doing the right thing by trying to make this work between the four of us, regardless of what her brother thinks. "They were nameless, faceless girls that meant nothing to us. She was the one we all wanted but could never have because we worried it would tip you over the edge. I thought you finding Nova and loving her would ease your asshole ways, but I guess we were all wrong because you're an even bigger dick than you were before."

Vox growls and shoots Hayze a scathing look but doesn't say anything as he swipes at the cut on his lip. It brings a smile to my face seeing his split lip. Serves the fucker right.

"Can we all just take this down a notch?" Vivian says as she breaks away from Hayze and moves toward her brother. She reaches for him but he steps back. Hurt flashes in her eyes and it takes everything I have inside me to keep from biting his head off for that stunt. "Vox—"

"Is this why you changed?" he asks.

"What?"

"Is this why you changed, Vivian?" he snaps. She jerks at the harsh tone of his voice.

"Vox!"

He snaps his head toward me and pins me with a murderous look. "Stay the fuck out of this!" The look in his eyes and the tone of his voice is indication enough that he is feeling everything he has buried for years so I snap my mouth closed and let this play out. "Did you screw my best friends behind my back?"

She inhales sharply and straightens. I watch as she locks down her fear of hurting her brother, but I also see the acceptance in her eyes and that makes me proud. She is finally accepting us and that has a fucking ton of weight lifting off my shoulders.

"No. At first, they were just the guys I thought were hot." Vox scrunches his face in disgust. "Then Archer and I... we hooked up." Vox shoots a look at Arch that promises pain. Archer knows he is going to get his ass kicked for that and he is man enough to nod and accept what is coming his way. "But then he put a stop to it. Hayze became a safe haven for me and somehow things changed between us but nothing ever happened until... the other night."

"What about him?" Vox grits out, flicking his head toward me.

I wait with bated breath to hear her explanation. She exhales. "He was my solace in the darkest moments. Archer is my protector, Hayze is the one that soothes my soul, and Ez, well, he's the one that keeps me grounded. I didn't realize I loved them all until last year when I thought Ezekiel died and

Hayze and Archer left me to help you. I thought I was being dramatic until I realized watching Ezekiel die broke my heart. I needed Archer and Hayze to hold me together but then they left and took what remained of my fragmented heart with them. I'm sorry, Vox, I never meant to love them, I swear, but I'm not sorry because I won't give them up, not again."

"Again?" he pushes.

"You took the three of them from me last year and I won't let you do it again. You have everything you wanted. You got the freedom you wanted from the Saints, I gave that to you. I saved Nova from the fate that was destined for her, *I* did that not you or them. Me. I am the Lordess of the Saints and it was always going to work out this way."

"No, the fuck, it wasn't!" Vox yells. "The Filthy Few was constructed to keep you from this fate. I never wanted this for you—"

Vivian cuts him off before he can finish. "You didn't but Edmund and Virgil fucking did!" she screams. All of us guys move to Vox's sides and stare down at the girl who has us eating out of the palm of her hand with that declaration. Tears shine in her eyes as she looks at each of us before finally focusing back on her twin.

"What the fuck does that mean? Dad and Edmund were trying to save you—"

"No!" she snaps, silencing Vox. "Edmund was only trying to save Taylor," she whispers, then sends me a broken look.

"What are you talking about?" I push as worry begins to gnaw at me, something isn't adding up here.

"When Nikoa reached out to me to be his informant, I didn't know what to expect but the more information I gathered for him the more secrets I uncovered."

"How did *you* become his informant?" Arch snarls.

She shrugs. "Who better to infiltrate the organization that

murdered her father than the sister of the leader of a masked crew who was hellbent on tearing them down. Not only am I smart enough to hack computers but I'm a really good listener, and nine times out of ten no one ever notices a woman in a room filled with powerful men. I learned things and in my own way I thought helping Nikoa would help the Filthy Few, but it turns out you all had it wrong from the start."

"Had what wrong?" Hayze hedges.

She smiles sadly. "My father and Edmund were only trying to save Taylor, not me." I reel back in shock at the bitterness that coats her tone and shake my head trying to deny what she is saying. Dad and Virgil were trying to save the girls!

"What?" I breathe out.

She turns all her attention to me and normally I would be happy to have her focus only on me but right now, I don't want it. The sorrow in her eyes is killing me. "You and I were always meant to be together. I was always going to be a Tempest, turns out you and I were promised to each other before we were even born."

I stare at her at a loss for words. I feel disgust crawling through me, causing my skin to itch. My father wouldn't have done this, he was a good man!

"Dad was trying to save you!" Vox argues.

Vivian stares at her twin, I see pity in her eyes. "You always thought dad was a hero. Hey, maybe he was to you but for me? I was nothing to him aside from a way for him to guarantee his future."

"Vivi, you need to break this down, baby," Hayze implores.

"There isn't anything to break down. Edmund and Virgil had planned to marry me off to Ezekiel so that their bloodline could remain in power. Do you know I own a sex club?" The four of us all jerk back. "I wish I could say I came up with the idea all on my own but I can't. When you are named lord or lordess you have access to all the records of the former leaders and guess what?" She doesn't wait for us to answer. "It was Edmund's idea and Virgil wanted to hold my wedding to Ezekiel at that hotel. Our father wasn't a good man, Vox, he was just like Thomas!" she screams.

I can't handle hearing more of this, I push forward and wrap my arms around her, anchoring her to my front. She tries to fight to get free but I don't budge even when she reaches under my hoodie and claws her nails down my back.

"Listen to me!" I snap, she freezes in my arms but doesn't pull her nails from my back. "I had no idea about what they had planned, but it doesn't have to change anything, Vivian. I married you because I want *you*, not some fucking title or power, I just want you!" She slowly begins to relax and when her nails release my poor back I sigh. She tilts her head back and stares up at me with tears rolling down her cheeks. I curse my father and hers for putting this doubt in her mind about me. "I love you, Vivi."

She exhales loudly and tears continue to fall down her cheeks. I start to worry she is going to push me away until she finally speaks. "Do you mean that?"

"Yes," I say with conviction that leaves no room for her to doubt my words. To my utter shock, she reaches up and locks her arms around my neck, bringing my lips to hers. I don't second guess it. I kiss her with a hunger that I don't mask, I need her to feel everything I feel. She needs to know she is the center of not only my world but Hayze and Archer's as well.

CHAPTER EIGHTEEN

Vivian

I break the kiss with Ezekiel and muster a smile for his benefit but I can tell he isn't satisfied. He doesn't call me on it as he steps aside and allows me to face my brother who looks like I just blew his world apart.

"I didn't just change because my heart got broken," I admit. I hate that Archer drops his chin to his chest and won't look at me but I'm not saying this to hurt him. "I changed because I was tired of fighting a losing battle. Even before I found out the truth about our father, I knew the Saints were too strong to take down. The only way to end them is to outsmart them, Vox."

"And how are you doing that?" The bite to his tone isn't lost on me but I choose to ignore it.

"By asking you four to trust me enough and believe me when I tell you I know what I am doing," I plead.

"Was Kelly getting murdered a part of your plan?" he snaps. I fight not to flinch at the accusation in his tone.

"No, it wasn't," I admit. "I don't know who is behind this but I am actively working on figuring that out but you guys being here isn't helping anything, I need you to go—"

"No!" Archer snarls, pulling my attention to him. "We aren't leaving you. I don't give a fuck about your plans or what you think is the right move. We aren't leaving your side." His promise has warmth spreading through me.

"Nova needs answers, Vivian. I can't go back to her with nothing." The anguish I hear in his tone isn't for himself, it's for the love of his life that he left behind to come here and try to avenge the murder of her mother. I mull over his words for a minute trying to think of the best course of action.

"I can't lift the banishment, there is no way the Saints would agree to that anyway," I announce.

"Why the fuck not?" Hayze growls. I pin the big boofhead with a deadpan look.

"Aside from the fact of you four being troublemakers? Maybe the fact that you four have a bigger claim to the lord status then the rest. The Night Of Saints is four weeks away and I have a lot of shit to do before then, including finding out who the fuck is stalking me and sending me heads."

"Wait, *heads?* As in plural?" Archer rasps out.

I shoot him a sheepish look. "Clive Bruce the District Attorney was the first." At my admission the four of them begin shouting. With no other option, I do the only thing I can to get all their attention, I scream. All four of them stumble backward. I shoot each of the dicks a glare of warning. "You don't call the fucking shots, I do. Am I clear?" None of them agree so I push on. "You don't like it, there's the fucking door, don't let it hit ya where the good lord split ya!" Vox scoffs.

"You may rule over those cockless bastards in the Saints, but not me." Utterly spent and over this dick measuring contest, I step right into my brother and harden my features.

"Then leave because around here I am the fucking king, not you. You shouldn't even be here and it's because of my mercy you aren't being hunted daily by The Brotherhood. Don't mistake that mercy for weakness, Brother."

"We agree to your terms," Archer says, trying to break the tension between me and Vox but we both ignore him as we continue to stare at each other. Months ago I would have conceded and allowed him to assume control, but not this time. This is my town, my house and this is my call. I won't allow him to fuck everything up when I am so close to winning!

"Back the fuck down or I will drive you back to Washington myself and let Nova kick your ass," Hayze vows. Vox's left eye twitches and I can tell he is close to losing his shit and the last thing I want is for him and the guys to destroy more of my house and each other so I try again.

"I know you don't like this and you don't have to, but all I am asking is for you to trust me. I know what I am doing and I promise you, I will find who did this to Kelly." He searches my eyes, trying to pull all my secrets from me. He's always tried to prove that the twin telepathy myth is true but it's not. He can read me as well as I can read him but we can't read each other's minds, much to my brother's dismay. I see the second he relents. His hands unclench from his sides and his shoulders lose some of the tension.

"I'm giving you three weeks, that's it. After that I'm going hunting and I don't give a fuck about the banishment. I want the cunts' head on a spike for what he took from Nova and for what he is doing to my little sister." I smile up at him, even though he is angry and hurt over all of this he can't help but still be my big brother and my heart swells with that knowledge.

"Deal," I quip, then wrap my arms around his waist and rest my head against his chest. The light chuckle that escapes him brings a small smile to my lips. His arms band around me as he places a kiss on the top of my head.

"Our conversation about these dickheads isn't over, but for tonight it is." I laugh when I hear the three grumbling about how much of an ass my brother is.

"I know but tonight I have somewhere to be." Instantly the mood turns sour and Vox's arm drops from around me. I sigh and take a step back, then look at each of them. "I have a meeting with the Saints. I can't get out of it so don't ask." When Archer opens his mouth I raise my hand silencing him. "No, you can't come with me so please don't ask." Arch and Ezekiel both glower but don't comment. "I'll be back as soon as I can. In the meantime, you can make yourself at home and clean up the mess you all made."

"I didn't do shit!" Hayze says with his hands raised.

"Me either!" Archer tacks on, both of them earn deadly looks from Vox and Ezekiel. Before they can start arguing again, I escape the room and dash upstairs to change, I have forty minutes before I need to leave and in that time I still have to shower. I choose an outfit that will ruffle some feathers at the meeting tonight, so I go with a pair of skin-tight white jeans, a white corset style top that makes my waist look tiny and pair the outfit with a pair of blood red six-inch heels. I toss the items onto my bed, then move to the bathroom. I strip off then pull the glass panel of my shower and step inside. I wait for the water to heat before stepping under the spray, careful not to wet my hair.

I start lathering my body with soap but freeze when I get the feeling of being watched. I slowly peer over my shoulder to see Hayze standing in the doorway with my discarded lavender thong twirling around his finger. The ravenous look in his eyes sends a shiver down my spine. His eyes lazily trail down my body then back up, there isn't any urgency in his perusal of my body and that turns me on. The way he is looking at me, like he has every right and there isn't a single thing that could distract him from the sight before him, has me darting my tongue out to moisten my lips. His eyes track the movement. As we are playing a game of who gives in first, I watch as he balls up my panties then brings them to his nose, inhaling deeply while still keeping his eyes locked on mine.

A gasp flies out of me when he lowers my thong and rubs it over his crotch, the cheeky fucker winks then stuffs them into his pocket. My nipples pebble and turn hard as I think about what he might do with those panties. A mental picture of Hayze pleasuring himself hits me, a moan tumbling from me when the image turns to one of him coming on my thong.

"Penny for your thoughts, Vivi baby?" His tone is husky and filled with need. My body is reacting to him without him even touching me. My pussy is pulsing and the urge to touch myself is fucking overwhelming. I'm aching for him and I know I won't be able to focus on anything at the meeting if he doesn't quell this ache, I need him. I decide to be bold and push the shower pane open on invitation but he still doesn't move. "You want me to come in there with you, baby, you're gonna have to say it."

I should be able to just say the words especially what happened the other night but I find myself feeling shy and slightly uncertain. All of this still feels so surreal to me. I know they have all said that they want me but if I sleep with Hayze without the others, will that change things?

"No, we all know there will be times where it's just one of us you want and we're okay with that."

I cock my head to the side confused. "Huh?"

He smiles but it's a slow sexy smirk that has me clenching my thighs together. "You said that out loud, little mouse." He pushes off the frame and takes a step toward the shower. My heart starts to beat faster and my body begins to heat. He reaches behind himself and tugs his hoodie and shirt off in the sexy way guys do. The second he removes them, my greedy eyes drink in the sight of his exposed skin and bite my lip to keep from moaning at the masterpiece before me.

"Hayze," I breathe his name like a prayer. He takes another step, then stops. He pops the button on his jeans and I suck a sharp intake of breath when he peels the zipper down but doesn't make another move to rid himself of his pants.

"Say the word, baby, and I'll make sure you get everything you need."

Jesus!

My body is burning up, my chest feels like it's going to cave in from the lack of oxygen thanks to him stealing my breath away. *I want this.* If I can fuck the three of them in the same room I can find the courage to tell him what he wants to hear. I refuse to deny myself the pleasure of them any longer, now that I've tasted them I can't seem to get enough.

"I want you," I say in a tone I don't recognize, my voice foreign to my own ears. I've never sounded sultry or sexy before but it seems that has changed. Hayze doesn't make me beg. He pushes his pants down his muscled legs and I gape when I notice he isn't wearing boxers, he kicks his shoes and pants to the side. My attention is rooted on his cock and how hard it is. It rests against his abs looking angry and red, he needs this release as much as I do. As if to entice him, I pull the elastic from my hair and shake out my waves—his eyes burn molten at the sight.

I'm not self-conscious or anything like that, but when you have a guy, or in my case *guys*, who look like them staring at you, even the most confident of women would falter for a second. I push all of my doubts out of my mind and decide to taunt him like he just did me. I reach up and cup my tits. His nostrils flare and his chest rises and falls in quick pants when I pinch my nipple between my fingers and release a soft mewl of pleasure.

"Fuck." His restraint finally snaps. He storms toward me and I back up to give him more room. The shower door has barely closed before he pounces on me. His large hand tangles in the back of my hair, yanking me flush against him while the other grips my ass in a firm hold. The second his lips touch mine, I moan into his mouth, then run my hands all over his body. Just as I attempt to deepen the kiss, he yanks my hair, forcing my head back. A hiss of pain escapes me but it quickly turns to a whimper when he begins to lick and suck on my neck.

"Yes!" I moan when he dips his head lower and licks around my nipple. Fuck, his teasing is the worst and best kind of edging. The feeling of his mouth on me and his hard cock resting against my bare skin is torture. My greedy little cunt keeps clenching on air, begging to be filled with his thick dick. I close my eyes and throw my head back, moaning when he finally sucks my nipple into his mouth. They're so sensitive to the point every flick of his tongue has me jolting and panting. "I need you inside me," I pant as I lift my leg and lock it around him, hoping for his cock to slide through my folds, but the sheer height difference between us makes it impossible. I growl in frustration until he releases my hair, then grips the backs of my thighs and lifts me.

He looks up at me with love and hunger in those beautiful eyes and suddenly all worries flee, there is nothing else that matters in this moment except for me and him... him and I, it's just us and everything else fades away.

"I want to draw this out, baby, but right now I just need to feel that pussy wrapped around me." Fuck, if he thinks he is going to get an argument from me he's out of his crazy ass mind.

"Please, I need you inside me now!" Hayze opens his mouth but is cut off.

"Fuck her and make her come." I dart my gaze over Hayze's head to see Archer leaning against the counter with his cock in his hand. I gasp, I hadn't even heard him come in, I was too lost in Hayze. Worry begins to take flight inside me until he meets my stare and I see nothing but raw longing in his eyes.

He's turned on by me fucking his friend!

"Keep your eyes on him while I fuck you, baby." I nod unable to get my voice to work. Hayze presses me flat against the stone wall, I don't even feel the bite of the cold thanks to how hot I am right now for him.

I pull my gaze from Archer and grip Hayze's face between my hands, forcing him to look at me. He stops moving and suddenly looks afraid that I'll end this moment. "He can watch but you get my attention. I want to feel you come inside me and mark me as yours."

CHAPTER NINETEEN

Hayze

We're all in uncharted waters here.

Yes, Archer and I have had threesomes before and shared girls but none of them meant anything to us. They were just holes we could use to get off but Vivian is different. I don't know if she realizes it but if it wasn't for how we felt about her, I don't think any of us would have overcome our differences and tried to make this shit work. Archer and I were content to live with the loss of losing two of our best friends, but now that we are back here, I know I'll fight to make my brotherhood with the guys work, not just for myself but for her because she is worth it.

Fuck, she is worth so much more.

"He can watch but you get my attention. I want to watch you come inside me and mark me as yours." I stare at her in surprise. My cock chooses that moment to twitch against her entrance and her eyes shudder. I say nothing as I slowly push inside her, the fact Archer is watching makes this ten times fucking hotter. I have a voyeur type of kink, I knew the second I followed her up the stairs that it would only be a matter of time before he figured out where I went and followed me.

I love the soft moans that escape her as I continue to ease inside her tight, wet pussy. Fuck, she's so wet for me I'm sliding in with no resistance. I lean forward and suck her nipple into my mouth, her head lolls back against the wall. When I finally bottom out inside her, she arches forward, pushing her tit further into my mouth as her pussy clamps down on my cock just as she cries out.

"Unless you want Vox and Ezekiel to hear you fucking her, I'd shut her up," Archer snarls. Vivian pulls my head, forcing me to release her nipple with a wet pop. She smashes her lips against mine and takes it upon herself to bounce up and down on my dick. I tighten my grip on her legs, letting her ride me. I groan and she swallows it like it's the air she needs to live. Fuck, her pussy is perfect and fits me like a glove. It was made for me and so was she. Her moans grow loud enough to the point that the kiss and the sound of the shower running can't mask them. I break the kiss and reach for the loofah on the shelf to my left. I shove the pink thing in her mouth, before she can try to spit it out I cover her mouth with my hand and thrust up inside her.

Her eyes rolls back into her head. I can see Archer out of the corner of my eye creep in closer to get a better look at her and I know it's only a matter of time before the fucker strips off and climbs in here with us. Vivian pushes down and starts meeting me thrust for thrust. I step back and push back until her head rests against the wall giving me better access, but it also puts me at a better angle to hit that G-spot inside her. I know the moment I hit her sweet spot, she screams out and her eyes widen in surprise.

"Oh yeah, baby, you're gonna come on my cock," I growl as I pick up my pace, my thrusts punishing and aggressive, but she fucking loves it. The sound of skin slapping skin is fucking euphoric. I feel a cold gust of wind on my back but don't stop fucking her as Archer comes to stand beside her. Her eyes are wide but have a dazed look to them, she's so close and his presence just adds to her heightened state of need. He reaches out and twirls her nipples between his fingers. She bucks against me and arches her back. "Fuck yeah, baby, I can feel it. Come on my cock like a good girl, Vivi baby." As if my words are her undoing she clamps down on my cock and screams into my hand as her orgasm rips through her tiny body. My balls tighten and I try to fight off the need to come, but when she keeps squeezing around my dick I fall over the edge of the cliff with her name on my lips. I come deep inside her pussy and relish in the knowledge I am deep inside her and she will have a part of me with her at that meeting tonight. "Fuck," I breathe out.

Archer steps back to allow me to push in closer. I remove my hand and rip the loofah out of her mouth, then before she can say anything, I kiss her. She melts into me instantly and locks her arms around my neck, holding me to her like she doesn't want to let go. When Archer clears his throat I break the kiss, resting my forehead against hers as I slowly ease out of her. She whimpers and I fear I've hurt her until she says,

"Now, I'm empty." I laugh at the cheeky minx. She smiles and shoots me a wink. I place a kiss to the top of her nose and slowly lower her to her feet. The second she is stable Archer shoves me backward and claims my place before her. "Archer—"

"Shut the fuck up, get on your knees." He sounds like a dick but he and I both know she loves it when he gets all dominant, I noticed it when we were back at CHU. Vivian loves to be fucked hard and rough. Without complaint she lowers to her knees and opens her mouth while locking eyes with him. "I'm not gonna help you, grab it and suck it." Her pupils dilate, she reaches out, grips the base of his cock and wraps her lips around him. Archer may be a tough fuck but even he can't fight against her. A deep guttural groan rips free and his head falls back as his hand tangles in her hair. He allows her to set the pace for a moment until his need overcomes him, he's too turned on from watching me fuck her to hold off his own release.

His momentum becomes hurried. She gags around him but he doesn't ease his thrusts. "Take him all the way, baby. I want you to swallow his cock and make him come down your throat so you have us both inside ya,." I find myself saying, her tear-filled eyes flicking to me, whatever she sees in my eyes has her own widening and her head bobbing up and down faster. She takes him as deep as she can. When she attempts to do it again, Archer thrusts forward drawing a long gag from her. I can tell that was too much, so I pull him back then pull her up by her arms. She stares at me with alarm.

I do the only thing I can think of, I lift her off the ground, she locks her legs and arms around me but this isn't what she thinks. I turn so her back is to Arch and rest my own against the wall. I grip the globes of her ass and part her cheeks. Her eyes widen in surprise and her mouth opens but I cut her off before she can speak.

"He's going to fuck this pussy and I want your eyes on me the whole time, baby. He's gonna make you come."

She shakes her head. "I can't."

"Yes, the fuck, you can and you will," Arch snarls as he comes up behind her. I know the exact moment he enters her, not only can I feel her tighten her hold on me but her eyes darken with carnal need.

"Archer!" she cries out when he thrusts inside her. I capture her lips and shove my tongue inside her mouth to quiet her screams as he fucks her like a savage. My own cock is growing hard and wanting to be balls deep inside her again, but I know she is already going to be late for this meeting, not that I care but I know she does.

"Play with her clit!" I do as Archer says, reaching between our bodies. I press the pad of my thumb against her clit. She pushes backward, resting against Archer. He doesn't slow his pace. Her head rests against his shoulder and when her mouth opens to cry out, he seals his lips to hers while I pinch her clit. Her entire body locks up. I lean down and capture her nipple in my mouth as her body tightens as the orgasm slams into her. I know she'll be clamping down on his cock, milking it for everything it's worth. I flick my eyes up and continue sucking her nipple as I see Archer's face contort as his own release tears through him.

His thrusts turn lazy and their kiss turns sloppy. I release her with a wet pop as Archer pulls back and smiles down at her. Her face is flushed and she has that just fucked look about her that has me smiling.

"Wrap it up, her ride's here." We all jerk in surprise at the sound of Ez's voice. I flick my gaze to him and to my own surprise I don't see jealousy or anger in his eyes, I just see... contentment and... hunger for her. Vivi pushes against us. We both help her to her feet, Archer wrapping an arm around her waist when her legs nearly give out.

"I have to wash and then get changed, I'm so fucking late!" she growls.

"No washing, you're going to that meeting with them inside you as a reminder of who you belong to. When you get home I'll help you wash them out of that pussy then lick it clean before filling you up with my cum so you don't forget there is three of us who own you now, little mouse." Ezekiel's words have her eyes popping wide and jaw hitting the floor. I'll admit the picture he just painted has my dick hard and ready for her again. Fuck, will this hunger for her ever lessen?

CHAPTER TWENTY

Vivian

I can't stop squirming in my seat, images of the guys drying my body while Ez stood there and watched flash through my mind. When I felt their come dripping out of me, I gasped which had all three of them focusing on my pussy and the mess they made of it. I expected them to wipe me clean but of course they did the opposite. Ezekiel was the one to gather the cum on his finger and push it back inside me, telling me to be a good girl and clench my cunt closed to hold it in. He promised to reward me if I listened and managed to get home with the cum still inside me. The three of them even sat on the edge of my bed and watched me change. I thought for sure they would all riot at my outfit choice but to my surprise each of them just told me how beautiful I looked.

To say that had me speechless is an understatement. On my way out the door I tried to avoid eye contact with my brother at all cost, but he isn't an idiot. He knew what we were doing upstairs and if the sounds of grunts and shouting I heard as I closed the door behind myself was any indication , I know they were all fighting about me.

"She isn't even listening!" I shake my head and push away all thoughts of my guys.

My guys?

I should be shocked by that revelation but I'm not. I love how it sounds and it has a certain ring to it if you ask me. But now is not the place to be having that revelation. I keep my face blank as I lock eyes with Donald Waiff. He is the owner of the banks in town, hence is the reason I needed to go to CHU to meet with Darius, Corvin, Beckett, Saint and Crue for their help.

"I am listening, Donald!" I grit out through clenched teeth. All I have done for the past fucking hour is listen to these ungrateful bastards go on and on about how they aren't seeing an increase in their profits or how their *extra* income is suddenly drying out. "I opened Lividica to help with this issue and like I have said so many fucking times before, I am not Thomas and I will not stoop to his level!"

"At least Thomas had our pockets lined and our families fed," Noel spits.

"Which one of your families was that again?" Noel's eyes widen and his mouth pops open but I'm not done. I push to my feet and stare out at all the members of this fucking sham of a brotherhood. "You all think I am an airhead bitch who doesn't know dick about money, politics or how to run an empire and I have allowed you all to think that because it was easier than arguing with you chauvinistic bastards." David tries to stop me but I'm not shutting up, they need to hear this and there isn't a fucking thing they can do about me being their leader until a month's time. "Newsflash, I know more about all of you then you know about me. Like how I know Noel has two families and he has tried his best to keep his wife and mistress happy but what he doesn't want everyone to know is his mistress is actually Cooper Fergusson's wife and the brand new baby dear old Coop just welcomed into the world isn't actually his son, it's Noel's." Cooper leaps over the row of chairs in front of him and guns for Noel, who is trying to deny what I say but it's falling on deaf ears.

"Lordess, I think you should go home while I smooth things over," David shouts over the noise in the room. I shoot my right hand man a megawatt smile and prance out of that room full of men with ego's twice the size of their heads. Tonight was supposed to be about me keeping the peace and assuring The Brotherhood that I had everything under control and they would see an increase in revenue soon, but I couldn't help it.

Kelly's death has triggered something in me, I can't pretend anymore. These men I have spent the past year with are cold-blooded murderers. They care for no one except themselves and I am done playing their game, it's time they all fucking played mine!

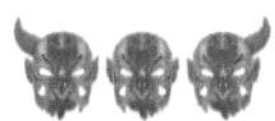

I PUSH through the front door of my house and sigh. Everything is silent but just knowing that there are people I love and care about inside these walls makes my house feel like a home. I don't feel trapped or isolated for the first time since moving in here. There's a warmth in here that wasn't there yesterday, the colors on the walls don't seem as dull and the home itself doesn't seem as daunting.

"Why are you smiling?" I shriek and nearly jump a foot in the air. I glare at my brother who is leaning against the wall in the corner, shrouded in darkness.

"Could you be any more of a cliché?" I snap.

"What?"

"You're hiding in a corner acting like I'm breaking curfew and you're here to bust me!"

He comes toward me and the instant he steps into the light my eyes widen. His cheek is bruised and he has a cut above his eye. "I guess you four had a disagreement when I left?"

He scoffs and rolls his eyes, then stalks off into the kitchen with me hot on his heels. I dart my gaze around the living room hoping to spot one of my guys.

"They're upstairs." I swing my gaze back to my brother who looks like he wants to break something.

"I wasn't looking for them."

His eyes narrow. "You've always been a shit liar."

"And you have always been an overprotective jerk but you don't see me complaining!" I bite back.

"A jerk that devoted his life to trying to save you from the very fucking brotherhood you now lead."

"What are you more pissed about, Vox, the fact I am the lordess or the fact I am screwing your friends?" He reels back and smacks into the edge of the counter. I pull a stool out at the breakfast counter and sit my ass on it while still glaring across at him. The asshole doesn't answer, instead he turns and opens the fridge and pulls a beer out. Clearly one of them went to the store because I didn't have any beer in there before. He pops the top and chugs back half the bottle before finally facing me again. Only this time when he looks at me, I see resignation in his eyes.

"When we were little, I thought you would always be by my side. It was supposed to be me and you till the end, Vi." The hurt that laces his tone robs me of air.

"What does that mean?" I whisper.

"It means, you aren't that little girl anymore and I'm not a little boy who thinks that our dad is going to come home."

Sadness envelops me for my brother, I may not think of our father as a hero anymore but he still does. "I want to be mad at you but I can't."

"Why do you want to be mad at me?"

He shoots me a sad look. "I want to be mad at you, so then I can displace the guilt of admitting it was me that broke us first."

I recoil. "You didn't break us."

"I did. I broke us when I kept shit from you because I thought I knew better. I didn't include you in our plans to take down the Saints because I thought I was doing the right thing by you. Turns out, I was wrong and I should have trusted you, but in my mind I was protecting you from the horrors of what the world was really like."

"You did protect me—"

"No, I didn't. It's my fault you married my best friend and became the lordess. I left you no other choice but to go behind my back and take matters into your own hands."

"Vox, that isn't true. I did what I did to protect you and save you all from living in hell. Helping Nikoa gather the intel I did helped me to see what the Saints were really like. I never wanted to be a part of them but when I was faced with a choice of you four dying under Thomas's rule and my best friend being forced to marry his cunt of a son, I did what I had to in order to ensure we all made it out."

"You still wanted to save me even though you thought I killed Ezekiel?"

Bitterness swells inside me at the reminder of what he did. "Yes, even then I still wanted to save you," I force out through clenched teeth then take a breath to tamper down my feelings of betrayal. We're both silent for a while lost to our own thoughts until he breaks it.

"Vi?"

"Yeah?" I say quietly.

"Why didn't you come to me when you started getting letters?" A whoosh of air escapes me. "Believe it or not, Nova and I actually have a bit of experience with getting random notes and shit."

"Because I didn't need you to fix this one for me, Vox. I know this may shock you but I am a big girl and I can handle myself."

"I know you are but you also have to know that I can't just let this go. I have to get answers, Vivian."

"Don't fucking—"

"Nova needs them!" It's not his tone that has me snapping my mouth shut, it's the mention of my best friend and the reminder of what she has lost.

"You should be with her, Vox. She needs you." He scrubs a hand down his face and sighs.

"I know. But the last time she lost someone, she pushed me away and blamed me. I... I just—"

"You left because you were scared that if you stayed she would do it again and this time, you wouldn't survive losing her." His shoulders deflate as he drops his gaze to the floor and nods.

"Yeah," he mutters. I rise from my seat and move around the counter to stand before him. He still won't look at me so I poke his side like I used to do when we were younger. It brings a ghost of a smile to his lips but I can see the torment in his eyes that are mirrors of my own.

"That girl is crazy in love with you and she would never leave you, but right now, you being here isn't where you *need* to be."

He shakes his head denying what I say. "No, I need to do this for her."

"Vox, you're being a coward and you know it. Nova needs you to be with her right now and you know it. She needs you to hold her. Ezekiel is her brother and I know for a fact he will do whatever he has to so his sister can get the closure she needs. I know the four of you are at odds right now but you have to know that no matter what, they will always have your back. Nova isn't just your girlfriend, she's Ez's little sister and he will protect her like you protect me."

"She's right." I spin around at the sound of his voice and fight not to smile at the three of them standing in the entryway, the fact they are all shirtless and wearing sweats that hang low on their hips has my mind growing foggy with X-rated thoughts. "I'll kill whoever I have to so my sister can get the justice her mother deserves. You can hate me for loving your sister but just know that I love mine the same as you love yours, and no matter how we feel about each other will never change that. But, Vivian is right, Vox, she needs you right now more than ever. I may be her brother but it isn't me she wants wrapped around her, it's *you*."

Vox eyes the guys and I can see he is warring within himself with his decision, but we all know what he will choose and I don't want him to feel guilt over his decision so I say, "I know you love me and want to be here to help, but you also love her more." He opens his mouth to argue but I push on. "There is nothing wrong with that. You should love her more than anyone and I want you to go back to Washington and be by her side while she grieves the loss of her mom—" I clamp my mouth closed when my front door bursts open and one of my guards rush inside. He was briefed on my way out earlier about my *guests* and knows his silence is key with who they are. "What is it ,Adam?"

"Miss, there is a car approaching, two occupants. What are our orders?" Within two point five seconds the guys claim control. I'm slung over Archer's shoulder while Vox, Hayze and Ezekiel race around the house turning the lights off and shouting at Adam to get outside. Archer doesn't put me down until we are in the corner of the living room. He pushes me into the corner and keeps me there with his body.

"Don't move, I mean it, Vivian," he orders.

"Screw you, Archer!" I bite back.

"They can't be worried about you while trying to kill whoever the fuck it is at this time in the middle of the damn night." His words hit me right in the chest and I snap my mouth closed. I wait with bated breath, my nerves are shot and I'm starting to panic as fear slowly grips me in its clutches. What if this is the person who sent me Kelly's head? Oh my God, are we all going to die? I reach out and grip the back of Archer's shirt in a vice-like hold. He turns and peers at me over his shoulder. "Shit," he curses beneath his breath, then whirls around and grips my face between his hands as he bends down until we are eye level. "I won't let anything happen to you, baby."

"Arch, I'm scared," I whisper, making his eyes soften.

"I'm right here, baby, and I swear to you, your brother and the guys won't let any cunt get near you." When we hear the sound of a car door closing, Archer turns away from me and faces the others. I peer around him when I can hear the sound of voices outside. If it was a bad guy surely they wouldn't be talking, right? Vox is hiding behind the wall with a gun in his hands, Ez is crouched down behind the breakfast counter while Hayze is across the room using the sofa as a shield. The front door opens and all the guys turn rigid but the instant she speaks, everyone moves.

"If you shoot me, I'll kill you all!" she says. Vox is the first to reach Nova, shoving his gun in his waistband, then he's wrapping his arms around her and crushing her tiny body against his. Ez moves toward them and waits for Vox to release her while Hayze and Archer move to flank me on either side.

"What are you doing here, witch?" Vox asks when he pulls back. Nova doesn't answer him, instead she pulls out of his hold and hugs her brother who seems to relax in her embrace. Seeing that brings a smile to my face.

"Nova, are you okay?" Ez asks her when she finally releases him. Her face is red and her eyes are bloodshot from all the tears, she looks rundown and utterly shattered. She darts her gaze around her brother and when she sees me, tears well in her eyes. My feet carry me across the room and within seconds of our arms wrapping around each other we both break down. She clutches me like a lifeline and I do the same to her. My heart breaks for Nova and the loss she has suffered.

"She's gone, Vi, my mom is gone! I'm sorry but I had to see you. I tracked Vox's phone and I just... need you!" she screams, then begins sobbing hysterically. I spy my brother out of the corner of my eye tugging on the strands of his hair helplessly, he has no idea what to do to ease her pain. It turns out we were all wrong, she didn't need him or Ez, she needed *me*.

"I know, sweetie. I am so fucking sorry. I wish I could change what happened," I say, meaning every single fucking word. Nova continues to cry into my shoulder as I hold her. I look at Vox and motion with my eyes for him to come to her. He looks like he's in agony but manages to do as I asked. The instant he places his hand on her back she rips out of my hold and clings to my brother. He picks her up and without another word or so much as a backward glance he marches them up the stairs, while the rest of us stand here staring after them.

"Well, I guess that means he isn't leaving." The three of us turn and pin Hayze with a look that has him scrunching his face. "What? You were all thinking it, so don't act like it was just me!" I shake my head, suddenly exhaustion weighs heavy on me and the need for my bed overwhelms me as I sway on my feet. For the second time in the space of ten minutes I'm lifted off my feet, but this time it's bride style. I don't fight Ez as he carries me up the stairs, I just nuzzle into him and sigh in contentment. I feel guilty for being so at ease while my best friend is in one of the guest rooms breaking apart in my brother's arms.

Ez kicks my bedroom door shut behind us and manages to lock it without dropping me. When I hear fists pound against it from the outside I can't help but chuckle. "Fuck off, dick heads, you had your turn," Ez snaps. My breath hitches and suddenly the sleep I was craving vanishes and I'm wide awake and wired. He places me on my feet at the edge of my bed and grips my waist in a firm hold. The smoldering look in his eyes sends a shiver down my spine and need coursing through me. "Did you do what I said? Were you able to keep them inside of you like a good girl?" Fuck the filthiness of this situation isn't lost on me and I should be worried about how turned on I am.

"Some of it came out," I admit.

"Where?"

"In my panties," I answer and blush.

"Show me."

CHAPTER TWENTY-ONE

Ezekiel

Her eyes are wide and her cheeks are tinged pink, but she has nothing to be embarrassed about. I release her and step back. She opens her mouth and closes it a couple of times. She's trying to think of a reason why she shouldn't show me so I wait, eventually she will realize that she has no other choice but to do as she is told. I've waited long enough and the sight of their cum in her panties will fuel the beast inside me that craves her and wants to claim her.

Hayze, Archer and I are three dominant males who crave control in all aspects of our lives but when it concerns her, all rules fly out the window. The three of us don't want to control her, we just want to exist inside her and be in her thoughts every second.

"You said I I could shower?" I step aside and sweep my arm out for her to lead the way into the bathroom. She purposely doesn't turn the light on when we enter but I'm not having that,

I flick the switch and ignore the undignified look she shoots my way.

"Vivian, why are you trying to hide from me?" She bites down on her lip and scuffs her toe along the tiled floor, clearly feeling uncomfortable but I'm not Hayze, I won't fold and allow her to hide.

"Because it makes no sense for the three of you to want me!" I recoil as if she's slapped me. This girl is out of her fucking mind. I eliminate the space between us and grab her face between my hands, forcing her to meet my stare. I make sure she can see how pissed I am. Her mouth parts on a gasp, then tries to pull free but I don't budge. "Let me go."

"Shut the hell up and listen." Her eyes spit fire but she does as she is told and remains silent. "Why the fuck would you think that?"

She scoffs. "Excuse me for having doubts. I mean the three of you did choose to leave me and not once did any of you ever give me a reason to believe that you actually do love me. I mean, can't you see how mind blowing this is?"

I get her reasoning but it doesn't change anything. "Is that the only reason you're being all shy?"

Her cheeks turn a brighter shade of red and I know for certain there is more to her anger than her believing that we abandoned her. "Why me, Ez?" she whispers.

"Why not you, Vi?"

She reaches up and grabs my wrists in a firm hold. "The three of you are gods in this town. I'm not delusional, I know you can pick and choose whoever you want to warm your bed. What do I have that those girls don't because I can tell you now, they would all be more experienced than I am. Before the other night, my only sexual encounter was with Archer and that was years ago. Aside from that, all I have to go off is Pornhub and my vibrator."

Jealousy spreads through me at the thought of a battery operated fucking thing touching her pussy. I make a mental note to find that fucking thing and destroy it.

"They see gods, you see us. They see our last names and what they can gain from it, you see who we really are behind the masks and under all the layers of bullshit we were forced to portray daily to keep the Saints happy. You have a brain and heart, they have neither. They can have all the experience in the world and we would still want you. It's not about the looks or the sex, it's about who *you* are. Your heart and who you are inside is the reason we are all falling over our feet to get you to love us and accept what this thing is between us. I know it's not conventional but none of us are willing to back down unless you want us too. If you only want one, then we will accept that choice."

She swallows audibly and stares up at me with a nervous look in her eyes. "But, what if I do want all three of you?"

A slow seductive smile crosses my face. "Then you will have us for as long as you want us, because none of us are going anywhere, baby. We want forever with you if you will have us."

She searches my gaze trying to find a reason to doubt me but she won't. "You mean that, don't you?"

"Every fucking word, Vivian. I love you. Archer loves you and so does Hayze. All you have to do is love us back and I promise you, baby, we will do whatever we have to do to make you happy. Let us prove to you that we are worthy. We will never leave you again. Vox knows where we all stand now and he either has to accept our choice or we will walk away from him. We're choosing the right twin this time."

"I hear divorces are tricky and we didn't get a prenup, so I guess you're stuck with me." Laughter rumbles out of me at her smartass reply.

"Divorce is for the weak. You and me are anything but that,

just knowing you have my last name makes me want to beat my fists against my chest every single fucking day." She smiles and this time, it's filled with an emotion I try not to let fill me, hope. So instead I kiss her. She melts into me and doesn't fight the pull this time, giving into it and kissing me back. I skim my hands down her bare arms and slowly begin pulling at the ties at the back of her corset. When it finally falls away, I step back and allow the material to fall between us.

I slowly lower to my knees before her and begin undoing her jeans. I peel them down her legs, leaving her in nothing but her panties. I lift my gaze to hers and that spurs me on when I see heat reflected in those beautiful baby blues. I keep my eyes on hers as I grip her panties and slowly tug them down. When she steps out of them, I bring them to my face and smirk at the sight of cum smeared in the crotch. I toss them to the side and push to my feet, rid myself of my sweats and smirk when I find her gaze glued to my hard cock.

"Come on." I guide her into the shower and turn the water on. I don't wait for it to heat before pushing her against the wall and claiming her mouth. She moans then begins trying to climb me. I grip her waist and force her to remain where she is.

"Ezekiel!" she growls in between kisses. I slip my hand between our bodies and slide a finger through her folds and groan. "Shit," she cries out when I push a finger inside her, her cunt tight and already trying to clamp down on my finger to keep it inside her. I press the pad of my thumb against her clit as I continue to fuck her and hook my finger at the perfect angle to hit that spot. She breaks the kiss and throws her head back to cry out when I stroke her G-spot.

"You like that?" Lazily she flops her head forward and hums. In an unexpected move, she reaches out and grips my cock in her hand. I hiss.

"Fuck, your dick is so beautiful," she purrs as she pumps

me. Fuck, the feeling of her hand on me has images of all the naughty *naughty* things I want to do to her flashing through my mind. "Ez, I'm so close," she moans, her grip tightens around my shaft and her movements turn hurried as I continue to finger her pussy. I apply more pressure to her clit and insert a second digit inside her. She screams out. I seal my lips to hers to quieten her as much as I can. I feel the moment she is about to explode and yank my fingers out. She cries out in outrage. I ignore her as I flip her around.

"Hands on the wall, legs apart. You're gonna come on my cock, not my hand," I snarl. She does as she is told and fuck, the sight of her ready and waiting for me is one that will be embedded in my mind for all time. I line myself up with her and in one swift thrust I am sheathed inside her. Her cries bounce off the walls. I reach around and cover her mouth with my hand and grip her waist with the other. "You feel that cock? Every last inch of it belongs to you. Every drop of cum is yours. You never have to doubt that," I grit out through clenched teeth. I pull almost all the way out of her before slamming inside her again. Fuck, she feels amazing. Every thrust feels like I'm coming home—she is my haven, my heart and my wife.

"Oh, fuck," she screams into my hand as I thrust inside her again. I can feel the walls of her pussy clamping down. Her body is taut and begging for release. I keep my thrusts steady and even, dragging out her orgasm. I need her to come with me. I want this moment with her to be utterly connected and soaring together when we both come.

"Don't come, baby, wait for me," I force out. She whimpers and nods as best she can. I slide my hand from her mouth and wrap it around her throat, then pull her back to me so I can claim her mouth. She kisses me with fever and hunger like I have never seen or felt before. The kiss is what tips me over the edge. I pinch her clit and within a half a second she is soaring with me. She screams into my mouth, the kiss doesn't do much to mute her sounds and I have no doubt everyone would have heard. My orgasm robs me of breath and shudders roll through me without consent as I empty myself inside her.

She breaks the kiss and sucks in some much needed breaths. I do the same but don't pull out of her, instead I wrap my arms around her and hold her against me. This right here is everything I have ever wanted—Vivian in my arms, in my bed and her being mine.

CHAPTER TWENTY-TWO

Vivian

I wake to the sound of my phone vibrating on the nightstand beside me. I reach for it blindly and hit answer without checking the caller ID.

"Yeah?" I croak out.

"You have a call from an inmate at Rikers penitentiary." I bolt upright in bed and cringe when Ez grumbles beside me. Alexander's voice came through the speaker. "Alexander Denver. Do you accept the charges?"

"Yes," I whisper as I slip out of the bed and snatch one of the guys' discarded hoodies off the floor and quietly slip out of the room just as Alex's voice comes over the speaker again.

"Vivian."

"Alex." I reply, then tug the hoodie over my head and quietly go down the stairs.

"Did I wake you?"

"No. Yes, but don't worry, I had to get up anyway," I say, then stifle a yawn.

His soft laughter brings a smile to my face as I pad through the kitchen to flick the coffee maker on, then lean against the counter.

"I'm sorry, it's after nine so I assumed you would be awake."

"I normally am but... I—uh—"

"I'm aware of your visitors."

"Are you having me watched?" I bite out.

"I told you I would keep an eye on you and I meant it." I inhale and try to relax. "Your lawyers have been in contact. I'll admit, I didn't expect for them to move so fast." Relief washes over me, I thought after my outburst last night I would have lost the support of everyone but it seems some of the members of the Saints do keep their word.

"Vance, Phil and Terry are the best at what they do. I have faith they will prove your innocence of these crimes."

"Hope is a dangerous thing in a place like this." I can hear the bitterness that coats his words and I find myself feeling sorry for him.

"Everything they said about you in the press, is that true?" I feel instant regret when those words tumble out of my mouth, but I would be lying if I said I haven't been thinking about it since I first went to visit him.

"Like I said, not everything you read about me is valid. If these lines weren't monitored, I might be inclined to tell you."

"But?" I push.

"But that would mean we would have to trust each other and right now, I don't think we're there yet." That brings a smile to my face. I go about pouring myself a cup of coffee and fight not to moan when I take my first sip.

"So, we need to be friends?"

"Believe it or not, Vivian. I already consider you a friend and because of that, you have my word that I will not rest until I discover who the traitor is in your midst." Call me crazy but I believe him.

"Thank you."

"Don't thank me, I don't deserve it. I have to go, be safe." He ends the call.

"Bye," I mutter as I drop my phone onto the counter and sigh. It's nearly nine thirty in the morning and I have to go to Lividica to go over a few things with Tate, then I have a meeting with David at the high school to check on the progress of the expansion.

"Hey." I snap my head to the side to see Nova coming in from the side door, I frown at the sight of her in a pair of runners and one of Vox's hoodies that falls to just above her knees. Her hair is piled into a messy bun above her head, but it's her eyes that have my chest caving in, those green eyes are filled with heartbreak.

"How are you feeling?" I ask.

She shrugs as she goes about pouring herself a cup of coffee, then rounds the counter to claim one of the stools opposite me. She nurses the mug between her hands but doesn't take a sip, she just keeps turning it in her hands.

"I need answers," she says softly.

"I'm trying, Nova, I swear—"

"I know. I know everyone is trying but do you know how hard it is to have everyone tell you that your mother is dead but how can I believe that when there is no body." My face slackens and I begin to feel sick at the thought of having to tell her the truth. "I can't accept this without seeing... her, you know?" She lifts those broken green eyes to me and I nearly crumble under the pressure of them, but then her eyes drop and she takes in my attire. "Is that my brother's?" she asks.

A whoosh of air escapes me and I smile sheepishly. "I guess I should be asking you now if you hate me for sleeping with *your* brother?"

A soft laugh escapes her. "Given the fact I had no idea he was my brother before you two went and fell for each other years ago, I can one hundred percent say no I don't hate you just... please don't hurt him."

I reach across the counter and grab her hand from the mug and hold it in mine. "I promise you, I have no intentions of hurting him or the other two but... this whole thing is so new and fresh and..."

"You guys are all still working out the kinks?"

I pin her with a look. "Pun intended, huh?"

She laughs and nods. "Oh yeah, pun definitely intended." Nova and I keep our conversation light and I invite her to tag along with me for the day just as Archer and Ez stroll into the kitchen. Both of them have showered given their wet hair, fuck. They look edible. "Eww, Vivian!" I snap my head toward Nova and frown at the disgusted look on her face. Before I can ask what she meant, Archer comes and places a kiss to the top of my head. Ez is next, but unlike Archer, he grabs my chin and forces me to turn to him. In the next second his lips are on mine. I don't even get to process the kiss before he's pulling back and winking at me, then steals my coffee and rounds the counter to sit next to Nova, who looks like she ate a lemon. "I get why Vox is pissed."

"What, why?" I ask as I'm tugged backward by the hood of my jumper. I land between Archer's legs who is sitting on the opposite counter, drinking his coffee.

"Seeing my brother do... that is disgusting." Ez shoots her a smile while I laugh. Archer is shaking with silent laughter behind me but doesn't comment.

"And seeing Vox go all Bam Bam on your ass isn't fucking gross?" Ez fires back.

Nova scrunches her face. "That's different, Vox is..."

"Vox," Ez, Archer and me all say at the same time. The four of us all laugh and it feels good to laugh after so long, but it dies off when my phone rings. Everyone goes silent as I answer the call.

"Hey Tate, I was coming by this morning—"

"Kim never turned up for her shift last night. I went by her place first thing this morning and her neighbor said she hasn't seen her since the night before last."

"Calm down, I'm sure she is fine. Let me get showered and I'll head over, then we can search for her and ask the other girls," I say.

"Yeah, okay, call me when you're here and I'll let you in through the back."

"Okay." I end the call just as Vox walks in, trailed by Hayze. Unlike my brother and the others who have showered, Hayze is still in his sweats and has the cutest bed hair. He yawns and stretches his arms above his head, knocking into my brother as he brushes past. Hayze comes straight for me and the sexy smile on his face makes me want to spend the day wrapped up in him. When he comes to a stop before me I wait for him to kiss me.

"Do it you cocksucker and I'll break your fucking jaw," Vox promises. Hayze rolls his eyes playfully and leans in, ignoring Vox's growl as he places a kiss on my cheek.

"I bet you wish Nova didn't come find him now, huh?" he whispers in my ear and without consent boisterous laughter breaks free of me. Hayze the dirty troublemaker shifts and pours himself a cup of coffee while everyone else looks at me expectantly. I begin to fidget under the pressure of my brother's gaze but Archer saves me when he leans down and wraps his arms around me.

"Don't fucking push me, Malik!" Vox growls.

I lean back against Archer and smile up at him. Hayze stands beside me looking directly at my brother in a challenge. "Get the fuck over it, Hatchett. You stamped your claim on your girl and this is us doing the same. Don't like it? Get a fucking hotel because Vivian is over biting her pillow." My jaw unhinges at Archer's taunts. Vox's face morphs into pure murder. Before my brother can take a single step, Nova is in front of him with her hands on his chest. Instantly Vox's attention is captured by the raven haired beauty before him.

"Come help me get ready. I'm spending the day with your sister," Nova says.

Vox's brows draw in. "No fucking way, you are not—"

"Tell me I can't go again and see what happens, dickbag," Nova snaps.

Vox snakes his arm around her waist and pulls her against him. "You really want to fight with me right now, witch?"

"Baby, I'm your only friend in this house, so don't piss me off or you'll really be on your own. Now, come help me change and if you're a good boy I might let two horns play with me tonight."

"Jesus fucking Christ, Nova!" Ezekiel bellows. Nova laughs as she drags my brother out of the room. I shoot Vox a smile before he disappears up the stairs. As gross as hearing that was, it makes me happy to know my brother finally found his soulmate. "I'm going to murder your brother," Ez vows.

"Pot meet kettle, brother," Hayze says, earning a snort from Archer and a glare from Ezekiel. Before they can all begin bickering, I excuse myself to shower and change. I barely make it a single step before the three of them are at my back. "What are you doing?" I ask.

"Helping you change," Archer says it like I'm an idiot for not knowing that.

"I can change on my own," I reply.

"But I haven't showered either and I volunteer to help you wash," Hayze adds with a wicked smile.

"I suppose I can be persuaded to dry you off," Ez tacks on.

I shake my head. "The three of you are going to be so bad for my calendar and appointments," I mutter as I climb the stairs.

"Never said we were angels but you already knew that," Hayze calls out.

"She'd rather be fucked by the devils anyway," Archer replies. As crass as their words are, I couldn't agree with them more, no one wants sweet sex. We all want to be fucked like we mean nothing then treated like a queen outside of the bedroom.

NOVA HASN'T BEEN able to stop gawking and pointing since we entered Lividica. Tate keeps shooting her looks of concern so I wave her off, we both need this time out from the guys. The four of them were broody bastards and were not above using sex to try and manipulate us into staying with them.

They all looked murderous when Nova reminded them that she wasn't formally banished, only they were so they had to remain indoors. Vox promised to destroy my town tonight as his alter ego if I didn't find a way to remove the banishment.

"I've tried calling her next of kin but they said they haven't spoken to her either."

I mull over Tate's words, I hate to admit it but I don't know much about these girls. Yes I was the one who hired them but aside from that I have had limited interactions with them.

"Let me call a friend. I'll see if he can help us locate her." I can see this situation is really worrying Tate. "I'm sure she's okay," I say trying to ease some of her worries but she just shakes her head.

"No. I can feel it, something is wrong." Bitterness coats her words and guilt begins to gnaw at me.

"These girls are lucky to have someone like you, Tate. I recall a few of them from the interviews. Some of them have no one who cares about them and knowing they have you would mean a lot."

"Yeah, a fat lot of good having me has done Kim," she snaps before stalking behind the bar to do lord knows what. I pull my phone from my pocket and move into the hallway, leaving Nova to continue inspecting the place. I dial David and wait for him to answer.

"Lordess."

"David, I need you to get our guys to search for one of the girls from Lividica."

"Send me her name and a picture if you have it and I'll send it to our guys in the police and get them to start searching."

"Thank you. I'll send it over now."

"What time should I expect you here?"

I check my watch, then answer, "I'll be there in about thirty minutes."

"See you then," he says, then I end the call and send him through the information he requested. David and a few other men are good guys and will be taken care of when everything is revealed. I pocket my phone and meet Tate at the bar. Her eyes are filled with terror for her friend and it pains me to see that look in her eyes.

"I have my guys looking for Kim now, they won't stop until she is found. In the meantime, I will have more security stationed around the hotel. I won't allow any of them inside here." She nods firmly.

"Thank you. I would like it if after the girls shift they could walk them to their cars as well."

"Of course. I'll send you Ray's number, he's the head of the security team that will be here tonight. Let him know what you want and he will answer directly to you." Her eyes widen in surprise.

"Oh, okay."

I smile reassuringly at her. "You have done more than I could have hoped for, Tate. I owe the success of Lividica to you and I promise you, I will never forget what you have done for me." Tate just stares at me with a doe eyed look for a second before it quickly vanishes and is replaced with her normal don't fuck with me one.

I practically have to drag Nova out of there. The entire ride back to our old high school is filled with her asking me hundreds of questions about Lividica. She was stunned to learn the sex club was my father and Edmund's idea. I just adapted their idea and made it my own, like opening a women's side of the hotel where they can live out their fantasies with men who will treat them right. The eight guys we have working that side are booked out fully for the next six months straight. We have no choice but to hire at least four more guys, which is what Tate will be focusing on.

As we pull into the school parking lot, I see Nova grow tense at the sight of our old high school. This place doesn't hold any good memories for her. I feel bad that they weren't able to graduate with the rest of us but I don't regret banishing my brother and the others. I just wish The Brotherhood would hurry up and locate Thomas. I know the dirty fuck is long gone by now but just knowing he is still breathing keeps me looking over my shoulder.

"I never thought I would be back here," Nova says as we come to a stop on the opposite side of the main building, where the expansion is happening. As I step out of the car I'm happy to see there has been a lot more progress than when I was last here. They have clearly pulled their fingers out of their ass since we brought in the other company to help speed the process up.

"Vivian." I turn to the side to see David waving me over, it still sounds weird hearing him call me by my name. I know he doesn't like using my name but when in public he has no choice. Nova walks beside me. David takes one look at her and his eyes widen at the sight of her. We come to a stop beside a table that has papers, blueprints, and numerous other items scattered on it.

"Mrs. Tempest." I smile at Brodie, he's the owner of the construction company I hired to build Lividica.

"How are you?" I ask him.

He smiles. "Busy at work and at home since my wife just gave birth to our third daughter."

"Oh my gosh, congratulations, Brodie." He smiles proudly and it warms my heart to see a man so proud that he is the father to another beautiful little girl. "Brodie, this my friend Nova Quinlin."

"Pleasure to meet you," he says.

"Likewise," Nova counters.

"Vivian, I was just speaking with Brodie and Ford in regard to the extra space you requested for dorm rooms to be added," David says in a tired tone.

"And?" I push.

"In order to accommodate the dormitories we would need to purchase the surrounding land. I did some digging and found that the land was recently purchased by the company *Ezy A.*" I roll my lips over my teeth, I can feel Nova's gaze searing into the side of my head and I know it is only a matter of time before the name sinks in.

3…

2…

1…

"Oh my God!" she shrieks, garnering everyone's attention. I whirl around and widen my eyes, telling her without words to keep her mouth shut. She listens to my silent demand but it doesn't stop the laughter from bursting out of her.

"Please, ignore my friend." Both guys nod but still shoot Nova a puzzled look as she keels over gasping for breath.

"So, in order for this to happen, we would need to acquire the land from that company," Brodie adds.

"No problem, leave it with me and I will have an answer for you by the end of the week." He looks surprised by my answer and a little stunned.

"I'll walk you back to your car," David says. I shake Brodie's hand and wish him well before following after David. "Why do I feel like I am being kept in the dark here, Lordess?" David asks quietly when we are away from prying ears.

"Because you are and trust me, it's better this way." He doesn't pry or try to push, he just nods and hands me a file filled with papers that need my signature and then runs me through the remainder of my tasks for the day. "Okay, I'll get onto all of that as soon as I get home. Is there an update on the *situation?*" I ask.

David sighs, reaches into his pocket and pulls out another pink envelope. I stare at it with wide eyes not wanting to touch the fucking thing. "This was delivered to the town hall this morning."

I flick my gaze back to him in shock. "What?"

"I believe whoever is sending these and doing *that*, knows more than we are giving them credit for."

"David, if they know about me, where I live and The Brotherhood that means it is one of the brothers!"

His lips thin and a murderous look flickers in his eyes. "I know." I've never heard David sound blood thirsty. "I will weed out the bastard myself, Lordess. Until that time, I would like it if you would remain at your home. I will have Tatum come to you. I have doubled your guards as well."

"Do you think they are going to come after me?"

The uncertainty in his eyes answers my question before he does. "Yes. I believe you are the grand prize and until The Night Of Saints we need to make sure you are protected and kept safe."

"You think whoever it is, *is* waiting for them to make their move and take me out."

"Yes, I believe that is the goal. Whoever is doing this wants you dethroned and out of The Brotherhood."

CHAPTER TWENTY-THREE

Archer

Vivian has been holed up in her office since she got home hours ago. Nova is in there with her and I am man enough to admit I'm getting pissed off. I get she has shit to do but come on, we've been without her all day and she can't even spare us an hour to just... hang out for a minute?

"You look like a wounded puppy," Hayze teases.

"Fuck off, jumper cables," I bite back.

"Why the fuck do you call him that?" Vox asks me.

"Because he's always starting shit." Ezekiel is the first to burst out laughing followed by Vox, even I can't help but smile. Hayze sits across from me on the other sofa, glaring.

"Oh fuck, that name suits the big bitch," Vox wheezes out, the sound of their laughter has both the girls poking their heads out of the office that is just off the living room where we are all hanging out, trying to act like the four of us aren't sitting here pouting because our girls aren't paying us any attention.

When the fuck did I become a whiney bitch?

Since I fucking allowed myself to fall head over heels in love with my best friend's little sister, that's when!

"Why are you two laugh-crying?" Vivian asks, looking slightly worried at the sight of her brother and Ez rocking back and forth clutching their stomachs.

"Archer's being a bitch, Vivi baby." I roll my eyes and turn to my idiotic best friend.

"Grow the fuck up," I snap.

"Fuck you, I don't have to grow up until I finish school, my mom said so." At the mention of school, Vivian drops her gaze and shoots Hayze a scathing look but he ignores it as he stands and crosses the room. Vox and Ezekiel finally manage to get themselves under control as Hayze comes to a halt in front of the girls. "Vi?"

"Yeah?" she answers quietly.

"Baby, we aren't worried about school, it was just a joke." Hayze tries to sooth her worries but we can all see she isn't picking up what he's putting down.

"You should be though. You and Archer have practice and you both are missing it because you're here with me," she claps back.

"Technically, so is Vox," Nova adds which just has Vivian looking more guilty. She has nothing to feel guilty about though, we all want to be here and there will be other schools. Granted they won't be the best in the country with the best football program but who cares.

"All of you should go back to CHU, I can handle this on my own," Vivian says, then disappears back inside her office. Nova comes to join us and she looks just as shaken by Vivian's dismissal of us as well.

"She doesn't mean that," Nova says just as Vox grabs her arm and tugs her onto his lap. He wraps his arms around her and buries his face in the crook of her neck. I envy the fucker, I wish Vivi would give into us the way Nova does to him, but I can feel she is still hiding something and it's something big. Why she won't trust us and let us help, I have no fucking idea.

"Yeah, she does," Ez says dejectedly. "She wants us gone so she doesn't have to worry. She has something big planned and from what I can garner, it's all got something to do with The Night Of The Saints."

"No. She's been upset since that guy gave her a letter." Nova yelps when Vox leaps to his feet and nearly knocks her on her ass. The three of us follow after him. Vivian is on the phone when we enter the office. She looks up from her laptop and the sight of the four of us standing here fuming with rage that she didn't tell us about the fucking note has her sighing.

"Vance, I have to go but I'll send you what I have and just keep working on the appeal." She ends the call and drops the phone to her desk. "What?" she snaps.

"You got a fucking letter and didn't think to tell us?" Vox shouts. Vivian doesn't flinch, she just turns... cold and her eyes take on a hard edge.

"Why the fuck would I tell you about the letter when it was addressed to me? You may be my brother, Vox, and in charge of your masked crew but I am the one calling the fucking shots around here. You will know what I choose to share when I choose to share it. Now, if that is all, get the fuck out of my office, I have work to do." She dismisses us by grabbing her phone and making another call. "Phil, it's Vivian. I just spoke to Vance..." Her conversation becomes white noise as my blood begins to pump and it's all I can hear ringing in my ears. My anger winds up winning and I lean across the desk, snatch the phone from her hand and end the call.

She stares up in outrage, but before she can utter a single

word I speak. "He's your brother but I'm not, and I have every fucking right to know what is in that fucking letter."

If looks could kill I would be six feet deep in the fucking ground from the way she is glaring at me.

"What the fuck makes you think you have a right to know?" she snarls.

"Maybe the fact that I've made myself at home between your legs?" I snap back.

"You're fucking dead, motherfucker!" Vox roars, but I pay him no mind knowing that Ezekiel and Hayze will hold him back while I deal with our girl.

"Is that what this is?" Vivian asks as she climbs to her feet and rests her hands flat on her desk, leaning forward slightly. "You think because we fucked you have a right to know all my secrets?"

"Yeah, I do," I answer.

A dark chuckle escapes her. "Tsk, tsk, Archy baby. We fucked years ago and you blocked me out but now that the shoes on the other foot you don't like it?" Her words hit their mark, shame and guilt war inside me for what I did to her.

"No, I fucking hate it. I hate that you will let us fuck you and penetrate your body but not your heart or mind." Vox continues spewing threats behind me, I can hear Hayze and Ez grunting as they fight to keep him back. "Let us in, Vivian!" I scream. She doesn't flinch or even bat an eye at my plea.

"No. I banished the four of you a year ago to fulfill a promise I made to myself and I will see it through. Your presence here won't change anything, my plan is in motion and all you are doing is trying to derail it and I won't allow that to happen." She tears her gaze from me to look at Nova, the look in her eyes is vicious.

"Vivian, I am begging you please don't!" Vox screams but his twin is too lost to her own anger to stop. Nova moves in front of Vox facing Vivian, my girl may look like a monster but Nova looks like a fucking she-devil.

"Whatever is about to come out of your mouth better be worth it, Vivi. You want to hurt him, I can see it in your eyes, and you know the only way to truly break your brother is through me. Make it worth it, Vi, because you know I won't go down without a fight," Nova declares. Vox is pleading with his eyes for Vivian not to tell her the truth. Ez and Hayze hold Vox back by his arms, refusing to allow him to move an inch.

"Send them back to CHU and I'll tell you where your mother is," she announces. The guys release Vox and move to my side.

"We aren't leaving you!" Hayze growls.

"Yes, you are. The four of you need to leave. You do better from a distance in the shadows where no one knows who you are. Go, don't come back. I banished you once and called the hounds off from tracking you but I won't do it again." Hayze and I begin to argue with her but Ezekiel just stands there locked into a stare off with her, I don't know what's happening but I know there is more to this than her wanting us gone. I can see it, beneath the malice and anger that she is terrified.

"A favor asked is a debt owed, baby. Ask it and we shall deliver," Ezekiel says in a vicious whisper that has her inhaling a shuddering breath. She shoots a quick look to Vox before turning back to Ez asking him without words. "He will leave and do what is asked of him by the lordess."

"Like fuck I will, I'm not going anywhere," Vox argues but Ezekiel ignores him.

"Where they rest for eternal life is where a favor is asked. The stone with the head is where you will be led. Be certain of the favor you ask, no second is offered. The debt will be collected when the favor is complete. A favor asked is a debt owed." Why the fuck is Ezekiel reciting the passage of the Filthy Few?

"Leave," she demands. Ez nods and turns to Vox.

"You once trusted me with your life and never once questioned my loyalty to you. I am asking you to do that once more, trust me now, brother, one more time." Vox stares at Ez for a long moment before looking at us.

"The four of us?" Vox asks Ez while still keeping his stare on us.

"We're going old school, time to leave, brothers," Ez announces. I take one last chance to look at Vivian, she meets my stare with a pleading look in her eyes to not fight and leave.

"This isn't over, not by a long shot," I force out through clenched teeth.

"Like Nova says, 4221, baby," Hayze adds. Vivian closes her eyes briefly. When she opens them again they are devoid of all emotion.

"That ring on your finger means something, remember that," Ez says, then stalks out of the room, leaving Vox standing there staring at Vivian, trying to read her thoughts.

"I've always dreaded this day. I never wanted you to not need me and yet here we are." Hearing the pain in Vox's voice has me feeling sorry for the big fucker. "Alter ego it is," he says, then storms out of the room, leaving me and Hayze alone with her and Nova.

"Look after him for me." I frown at Nova.

"What?"

"I'm staying, Archer. Make sure he doesn't do something dumb and keep him safe for me." I can hear the anguish in Nova's tone, this girl is fucking strong. She has survived the death of her best friend and here she stands days after losing her mother, vowing to help Vivian in her time of grief when she should be mourning the loss of her own mom. I close the space between us and wrap her in a hug.

"You keep my girl alive and I'll keep your boy from killing every fucker to get to you."

"Deal," she whispers as I release her and face Vivian once more. She refuses to meet my stare and that shit burns.

"Hayze, we're out," I say as I walk my ass out of that office and away from the one person who has the power to bring me to my knees. Vivian is many things but she isn't a malicious bitch. That person in that office is a fraud. I don't know what's going on but I trust Ezekiel enough to know he wouldn't have walked away without a fight if he didn't have a plan.

CHAPTER TWENTY-FOUR

Vivian

Nova and I are laying in my bed staring up at the ceiling, neither of us can sleep. She hasn't tried to push me for answers or asked why I sent the guys away. She's trusting me blindly and the pressure of that alone is crippling. I reach over to turn on the bedside lamp, open the top drawer and retrieve the letter I received today and hand it to her. She stares at it for a while then shakes her head.

"Read it to me." I take a deep breath and do as she says.

"My my my, how courageous you have become, who knew all it would take was three cocks in your wretched holes. There is another who knows how to take cocks, you will meet her real soon. Have no fear, my dear, you will be mine before too long and this time there will be no surprises. Try not to fuck in the shower next time, I prefer to watch you pleasuring yourself while you scream each of their names. Next time you take a cock it will be my name you scream."

"Vivian..." Nova stares at me in horror, I deflate and nod unable to voice my thoughts. "What the fuck is it with this town and sending fucking letters?" she mutters more to herself.

"Whoever has been sending me these notes has been growing more confident. David and I believe it's one of the members of the Saints."

"How do they know about you and the guys?"

I shrug. "I think they have been watching me. This fucker knows my schedule. He's left notes at Lividica, my house, the town hall and even posted one to David."

"What else have they sent? What did he mean about you meeting a girl soon?" I shake my head.

"I don't know what he meant about the girl but he has... he has killed before." Nova slowly pushes up into a sitting position and faces me, searching my eyes. I know she is going to find the truth without me having to say a word.

"Lordess!" At the sound of one of my guards yelling my name I jump out of the bed, tear my door open and race to the landing peering over the edge to see Nial standing there with a pink box fitted with a beautiful pink bow on top. He doesn't need to say anything else, I know what's inside of that box.

"Vivian, what's going on?" Nova asks as she follows me down the stairs. My suspicions have been proven correct, the very same day I kick my brother and the guys out a box arrives. He is watching me right now and that knowledge has my skin crawling and the hairs on the back of my neck raising.

"I've called David, he's on his way," Nial says. I nod and motion for him to place the box on the dining room table.

"Why are you calling David over a gift box?" Nova asks. I'm left with no choice but to tell her the truth. She's going to witness what is in that box herself in a few minutes so it's better I tell her now before she pieces it together herself.

"He sent me the head of the district attorney in a box

exactly like this." Her eyes widen and her mouth pops open. "He... Nova, I'm the one who told Vox that your mother was dead."

She recoils as if I struck her. "What the fuck, Vivian?" she snaps. I try to reach for her but she steps back out of reach. "Why the fuck would you tell him that?"

"Because the DA wasn't the only *gift* I received from him while I was away at CHU," I say quietly. Nova looks from me to the box, I wait for her to grasp my meaning. Nial and I both remain silent, giving her the time and space she needs to come to terms with this. When she finally looks at me her eyes are brimming with unshed tears and my heart aches for my friend.

"You told Vox she was dead because he sent you my mom's... he sent you... you have my mom's... Oh God," she cries out as she falls to her knees distraught. I rush forward and drop to my own before her and wrap my arms around my best friend. She screams and wails while I hold her tight, never once letting her go even when she tries to break free. "Mom!" Fuck, the raw pain in that one word is felt deep into my soul. My own mother is back in Washington helping Olivia search for Kelly, neither of them wanted to believe their friend was dead and still live in denial about it even though Vox has told them what happened.

"I swear, Nova, whoever is doing this will fucking pay," I promise. My friend clings to me and soaks my shirt with her tears. I fight against the urge to call my brother. I know she won't admit it but right now, she only wants him so I do the next best thing and pull my phone out and Facetime Vox. He answers on the third ring and the instant he hears Nova sobbing his face morphs into one of unfiltered rage.

"Who the fuck hurt her?" he snarls.

"I did," I admit, for the first time in my life my brother

stares at me like I am a stranger. Never once has he ever faced me with a look filled with malice until now.

"What the fuck did you do?" he asks in a clipped tone.

"I received another package tonight, I had no choice but to tell her about the... previous one I received." His features sober instantly and worry enters his blue eyes.

"Is she okay?" I turn the camera so he can see her crumpled against me. "Witch?" His tone is filled with anguish. Nova slowly lifts her head and the instant she sees my brother a sob tears out of her.

"Vox," she calls for him.

"I'm coming, witch. Hang on, baby." She instantly shakes her head and swipes her face to wipe her tears.

"No. I'll be okay... just, don't hang up, okay?" she begs.

"Never, baby. I'll stay on the phone as long as you need me too," he promises. Before I hand the phone to her, I help her to her feet then turn the camera to me. Vox still looks pissed off and I know it's because I forced them to leave.

"I'm sending her upstairs, she doesn't need to see this," I tell him. "Stay on the phone with her." I don't wait for him to respond, I hand Nova the phone. "I'm so sorry, I'll be up there as soon as I can." She nods and takes the phone from my hand and heads upstairs looking like she has the weight of the world on her shoulders.

"Is my brother with you?" I hear her ask just as David walks through the front door. The moment he and I lock eyes a silent conversation happens. We both know for certain now that whoever is doing this is one of the members which means we can't trust anyone aside from ourselves. I can't even trust the lawyers I have tasked with getting Alexander out of jail now.

"Have you opened it?"

"No, we waited for you." David seems to only notice Nial then and nods a hello before stepping up to the edge of the table. My breath lodges in my throat as he undoes the bow. When it falls away, a small pink note can be seen. David looks at me but doesn't make a move to grab the note. I square my shoulders and keep my head held high as I tentatively reach out and grasp the small postcard size note.

I wonder if she would take those vermin as well as you?
I guess we won't get the chance to find out.
Nowhere you go, nowhere you hide will be safe from me.
I know your every move.

I read the note aloud, refusing to feel ashamed about the first part of the note, I regret nothing. As David reaches out to remove the lid, I stop him with my words.

"I already know who it is," I say quietly.

The shock is evident in his gaze. "Who?"

"The girl I called you about, Kim. I think it's her in that box." Sadness coats my words, she was so young. Twenty-six with her entire life ahead of her but because she crossed paths with me, she was murdered and I will have to live with the guilt of that for the rest of my life. I close my eyes not wanting to see her face when David lifts the lid. His resounding sigh is all the answer I need.

It's Kim.

"Give her a burial and make sure there is evidence for her parents to find, they don't need to be wondering what happened to her." When Nial leaves the room with the box, I finally take a full breath and flop into one of the dining chairs and bury my face in my hands. "Lordess, we need to do something. That's the third one and I am afraid to say it—"

"There will be more unless I start giving into their demands. I know," I answer. David shoots me a solemn look.

"I think we need to start looking through all the members and making a stockpile of the ones who want you out the most."

"Yeah, let's do it now." I'm already so far behind on all my college classes with no hope of catching up, so I may as well devote my time to something useful, I mean there isn't any point in studying or submitting essays if I'm dead.

David makes a call to have all the records of current and past members delivered to my house. While we wait, I decide to go and check on Nova. My bedroom door is slightly ajar and I pause when I hear her talking.

"I love you, witch." Hearing those three words come from my brother fills me with a sense of pride. Him being away from this place for the past year has been the best thing for his relationship with Nova.

"I love you too," she says through her tears. I decide to leave Nova to talk to Vox and head back downstairs to wait for all the files to be delivered. David is sitting on the sofa with his phone in his hand, at the sound of me approaching he looks up and forces a smile.

"It's going to be a long night so I've ordered some Thai and coffees."

"Have I told you that you are worth your weight in gold, David?" This time when he smiles it's real. I drop into the single seater opposite him.

"I just received a message from Tate." At the mention of her I sit up straighter.

"What happened?"

"Another girl didn't turn up for her shift."

"Fuck!" I run a hand through my hair. "What's the chance that she's sick?" I ask hopefully.

"Slim to none considering she was just hired last week to

take over the Explorer room." Every room in Lividica is dedicated to a certain type of pleasure. The Explorer room is for men to try new things that they wouldn't dare do with their wives. We even have a room dedicated to golden showers.

"Let me guess, no one has seen her since she left the interview?" David nods. "So, we know for sure the fucker is in town and no doubt watching us right now." Again he nods. "I want you to get a team out here first thing in the morning to do a sweep of the house."

"You think this place is bugged?"

I shrug. "I'm not putting anything past this sick fuck, I want us to take extra caution. We need to change our routine every day."

"I've already changed my meeting times for the week and I have my assistant Cornelia handling most of my in person checks."

I reel back in surprise. "You have an assistant?"

He laughs and I find myself smiling at the sound of it. Given the horrendous situation we are in we need to find a reason to smile. "Yes." David goes on to explain that he actually has his own accounting firm which floors me given the coupe I have staged. When the boxes are delivered, I almost want to cry at the sheer amount of them. Each folder has pages of information on every member and their families. I comb through the stacks that are in alphabetical order trying to find Ezekiel, Hayze, Archer and Vox's files but the files aren't in there. "I already had their files removed from the archives after you banished them."

I whirl around and face David in surprise. "Why would you do that?"

"Because I knew they would become targets by the other members. If they weren't targets, they would be the ones they would go after to try to overthrow you and I couldn't allow that." His declaration renders me speechless. What David has done breaks a lot of rules that could have him banished or killed by the other members, if they were to discover what he did.

"I... Why would you help me? You didn't even know me well then."

"Call me insane but I had a feeling that you would be the leader the Saints have needed for years. I have been a member of the Saints for longer than you have been alive and believe me when I tell you that some of these men shouldn't be free to walk the streets."

"David—"

"Can I be curt with you?"

His tone has me feeling nervous. "Yeah."

"Are you planning on turning me over to the feds when you take down the Saints?" My mouth pops open and I gape at my right-hand man in equal parts shock and terror. "I may be old, Vivian, but I am not stupid. I have had the past twelve months to get to know you. Believe it or not, in that time I would like to think that I have gotten to know you very well."

"David... I-I... we can't discuss this," I mutter. I don't know if my house is bugged and I can't risk it. What he has just suggested could get us both killed. My status in The Brotherhood won't save me if I am caught betraying the cause.

"Very well," is all he says and returns to his task while I am left standing here reeling. Maybe I'm not as smart as I thought. If David has suspicions, then that means the rest of the Saints do as well and that makes holding off until The Night Of The Saints ten times fucking harder.

CHAPTER TWENTY-FIVE

Vivian

One week later...

Have you ever felt so in over your head that you can't even think straight? Yeah, that's me right now. My days are filled with digging through records and trying to catch up on my college classes while making sure Nova eats, showers and gets out of bed. I won't lie, I am fucking nervous and worried about her which is why I have forced her to accompany me tonight to Lividica's first ever masquerade night. All the girls and staff are decked out in masks, they range from sexy, scary, morbid and downright fear inducing but tonight we have merged the women's den with the men's and allowed everyone to interact as one.

Tonight is a huge test to see if we can combine the two areas every once in a while. We have had numerous requests from both sides to merge so that couples can finally have the threesome or foursome they have been dreaming about with their significant other. I have to admit though, I think the only reason I agreed to this is because I miss my own guys and how the time we spent as a foursome has ruined me for any other.

Security has been doubled here since the death of two of my girls—two days after Kim's head was delivered to my house another one arrived. Since then, I have moved all my girls, Tate, Andre and the men into the hotel. Security escorts them to their rooms after shift. Tate still has no idea about what is really going on and I can tell she knows I am hiding something which has put a slight divide between us.

"Vivian?" I turn away from the crowd of people and face David. My brows raise in surprise, he's dressed in an all-white suit with a red tie. The mask he wears is one of those fancy rich people ones on a stick.

"You look good."

He waves off my compliment. "I have brought in extra men tonight to help with security in case something happens."

"Thank you."

"I've also instructed them to escort each guest out and to make sure they leave here safely. The last thing we need is for something to happen tonight and dampen the success of this venture." I smile at that. I promised myself if tonight went off without a hitch I would consider David's proposal to open another hotel like this near CHU where he is trying to push me to go. I also have plans to open a few more of these hotels in New York, Miami, Chicago and Texas.

"I found three other prospective birds." David's face morphs into one of pure malice.

"Send me their names, I'll have the men take a closer look." I nod and pull out my new phone and text him the names. When David had my house swept we found eleven bugs, none of them recorded audio thankfully but the fact the sick bastard has been watching me had my skin crawling. David and Nova tried to urge me to leave and stay at the hotel but I refused. I won't let this bastard scare me out of my own home. I tossed my old phone, not trusting it to not be bugged and had David collect me a new one. I've had my home fitted with motion sensors, spotlights, state of the art security system, new locks and I'm currently having a fence built around the property. These are all measures I should have taken earlier but I thought I was smarter than my stalking bird.

"We have three weeks, David."

He nods stiffly. "I know, do you think your *friends* could help out with tracking this person down?" I shake my head. After the bugs were found, I confessed all my secrets to David fully prepared for him to out me and have my head on the chopping block, but he floored me when he offered to help me achieve my goal.

"My friends won't lift a finger until I turn over the documents. I can't do that until we finish the last part." David sighs tiredly and nods. "You know what they are like, I have to give something to get something."

"On that note, I have things to attend to but there is someone at the bar requesting an audience with you." I frown and turn to peer around the crowd to see who it is but I can't see. "Go, I'll keep an eye on Nova." I smile thanks to David and tell Nova I'll be back in a minute. She doesn't say anything. I feel like a horrible person for making her come here, I thought getting her out of the house would help but I think all I have done is made it worse. She barely speaks and I don't know what else to do.

"We'll leave as soon as I get back," I promise. She flicks her eyes to me and it fucking shreds me inside to see blame in her green eyes. I can't fault her for being angry at me and blaming me for the death of her mother. When I refused to allow her to see her mother's head, she went nuts and started throwing anything she could get her hands on, I just narrowly missed getting a saucepan to the head.

I leave her with David and head to the bar. When I finally break through the crowd I don't see anyone waiting for me. I lean over the bar and call out to Tate who is run off her feet with the amount of people here tonight. She has three other's helping her but Tate is the type of woman who likes to do everything herself and refuses to ask for help. She shoots me an annoyed look so I raise my hands and wait for her to finish serving her customer.

"What do you need?" Her tone is curt but I get the sense her sour mood isn't because of me or work so I ask.

"Are you okay?"

She sighs and rubs her face in frustration before looking back at me. "Sorry. I just... I was supposed to meet my dad tonight—"

"Oh, shit, leave and I'll get someone to cover you—"

"No, Vivian. I mean I was supposed to *meet* him tonight for the first time and he never showed up."

"Oh," I breathe out unsure of what else to say.

"Yeah." Her tone is sarcastic. "For months he has been messaging me like fifty times a day and now when the time finally comes for him to meet in person, he blows me off." Anger thrums inside me for my friend.

"He is an asshole for blowing you off. I'm sorry, I had no idea that happened."

"I told him not to be late and when my break was. He thinks I work in the hotel as a manager and he said he was proud of me for making something of myself, so I don't get it." She looks a lot younger than her age right now, I would even go as far to say she looks younger than me.

"I can relate to feeling disappointed in a father you didn't know. Mine died before I could really remember much about him, but the things I have found out about aren't good. I hope he has a really good reason for blowing you off tonight because you are fucking amazing, and if he can't see that he has a kickass daughter, then that's his loss, babe. Not yours." My words seem to erase some of the sadness in her eyes.

"Thanks, Vivian."

"Don't mention it..." I let my sentence trail off when Tate's eyes widen and her mouth parts on a silent intake, gone is the upset look on her face as she stares at someone over my shoulder with a strange look.

"Hello, Vivian." I splutter and whirl around at the sound of his voice. Without thought I squeal and throw my arms around his neck and hug him. It takes him a second before he awkwardly returns my embrace. He's the one to break the connection and take a step back, he looks flustered as he rubs the back of his neck. I take in the sight of him and marvel at how different he looks. He wears a black suit and even has a tie on, but rather than looking sophisticated, he looks like a punk kid ready to crash prom. His hair is tied in a bun which just showcases the tattoos on his neck, he looks effortlessly handsome.

"I can't believe you're here!" I breathe out, then cock my head to the side. "Wait, how are you *here*?" I dart my gaze around the room, worried someone was going to come rushing in to take him away.

"I was released two days ago. Turns out your lawyers are better than mine or I guess the fact that the judge is buddies with Vance didn't hurt either." I can't help but just stare at him. God, how fucking crazy is this moment?

"Come, have a drink with me." I offer and motion for him to join me at one of the tables. He follows my lead but when I raise my hand to signal Tate, he shakes his head.

"I don't drink."

"Really?" I blurt.

"Yes. If my sources are correct, you are underage as well." I snort and roll my eyes which has him smirking.

"I own the place, that kind of gives me certain perks."

"Hmmm," is all he says, then looks around the room. His lips pinch to the side and I find myself worrying that he doesn't like Lividica. "You designed this place?"

"The interior yes, but not the architectural side obviously."

He nods. "You did a hell of a job."

His praise has me preening. "Thank you. Now, I have to ask, how did you get in here?"

A sinister look enters his eyes. "Halo is fucking deadly at what he does and getting my hands on a membership to this place wasn't out of his reach."

"The membership is a hundred thousand dollars!" I whisper shout, I don't know why I am so outraged he paid the fee when I was the very person who set the damn price.

Alex shrugs. "Money isn't an issue, Vivian. Never has been and I don't foresee it ever being one." The intense way he looks at me has me squirming. "You seem... different."

"I haven't exactly been partying and living the life of a normal nineteen year old," I admit bitterly.

"Why not?"

I shoot him a deadpan look. "You know who I am and what I do. Given the title I carry, I don't exactly get much free time. I mean for fuck's sake, I'm taking college classes online rather than attending in person."

"You can change all of that."

"How?"

"All you have to do is walk away." I open my mouth to argue but he pushes on. "It's that simple. Turn your back on your past and grasp your future with both hands and you would be surprised at what you could achieve without your past holding you back."

"Are we still talking about me?" I counter.

"I guess not."

"Why are you in town?"

"Omen and Vatican have been tracking you." I jerk in surprise. "I tasked them both with keeping an eye on you but it appears the fucker was smart enough not to show tonight."

"Huh?"

"Vatican thought for sure that he would show tonight."

A cold shiver runs down my spine. "Why would he think that?"

"It's a masquerade ball, you could be anyone tonight and no one would know if you were telling the truth or not."

"He's grown bolder."

"How so?"

I look around to make sure no one is paying us any mind. The only person who seems to be watching is Tate but her attention is focused on Alex, not me. "He took out two of my girls and sent me *gifts*."

He nods his head. "I know you have upped your security and altered things at your home, those measures are putting a wrench in his plans."

"Why do you sound so angry about that?"

His eyes darken and I suddenly feel severely outmatched. "Because it means he will grow desperate. Desperate men do stupid things and that doesn't bode well for you." Whatever he sees on my face has him reaching across the table to place his hand on top of mine to ease some of my worries, but then a tingle of awareness shoots through me and the hairs on the back of my neck stand up.

They're here.

CHAPTER TWENTY-SIX

Hayze

We've hidden in the shadows most of the night, going unnoticed and passing ourselves off as security. Vox nearly blew our cover when he saw Nova walk in with Vivian, both of them beautiful but Vivian took my breath away in her dress. It's a weird design of a dress, only a strap to keep it up over her right shoulder and the rest flows around her like toga, but there are sections missing that show off her flawless skin. She captivated the attention of all the men in her vicinity but it wasn't just the dress that had me stumped, it was the masks they both wear.

They are wooden like our own, but they are painted red and only cover half their faces, Nova's has two horns to match Vox's, which pleased the big fucker but Vivian's has an antler type horn on the side leaving the other side bare. She wanted to represent the three of us.

"Who the fuck is that?" Ezekiel snarls from beside me. I

follow his line of sight to see some cocksucker standing behind our girl at the bar but what has me seeing red is when she spins around and beams at the sight of the cunt and launches herself at him. Without meaning to, I take a step forward only for Archer to yank me back.

"Calm down, we have a job to do tonight," Arch warns.

"I have to get Nova out of here," Vox says in a tone that borders on painful. I look toward Nova and feel for her because she looks so distraught. She's in a room full of people yet she looks so alone aside from David who stands guard beside her. When Nova suddenly snaps her head up and begins to frantically scan the room, I know it's because of that tether she has with Vox, she knows he's here. "Come to me, witch," Vox murmurs and then suddenly she stares directly at us. I know for a fact she can't see us in the dark corner but she sure as hell feels Vox. When she moves toward us, David grabs her but she yanks free of his hold and says something to him, then she is gliding across the room.

Even with his mask firmly in place I can tell Vox is smiling. He loves knowing that he can't hide from her, those two can track each other without much effort and it's a skill I fucking envy. She walks blindly into the darkness and within a split second of being shrouded in the dark Vox has arms around her and she clings to him like a lifeline.

"Hello, my little witch." Nova says nothing as she pulls back and pushes his mask up and removes her own, only to claim his mouth. The three of us turn away from them and focus back on Vivian. I was fully prepared to stand back and watch this play out until he placed his hand on top of hers. I lose all restraint and storm toward them, watching as she sits up straight and tenses. Oh, so you can feel us like Nova feels Vox.

I feel Arch and Ez at my back but neither of them stop me, it's too late anyway, she knows we are here and the fucker she is sitting with has spotted us. I come to a stop behind Vi. Ez and Arch flank me on either side. Without having to be told Vivian slowly withdraws her hand from under his and returns it to her lap. The three of us continue to glare at the fucker who sits there without a single flicker of any emotion, he looks like a fucking creep.

"Alex, meet my..." I wait for her to call us her *friends* and shred my fucking dignity to pieces. "Guys." I want to beat my fucking fists against my chest hearing her call us *hers*. "Ez, Arch, Hayze, meet my friend, Alexander Denver." Ice fills my veins.

The Butcher!

Before any of us can say anything he speaks. "Remember we are in public and much like yourselves I have an identity to protect, so how about we have this conversation at a more private location?" His tone is calm and even.

"The penthouse is free, we'll go there," Vivian says, pushes back from the table and stands, but still she won't face us. Alex stands and motions for her to lead the way. She does but we all crowd her and form a barricade. As we pass David, I nod in his direction but he looks to Vi who just nods and smiles, letting him know everything is fine. When we make it into the main lobby and she heads for the elevators, but I grab her wrist and force her to stop. She slowly turns to face us and the moment she does all the breath rushes out of me at the look on her face.

"Vivian, I must go. I'll be in contact soon, enjoy your night." Vi turns to watch Alexander storm out of the hotel, a blacked out jeep is waiting for him. None of us utter a word until the jeep disappears from view. It's as if time has come to a standstill as we all wait for her to finally look at us. It feels like hours have passed before finally she gathers the strength she needs to turn to us. I know the fact we are wearing our masks doesn't seem to make it easier for her to look at each of us.

"You shouldn't be here," she mutters.

"I got your code and I spoke the terms of the Filthy Few to be certain. We know why you did it and said what you did but this time it's you that needs to listen to us," Ez says in a tone that leaves no room for argument.

"Now, are you going to lead us up to this penthouse or am I throwing you over my shoulder again?" I ask, earning a sexy smirk from her.

"In this dress? I think not," she rebukes.

"I'm more interested in what's beneath the dress." Archer's comment has her cheeks staining red. She leads us toward the elevators and presses the buzzer. The tension between the four of us is tangible, you can taste it on the tip of your tongue. There's so much sexual need pulsing in the air and I know I'm not the only one who can feel it. Vivian proves me right when she starts swaying side to side and clicks the buzzer twice more. The doors finally open and she growls which has me smiling at her frustration.

The three of us stand where we are forcing her to make the first move. She spins around and faces us with an annoyed scowl on her beautiful face. "Get the hell in here before your presence blows my plan out of the fucking water." The three of us all push and shove to get inside first but fucking Archer winds up winning and getting to her first. Just as the doors begin to shut an arm darts in between the metal, forcing them apart. I'm ready to tell whoever it is to fuck and catch the next one until I see the two horned fucker.

"Can't you take the stairs?" Archer grits out as Vox forces his way inside with Nova tucked under his arm. I stare in confusion when Vivian shifts as far away from Nova as she can and refuses to look at her. Did something happen in the week that we were gone?

"Fuck off, dickhead, we all need to talk," Vox clips out just as the doors shut. The sexual tension that was pulsating between us a minute ago evaporates and is replaced by awkwardness. I for one would rather be edging than sitting here not knowing what to fucking say.

When the doors open we all file out into the grand entry of the penthouse, clearly no expense was spared when designing this place. All the furniture is pristine and new, the view of the city from here is photograph worthy. My perusal of the place is cut short when Vivian clears her throat and sits down on one of the three seaters. Fuck the tension, I dart forward and shove Archer out of my way as I drop down beside Vivian. Ezekiel claims the vacant spot on her other side, forcing Archer to the opposite sofa with Vox and Nova. I take my mask off and place it on my lap, then shoot him a smirk and wag my brows.

"Fuck you," Archer snaps.

"Stop fucking acting like children or I'll make you all sit on the floor," Vox snaps as he removes his own mask.

"Think the fuck again, asshole, my ass is staying planted right beside my wife." Vox turns and glowers at Ezekiel.

"Stop calling her that!" I roll my eyes. Vox has to get the fuck over it, Archer and I did.

"You called him your brother-in-law back at CHU, a bit contradicting don't ya think?" Archer taunts as he twirls his mask between his hands.

"You motherfuckers—"

Vivi cuts her brother off before he can continue his pathetic attempt at threatening us. "Everyone stop!" The command in her voice has my cock leaping to attention. "I don't have time to sit here and argue over who hurt who's feelings—"

"No, but you can ignore mine!" Nova claps back. Vox frowns and looks between his girl and Vivian, clearly just noticing the tension between the two girls.

Vivian releases a long sigh. "I'm sorry—"

"Don't fucking lie to me Vivian!" Nova screams and tears her mask off, tossing it on the floor. "If you were sorry, you would have done as I fucking asked instead we are all here because of you!"

"*Me?*" Vivian snarls in an icy tone, she snatches the mask off her face and tosses it across the room. "I never fucking asked for any of this! I'm not going to sit here and pass the blame and take shots at you because I know you are hurting."

"Fuck you!" Nova screams.

"Witch!" Vox roars, Nova swivels to face him. She is furious and that is obvious but Vox won't back down. "You asked me not to hurt your brother and I didn't, now I am *telling* you to leave my sister alone."

Nova scoffs. "You're going to take her side?"

He shakes his head. "I'll never pick a side when it concerns the two of you but I also won't stand by and watch you lash out at her because you're angry."

"She won't let me see my mom!" At Nova's admission Vox swings his gaze to Vivian.

"I refused to let her see Kelly and ever since she has blocked me out. I get why she is blaming me but I wouldn't want that to be her final memory of her mom," Vivian utters in a tone laden with guilt. I wrap my arm around her shoulders and pull her into my side. She relaxes into me instantly, I place a kiss on the top of her head at the same time Ez interlocks his fingers with hers.

"Witch—"

"Don't, Vox," Nova chokes out as her tears begin to fall. "She was all I had."

"No, she wasn't. I'm still here Nova and I'm not going anywhere," Ezekiel vows.

Nova leans her head against Vox's chest and clutches his

shirt in her hands. "I'll never leave you, witch, I'll always be here," Vox promises.

"I can't lose anyone else." My heart beats wildly in my chest for Nova, she has suffered more loss in a short amount of time than most do in their lifetime and I feel for her.

"Then you all need to leave." All of us turn to Vivian. "I can't guarantee any of your safety if you remain in Hollow Hills. I think it's best if you all return to CHU."

"Fuck that. We left you once already and now that we are back we aren't going anywhere." Archer's tone is filled with venom and Vivian is smart enough to know if she tries to fight him on this that he won't back down. It's about time she realizes she isn't in this on her own. I know she thinks she is a badass and can hold her own but she doesn't need to anymore. Vivian has always tried to act like she didn't need anyone to care for her and most of the time she doesn't, but when she has those moments where she doubts herself, she needs someone to remind her how fucking incredible she is.

"We didn't just come here to watch your back, little mouse," Ez admits.

"What do you mean?" Vivi pushes.

Ez looks at me and I give him a subtle nod. "When we left you, we have been spending every minute trying to figure out what the fuck is going on and how the fuck they bugged your house."

"I was hoping you would understand what I was trying to do. When you spoke the rules of the Filthy Few, I knew then that you understood and would fill the others in," she admits.

Ez smiles comfortingly. "The fact you had cameras in the house means whoever the fuck is behind this knows who we are and that we are the Filthy Few." The undercurrent of worry in his tone is valid, rumors had spread amongst The Brotherhood that there were some psychos going around wearing masks and targeting some of the brothers. Those whispers quickly disappeared when we stopped hunting them and focused our attention on Nova. If whoever is behind these attacks is a brother, then they would be able to connect the dots and know the rumors weren't bullshit.

We could be blackmailed.

"I promise you, nothing will happen to the four of you, I made sure of that." Her tone is filled with confidence and I start feeling like she has done something to make what she says true.

"What did you do, Vivi?" Archer asks as he leans forward and stares directly at her.

"What I had to. Now, can you explain why you wanted to be here instead of staying away and don't say it was because you're worried about your identity," she throws back at him.

"The truth is, I couldn't give a fuck about anyone knowing who I am beneath the mask. I couldn't stay away from her any longer and it wasn't like those three fought me on the idea of coming back," Vox says as he runs his fingers through Nova's hair. Vivian melts into me further and I suddenly forget about the shit we are up against. This girl is a distraction and I can't find it within myself to be mad about it, because she is the best fucking distraction.

"What about your schooling and football practice?" Vi asks.

"Turns out the bitch ass friend you made at CHU has some pull," Ezekiel grits out. When I called Coach to tell him we had some personal shit to take care of and that we lost a close family friend he was all for us taking as much time as we needed. I thought it was fucking weird but then he told me that Dawson vouched for us and said we didn't need the extra training like some of the others.

"Dawson is sweet." Vi defends the fucker and all she gets in response is growls and scoffs from the three of us.

"Why was The Butcher here, Vivian?" Vox asks.

"Honestly? I don't know, after I met with him at the prison—"

"You did fucking what?" Archer shouts.

"You best be fucking joking!" Ez snaps.

"Are you out of your fucking mind?" Vox snarls.

"Baby, are you on drugs?" I ask.

Vivian leans forward and shoots us all a scathing look that has me worrying she may take her anger out on my dick. No, that's a lie I would really love to angry fuck her, she looks like she would be wild in bed when she is pissed off.

"All of you can kiss my ass! I know what I am doing and it's about time all of you stopped doubting me because it's fucking annoying. Yes, I met with Alexander. At first I thought he was the one behind the letters and the... *packages* but after meeting with him, I learned he isn't the monster he was painted out to be. He's actually helping me!"

"How does he know who we are?" I ask.

"Apparently my hacking skills aren't as good as his guys and he was able to figure everything out on his own." The fact she sounds more put out about her lack of hacking skills rather than a murderer knowing our identity is grating on my nerves.

"You can't trust him!" Vox snaps.

"Why? He's proven to me he can be trusted and if he is offering his help to take down Nexus and Thomas, I will gladly accept any help he is offering because we haven't been able to locate either of them. I am done looking over my shoulder wondering if Thomas is going to come and kill me because I took his spot..." Vivian clamps her mouth closed but her eyes widen to the size of dinner plates as she stares at Nova. What's more unsettling is Nova looks at Vivi with the same look, she slowly pushes away from Vox and stares directly at Vivian.

"You thinking what I am?" Nova breathes out.

"Yeah. Yeah, I think I am."

"Me and you?" Nova says.

"Just us, it has to be," Vivian replies. The guys and I all share a confused fucking look, these two were pissed at each other a minute ago and now they are staring at each other with varying looks of triumph and speaking in code.

"How?" Nova pushes.

"We wait," Vi replies.

"What the fuck are you two talking about?" Arch asks, looking as dumbfounded as I feel.

"Nothing," Nova answers quickly then turns to Vox. "Spend the night with me?" Vox looks skeptical, he knows his girl is trying to distract him with sex and a part of him wants to argue but the red blooded man inside him is beginning to win the fight.

"Take the downstairs bedroom," Vi offers.

"And where are you sleeping?" Vox barks at my girl with an accusing look in his eyes.

Nova answers before any of us can. "With your best friends." Vox nearly chokes on his fucking tongue. "You can stay here and cock block your sister or you can come to bed with me and take my mind off everything. Choose wisely, dick bag," Nova growls.

Vox weighs his options for all of two seconds before standing and dragging Nova out of the room. The instant they disappear Vivian stands, rights her dress and smiles deviously at the three of us.

"The master has a California king bed..." Point five of a second is all it takes for the three of us to be on our feet and chasing her upstairs, the sound of her laughter has smiles gracing all of our faces.

CHAPTER TWENTY-SEVEN

Vivian

Standing here and looking at the three of them sprawled out over the bed fast asleep is a sight I will forever cherish. Last night the three of them took their time worshiping me and showing me without words that they mean what they say about wanting this thing between the four of us to work. Being with them last night showed me that there is something worth fighting for aside from the freedom of those I love and getting the revenge I crave against The Brotherhood for all they have taken from me and so many others. A year ago this sight before me was never a possibility.

I had always thought I would be a one man type of woman but I was wrong. Hayze was right, if Archer didn't break my heart I would never have seen him or Ezekiel as anything other than my brother's friends but as the months went by, I started seeing him and Ez as... more. I just had no idea they both felt the same way about me and fuck, I'm so glad they do because after having the three of them I could never choose.

I want them all.

I just hope they can understand why I have to do this. I want this finished and I want to be by their sides every single day. I want the college experience with my guys. I want to sit in the grandstands and cheer them on while they play football. I want late nights on the couch eating pizza and watching reruns of their games while they pick apart what they need to improve on. I want it all with them. I want my happy ending and I am going to do everything in my power to get it because I am in love with the three of them and there is no point denying it anymore.

I'm in love with my brother's best friends.

And, they love me too.

I give myself one more minute to just drink in the sight of them. It takes every ounce of my willpower to walk away. I feel a lump forming in my throat but I refuse to give into the emotion, one day they will see I did all of this for us. I head for the elevator and it doesn't surprise me to see Nova leaning against the wall waiting for me. Neither of us say anything as we wait for the doors to open, our moods somber as we step inside the metal box and allow it to carry us away from the men we love.

"Vox will come for me, you know that, right?" she says as we walk out of the hotel and climb into the back of the car I had David send for us.

"And my guys will come for me which is why we aren't going to my house. Give me your phone." She hands it over without complaint. I roll down my window and toss hers and mine out the window.

"You couldn't have just turned them off?" she snaps in annoyance.

"They can still track them while they are off. You know you don't have to do this, right?"

"Yes, I do. If we are right then I want to look that bastard in the eyes as he falls while we rise. He doesn't get to walk away this time."

"Agreed."

"Are you sure it's even him?"

I sigh and lull my head back against the headrest. "Honestly, no, but he is the only person who knows all our weak spots and he is the only one to gain something out of the death of your mother." Ever since the notion struck me last night I haven't been able to stop thinking about it. Kelly is the only person out of the four he has killed that meant something to me which means, he did that to provoke Nova. He wants us both and he wants the guys out of the way.

"Vivian?" I lull my head to the side and face my friend, she looks utterly spent and I cringe to think of why she looks like she hasn't slept.

"Yeah?"

"Why do you have a company named after my brother, Hayze and Archer?" I've been waiting for her to bring this up. I tell the driver to turn up the music in the hopes he won't be able to hear our conversation over the music.

"When I took over the Saints, I had a plan from the start."

"Which is?"

"Nikoa told me once that the only way to take down the Saints was from the inside. He said you could cut the head off the snake but another one would just grow back and the cycle would continue. When I was informing for him and gathering intel I decided to take a deeper look."

"What did you find?" she hedges.

"Money."

Her brows furrow. "Huh?"

"The guys thought that they could torture members for intel on Thomas and hey, they did get what they wanted but it wasn't enough. The Saints have enough money to own the town. Hell, they pretty much do already."

"I'm not following, Vivian."

"The only way to truly kill the snake and make sure it never comes back is to take away every resource it has and that's what I've been doing. *Ezy A* is a company I opened before I took over the Saints." Her eyes widen in surprise. "That company has been funneling the income from the Saints and investing in other companies, legitimate companies. Like Lividica, they think with how busy it has been since the grand opening that they are making huge amounts of money. They have even put money into The Brotherhood's accounts to go toward building more hotels just like Lividica."

"Won't they know you are ripping them off?"

"No. When the accountants check the bank balance they will see millions of dollars on the screen but it's all smoke and mirrors. The account they are actually viewing is mine."

Nova gasps and reels back. "Vivian, they will kill you for this!"

"They can't touch me. The money I have taken from them is already invested and I am already building other hotels. They think they are about to triple their incomes but none of it is under The Brotherhood, it's all under Ezy A. The more money they keep sinking into The Brotherhood means they are emptying their accounts. Once they are all broke they won't have a leg to stand on. All I have to do is push a button and the remainder of the money's gone. They have all been restless because none of them have seen a return on their revenue but with the promise Lividica has shown and the lies I tell about the new builds costing more money than we thought, they keep buying my lie. David owns an accounting firm and is helping me. He is the only person that knows what I have planned. You can't tell Vox," I beg.

"I won't say anything but, Vi, they would have helped you."

I shake my head. "No, the money isn't the only thing," I admit somberly. She studies me for a long moment then suddenly she gasps and reaches out to place her hand on my arm.

"What the fuck have you done?"

"What I had to do, Nova. They are all killers, they ruined families and destroyed countless lives. We live in a corrupt world and I am the leader of the worst of them. They need to pay for what they have done, so I struck a deal."

She stares at me with a horrified look on her face. "They won't let you go, they will need a fall guy."

I nod, pain washes over me but I push it aside. "I know but I made sure the four of them, our families, yourself and a few members of the Saints that I know and trust will be granted freedom and they will never come after any of you. It's okay, Nova, I know it's a cruel existence and it feels like there is no point hoping at all, but I am at peace with my decision." Tears fill her eyes. I smile sadly, unable to appease her worries more than I have. She reaches for me and wraps her arms around me in a tight hold. I hold her close and breathe in her scent, utterly grateful that she came into my life.

WHEN WE ARRIVE at the new house, Nova has her face plastered against the window. Unlike my house, this place is gated, patrolled, bullet proof windows, alarm system, cameras, motion sensors and the rest. This place will make it hard for the fucker to get to me now. Nerves begin to thrum through me when I climb out of the car and see David standing in the entrance. Nova follows after me.

"Welcome to your new home, Lordess," David says as he steps aside and lets us pass by. The house isn't anything overly huge, four bedrooms, two baths, two entertainment areas, heated pool and gym.

"Thank you, David," I say as we follow after him into the living area. I freeze when I see the box on the little table. David nods confirming that it is what I think it is. Nova stands beside me looking out of place. I grab the box off the table and turn to face her with it in my arms. She looks at it then looks at me and shakes her head.

"I don't want whatever is in there."

I scoff and roll my eyes. "This isn't *that!*" I chastise her. She just purses her lips. "This is me trying to make my wrong right. I couldn't let you see Kelly that way, Nova." Instantly her gaze drops to the box. "David and I had her... cremated." I tense in preparation for her to rage and yell at me for making that decision for her. I warred with it for a long time given the fact Vox cremated Waylen without her consent as well.

She shakily reaches out and lifts the lid to expose the cream colored urn, she reaches in and pulls it out. I had it engraved for her as well, on the front of the urn it reads.

Kelly Quinlin,
Beloved mother of Nunu.
A mother holds their child's hand for a while,
But, she holds their hearts forever.
Rest peacefully, until we meet again.
4221...

TEARS ROLL DOWN her cheeks unchecked as she rubs her thumbs over the inscription. I look to David for confirmation that I did the right thing. He smiles and nods, then silently excuses himself to give us some time alone.

"I never needed friends because I had her," she chokes out. "When Waylen came into my life I thought everything was perfect. I had my mom and my best friend and that was all I needed. When she met Thomas I was happy for her because it was the first time she had ever done something for herself. She revolved her whole life around me and she never complained once."

"Your mom was an amazing woman," I say quietly.

"She was the fucking best." Her pain is evident in her wavering tone. "She didn't deserve this, nor did Waylen, but loving me got them both killed." She flicks her green eyes to me and the shattered look in them robs me of air.

"No, it didn't. Loving you is what gave them the courage to want more from their lives. Kelly was so proud of you, Nova, you could see it in the way she would look at you. I didn't know Waylen well but from the brief encounter I had with him I could tell he would have jumped off a cliff for you. Being able to love you is a gift."

"Yeah, the gift of death," she bites out.

"No. Those bastards took them from you and we are going to take everything from them, I swear it."

"I want them both to pay!"

"And they will, we will make sure of it."

"For Mom and Waylen."

"For Kelly and Waylen," I promise. I don't include my father or Ezekiel's because they knew what they were doing when they became the lord. They could have chosen to take the Saints down a different path but they didn't. Like all the others, they wanted power and money and that is ultimately what led them to their deaths.

LATER THAT EVENING David and I are sitting around the dining table working on our laptops when his phone rings. He answers it and when I see his face contort I know something is wrong. He ends the call and faces me.

"What is it?" I ask.

"Your brother and his friends have managed to get inside Lividica and Tate wants to break their necks."

I cringe. "What have they done?"

"Nothing to any of the girls but the club is about to open and they can't be found by the brothers." I sigh and hold my hand out for his phone. He gives it to me and I redial Tate's number.

"I'm gonna break the blonde one's nose!" Tate says when she answers.

"That blonde one happens to be my husband, Tatum," I growl.

"Vivian?"

"It's me. Now tell me exactly what they are doing?"

"You mean aside from being assholes?" she bites out.

"Yes!" I snap.

"They are being loud douchebags and demanding you and Nova get your asses here or they are going to—wait."

"Wait, what?" When she doesn't reply, worry begins to stir inside me, I can hear shouting in the background. "Tate!" I shout.

"What?"

"What's going on?"

"Ah, that Aztec God from last night is here talking to them." I scrunch my face.

"Aztec what?"

"The guy you were talking to last night." She sounds annoyed which just pisses me off.

"Alexander?"

"I don't know, you hugged him and then went and talked to him," She answers.

"Shit. Hang tight, I'll sort it out." I end the call with her and open my iCloud on my laptop. I find Alexander's number and quickly dial it. It takes him five rings before he finally answers.

"How did you get this number?" he growls.

"Alex, it's Vivian."

"You seem to have disappeared and left a mess behind," he says.

"Is that my girl?" I hear Hayze say.

"I know. They can't find me Alex—"

He cuts me off before I can finish. "Because you want *him* to find you and you know he won't do that if you have round the clock bodyguards with you."

I gasp. "How did you know that?"

"Because it's something I've done before. I'll handle this situation but I want something in return."

Of course he wants something from me!

"Name it."

"Nexus Valerian is mine, no one is to touch him."

I don't hesitate. "Deal." Alex ends the call without another word.

CHAPTER TWENTY-EIGHT

Ezekiel

"Was that my wife?" Alexander just stares at me which fuels my anger to new heights. Waking up this morning I expected to get lost inside her again but she was gone. The instant we heard Vox calling for Nova we knew that it had something to do with them speaking in code last night. The only way we thought to find them was causing a scene here. Vivian loves this place and we knew someone would call her or David.

"You four can stay here or come with me." Alexander says, then turns and stalks out without another word. We all exchange a look before deciding to follow the fucker. He seems to be the only one who can contact Vi which means all we need to do is get his phone, then we can track her. They were smart to ditch their phones, it was the first thing we tried to track this morning. When we get outside, Alexander climbs into the passenger seat of a car then takes off.

"Motherfucker!" Vox snarls.

"Get in." The four of us swing our gazes to the left to see a guy who looks like he lives on the streets standing next to a blacked out Escalade. "You have three fucking seconds then I'm driving off without you idiots." I grit my teeth and storm toward him with the others following after me. Archer rides shotgun while the rest of us climb into the back. I look in the back to make sure no one is hiding in there and that this isn't an ambush. As soon as fuck face climbs behind the wheel, Archer pulls his gun out and rests it on his lap.

"Who the fuck are you?" Arch hisses.

The guy doesn't look at him as he continues to drive, the fact he seems so at ease with four strangers who are clearly strapped in his car doesn't settle my nerves.

"My name is Omen and believe me when I tell you that you will need more than that little Glock to scare me, asshole, so you may as well put it away."

"Why the fuck would I listen to you?" Arch fires back.

The guys just shrugs. "You need a gun to intimidate, all I need is my name. You and I come from two different worlds. You were born with privilege, I fought for it and mark my words, *Archer*, if I wanted you dead I wouldn't need a gun to do it." He knows who we are and that puts us a step behind them. Whoever the fuck this guy is he is clearly with Alexander which means...

"You're a part of the Denver Kings." It's not a question, just a statement. We've all heard stories about them but much like their leader no one has ever seen pictures of them. They have no gang insignia or tattoos to tell you who they are, they operate like they are ghosts.

"No idea what you're talking about, we're a long way from Denver." His blatant brush off just pisses me off. The remainder of the drive is spent in silence. Archer still won't stow his gun. When we finally slow down, I peer out the window to see we are out of Hollow Hills now and somewhere up in the mountains. A barn comes into view and instantly I go on high alert, if this fucker thinks we will go down without a fight he has another fucking thing coming.

"I'll blow your brains out before you can blink if you try anything," Archer promises when Omen puts the car in park. The fucker just smiles and tugs the hood of his hoodie up before climbing out of the car and walking toward the barn. The car Alexander left in is parked next to ours. I look around and can't spot anyone, the only light out here is coming from inside the barn.

"What's our move?" Hayze asks.

"We go in, keep our guard up and get answers, then we leave," Vox says.

"This was a bad fucking idea," Archer echoes my thoughts. The four of us climb out. We all draw our guns and move in a line toward the barn. It feels weird not having our masks on as whenever we have gone into situations like this we have always worn them. Tonight, we're not hiding. Vox is the first to slip through the door followed by Archer and Hayze. I take one last look behind us to make sure no one can sneak up on us before following them inside.

"Jesus Christ," Hayze spits out. I stand here stunned and chilled to the fucking bone at the sight before me. When we followed Omen inside I thought we would walk into an ambush or something but not... this!

Four guys are strung up from chains, they are bloody, beaten, naked and look like they are at the stage where they would welcome death. I look around the room. Alexander stands just behind the four strung up with his gaze laser focused on us. Omen stands off to the side with his hood up, concealing his face. Three other guys stand off to the side dressed similar to Omen, each of them have their faces concealed and it's then I begin to understand. We wear masks to hide our identity but these guys use their hoods and clothes that blend in so no one would bat an eye at someone who dresses like they are homeless.

It's the perfect fucking cover.

"Want to tell me why we are here?" Vox's tone is filled with venom. If he notices it Alexander doesn't show it.

"You're here because it seems the four of you little fucks can't stay out of things that don't concern you." My hackles raise and I shoot Alexander a cold look that he ignores. This fucker is like a statue, he gives nothing away and makes it seem like nothing bothers him.

"Anything to do with Vivian concerns us and if you can't get that through your fucking head, I'm down to beat it into you." The pure fucking violence in Hayze's tone shocks the three of us. Vox even stares at him like he has no idea who the fuck is standing beside him.

Alexander smirks but it's condescending. When one of the guys who is strung up makes a sound, the smirk vanishes and the look of a cold blooded killer overtakes him. It's fucking chilling to witness the immediate change in him. Last night the killer before me was nowhere to be seen when he was hanging out with my girl. I'll be honest, he doesn't look like I thought he would. I had expected him to be deranged and Hannibal Lector type of crazy but not... this. He seems so fucking normal.

Alex glides toward the guy and the instant he feels The Butcher at his back, the guy begins to sob. Alex flicks his gaze to us as he leans in and whispers something in the guy's ear that has him clamping his mouth closed and silencing himself. Tears still cascade down his cheeks and the terrified look in his eyes will plague me. When we were the one dishing out the torture and slicing people it was different, felt different even but being on the other side of it just feels wrong.

"Do you know who they are?" Alex asks as he walks around the men, each of them flinch away from him as he walks by. Two of them seem familiar to me but the two older guys on the end, I can't recall ever seeing them before in my life.

"Should we?" Archer volleys back. I snap my head to the side when I see Omen move in closer. I tighten my hold on my gun at my side ready to strike if I have to.

"Considering they were in your—no, *her* brotherhood, I had hoped you might recognize them but it seems I was wrong." I keep the shock from splaying across my face, these four guys are members of the Haven Saints. "Don't feel bad for them, you should have heard what they had planned for sweet Vivian," he coos as he draws a blade from his side and runs the point along their backs as he circles them again. All of them arch forward and try to escape his torture but its futile, they can't break those fucking chains and even if they could, they would never make it out of here.

"Stop playing fucking games and tell me why the fuck we are here," I snarl. I'm fucking fed up with his bullshit. I don't give a shit if he is known for butchering people, I'll sink a bullet in his skull before he gets to me. Alexander stops moving and faces us, the bloodlust I see in his eyes is fucking off the charts. He loves what he does to his victims and the fact Vivian helped him get out of prison doesn't sit right with me.

"You're here because he has been watching you and won't make a move until the four of you are out of the way."

"Who the fuck has been watching us?" Vox snaps.

"Thomas Valerian." At the mention of him we all inhale sharply. "Before you idiots start denying it, I've been tracking him and he's in town but it turns out your girl's Saints are still loyal to their former lord."

"That fucking cunt, he was the one who killed Kelly," Vox grits out, then starts pacing in front of us.

"Wait, what fucking move is he about to make?" Archer asks with a hint of worry in his tone.

Before Alexander can answer I do. "He's taken us off the board so Thomas can get to Vivian, this cocksucker wants it to happen in the hopes Thomas will draw Nexus out of hiding." A dark smirk crosses Alex's face.

"You motherfucker!" Hayze roars.

"I'll kill you before I let that cunt touch my girl," Archer vows.

"You make a move against him and you will be the next four we string up," Omen promises.

"Fuck this, let's go." Hayze turns to leave but the exit is suddenly blocked by three other guys holding machine guns.

"I can't let you leave." I whirl around and glare at the son of a bitch.

"She fucking trusted you!" I roar.

A flicker of remorse crosses Alexander's face before he masks it. "I'm following her wishes." I stare at him open-mouthed and rendered speechless.

"My sister wants this?" Vox sounds panicked.

Alex nods. "She trusts me enough to know I won't kill you four. She is the one who struck this deal with me the night I left you all. She named her terms, I agreed to them all in exchange for Nexus-fucking-Valerian."

"You just offered my fucking sister up to the fucking devil! If anything happens to her or my girl, I'll fucking slaughter you all," Vox booms.

"He'll kill her," Archer yells.

"Get the fuck out of my way, now!" Hayze bellows, he has a gun pointed at one of the guys carrying a machine gun behind us. I look around the barn and there is only one exit point which is now blocked by those fucks with guns. Panic is taking root inside me and the need to get to Vivian is starting to cloud my rational thought. If he gets her... I shut down that train of thought, refusing to even think about what he might do to my girl.

I close my eyes and take some deep breaths ignoring the arguing going on around me. She did all of this to save us, she knows Thomas is coming for her and instead of running she went right to him to end this so we would all be truly free. We all knew that Thomas wouldn't stop when she banished him but we were so caught up in being broken hearted that we never went on the offensive, now we are stuck playing defense.

"You lost your sister to a Valerian." At my statement everyone grows silent, I lift my head to meet Alexander's murderous scowl.

"Tread fucking carefully," he warns as the three that have been hiding in shadows suddenly move until they flank their blood crazy boss.

"Are you really going to force us to watch as a Valerian takes someone we love from us? She is Vox's sister, his fucking twin. Will you really make him suffer the same fate as you?" I'm begging him right now and I couldn't give two fucks about it. If I have to get on my fucking knees and beg harder I will if it means I can get to my girl and save her.

Alexander just stands there staring at me with a blank look. "Please." I swing my gaze to Vox, shocked he even knows that fucking word. "She's my little sister. I know I have done a shitty job at trying to keep her safe and away from all of this but I can't lose her. My girl is with her. I love them both and I won't fucking survive losing either of them."

"She made her terms clear," he claps back.

"Fuck her terms," Archer shouts. "I'm telling you to change those terms and let us go. If I have to shoot my way out of here, then so be it, but I'm not going down without fighting."

"Have any of you bothered to stop and actually fucking think!" one of the hooded cunts behind him says.

"Vatican," Alex warns.

"No. They want to play fucking hero then let them but this will never work for you miserable pieces of shit unless you let it play out the way she wants. Unlike you fuckers, she hasn't let her emotions cloud her judgment. She isn't going into this blind, nor is her friend. They both know what is about to happen and are ready, you go to them now and you will ruin everything Vivian has set into motion."

"What exactly has she set into motion?" Hayze fires back.

"Nice try," one of the other fucking hooded cunts says. I'm starting to understand why people hated our masks so much, its fucking frustrating arguing with someone you can't fucking see.

"Stay a while and observe, you might even learn something," Alexander says. "He won't make a move tonight, she switched locations and he needs time to find her."

"If you're tracking him, why not just take the cunt out?" Vox asks.

"We're tracking his associates, not him. That gutless bastard is smarter than we gave him credit for. But, we know he is working with high ranking members in The Brotherhood and they are the ones who are helping him, aren't they?" Omen snarls as he yanks one of the guys who is chained up by his hair.

"Yes!" the guy cries out.

"Believe it or not, Vox," Alex says, drawing Vox's attention to him and this time I do see a flicker of emotion on the fuckers face. "I wouldn't want anyone to suffer the loss of a sibling. Your sister will make it out of this *alive*, I will make sure of that. You have my word." Call me fucking deluded but I actually believe the fucker and judging by the look on Vox's face, he does as well.

CHAPTER TWENTY-NINE

Vivian

For two days Nova and I have stayed holed up in this house. The constant fear and the worry that at any moment Thomas will show his face has us on edge. I heard from Alex that he has the guys. Nova was pissed when I told her about that but she understands and knows it's safer for them to be away from this. We have no idea who Thomas is working with or how many men he has on his side. Alex has been helping us and keeping track of the men we know are aiding Thomas. So far the man himself hasn't shown his face or even sent a letter, but I can feel it in my gut that he knows exactly where I am.

Why is he waiting?

"Answer me this." I turn away from the window to look at Nova who is laying on the couch.

"What?"

"The deal you made, why not just give them all up now?"

"Because they want Thomas. He is the ring leader and without him the deals I made mean nothing." Those fuckers are slimy and the fact they can't just be happy that I handed them myself and a secret society filled with smugglers, dirty feds, crooked politicians, embezzlers and murderers is fucking bullshit. They want the head of the snake. I get that, I do, but they also think they are going to get the assets that the Saints have amassed over the years. They are in for a rude surprise when it comes time for that. David knows when to funnel the final amounts out of the accounts and there is no way they will be able to trace it back to us or anyone else. They will be searching for that pot of gold for years without finding it.

"Fucking greedy assholes." I hum my agreement. "What if it isn't Thomas doing this?" That question has been plaguing me daily.

"I can't explain it but I just have this feeling in my gut that it's him. I know it sounds crazy—"

"No, it doesn't." She sits up and faces me with a somber look. "I get it because I feel the same way. I just hate not being a hundred percent sure, ya know?" I nod. I know she has compartmentalized her grief and is clinging onto her anger and the need for vengeance against Thomas, but she will have to deal with that grief sooner rather than later or it will eat her alive.

"Tatum has arrived," David calls out. He's been here every day with us and honestly I am grateful as fuck for him. He doesn't need to be here but he doesn't want to leave us alone too much.

"Bring her in," I call out. I haven't been able to catch up with Tate since the guys barged into Lividica and put my two doormen in the hospital. They will fucking pay for that. Tate saunters into the room looking angry at the world. Nova looks to me in question, I shrug my shoulders unsure why Tate is in such a terrible mood. Tate flops down onto the sofa unceremoniously and sighs. "Make yourself at home," I tease.

She rolls her head to the side and looks at me, fuck she looks so much younger in the light of day. What lotion does she use? "I never should have tried to find my family. If I'm here because you are going to fire me then please don't, I swear I won't get distracted at work again. I need this job, Vivian—"

"Stop!" She clamps her mouth closed and slouches into her seat further. "No one is getting fired." Her face perks up.

"Really?"

I nod. "Yeah."

"Then why am I here?" she asks, looking around the room as if she is only just realizing we aren't at my house. "Did you move?"

"Temporarily," I answer curtly.

"Okay..." She drags out that one word.

"You're here because I wanted an update on the club." She seems to switch from moody to excited at the mention of the club. She gives me a rundown on everything that's happened and tells me that my masquerade night was a success. She has hired five more guys and three more girls to fill the demand.

"If you haven't thought about expanding, you really should because we can't keep up with the demand of both sides of Lividica," she says in a dreamy tone.

"I do have plans to expand but not in Hollow Hills. I have other locations but they will take time. Until then we need to make this club work because everything is riding on the success of Lividica."

"Well, you will need to find a manager for each of those places," she says but I can see the cogs in her mind working overtime as she tries to think of the perfect person for the jobs, but I put an end to her pondering.

"Tatum, I asked you here because I will have to go away for

a while soon and you are the only person who knows how to run both sides of the business."

She frowns up at me. "I don't understand, Vivian."

Nova smiles and leans forward. "What my friend is trying to say is that she has already found a person to take over running *all* the clubs." Tatum's face falls, she drops her gaze to her lap.

"I hope they do a good job," she mutters.

"Oh, I know they will because if they don't, I won't be as welcoming when they march into my house and flop all over my sofa." Her brows pinch for a second until my words sink in.

"Wait!" she screams, then jumps to her feet. "Are you offering me the job?"

I smile and nod. "Yes I am." Tate screams and starts jumping on the spot clapping her hands like a kid in a candy store.

"Oh my God! This is fucking amazing, holy shit I can't wait to tell my brother."

"You have a brother?" I ask.

She nods excitedly. "Yes! He was abandoned by my dad as well. He found me and has been staying at my place." She waves her hand. "Never mind about him, he's a hermit and never leaves the house." I pinch my lips to the side. It worries me that since Tate has started working for me and gets paid *really* well, then suddenly she has a long lost father and brother reaching out to her. I fucking hope they don't use her for her money.

"The new job comes with a pay raise." Tate's eyes widen.

"Vivian, you pay me a shit load of money now, I don't need more—"

I raise my hand, halting her spiel. "You will be flying between locations and holidays will be few and far between so take the money, it's the least I can do."

"How much money are we talking?" she asks shyly.

"An extra 100k a year." Her jaw unhinges and her eyes widen to the point it looks like they might actually pop out of their sockets. Nova laughs at Tate's reaction and I can't help but smile as well. The reason she is getting paid so much is because she is a hard worker and I know how deeply she cares for all the girls and guys. She keeps them safe and keeps tabs on all of them. I've even heard from David that she paid Montana's rent because she was short a couple of weeks back. She doesn't do that stuff for recognition she does it because she is a good fucking person and I couldn't think of a better person to run my empire while I'm away. I know she will be fine and if she needs help, David will be there to guide her.

Sadness thrums inside me. I know I'm doing the right thing but it doesn't make it any easier knowing that life will go on without me. I just have to keep reminding myself who I am doing this for. At the start it was for my family's freedom but now, I just want to make sure my guys will be okay. I want them to be safe, happy and able to live a life without worry of having to be called into the Saints when they turn twenty-five. The fact they chose to attend CHU and not some Ivy league school like they were told they would have makes me smile. They were already starting to take control of their own lives and live freely.

"I swear I won't let you down," Tate promises, pulling me from my thoughts.

"I know you won't. I have faith in you, Tate. Just promise me you will take your time with getting to know your dad and brother."

Her features pinch. "My dad has been blowing me off, he was so interested and everything to do with my life and wanted to know everything about me and my friends. Then when he didn't show, he went silent until yesterday. He wanted to meet me today but I blew him off." Pride swells inside me.

"Good. Make him earn your forgiveness," I say proudly.

"Amen to that," Nova adds. We spend an hour chatting with Tate before she leaves to get ready for work. David takes his leave with her and promises to check in a couple of days. Nova and I wave him off. Nova and I spend the rest of the night hanging out and watching rom coms to keep our minds off the men who took hold of our hearts. She tells me stories about what she and Vox have been up to while we were separated but I'll be honest, I'm more interested in the stories she tells me about her and Ez.

NOVA and I have the day to ourselves since David isn't coming over. He wants to keep changing his routine so no one can track him here. During the day we only have two guards while the others head home to rest up for the evening shift. I feel bad for them having to stand outside all night. With it being too cold out we rule out swimming, I don't care if it's heated or not it's too cold today. It's overcast and windy as hell. I can hear the wind howling and that shit scares me. I would much rather be tucked up in bed cuddling Hayze while Ez plays with my hair and Archer runs his hands over me—

"You have that faraway look in your eyes." I shake my head to clear away my thoughts as I face Nova.

"I was just thinking about the guys," I admit.

She smiles and winks. "Finally ready to admit you're in love with my brother, Hayze and Archer?"

My lungs deflate but a smile spreads across my face. "Yeah. I am so fucking head over heels for them and it scares the hell out of me."

Nova stares at me with a knowing look. "Someone once told me, *sometimes you have to fall in order to know where you stand*. I kind of think that person might know what he is talking about because when I fell, I was terrified but at the same time so excited at the prospect of what we could become."

"My brother said that, didn't he?" She chuckles and nods.

"Yeah. Yeah he did but it doesn't make it any less true."

I roll my eyes. "I'm scared of them hurting me again," I blurt out. Her eyes soften as she makes her way toward me, then grabs both my hands and holds them.

"Love hurts but it is the greatest pain we will ever feel in our lives, because having the power to love and be loved is what makes life so special. We only get one chance at living, so embrace that bitch and dive head first into whatever this is you have with them. Life is too short and I don't want you to waste a minute of it."

"How the hell am I going to handle three of them?"

Nova laughs and this one is a full belly laugh that has me smiling wide. "Girl, I can barely handle your brother and there is only one of him. Good luck to you and RIP to your pussy because if those guys are anything like Vox, you won't be getting any more sleep." I cringe at the mention of my brother.

"You suck at pep talks, you know that, right?"

She just shrugs. "This isn't a pep talk, this is me telling you to let go of your past and embrace your future. Live in the moment, Vivian. I don't know about you, but this past year has shown me that loving your brother has made my world so much brighter. On my down days he is my strength, when I need to be held he is always there. Fuck what people say or think about you four, they are only jealous because you have the three of those boys eating out of your palm and ready to jump when you tell them."

"God, I miss them," I admit.

Sadness clouds her green eyes. "Ditto. But I miss Vox the most, it's so hard not having him with me every second of every day."

"You really do love my brother, don't you?"

Her eyes turn misty. "More than he will ever know. He isn't just the boy who stole my heart, he is my... person. With him by my side I know I can get through anything. Not having him with me right now kills me because he is my go to, he is the person I turn to for everything and it feels strange to be without him again after so long."

"I'm so sorry you are back in this shit because of me."

"I'm not. That motherfucker took my world from me and his cunt of a kid stole my best friend and robbed him of life, so I want them to pay. I need to put the past to bed as much as you do. I have been living half a life since we left here, always terrified they would show up and blow my life apart."

"We end this," I promise.

"I swear on my life I will look after them."

"I know you will just please... don't let them hate me," I plead.

She pulls me in for a hug. "They can't hate what makes them breathe. You are the air they need to survive. Without you, they have nothing."

CHAPTER THIRTY

Vivian

The feeling of being watched has me snapping my eyes open. I remain still and try to calm my racing heart. You know the feeling you get when someone is standing behind you? Yeah, I have that feeling right now. My stomach is in my throat, fear is clutching me in its vice-like hold, strangling the air from my lungs. I draw on all the strength I can muster and sit up but keep my gaze ahead trying to garner myself some time to prepare for what is about to happen. I don't need superpowers to know this feeling isn't a figment of my imagination, I *know* I am not alone in my bedroom.

I exhale slowly, then turn my head. I bite back my scream, I knew he was there but a part of me still wanted to doubt my gut feeling. I can't do that now that I have locked eyes with the monster. His sinister smile is filled with pure malice. He steps forward and is illuminated by the moonlight trickling in through the windows.

His green eyes look hollow, soulless. His black hair is a mess and just adds to the unhinged aura he has clinging to him. I run my gaze over him and instantly regret dropping my gaze. My breath hitches and lodges in my throat.

"You scream. We die." I swallow audibly and nod. "Do you know what this is?" he asks as he waves his hand. I nod as terror envelopes me. "Say it," he demands.

"I-it's a suicide s-switch," I stutter out. The devil just smiles. He's wearing a vest wired with explosives and has a suicide trigger in his hand, his thumb is on the button. If he releases that thing, we're all dead.

"You do as you're told and I won't kill everyone in this house." Horror splays across my face as I think about Nova sleeping next door.

"Okay."

"Get dressed. You try anything and you won't like what happens," he threatens.

"I won't, I swear." I climb out of bed and rush into my wardrobe. I ignore him watching me as I change quickly into a pair of yoga pants and a random shirt, then I pull on some trainers.

"Lead the way." I do as he says and slip out of my room with him right behind me. I shoot a glance at Nova's closed door, grateful that she is a heavy sleeper and hasn't woken. The silver lining through this whole thing is that he doesn't seem to want her. I don't doubt that he knows she is here. When we reach the living room he shoves me toward the front door. Hope fills me. Nial and his partner are outside, they may not be able to shoot him but surely they would have been trained for a situation like this and at least know how to subdue him.

My hope dies when we step outside. A scream lodges in my throat at the sight of Nial and his partner laying on the ground in a pool of their own blood. Both their throats have been cut.

Tears fall instantly, they died trying to protect me. I look around wondering where the fuck the night time guards are, there should be more of them but then it hits me.

The guards are loyal to Thomas.

As we round the corner I spot a car idling there with the back door open. "Get in," he snarls. I do as he says and balk at the sight of the person in the driver's seat.

"Leo!" I screech in astonishment. I haven't seen him since my brother and the guys beat the shit out of him and he was forced to take the remainder of the season off and missed out on playing in front of scouts.

"Shut up, bitch, this is payback," the asshole spits out as Thomas climbs in beside me. I press against the door as far away from him as possible. Leo drives like a fucking lunatic and I'm forced to grip the door handle or risk slamming into Thomas and his finger slipping off the trigger. I keep watch and make sure to stay alert, as we exit the city limits panic begins to take root inside me.

"Where are we going?" I ask. Thomas strikes out and back hands me right in the mouth. I cry out as the metallic taste of my own blood fills my mouth. I cup my hand over my mouth and turn to him.

"You stay fucking silent, cunt." He sneers, I flinch away from him as tears fill my eyes. I didn't think this through. I thought I could handle him finding me and finally taking him down, but I was wrong. I'm fucking terrified and no one knows where the fuck I am. David and Nova are the only two who will know I am missing and that won't be until they wake which is hours away.

I close my eyes and picture three faces, their smiles bring me some comfort. A pang hits me as guilt swims inside me, I won't get the chance to tell them how much I love them and that I did all of this for them. All the lies and secrets, it's all for them.

When the car jerks, I snap my eyes open to see Leo has taken a dirt road, I can't see anything aside from trees and open land. We are in the middle of fucking nowhere, even if I do escape where the fuck can I run?

It feels like this road goes on forever but he finally comes to a stop out front of an old hunting cabin that looks like it has been vacant for years. Leo kills the engine, then climbs out. I don't dare move even when he opens my door. I cry out when he reaches inside the car and drags me out by my hair. I try to lengthen my strides to keep up with his longer ones but it's no use, I can feel strands of my hair being torn out. We stop for a second as he opens the door, then I'm being dragged by my hair again. The inside of the cabin is dark and I can't make anything out, but Leo doesn't seem to need any light, he yanks me forward and I cry out but then he releases me and I fall to my knees.

"You'll get what's coming to you," Leo vows before slamming the door closed. I hear a lock click into place and whimper. I look around the dark room trying to see but my eyes have barely adjusted as I hear something move. I shuffle backward and try to slow my breathing.

"Who's there?" I rasp out.

"Vivian?"

I gasp and begin crawling on my hands and knees across the room. When the tips of my fingers brush against something I stop and slowly run my hands up her legs. "Tate?"

"Y-yeah," she stutters out.

"What the hell are you doing here?" I whisper shout.

"When David and I left we were run off the road, when I woke up I was in here." I inhale sharply as horror washes over me.

"Where's David?" I snap as I grip her arms and shake her, a stifled whimper escapes her and I force myself to release her and calm down. "Tate, where is he?" I ask in a calm tone.

"I don't know. I haven't seen him or anyone since I woke up. I don't even know where the fuck we are, Vivian!"

Fuck!

Oh my God, our rescue now relies on Nova who has no fucking idea what to do in a situation like this! No, that isn't true, she would call Vox and my guys, they will find me. I just need to keep us all safe until they get here. I shuffle over beside Tate and lean my back against the wall as a resigned sigh escapes me. Why the fuck did I have to go and play hero? Why couldn't I just tell them the truth instead of trying to prove to them that I am strong?

Oh, that's right because you had to try and prove you were able to fight your own battles so they wouldn't see you as weak!

I close my eyes and try to breathe through the melancholy. I put myself here and there is no one else to blame except for myself. I shouldn't have tried to play savior, I should have just trusted in my guys to have my back but I let our past cloud my judgment. Now my error doesn't only affect me, it has cost two other people I care about.

"What do you think our chances of getting out of here alive are?" Tate's softly spoken question pulls me from my inner turmoil.

I release a loud sigh and lull my head to the side, I can just make out her silhouette. "I'll do everything in my power to make sure both you and David get out of here." My stomach twists, not knowing if David is safe or if he is actually here is making me feel sick with worry. The old man has become someone I truly care about and dare say... been a father figure I never knew I wanted or needed. He has always been by my side and trusted in me to make the right choices and lead The

Brotherhood in the right direction. Now he may face a fate I wouldn't wish on anyone I care about.

"You'll be fine, you have money and a family that will want you back." The edge of bitterness I hear in her tone has me feeling sorry for her and the situation she is in. I may fight and bicker with my mom and brother but I can't imagine not having them. Family means everything to me.

"I won't leave you Tate, I promise."

"Yeah, everyone always promises not to leave until they do." I reach over and place my hand on her arm, choosing to ignore how she flinches.

"I'm not everyone and I will never leave you."

"You don't even know me, Vivian!" she bites out in a harsh tone.

"Then tell me."

"Why, because now you suddenly care?"

I balk at her cruelness. "Tate, I have always cared about you."

"No, you have just cared about how I run your hotel. You and I aren't friends, you're my boss."

"Fine. I admit I have done a shitty job of proving to you that you are more to me than just an employee. But, there is so much more happening that you don't understand."

"Given the fucking situation we are both in, I believe I deserve the truth." I debate for a half second about telling her everything, then decide she is right.

"What I am about to tell you is going to blow your mind and you cannot tell anyone about this. I mean it Tate, not a fucking single soul."

"I swear." So, I tell her everything about the Saints and who Thomas is and what he has done. I even told her about Alexander and the deal I made with him. The part I struggled with was admitting that the masked men are my brother and my guys. To my shock, learning about the Filthy Few shocked her more than anything else.

"You see, someone will find us. I made sure of it, we just have to survive until they arrive," I say quietly.

"Jesus Christ, of all the towns I could have run to, I chose the wrong freaking one!" Tate exclaims.

I snort. "Yeah. Hollow Hills isn't exactly what everyone thinks it is, especially if you have a certain last name."

"So you and this Alex guy and the Filthy Few plan to kill every Valerian?" The hint of... remorse I hear in her tone staggers me for a second until I realize not everyone is used to murder like most of us.

"Yeah, it's the only way to be sure that we will all be safe. Alex's terms were clear, he helps me with Thomas and I make sure the Filthy Few don't touch Nexus."

"Does this guy Nexus know about all of this?"

Something in her tone puts me on edge. "Yes. He knew from the moment I banished the guys and his father that his end was coming, he just doesn't know it won't be by the hands of the man who's sister he drugged, raped and murdered."

A soft whimper escapes her. "I'm sorry."

"For what?" I ask.

"I just... Vivian, I lied," she blurts the last part.

"About what?"

"I'm not twenty-three."

My brows raise. "How old are you?"

"Seventeen," she whispers.

"What the fuck!" I shout.

"Shhhh!" I clamp my mouth closed and snap my head toward the door to make sure no one rushes in here to silence me, for a solid minute my heart continues to beat faster than a racehorse can run.

"Your ID and social security number say you are—"

"I know what they say, they are fakes." I fucking gape at the lying little shit. I knew she looked young but I never thought she was lying about her age.

"Oh my God! I made you manager of my fucking sex club and you aren't even legal to drink. I'm going to fucking prison and I'll lose everything!"

"No, you won't."

"How the fuck do you know that?" I snap.

"Because after we get out of here, I'll quit and you can find someone else. I'm sorry, Vivian, but I really needed this job."

"So you thought lying was the best option?"

"Would you have hired me if you knew how old I was?" she claps back. I take a deep breath and hold it a moment to try and calm myself down. There is no point worrying about this now when we have more important things to deal with like getting the fuck out of here alive.

"We'll figure out that shit later but for right now, I need to find a way to alert Alex."

"And how the hell are you going to do that?"

"I may need your help with that one?" I admit guiltily.

"Why do I get the feeling I'm not going to like this?"

"Because I need you to break my arm or something so they are forced to move us so Alex can track them on the cameras."

"What fucking cameras?" she hisses.

"The Brotherhood has the entire town wired with cameras so we can keep an eye on everything. Alex can't hack them all but I know the ones on the way to the hospital he has access to. I need you to hurt me enough they take me there, it's the only way we are going to get the fuck out of here."

CHAPTER THIRTY-ONE

Fuck!

Tears instantly stream down my cheeks and I cry out in agony as Tate lands another punch to my face. When I asked her to break something I didn't think it through. Alex had suggested I ram my shoulder into a wall to pop it out of its socket when we spoke about this and now I'm starting to think his way would have been less painful.

"Stop!" I beg. She doesn't listen which is what I told her to do before we started this beating, but now I am regretting that choice. When she manages to hit me in the temple my eyesight turns hazy and I grow limp beneath her. I can hear her ragged breaths and my own heartbeat thumping but it's starting to grow distant. I welcome the darkness that wants to consume and pull me under its wing. Everything becomes blurry, I feel Tate's weight vanishing from on top of me then I'm being lifted. I can hear muffled sounds but nothing makes sense. My legs refuse to work and then I'm being dragged. I hear shouting but I can't make out the words.

I'm shoved forward and land in a heap, I grunt in pain and close my eyes, trying to regain my equilibrium and get my wits about me which I am ashamed to admit takes me a lot longer than I had hoped. When I open my eyes again it's bright and the drastic change from darkness to light burns my eyes forcing me to close them again and slowly blink them open. The ringing in my ears slowly starts to ebb and I sigh in relief. I look around and instantly lock eyes with Leo. It pains me to see him here. He and I were never friends or anything but we went to school together. He played on the football team with my brother and Hayze.

I continue taking in my surroundings and glare at Thomas when I see him dragging Tate out of the room we were locked in. Rather than throwing her on the ground beside me, he shoves her onto the threadbare sofa. She bares her teeth at him. She may be young but she clearly has spunk and I like that. I feel blood trickling over my upper lip and swipe it away with my arm. I flinch when I jostle my nose. I didn't feel any bones break which is infuriating considering it hurt like a bitch and I won't get my trip to the hospital like I hoped.

"Both of you bitches are stupid as fuck," Leo bites out.

"Coming from you, the insult means nothing," I fire back with a dark smirk on my face. Leo's eyes darken and without warning he lifts his leg then stomps down onto my outstretched one. White hot pain rips through me. I throw my head back and scream as crippling pain blazes throughout my body—I felt the bone break this time. Tears cascade down my cheeks as I try to scoot away from him along the ground but the fucker isn't done. He grips the ankle of the leg he just broke. "No, please, stop— Ahhhhhhh," I scream out when he drags me toward him, the pain blinding and robbing me of air. I sit forward and try to bat his hand away, but the sight of the top of my calf has bile rushing up my throat. There is a perfect boot indent on the top of my leg.

"Run your mouth again and I'll snap the other one," Leo promises.

"Touch her again and I'll slit your fucking throat!" Tate screams. Leo whirls around to face her but she doesn't cower when he cocks his arm back.

"Don't!" I scream but it's too late, the motherfucker punches her and she flops to the side from the force. "Leave her alone!" I scream when he grabs her hair and pulls her head back then attempts to hit her again.

"Enough," Thomas snaps and forces Leo to stop before he can hit Tate again.

"I'll break you too, bitch," Leo spits in Tate's face.

"It'll take a lot more than that to break me, you little pussy. I've lived through this shit my whole life." Her declaration has me frowning, but then my attention is brought back to my leg when another wave of pain rolls through me, forcing me to clench my teeth or risk crying out.

"Get them in the car, the meet is scheduled. Time to recover what was almost lost to us." Thomas's ominous words have a pit of dread forming inside me but the prospect of getting out of here and going to the car where we could be seen by Alex outweighs the need for me to fight Leo when he yanks me up by my hair. I scream and cry in pain as he forces me to walk and put weight on my leg. By the time he shoves me into the backseat of the car, I am so sweaty and riddled with pain I nearly pass out. What I can't stop though is the vomit rushing up my throat, I have no choice but to throw up on the floor of the car thanks to the back door being locked.

When Tate is thrown in, she immediately reaches for me,

her eyes meet mine and my bottom lip begins to tremble. She darts her gaze out the window then turns back to me.

"You need to worry about yourself and get yourself out of here, don't defend me." I shake my head and bite the inside of my cheek when pain begins to bloom inside me again. "Vivian, I can hold my own. I may be young but I have been in enough foster homes where fuckers think they can touch what isn't theirs, I know how to protect myself." She clamps her mouth closed and sits back in her seat as both the front doors open and Thomas and Leo climb inside. Leo instantly swings his head toward me when the stench of my vomit reaches them.

"You fucking cunt, you'll be eating that shit," he grits out. I flinch back and remain silent. I wish more than anything Ez, Hayze, Archer and Vox had just killed this piece of shit. Tate slides her hand along the seat and locks her pinky finger with mine, that small gesture has the vice strangling my chest easing slightly. I breathe through the pain and grind my teeth as we hit bumps so I don't cry out, the last thing I want to do is give Leo the satisfaction of hearing me whimper.

I try to compartmentalize my pain by keeping track of the scenery outside. When we come to the intersection near the hospital, hope begins to build inside me.

"Look at that, Vivian. Help is right there, just a measly block away where they could fix your leg and take away the pain." I suck in a sharp inhale. "Look at how close you were to being seen." He knows. "So close, yet so fucking far," Thomas taunts just as Leo turns right and heads in the opposite direction. The small flame of hope that was burning inside me dies out, Thomas knows about the cameras. He was a step ahead and I was too fucking jaded and self-absorbed to realize that I have been betrayed by my own brotherhood. They would have been the ones to tell him the system was hacked. A year of my life I spent trying to clean up his mess and make something better for this place. Turns out none of those bastards wanted change, they were happy to live off the blood and torture of others.

Knowing this for certain now makes the choices I have made easier to live with. This will all come to an end and I just have to pray that I will be around to see how this shit plays out because I want to watch them all be taken down and burn in hell.

"How did you find me?" I force out through gritted teeth. Thomas's answering laughter grates on my nerves and has my hackles rising but I refrain from snapping at him.

"It's been eating at you to know how I have been a step ahead, hasn't it?" I don't answer, he doesn't need me to. "Did it keep you up at night wondering if it was The Brotherhood who sold you out?" I dig my nails into the palm of my hand to distract myself from this bastard's taunt. "What if I told you it wasn't The Brotherhood who led me to you and that it was someone you trusted who gave you up?"

My interest is peaked, the sinister laugh that escapes Leo tells me he knows who it is and clearly it is someone who I would never expect. A pang of unease crawls its way up my spine.

"Who?" I'm proud of how strong my voice sounds even though I am crippled with pain and feel the cold sheen of sweat dotting my forehead.

Thomas turns the rearview mirror so he can meet my gaze, the look of spite in his dead eyes sends a chill down my spine. "How well do you really know Tatum Lawson?" A gasp escapes me as I yank my hand back and snap my head toward her. She's staring at Thomas like a deer caught in the headlights.

"I don't even fucking know you!" Tate shouts, then looks at me with a pleading look. She tries to reach out to me but I flinch away. "Vivian, I never told them anything, I swear. I don't even know who they are. You have to believe me," she begs.

I want to believe that she wouldn't betray me but how the fuck can I trust her, she said it herself I don't even know her really.

"Tatum, dear?" Thomas calls out, drawing her attention back to him. "I'm so glad we could finally meet. It's a shame your mother was a lying cunt and that you don't have a cock or I would have raised you myself." My face scrunches in confusion, Tate on the other hand turns pale like she has seen a ghost.

"What the fuck is he talking about?" I growl, Tate still won't take her eyes off Thomas. "Answer me, dammit!" I scream. She jolts as if I just zapped her, then turns to me with tears clouding her eyes. She opens and closes her mouth three times but no words come out. "Tate?" I push.

"He's my father," she whispers so low I would have missed it if I wasn't paying such close attention. Her revelation has me turning to stone beside her.

Thomas is her father.

She sold me out.

Nexus is her older brother.

"You see, I never had to reach out to my brothers, my own daughter getting a job with you was something I couldn't have planned, but it worked out well. All I had to do was prey on her need for acceptance and she gave me everything I required without knowing it. Calling her to your new safe house wasn't smart," he mocks.

"You tracked her phone," I mutter. Thomas laughs and the sound chills me to my bones. Tate is silent and continues to stare at me like she is in a trance. I invited the wolf's pup into my den without even knowing it. I told her everything, I gave her all the intel and she passed it onto her estranged father without even knowing she was being groomed. Thomas continues spilling the beans about how easy it was to get all the Saints to fall into line and follow their true leader. My mind is too consumed with the knowledge of Tatum being his daughter to register what he's saying. Even when Leo finally stops the car I don't register where we are until he drags me out of the car by my arm and I'm screaming when my leg hits the ground.

Peace & Love Crematorium.

I don't have the strength to question why we are here as well as trying not to pass out from the pain, so I keep my mouth shut and do my best to hop on one leg. It does nothing to ease the agony, the constant jostling of my leg is torture of the worst kind. When he drags me inside through the side door, I miss the step and land on my ass. Leo, being the cunt he is, doesn't lift me he just grabs a handful of my hair and drags me along the linoleum floor, screaming as I try to untangle his fingers. I can feel the strands ripping out of my head and the feeling is indescribable. I refuse to give up fighting even though I know it's useless, but I won't go out like a pussy.

My guys and brother taught me better than that!

When Leo finally comes to a stop, I nearly whimper in gratitude but the sound lodges in my throat when I realize we are in the room with the cremators.

They're going to burn us alive.

I see three cremators and my stomach sinks, I'm going to die here. Tate is dragged in behind screaming and throwing punches blindly as Thomas yanks her by her head. The sight of blood trickling down the corner of his mouth brings a smile to my face.

Atta girl, Tate.

Thomas shoves her to her knees beside me but doesn't release his hold on her hair as he forces her to remain there.

"You ungrateful bitch." He sneers and he wipes the corner of his mouth with his thumb. When he sees blood on his finger he snarls, then releases Tate's hair only to backhand her.

"Stop!" I snap. My outburst costs me. Thomas kicks my injured leg, drawing a sharp pain filled cry from me.

"You bitches will learn. I had planned to keep you and teach the ways of The Brotherhood and marry you to a good friend but now, you will die alongside her and her traitor of a fucking friend," he says to Tate. My stomach is tied up in knots, does he have Nova? Panic starts to set in again for the hundredth time tonight, I can die without complaint so long as Nova and Tate are safe.

"I'd rather rot in fucking hell than ever have anything to do with you," Tate fires back with venom dripping off each of her words. Thomas's answer comes in the form of a slap across the face. Tate topples to the side but doesn't make a sound which just seems to further aggravate Thomas, so he kicks her in the side. The force of the kick has her wincing and clutching her ribs.

"Get the others," Thomas barks at Leo who scurries off like a good little dog. I remain silent but keep my eyes on Tate and Thomas, the latter pulls his phone from his pocket and begins typing. When the door Leo disappeared through opens again, Thomas smiles. It shouldn't surprise me to see Drew Anders and Ford Booth among the men who enter the room, but it does. Both of them leer down at me. I keep my face blank of everything and stare each of the traitors in the eye as they come in. There are too many of them to fit in here, so Thomas instructs them to head into the viewing room and turn the speaker on so they can hear and watch through the glass window.

Some of the members of the Saints that are here tonight I knew were lying sacks of shit, but some of the others I thought were real and almost considered them friends. It hurts to see them here ready to watch me die.

"Brothers, we are here tonight to put an end to the reign of this wannabe lordess." The men cheer like a paid crowd. "The Brotherhood will be returned to its former glory and we will reclaim what she tried to take from us." More cheers ring out.

"Kill her!" Ford calls out, shocking the fuck out of me but I don't let it show. Thomas cackles like what he said is something so normal.

"You are all fucking sick," Tate snarls with disgust thick in her tone.

"That the bitch you gonna give me, my lord?" Drew asks. Tatum's eyes widen in horror.

"I had planned to, but it seems she isn't trained as well as I thought," Thomas answers, feigning pity.

"I'm not scared of a little work. I've wanted to break that sweet pussy in since I saw her at Lividica." Drew mentioning my club has me gritting my teeth, no matter what they do to me they will never get my club and that knowledge keeps me from ripping these cocksuckers a new asshole.

"We'll discuss this matter later, my friend." At Thomas's answer, Drew smiles sinfully down at Tate who visibly shudders in revolution. "Now, on to the matter at hand—"

"Why the need for the show? You had them all on your side, so why not just get them to tell you where I was? Why drag this fucking thing out and hurt so many innocent people just to get to me?" I cut in and ask, none of this is making sense to me.

Ford tries to come at me with his hand raised but Thomas stops him with his words. "After your little stunt I had to prove myself worthy to the brothers and show them that a true leader won't stop until he wins. Plus, some scumbag we called a brother was hiding your tracks." I reel back in confusion.

"The deaths were my way of showing you what happens to traitors."

"Kelly wasn't a traitor, you bastard! She was your fucking wife and my best friend's mother. She had nothing to do with this—" My reply is cut off when Thomas slaps me across the face. I fall to the side with the grace of a toddler.

"Don't touch her!" Tate shouts but is silenced by a backhand from her father. Thomas forces me back to a sitting position by the hold he has on my hair. My scalp is raw and aching but I refuse to make a sound. He kneels down and gets right in my face. I can smell the whiskey on his breath and it takes strength not to gag at the smell of it.

"You listen to me, you little cunt, that bitch was a means to an end. Killing her was for me, it was my way of saying *fuck you* to that little bitch of a daughter of hers. Killing her was joyous. I knew her death would ruffle you all and force those other little cunts to come back to Hollow Hills, what I didn't expect was for them to be those masked fucks." My nostrils flare and I bite the inside of my cheek to remain silent. "Oh, don't worry, we'll be hunting them next. We know they have been picking off brothers and now they will be judged for their sins."

"You lay a single fucking finger on my men or my brother and I will fucking ruin you and make hell seem like a vacation."

"Bring him in!" Thomas shouts right in my face, then releases me with a hard shove. I catch myself on my elbows just as Tatum shuffles forward and wraps an arm around me to help me up. My discomfort is muted when Leo leads a handcuffed, beaten and bloodied David into the room. My bottom lip instantly trembles at the sight of my friend. His right eye is swollen shut and blood is crusted on the side of his head. His shirt is stained with blood, leading me to believe there are more wounds beneath his clothing that I can't see. His face is littered with bruises but it's the look in his eye that has me whimpering.

He limps forward, wincing in pain but doesn't make a single sound as he stares down at me with a regretful look.

"Everything is done, you did it, Lordess." His voice is laden with pain and it breaks my heart to see him like this.

"I'm so sorry," I choke out. He tries to smile but winces in pain.

"How touching," Thomas mocks, causing all the others to laugh. "David or should I say *Special Agent Green*." My eyes widen in shock as I stare at him. "Oh, she didn't know?" Thomas asks in a sickly sweet tone.

David blanks his face of all emotion as he turns to Thomas with a sinister look in his eye. "You gonna keep talking or get this over with?" I look at Thomas who is turning a shade of red from his anger, my mind is still reeling that David is an undercover fed.

"You will pay for the crimes you have committed against this brotherhood. You will burn in hell for what you have tried to do," Thomas sneers.

"The word *try* implies that I didn't accomplish what I set out to do. I accomplished my job and more. Do your worst because you're running out of time." Thomas's face hardens, his eyes narrow and it's obvious for all to see that David is getting under his skin which makes me proud.

"Heat the furnace!" Thomas barks. My eyes widen in horror. Vaughn, one of the newer members of The Brotherhood, does as he's told and that's when it hits me. His mother is Belinda, the owner of this place, the very same place I sent Kelly to be cremated. "How long before it's ready?"

Vaughn turns to Thomas. "A couple of hours to fully destroy the evidence but three minutes to be hot enough to burn him alive."

I choke out a scream. "No, please don't hurt him!" I beg.

David looks down at me with a resigned look on his face while Thomas smiles wickedly. "Take me instead," I plead.

'No!" David shouts. "You will not trade your life for mine. I have lived and had my time, your life is just beginning. It has been an honor to stand by your side, *Lordess*. Don't judge me for the secret that was kept from you, judge me by the person you know me to be."

Tears flow freely down my cheeks as I stare up at my friend who has stood by my side and never once judged me or tried to change who I am, even though he is a federal agent and about to be put to death because of me. The pain in my leg lessens as the pain in my chest intensifies.

"I'm... so... sorry," I choke out through my tears.

"I'm not. I would have chosen this end a hundred times over if it meant the final result was still the same because you are worthy of it. Embrace the wonders of life and allow those that love you to protect and cherish you because we all need somebody. Thank you for being my *somebody* and reminding me that I am worthy of more than the badge I have worn for more than half of my life. All you set out to do has been done, hold on a little longer for them to get here because this will be *filthy* soon enough." His meaning hits me like a ton of bricks. They know where I am and they are coming for me, but they won't make it in time to save my friend. Thomas shouts for Leo to take David to the cremator. He shoots me one last loving look before he stumbles forward.

I scream and shout, I even try to stand but Tate holds me back. I try to free myself of her hold but she clings tighter to me. "They'll shoot you," she shouts, but I ignore her plea as Leo and Vaughn force David onto a trolley looking thing. Two others step forward and hold David down while they strap him to it. He tries to fight but it's useless, he can't get free.

"Thomas, please, I am begging you!" I scream. "David, I'm so sorry!" I shout.

"A favor asked is a debt owed, Lordess, my debt has been repaid!" he shouts out, stunning me silent for a second until Vaughn pulls the door to the furnace open. I struggle harder to get free but Tate wraps her arms around me from behind. Sobs claw their way out of me as I watch them wheel that fucking trolley to the entrance, the temperature so stifling I can feel it from here. It's like a heatwave. When they begin to push David toward it, he starts screaming. He isn't even inside before the stench of singed hair assaults my nostrils.

"David," I cry again as Leo pushes the tray forward. David's screams will haunt me every night for the rest of my life. Vaughn slams the door closed and locks it but it doesn't mute the screams of my friends' excruciating pain. I close my eyes and try to block the sound out but there's nowhere to hide or run to escape them.

"I'm so sorry, Vivian," I hear Tate whisper after a while and that's when I realize the screams have finally stopped. The ghost of his screams can still be heard. Soon I will meet the same fate as him and I can't find the strength within myself to fight the inevitable.

CHAPTER THIRTY-TWO

Archer

"What exactly am I watching?" I clip out, sitting here for hours watching all these monitors has my eyes fucking aching.

"When they pass a camera the software Vatican designed will ping their facial features and alert us, we'll be able to track them and determine what direction they are heading." I kick my feet on the makeshift desk and cross my arms over chest, my anger still simmering over the fact Alex the cock head wouldn't let us leave, then Ezekiel and Vox pleaded with us to remain calm and not fuck this stupid plan of Vivian's up. When I get my hands on her I am going to wring her pretty little fucking neck, and then punish her in the only way I know how.

Orgasm denial.

That should do the trick. I smile to myself and picture just how I plan to do that. My blissful state is interrupted when fucking Halo jerks forward in his seat. I nearly fall out of my own when I try to match his move, the bastard has his face practically pressed against one of the monitors. I try to peer around him but I can't see shit. I shove his shoulder but he just growls and remains where the fuck he is!

"Dude, either move the fuck over or tell me what you are seeing?" I snarl.

"Vatican, Omen, get Alex now," Halo calls out. When I try to shove him out of the way again, the fucker pulls a blade and has it pressed against my throat. He moved so swiftly I didn't even anticipate the move. "If you get in the way of me doing my job, I will put you in the ground and not lose a wink of fucking sleep over it, clear?" He doesn't wait for a response as he turns back to the screen effectively dismissing me, which grates on my already frayed nerves. Within a minute everyone has gathered around us. Vox nudges me to try garner my attention but I ignore him, too focused on trying to catch a glimpse of the screen,

"What have you got?" Alex asks.

"I have a sighting of Thomas himself with another cunt I don't recognize," Halo answers as he sits back so we can all view the screen. The instant I see Thomas's face, white hot rage runs through my veins, but then I flick my gaze to the guy beside him and lean forward to make sure it's who I think it is.

"Get out of the fucking way," one of Alex's minions snaps but I ignore him. I pull back and turn to face Vox, Ez and Hayze who all wear varying looks of surprise.

"How the fuck is Leo involved in this?" I ask.

"He was never a member of the Saints," Hayze adds.

"Vivian would never have inducted him," Ez announces. I nod my head in agreement. Vivi would never have allowed Leo to join after what he did.

"That traitor would have helped Thomas so he could get revenge against us for what we did to him." The anger that laces Vox's tone can be felt, knowing Thomas is behind this is one thing but to learn that someone we once went to school with and played on the football fucking team is helping this cunt, has my stomach churning. It's clear we can't trust anyone but ourselves. This whole town is filled with two-faced bastards that are only out to help themselves.

"I'll kill the son of a bitch for helping him," Hayze vows.

"There's another angle," Halo says, then clicks a couple buttons on his keyboard so the screen shifts and a new picture appears, but it's the side of the car. My blood turns cold, I can see her through the center of the front seats, huddled in the backseat with a terrified look on her face that has every emotion inside me firing on all cylinders.

My baby.

I just got her back and I won't fucking lose her. I can't be without her again. Turning my back on Vivi the first time was excruciating and the pain nearly crippled me but this time, it would kill me. I can feel the raw emotions wafting off the guys and I know they are feeling everything I am. No one needs to say a single word, we all know we are about to go to war for that girl and there is nothing anyone can do to stop us. Vox pulls his phone from his pocket and dials someone, he stands tense and poised as if he's ready to strike at any moment.

"Witch?" My attention is captured at the mention of his pet name for Nova.

"Is she okay?" Ezekiel asks with worry lacing his tone. Vox puts the call on speaker so we can all hear.

"Vox, I'm okay but Vivian is gone." Panic is evident in Nova's voice.

"I know, baby. Where are you?" he urges.

"I'm at the safe house. She was with me last night and when I woke up to grab a glass of water I checked in on her but her bed was empty. The two guards are dead and I'm... scared," she admits, which just causes Vox to grind his teeth and clench his phone in a vice-like hold.

"Where are you, baby? Send me your location, I'm coming to you now," he says.

"Go to my sister and we'll go after Vivian," Ez says. Vox snaps his head up and stares at Ez. A range of emotions are flickering through his eyes but it's clear he is battling with the instinct to protect his twin, but on the other hand every part of him wants to race to the girl he loves and make sure she is safe.

"Vox?" The sound of Nova's voice seems to shake him out of his battle.

"Yeah?" he answers.

"Go after your sister. I would never make you choose between—"

Vox cuts her off. "I love you, witch." Then he looks between me, Ez and Hayze with a hard unyielding stare. "It's because I love you that I know these idiots will do whatever it takes to save my sister, because they love her like I love you." The three of us nod our heads, promising him that we won't let him down and we *will* save our girl. "Hang tight, baby. Send me your location." Vox ends the call and straightens. I can feel Alex and his four sidekicks staring at us but we ignore them. "So fucking help me, man, don't make me regret trusting you three to save my sister. Vivian is tough but she isn't unbreakable. Save her... please."

Hayze lays a hand on Vox's shoulder, no trace of his usual humor is to be seen as he stares him down. "On my life, we won't let anything happen to her. Go save your girl so we can save ours."

Vox nods then looks to Ez. "Bring her back."

"You have my word, brother. Keep my little sister safe until I get back," Ez instructs.

Vox turns to me next and I don't cower under the scrutiny

of his stare. "You make sure you treat her right, asshole. Don't fuck her over because I will kill you if you break her heart."

I nod. "If I hurt her, you would have to beat these two to get to me." My answer seems to appease him. When his phone pings with a message, I know its Nova sending him a pin to her location because his shoulders droop.

"I gave you my word that I would protect your sister, I meant it." Vox looks at Alex in surprise. "Calvin and Gary are out front, they will ride with you to get your girl and watch your six. We now have an idea of Thomas and your sister's location, we'll bring her back," Alex promises. Vox steps forward and stops a foot away from Alex. The pair stare at each other and I start to wonder if Vox is going to take a swing, but then he stuns us all when he holds his hand out for Alex to shake.

"Thank you. The Filthy Few will now owe you a debt." I cut a glance to Hayze and Ez to find both of them standing there looking equal parts shocked and in disbelief. The Filthy Few have never offered a debt without being asked a favor.

Alex places his hand in Vox's and shakes it. "Get out of here and get your girl, we have a bunch of whacked up snobs to kill and a girl to save."

"Wait." Everyone turns toward Omen who is pointing at the screen. "We have *girls* to save."

"What?" I mutter as I lean forward. I have to squint slightly to see properly but the moment I do, I recognize the girl in the backseat. "That's the bartender from Vivian's club."

"Tatum," Alex says aloud, the hint of hatred that laces his one word answer has questions brewing inside me but I don't say nothing.

"Either she is a part of this bullshit or she is a victim as well," Halo adds.

"I'm not jumping to conclusions, we need facts. You all

know the drill, we run on facts only and not speculation. Am I clear?" I watch in fascination as the four guys all mumble their yes's and nod their heads. It isn't hard to see that Alexander has their loyalty and it's not the type of loyalty you buy, it's earned. Vatican, Halo, Omen and Pope would die for him. "Get geared up, we roll out in five." He then turns to Halo and focuses on him. "Find me the exact route they took and give me a location. I want all our forces mobilized and ready to go in on my command."

They all take off to get ready, leaving the four of us alone. We each wish Vox good luck and promise to update as soon as we have Vivian. When he leaves, the three of us seem to drop our facade and show each other our true emotions.

Fear.

Worry.

Doubt.

We're worried we won't get to her in time.

We fear Thomas has had too much time to inflict pain on our girl.

We doubt ourselves because we're terrified that once this is all over and she no longer needs rescuing, she'll change her mind on how she feels about us.

"We watch each other's backs," Ez says, trying to take control of the situation and redirect our wayward thoughts. "We go in there with one purpose—save Vivian."

"What about Thomas?" Hayze asks.

"She is our main priority. We get her out and then we go back and take out as many of those sons of bitches as we can." Ez's ominous tone says more than he is willing to admit. He doesn't plan to come out of this fight alive, he wants to take the head of the snake so Vivian can be free for real this time.

"We're with you," I say firmly, his face contorts in remorse but he nods regardless.

"Until the end, brother," Hayze tacks on.

"No matter what, I want you both to know that you will always be my brothers and growing up with you both and Vox is what kept me alive. We may not share blood, but you three are my family."

"As you are mine," I say with conviction.

"Stop with this sad shit, I have too many reasons to live and the main reason is waiting for us to save her. So, get your fucking heads in the game and let's go get our girl, so we can punish her ass tomorrow for thinking she doesn't need us." Both Ez and I smile at Hayze, he always knows how to lighten a mood and keep our spirits up.

Ready or not, baby, we're coming for you...

CHAPTER THIRTY-THREE

Vivian

I hear the buzz of their voices in the background but my mind is numb from the pain of loss. I know Tate is holding me but I can't feel it, I can't even feel the throbbing pain in my leg. Everything is redundant right now, all the plotting, planning and lies I have told over the past twelve months has been for nothing. I still lost someone I cared deeply for. Tate begins shaking me trying to garner my attention, the buzzing of their voices becomes clear.

"By the power vested in me by the Haven Saints, I sentence you, Vivian Tempest, to death by fire." Thomas's declaration should inspire fear of some kind but I can't find it within myself to feel anything.

"Vivian, snap the fuck out of it," Tatum hisses in my ear as the crowd of gathered men cheer and pump their fists in the air like this is some rally. "Don't let his death be in vain, you owe him that." Her words strike a chord inside me, the numbness slowly starts to bleed way to a burning sensation that has me gasping for air. The feeling is so strong it almost consumes me with the need to suffocate the life out of Thomas and watch as his soul leaves his body so it can burn in fucking hell.

"You thought you were better than us, you dumb cunt—"

A humorless laugh escapes me, forcing Thomas to snap his mouth closed. "A dumb cunt? Is that what you think I am?" I taunt.

"I don't *think*, I know it's the truth," he grits out.

"Hmmm." I hum then purse my lips and tilt my head side to side. "I must have done pretty well for a dumb cunt since I bankrupted your pathetic little society." Thomas's face isn't the only one that falls. Murmurs begin to break out around us.

"You're lying, the build for the school is funded by The brotherhood," Ford says with false bravado.

"Yes, but the land surrounding the school isn't owned by The Brotherhood now, is it?" I fire back. The bastard stands there, clenching his fists at his sides.

"She's lying, I would know if the money was missing," Gavin, the Saints accountant, says with a smugness I can't wait to destroy when I drop the bomb.

"Are you willing to bet your life on that, Gavy boy?" I sass back, earning a scowl from him.

"Enough!" Thomas roars, silencing the room but I can see from the way Leo is staring at me with judgment that he knows I'm not bluffing. "The bitch is a skilled liar like her sorry excuse of a brother. Get her ass up now, I want this over with," Thomas orders. Three men attempt to come toward me but Leo's words have them halting.

"She's not lying." Everyone turns to him but he keeps his seedy gaze on me. Leo is going to be one of the first I kill.

"How do you know that?" Thomas barks.

"Because she was the smartest in all our classes. She may be a foolish bitch but she's a clever slut and I know this little bitch would have had a backup plan." Just to be more of a vindictive bitch, I clap my hands slowly drawing it out just to fuck with them.

"Look who is finally keeping up with the rest of the class," I taunt. Leo being the fucking cockroach that he is, steps forward and kicks my broken leg, forcing a sharp cry of pain from me. I snap my mouth closed and breathe through the pain, I just need to keep them talking long enough for the cavalry to arrive. I hope I'm not misunderstanding what David meant. I have no idea how he managed to pull off the last part of my plan before being taken, but nothing surprised me with him, he was a magician when it came to getting things done.

"You either start explaining or we start breaking more bones, you conniving little cunt."

"You think calling me a cunt is an insult but in truth, Thomas, cunts are useful things to have, so it's really a compliment if you ask me." At my mocking reply he turns a shade of red. He's getting pissed off because I'm making a mockery of him in front of all his spineless brothers that think the sun rises out of his flat ass.

"You may think you are steps ahead but you and I both know that I have the power to take down your disloyal brother and his band of misfits. I have all the evidence I need to end them and their mask-wearing cowardly ways. Unlike the four of them, I don't need to hide my face, a true leader leads from the front."

"A true leader would know when his ship is sinking as well," I toss back at him.

"My ship is fine," Thomas snarls.

"No, you're on the Titanic and it's about to hit the iceberg and you can't even see it happening." It fills me with great joy to see the doubt in his eyes. "You can kill me but The Brotherhood will never survive the aftermath of my death. I knew these fuckers weren't loyal, so I made sure to have a contingency plan in place especially with the Night Of The Saints fastly approaching."

Thomas cuts a glance to Ford who looks ruffled, he can try to hide it as best as he can but I see through the facade. I run my gaze over all of them, each one of them looks uncertain and when you have your back up against the wall with no other allies, all you need to do is build doubt in their minds and they will turn against their leader. The greed each of these selfish assholes possess is sickening, they would sell their soul to the devil if it meant they could remain rich and untouchable.

"She's bluffing. The Saints have covered the cost for the expansion, she has no money." Ford is trying hard to believe the bullshit he is spewing out of his mouth but it's obvious to all that he is grasping at straws.

"Fuck this, take her now!" Thomas roars. Fear erupts inside me as Leo and Vaughn step toward me. Tate's hold on me tightens but I know it's futile, she doesn't have the strength to fight these fuckers and nor do I. I thought I could hold them off until help arrived. Leo sneers down at me as he extends his arms to grab me, but the lights cut out. I know we are in a crematorium and given everything that has happened and about to happen its only now that it registers to me that we are in a place of the dead and it could be fucking haunted!

"Fan out, find the circuit breaker," I hear someone shout.

"Fix this!" Thomas bellows. Chaos breaks out as everyone begins shouting, they all reach for their phones to try to light the area but it's not enough. I feel Tate yanked backward and I grunt in effort to remain upright.

"Get the fuck off me!" she snaps.

"Shut the hell up, it's me." I freeze at the sound of his voice. "Let go now, I need to get you out of here, he'll kill you after he finishes with her," Nexus whisper shouts loud enough for only us to hear.

"I can't leave her," Tate argues. If I survive the night I know I will probably regret my decision but for right now, I won't because I can't have her death on my hands. Giving into this means letting this rapist go free for a second time.

"I can't carry her, I can only get one of you out," Nexus argues.

"He's right," I hiss. "Go, Tate." I push.

"Vivian, I won't leave you to die," she claps back.

"It's better me than you." I twist and force her arms to release me, I can make out their silhouettes but that's it. "Take her and keep her safe." I can feel Nexus's gaze on me and it makes my skin crawl but I swallow down my hatred for him. Him being here and going against his father to save her shows me that heartless bastard actually does care about someone aside from himself, which I never thought was possible.

"I'm sorry," Nexus bites out, then I feel Tate's heat vanish from behind me. I sigh in defeat. I'm happy she will be safe and live to fight another day but a part of me is envious my rescue party isn't here.

"Ahhhh," someone cries out followed by another painful shout. All the phone lights turn toward the front of the room, where the noise came from. The sound of the men pounding on the glass in the viewing area sounds out. Everyone swivels to face the glass but we can't see anything.

When another round of screams rents the air, everyone grows still, my heart beats faster as equal parts hope and fear swirl inside me.

Did they reach me in time?

When the lights flicker on, I slam my eyes closed to stop the burn from the sudden assault of brightness. I quickly blink them open and gasp at the sight surrounding me.

They came!

My guys stand in front of me, forming a shield. The three of them wear their masks and have both Ford and Leo on their knees in front of them. Hayze and Archer have their guns pressed against the backs of their heads. I twist to look behind me, surprised to see Alex and a couple more guys who I assume are his men.

"Where you will rest for eternal life no favor will be asked. Your stone will have no markings. A favor was asked by one and it has now been granted. The debt to be collected is your life. A favor asked is a debt owed," Ez says. He doesn't use his voice distorter, there isn't a need as they would all know their cover has been blown now. I asked the favor to help me take down the Saints and they are here to grant it. Tears well in my eyes at their presence, they didn't leave me. They came for me because they love me and that notion has the tears spilling down my cheeks.

"You fucking fools, you can kill them but we will slaughter all of you before you get a chance to fire a second round," Thomas says with a cocky lilt to his voice. I can see him through the gap between Archer and Ez and he looks pleased at the sight of them which worries me. "I knew you would come to save your whore—" Hayze lifts his gun from the back of Ford's head to point at Thomas.

"Call her that again, I dare you." The venom that drips from his tone has me growing warm. Hayze broody and angry is a fucking sight to see.

"Welcome to your final night," Thomas says with a wicked smile. The men surrounding him don't seem to relax like their leader. When Alex circles around me to come stand beside Archer Thomas's eyes widen at the sight of the imposing man. "*You,*" he breathes out.

"You seem surprised to see me, Thomas," Alex says in a calm tone.

"You're supposed to be locked up," Thomas splutters.

"Yeah, no thanks to you," Alex growls. "You see, the problem with severing heads and sending them to the lordess without claiming the kill had her thinking *The Butcher* had come after her." Thomas cuts his gaze to me, I smile. "You and your men have two minutes to surrender and drop to your knees or we put bullets in each of your heads." Before Thomas can utter another word, Ez pulls his gun in one swift move and shoots Leo in the side of the head. I scream in fright. Archer pulls the trigger and shoots Ford in the back of the head pulling another scream from me. Everyone begins shouting and shifting around the room but freeze when Alex steps forward toward Thomas.

"Don't kill him!" I blurt out. My three guys turn and stare down at me. I look at each of them imploring them with my eyes to trust me. I think they will agree to my terms but the second Archer's gaze travels down my body and he sees my leg everything changes. He whirls around and goes to charge Thomas but Alex intercepts him.

"Get the fuck off me," Arch roars.

"You can't!" Alex shouts back.

"He fucking hurt my girl and he'll fucking pay for that shit." Archer fights harder against Alex's hold. I turn to Ex and Hayze.

"Please, I need Thomas alive or all of this is for nothing. I am begging you, please, trust me." Both of them look at me for a long moment before turning to each other. I hold my breath, praying they listen to me. When they both dart forward to pull Archer back and subdue him I finally exhale. But then the sound of sirens in the distance has the tension in the room ramping up.

"You have one minute! On your knees and live, or we take you all out. Decide now!" Alex roars so loud I flinch at the raw hatred in his tone. When he's spoken to me he's always been calm and soft but this is the side of him people fear and I can finally see why.

"We have to get out of here," Ezekiel grits out. Archer seems to finally calm down at the sight of a lot of the men around dropping to their knees. Drew drops to his knees beside Thomas, earning a glare from the former lord, but his eyes are fixed on the lifeless body of his partner.

"You fucking fools!" Thomas shouts. "We outnumber them."

"No, you don't. Your men in the little room are locked inside, I have the entire building surrounded. You will not make it out of here a free man." Alex continues barking orders as my guys all kneel down around me. I reach out and touch each of them feeling overcome by my emotions.

"I love you," I blurt out, making all three of them still in surprise. "I'm so sorry I pushed you all away and I swear I won't do it again. I love you guys so fucking much," I choke out as a lump forms in my throat. Hayze cups my cheek and I melt into his touch.

"We love you too, Vivi baby." His words have my chest constricting.

"We need to get you out of here so we can yell at you," Ez says as he reaches forward to lift me but I jerk back.

"Vivian, now isn't the time we need to get out of here, the cops are almost—"

"I know," I say, cutting Archer off.

"Then shut up so we can get out of here," Ez snarls in warning.

"She can't leave," Alex says. All three of them turn their heads and stare up at him. I spot Thomas still standing and it grates on my nerves. He should be kneeling and pleading for his worthless life.

"What the fuck are you talking about?" Archer fires back.

Alex flicks his gaze to me and nods encouragingly. I take a deep breath, knowing my time is nearly up and touch each of them, drawing their confused stares back to me. I force a smile to my face to try and ease some of their uncertainty but I can see they aren't buying it.

"You have to go and leave me behind," I say quietly.

All three of them just stare at me like I'm a strange being they have just discovered. "No, you just said you won't push us away anymore—"

I grab Hayze's hand silencing him. "And I meant it, but this is the final piece of the plan." The sound of the sirens grows closer. "To end the Saints for good I made a deal—"

"What fucking deal?" Ezekiel shouts, I can hear the hint of fear in his voice and that shit kills me.

"I want to explain everything but I can't. There isn't enough time but I need you three to trust me, I know what I'm doing. Please, I am begging you to leave now."

"No."

"We aren't leaving you."

"You made a deal with the feds," the three of them fire off at the same time.

"Go, or else everything she has done is for nothing," Alex snaps.

"Please," I say as I reach for Ez and Archer clutching their arms and imploring them with my eyes. "I need you to go."

"Vivian, no I am not leaving you," Archer snaps.

I flick my gaze to Alex. "Please." He sighs then nods to his men who all rush forward and grab my guys. The three of them fight against the four guys who are pulling them away. Hayze manages to elbow the guy dragging him backward and gets free for a second until the guy tases him. "Don't hurt them!" I scream as Hayze begins convulsing on the ground. I sob at the sight of him jerking on the ground in front of me.

"Vivian, I'll kill them all for this!" Archer roars.

"Don't fucking do this," Ezekiel begs as they are dragged from the room. Hayze is lifted and tossed over the guy's shoulder like he weighs nothing and the sight of him passed out has me crying harder. Just as the guys slip out the door Thomas tries to make a run for it but Alex moves swiftly like a panther, and fires a single shot that pierces Thomas's leg. He screams out in pain as he drops to the ground. Alex turns back to me and holds his gun out to me.

"Take it, they'll all try to run as soon as I walk out the door. I'll leave some guys here to watch the exits to make sure none of them escape." I gingerly reach out and take the gun from him but Alex doesn't stop there. He moves behind me and grabs me under my arms then drags me across the room and leans me against the wall so I have all the members of the Haven Saints in my sights. "Any of them move, shoot for the chest. It's the biggest target."

I meet his gaze and nod. "Thank you, Alex."

He exhales tiredly. "I upheld my end now, now make sure you call off the dogs."

"You have my word."

He searches my gaze for another second. "Stay alive, Vivian Tempest," he whispers.

"Same to you, Alexander Denver." It surprises me how much I mean that.

"I'm always a phone call away," he says, then turns and runs out of the room. The second that door clicks shut behind him, the tension and the atmosphere switches.

"Get her!" Thomas roars. I suck in a ragged breath and lift the gun in front of me waiting for one of them to make a move.

"Get the fuck up and kill her or we are all going down." It should come as no surprise that Drew is the first to stand, the sirens are deafening now which means they have to be here. When three others follow Drew's lead, I dart my gun between the four of them. Drew sneers as he takes a step forward, I close my eyes and squeeze the trigger without a second thought. The shot rings out just as we begin to hear shouts. I open my eyes and gasp, Drew stands there with wide eyes, he looks shocked as he reaches up and places a hand over his stomach where blood is soaking through his shirt. He looks down at his wound, then back to me with surprise as he drops to his knees just as the door is kicked open. Men in black clothing with rifles, helmets and masks that cover half their faces barge into the room. One of the men spots me and turn their rifle to me.

"Drop the fucking gun now!" he yells. Another three guys point their guns at me. I raise my free hand and slowly lower the gun to my side and raise both hands. "Push it away, now!" I do as he says and the instant the gun is away from me, he rushes forward and drags me forward. I scream out in pain when he forces me onto my stomach and yanks my arms behind my back, tears of agony rolling down my cheeks just as bile rushes up my throat from the pain of my leg making itself known again.

The pain becomes too much and when I see black dots dancing in the corner of my eyes, I welcome them and allow the darkness to consume me.

CHAPTER THIRTY-FOUR

Vivian

I groan as I slowly wake and pain immediately travels throughout my body. A small whimper escapes my lips as I slowly blink my eyes open. My head feels hazy and my mouth feels like it's filled with cotton balls. I look around the room and frown, the walls are all sterile white and I hear the beeping of a machine. I lull my head to the side and my eyes snap wide at the sight of the machines beside me. I try to move my hands so I can push myself up but freeze when I can't move them. I use my upper body strength to half sit up. I look side to side and begin to panic when I see both my wrists are handcuffed to the railings of the hospital bed I'm on.

I look around the room, it's bare except for the machines and two plastic chairs. I may not have been inside a lot of hospitals but I know something about this is off, this is not a standard sized room. I look down at my legs and my eyes widen further when I see my leg is elevated and resting on some pillows, my other one is covered by a blanket. I brace myself for the pain and attempt to wiggle my toes on my broken leg, the second I do I cry out in agony as pain shoots through me.

Hysteria works its way up my throat. I try to take some calming breaths and reason with myself that this isn't as bad it seems. Surely if Thomas and the others made it out of there and had me as a prisoner they wouldn't have wasted time performing surgery on my leg. Just as I begin to calm myself I hear voices and instantly my gaze flicks toward the closed door. I watch the handle with rapt attention. I inhale through my nose and exhale steadily as I wait with bated breath. When the handle turns, I hold myself still as the door opens. I don't know what I expected to see but it wasn't this. My eyes widen and the breath rushes out of me deflating my lungs in the span of a second.

The woman smiles at me as she enters the room, followed by two men in suits who both look like carbon copies of each other—short-cropped, army type haircut and dark eyes that look like they have been to hell and back—but it's the woman who commands the room. She oozes power and authority, the lady suit she wears only seems to enhance her image.

"Hello, Vivian, how are you feeling?' she asks in a monotone, it takes a moment for her words to sink in.

"Water," I croak out. She turns to one of the men who crosses the room again and ducks his head outside. A moment later he closes the door and walks toward me with a capped bottle of water and straw. He unscrews the lid and pops the straw in, then brings it to my lips. I guzzle the cool liquid greedily and don't stop until I start coughing. He removes the bottle as I flop back against the pillows.

"Now, we have a few questions for you—"

I cut her off before she can continue. "You're David's assistant," I rasp out. Cornelia smiles but it's not genuine.

"That was my cover," she says.

"Cover?" I hedge.

She sighs as if this conversation bores her. Fuck her, she can answer my questions before I answer any of hers. "Yes. My cover was Cornelia Gomez, David's assistant. My real name is Deputy Director Fiona Williams. I was Tracer Adams'—who you know as David—handler."

Tracer Adams.

Knowing that David wasn't his real name stings more than him being an undercover agent. Him being a fed isn't what hurts most, it's the fact he lied to me and didn't trust me enough with the truth.

I harden my features and glare at the bitch. "You're full of shit, you weren't his handler. I know the Director of the FBI and he is one of the Saints. Why don't you stop wasting both our time and just tell me what the fuck Thomas wants."

Her brows raise and a hint of a smile tugs at the corner of her mouth. "Who said I was FBI?"

"What Deputy Director Williams is trying to say is that only Special Agent Tracer was FBI." I look at the guy with the mole on his cheek and narrow my eyes. He sighs in annoyance and adds, "We are CIA."

I reel back in surprise. "But... I made a deal with the feds," I mutter.

The three of them nod. "Yes, and that deal has been passed onto us as this was our case not theirs," Fiona says.

"I don't understand," I admit.

"Tracer was a fed but the CIA was investigating the Director of the FBI. When you reached out to the head office, they offered you a deal which wasn't theirs to offer. The CIA has the lead on this case..." She lets her sentence trail off giving me time to process what she means. When it sinks in, I close my eyes as tears prick the backs of them.

I open my eyes and look at her with defeat. "My deal for immunity is off the table, they told me what I wanted to hear so I would flip on the Saints."

A somber look takes over her face. "Yes."

Pain lances my chest, I thought I did everything right. I made sure that my loved ones would be safe, they fucking promised me. I turn away from her and stare up at the ceiling resigned to my fate, I'll spend the rest of my life in prison. I fight back the tears that want to fall as failure courses through me, all of this shit was for fucking nothing.

"How long before I'm moved to the prison?" I force out.

"That depends on you, Mrs. Tempest." I slowly turn my head back toward her. She nods to both the men and they both leave the room. She doesn't say another word until the door is closed behind them. "What I am about to tell you is classified information." I nod stiffly encouraging her to continue. "The Director of the FBI wasn't our only target in the Saints. Tracer was planted inside the organization years ago when we learned of a gang—for lack of a better word—who were embezzling money. The deeper Tracer got he realized that the gang wasn't recruiting random people or men of wealth... They were recruiting, politicians, FBI agents, cops and many more high ranking members. Did you know that the President's press secretary is a member of the Saints?" My eyes widen and my jaw unhinges.

"Who?" She shakes her head and taps her nose at my question.

"That is on a need to know basis. There are more members of this society than you are aware of, which is why the feds hindered their deal on Thomas being apprehended alive."

"Because he's the only one who knows the full list of members," I answer, she nods and smiles.

"Tracer had been trying for years to get his hands on that

list but was never able to. The information you have provided is great but we need more, we need Thomas to flip and give us the names of the members he has planted all over the world."

"The world?" I balk.

She sighs and nods. "Yes. The Haven Saints is bigger than you clearly knew, which is why Thomas was doing everything in his power to regain control. Not all members are privy to the vast expanse of The Brotherhood from what we can gather, but the higher ranking members are remaining tight lipped."

I bristle. "Of course they are because they only care about their money."

Her eyes narrow and she looks at me with an accusing glare. "Well, I'm glad you brought that up because a lot of the members are refusing to say a word until *you* return their stolen money."

I furrow my brow in confusion. "I didn't take their money," I defend.

"The day Agent Adams went dark, all accounts linking to the Haven Saints were emptied. We have our best on the job trying to track the location of the millions stolen, but so far... we have nothing. Care to shed some light on that, Mrs. Tempest?"

I swallow and dart my tongue out to moisten my lips but then his words sound out in my mind.

All you set out to do has been done.

David—Tracer, he did it. I fight back the smile and close my eyes, sending up a silent thank you to my friend for finishing what I started. He gave his life for a cause he believed in and I'll be damned if I tarnish his memory by admitting to anything.

"I have no idea what happened." Her lips purse at my answer and I can tell she doesn't believe a word out of my mouth and I couldn't give a fuck. She can't prove shit, which is why she is here trying to get a confession out of me.

"Figured you would say that." I fight not to tense and keep my features impassive. "Here is how this going to work, you are going to remain in our custody—"

"You can't do that!" I shout.

A smug look overcomes her. "Yes, I can, actually. You see, the unit who was sent to extract you and Thomas Valerian doesn't exist. They are a black ops team that aren't on the books. No one knows where you are or if you are alive. We brought a few of the members here and the rest we kicked to the feds so they could take the spotlight for the bust."

"What the hell does that mean?" I snarl.

"It means, the CIA wants the highest ranking members, the feds only want the credit for performing a big bust."

"This is bullshit, my family won't stop looking for me."

"Oh, I'm sure your *boyfriends* will try but they won't find you."

"Fuck. You."

Her face contorts with anger. "Give us the location of the money and tell us the plans of the Saints and we might be inclined to make another deal."

I scoff. "I want my original deal."

"Not going to happen."

"Then good luck, Fiona. I wish you nothing but all the misery in the world, you heartless bitch."

"Listen to me, you little shit—"

"No! You listen to me. Twelve months ago I dethroned Thomas Valerian so my family and friends would be free of his tyranny. I sacrificed everything so they could live a good life. I knew about the FBI being members which was why I was so careful and only dealt with the one person because I didn't know who I could trust. All I tried to do was take down the Saints and end them so all the families forced to serve them would never have to again. They are a plague and I wanted them exterminated. I just wanted to be free," I whisper the last part.

"Then why not run with your brother and your boyfriends?" The judgment in which I can hear in her voice when she says boyfriends pisses me off.

"Because I knew Thomas would still come after us unless one of us ruled. Given the rules of The Brotherhood, I was the only one with the strongest claim so I gave up my life and freedom so they could have theirs."

"Why?"

I sigh. "Because, I was in love with my brother's best friends and wanted them to have a chance at a happy life even if it wasn't with me. I wanted my best friend to be free. I wanted my mother and brother to not have to worry or constantly look over their shoulders because of the choices my father made."

"You know about your father?"

I nod. "Yes, my brother still thinks he was a good man but he was just like the rest of them—"

"You're wrong."

"What?"

Fiona leans forward and smiles cunningly. "Your father was the one who appointed Tracer as the keeper of rules. Edmund and Virgil were the only two people inside the Haven Saints who knew Tracer Adams's true identity." I cover my mouth with my hand and stare at her with wide eyes, utterly floored at hearing this. "Your father and Virgil were trying to achieve the same goal as you, they wanted freedom but were taken out before they finished what they set out to do. I don't claim to understand them or what they went through, but Tracer made it clear in his reports that their names were to be cleared if this got out to the press and it has."

"Oh my God, my family?" I breathe out.

She rolls her eyes. "That part of your deal was honored." I

gape up at her. "Vox Hatchett, Ezekiel Tempest, Hayze Draven, Archer Malik and Nova Quinlin have all been sent back to Crestview Heights University and have full immunity. Your mother and your friends' parents have not been charged. Shane Draven and Henry Malik have been cleared of all charges as well."

Tears form in my eyes. "They're really free? Like for real this time?" I mumble.

She nods. "Yes. All of them have been cleared and their names will not make it to the press, they can all go on and live normal lives."

"What about... the Filthy Few?"

Her eyes harden. "Who?" she says in a suggestive tone, I clamp my mouth closed and nod.

"Thank you," I say, meaning it.

This time when she smiles it does reach her eyes. "I'll keep my word so long as they throw those masks away and never, and I do mean *never* wear them again or I will have them prosecuted. I'll make sure they get the fucking book thrown at them, am I clear?"

"Yes, ma'am."

"Don't be a wise ass, Vivian," she snaps.

"What happens now?" I ask.

"Now, you heal up and then you help us or we throw you in a jail that doesn't exist on any map where you will spend the rest of your days rotting away, where no one will find you." My brief moment of elation over my guys and Vox being spared is snuffed out.

"What if I don't have the information you need?" I ask.

"For your sake I hope you do, because there needs to be a fall guy and I assure it won't be Thomas." Dread pools in my stomach, when I made the deal with the feds to flip on the Saints, I never thought it would end like this. I just pray that I have the answers she needs so I can be set free to go after my guys if they will still have me.

"Ask me what you want to know. I'll tell you what I know but I swear, I have no idea what happened to the money from the Saints."

Lying to the head of the CIA is probably not a good idea, but I'll be damned if I lose everything I worked my ass off to give my guys.

CHAPTER THIRTY-FIVE

Hayze

Three weeks later...

Every day I wake up with this ache in my chest. It feels like a bullet has lodged itself inside me, every minute of every day I'm filled with pain. Every time I close my eyes all I see is her face, the way she looked at us that night was how I have always dreamed of her looking at me with nothing but love and devotion. Then, she ruined it when she went behind our backs and had Alexander and his fucking bitches drag us out of there.

When I woke up I tried to fight to get free but they had my hands and ankles bound. Ez and Archer were both bound like me in the back of the van. I've never felt so powerless in my life until that moment. Alex took us to Vox. The second he saw the three of us being lifted out of the back of the van... he knew.

He knew we failed him.

We promised him that we would save his twin and bring

her back to him but we didn't. When we argued last year and everyone went their own ways it was different. We all knew deep down that we would come back together after we had a chance to cool down, but not this time. The three of us stood there waiting for him to throw punches or scream and yell but he didn't do any of that.

It was much worse.

He didn't say a single word. A lone tear traveled down his cheek and the sight of that shit broke me. He turned his back, hopped in his car with Nova and left. On top of losing my girl, I lost my brother as well and this time we have no one to blame but ourselves. The fucking feds forced us out of Hollow Hills and threatened to arrest our families if we didn't return to CHU. None of us wanted to leave without her but we also couldn't let our families pay for our fuck up.

Every day the guys and I have tried to call Vox—he sends our calls to voicemail. Nova sends us updates on him but none of them are good. He tried to give up his place on the team but Dawson refused to allow it, the fucker wouldn't even let us. Our original thoughts about him seem to have been wrong, the guy comes round every afternoon and drops off tapes of previous games, food and he even invited us to his family's cabin for Thanksgiving. None of us agreed.

We've all been running on autopilot. We get up, train, go to class, train, come home and then do it all again the next day.

"Did you see how he blitzed them at the fifty yard line?" The sound of Dawson's voice pulls me from my inner thoughts. I look up at the TV and frown, I didn't even realize he had put a tape in of some of the games from last year. I look across at the room, both Ez and Archer are sitting on three seaters gazing out the window, lost in their own thoughts.

This is our life.

We are shells of the men we once were because without

her, we are nothing. We are empty. Soulless. She was our light and now that she isn't here, we have nothing to look forward to. Football doesn't even make me happy. The only plus side to practice is we get to see Vox. He doesn't glare or try to fight us, he just keeps his head down and stays silent. Even on the field, he doesn't utter a single word.

Dawson sighs when he looks over at the guys. I don't know what this dickhead's deal is or why he is even here and trying to be our friend. A knock sounds at the front door and I furrow my brow. Ez and Archer both look at me but I'm not moving to answer it, unless it's Vivian on the other side of that door, which I know it isn't because my body isn't on fire like it always is when she is near. Dawson grumbles and mutters something under his breath as he stands and goes to answer the door.

"Hello?"

"Hi, my name is Carmichael Lockery and I am the attorney for Mrs. Vivian Tempest—" At the mention of her name, the three of us are jumping over the sofas and running to the door. Dawson sees us coming and his eyes widen in surprise before he jumps out of the way. Carmichael looks frightened at the sight of us charging toward him.

"Where is she?" I snap. The guy jolts and opens his mouth but no words come out.

"Speak up!" Archer snaps.

"Where is my wife?" Ezekiel roars. The guy takes a step back and before I can rush him, Dawson cuts in front of us and raises his hands.

"How about you guys take it down a notch and invite Mr. Lockery inside so he can explain why he is here?" Dawson peers over his shoulder at the guy. He forces a nod and gulps.

"Y-yes," he stutters. Dawson nods then turns back to us.

"Guys, have a seat and I'll walk him in, huh?" Fucking beats me why we listen to the idiot but we all turn and storm back into the living room. The three of us claim the sofa and sit there, waiting for the other two. The second Dawson enters with the fucker he offers him a seat. I'm about to start screaming at the cunt soon if he doesn't start explaining why he is here! I can feel the tension wafting off the guys, we all want answers.

"Thank you for seeing me. We can begin as soon as Mr. Hatchett arrives," the fucker in a suit that doesn't fit him properly says.

"Vox?" Ez asks.

Carmichael nods. "Yes, this involves him as well and per Mrs. Tempest's instruction this must be read whilst he is present." The guys and I share a look just as the front door opens. In true Vox fashion, he saunters into the room with a hard look on his face, Nova trailing in behind him. He stops at the edge of the room and looks from us, then turns to Dawson and Carmichael. Nova interlaces his fingers with hers and I see him relax slightly. Envy rears its ugly head inside me.

"What the fuck is this?" Hearing Vox's voice after so long is like a balm to my battered spirit, call me crazy but just being around him at practice seems to ease some of the pain in my chest. In the brief moment he'll look at me, I see her in his eyes. They are twins and have the exact same shade of color. Knowing that he is her exact other half makes me feel closer to her and I know that's wrong and unhealthy but I am fucking breaking, I'm dying slowly without her. I'm not the only one, Archer and Ezekiel are exactly like me. They do nothing except try to search for her. We all reached out to Alexander and asked for Halo's help in tracking her.

After the threats we spewed at them I was sure they would tell us to get fucked, but Alex said he felt just as responsible for her going missing. She told him that she had made a deal with the feds and that she would be released in a day or two after giving her statement, but it's been three fucking weeks. Halo has had no luck in tracking her. He said she is being hidden. There was another option but we refused to believe that she was gone. We would fucking know if she was... I push that thought away and focus back on the man with the briefcase sitting on his lap.

"Would you please have a seat—"

Vox cuts Carmichael off. "No, you better start explaining why the fuck I was dragged here by my girlfriend—"

"He has something from Vivian," Ezekiel says. Vox snaps his head toward Ez so fast I'm surprised he didn't snap his neck.

"What?" he snaps.

"Just sit the fuck down so he'll explain!" Archer roars. I can see Vox wants to fight him but his curiosity is peaked, he wants to find her just as much as we do. Nova drags him over to the single seat and pushes him down. He tries to stand back up, so she does the only thing she can, she drops onto his lap, forcing him to remain where he is. Vox glares at Carmichael. To his credit the guy doesn't cower, he just opens his briefcase and pulls out an envelope that he places on top of the closed lid. Either he can't feel the six sets of eyes on him and the tension that is suffocating or he is ignoring it. He slowly peels the top open then proceeds to pull the contents out slower than a fucking snail. I'm not the only one getting pissed off. Vox, Ez and Hayze all look like they are about to jump out of their skin if this fucker doesn't hurry his ass up.

"Now, let me start by saying this isn't usual for me, I don't normally do this type of thing but given that David was a long-time friend—"

"Wait, David?" Archer cuts in.

Carmichael shoots him an annoyed look. "Please allow me to explain, then I will answer your questions. Like I was saying, David was a longtime friend of mine. I can't discuss all the details but a month ago he came to me with a package on behalf of Mrs. Tempest." My breath fucking stills at the mention of our girl.

"What did she give you?" Vox asks as he shifts forward in his seat, wrapping his arms around Nova's waist to secure her to him.

Carmichael shuffles through the papers until he finds the one he wants. "This is a letter from Mrs. Tempest." I look at Vox who is staring at me with wide eyes. The room is eerily silent and filled with anticipation as we all hope this letter will give us answers and a clue to where she might be. "I'll begin reading it now."

If you have this letter, then I guess things didn't go to plan.

I know you guys are all probably angry and hurt over the choices I made.

I'm sorry.

I never meant to hurt any of you, especially my guys.

I hope I get the chance to tell you to your faces but I fucking love you three.

That's right, I love you.

I just hope if this letter does reach you that I somehow survived the fall out. Carmichael is a friend of David's who has been instructed to deliver these documents to you all if I don't make contact with him by the Night Of The Saints.

Please don't hate me or be angry. I did all of this so we could have a better life and be free of the Saints. I never wanted to lie to any of you or hide things but it was safer for you all if you didn't know the truth.

This is a long letter so listen closely.

Vox, my twin, my big brother, my best friend. I love you. I'm so sorry I hurt you by not telling you what I had planned and marrying Ez behind your back. I love him, Vox, and I love Hayze and Archer as well. Please don't take out your anger on them, they need you! You are the last piece of me they will have. Look after Mom and tell her that I love her, make sure she knows I'm so grateful for everything she did for us and loving us the way she did. Being away from her all this time has been harder than I thought possible. Make sure you look after her.

Nova, thank you for being my best friend and loving my brother. Thank you for making him happy and showing him that he is worthy of love. I'm so sorry for your loss, sweetheart. Your mother was an amazing woman and I am truly sorry if my plan was the reason her life was cut short, I will forever live with that guilt.

My guys, the loves of my life, my happy ending. God, I wish I was with you three, I want to be there right now holding you and seeing the looks on each of your faces as you hear me tell you I love you. I never thought I would ever be lucky enough to find a man who loves me and I wasn't lucky, I was blessed because I got three. Thank you. Call me crazy but knowing the three of you had my back and loved me even when you could have thought the worst of me means more than you will ever know. I won't say to move on and be happy because it would be a lie. I do want you to be happy but I don't want your happiness to be because of another woman. When you hear the next part, please keep an open mind as all the lies I have told have been for this reason, I did all of this for you. For a chance at a life with you three, I could write so much more and I want to but words will never be enough to express the connection I feel with each of you. You guys gave me a happiness I never thought I would experience and for that, I will go into the next life smiling because of you three.

I love you all with all my heart, never doubt that.

A pain I have never felt before blooms inside my chest and robs me of air, I feel my eyes prick with tears and I fight those fuckers back. I never thought I would be the type of guy who cries over a girl, yet here I sit using every ounce of strength I have not to let my brothers see me cry.

"I will now read you the instructions from Mrs. Tempest." We all nod, none of us able to speak or even utter a simple grunt. "All rights and ownership of my company *Ezy A* is to be disclosed to Ezekiel, Vox, Hayze and Archer."

My brows slam together. "What company?" I ask.

Carmichael smiles sadly. "Mrs Tempest opened a company under the name of Ezy A two years ago." I reel back.

"You got that wrong, she didn't own any company two years ago," Archer snaps.

"I have it in writing, Mr. Malik, the company was opened by Vivian Hatchett but she was never the owner." We all share a confused look. Up until a year ago, Vivian had never done anything without us knowing, this can't be right. We would know if she started a company, right?

"He's right." We all turn to Nova.

"What the fuck do you know about this, witch?" Vox growls at his girl.

Nova ignores the bite in his tone and looks to the three of us with a soft smile. "I found out about Ezy A when I was with her in Hollow Hills. She didn't need to say anything, I knew what the name stood for which then made everything else she was doing make sense."

"What does it stand for?" Ez asks.

"Ezy stands for Ezekiel and Hayze and the A is pretty clear," she says smugly.

"Archer," the man himself mutters.

"Vivian didn't do what she did on a whim, she had this planned for years. She was a lot smarter than anyone gave her credit for," Nova says.

"The owners of the company are Ezekiel Tempest, Archer Malik, Vox Hatchett and Hayze Draven," Carmichael announces. "All of the assets of the company are yours to do with as you please. She has left instructions and notes on everything she has done and has planned for you all to follow. I will leave these documents with you all to read over and do with as you please. I'll see myself out." He places the papers on the small table in the center of the room and stands.

"I'll walk you out," Dawson says, then turns to us. "I'll catch you guys later." We nod but don't say anything. When the door clicks shut Nova jumps off Vox's lap and drops to her knees beside the small table and rummages through the paperwork. The guys and I all remain silent, mulling over everything we have just learned. My mind is reeling but guilt is eating at me.

"She planned to give herself up to save us years ago," Ezekiel mumbles with hurt thick in his tone.

"How did we not see this?" Archer asks no one in particular.

"Because we were all too caught up in our own lives. She saw everything we couldn't because we were too stubborn to admit that we had no idea what we were doing, but my sister did. She knew it had to be her that ended this. My little sister was better than all of us. She didn't need to kill, torture or lie to defeat the Saints, she just had to be her." Vox's tone is riddled with remorse.

"You evil genius, Vivi!" Nova exclaims, drawing all our attention to her.

"What did you find, witch?" Vox asks as he slides further forward in his seat, trying to see the paper Nova is holding.

"You guys are right. Vivian did plan all of this out long ago," she says in a faraway tone as she continues to read.

"Nova, explain what you mean... please," Ezekiel forces out through clenched teeth.

Nova looks up at her brother with a proud smile on her face. "Ez, she meant it when she said she did *everything* for you guys. Everything she built, the hotel, the investments she made, they are all owned by you guys."

CHAPTER THIRTY-SIX

Archer

I can't even explain how I am feeling right now. On top of the pain I feel over not having her here, I now feel like a failure—we all failed her. While we were all playing hero and trying to take down the Saints as fast as possible, she was playing the long game. She saw through our flaws and concocted a plan of her own. She beat us all at a game we had no idea she was playing.

"The four of you own *Lividica*." My jaw unhinges.

"The sex club?" I blurt.

"I think what you mean to say is, your million dollar hotel that is currently being expanded to four other locations. Vivian has gifted you all financial freedom, she has set you all up for the rest of your lives," Nova says in wonder.

"How did she fund the build?" Hayze mumbles.

Nova continues to read over the stack of papers and we all sit here watching her facial features change from pride to mirth and then pure smugness. "She took a leaf out of their book. She embezzled the money from the Saints. She had the money run through an offshore account that is owned by a shell company then paid Ezy A for a service so the hotel build was funded by..." She lifts her head and looks between the four of us. "All of you. She found a way to funnel all the money from the Saints so they would never be able to rebuild and gave it all to you guys. The way she has done this makes it so nothing will track back to any of you guys. The FBI and anyone else that tries to come for the money won't be able to find it without these documents. Vivian was the trojan horse they never saw coming." The pride in which she speaks is clear as day, Nova is in awe of Vivi. Which makes me feel like shit. I never once gave a thought to my girl as I was wearing that mask and off doing things I shouldn't have been doing because I wanted to be free of the noose around my neck.

"Wait a second." We all turn to Ez, who scoots forward and drapes his forearms over his thighs while looking at his sister. "She bankrupted the Saints?" Nova nods, then Ezekiel smiles so fucking wide, displaying all of his teeth. The fucker could pose for a Colgate commercial.

"Why the fuck are you grinning like an idiot?" Hayze asks.

"Because my sister just destroyed not only the Saints but every fucker in The Brotherhood." Vox is puffing out his chest like he just won the championship game.

"And...?" I push, getting pissed off that Hayze and I seem to be the only ones not grasping what the fuck is going on.

"The Saints can never rebuild because they don't have the funding. All the members are now broke... every single one of them. On top of their names being blasted in the press, none of them will be able to afford a lawyer. They will be represented by public defenders and will be buried by the prosecution. They are all going to jail because Vivian was brave enough to do what she did. She saved us all," Nova says wistfully. I hang my head in shame, she should never have had to sacrifice herself for us.

"Those papers don't happen to mention where she is, do they?" Hayze asks with hope in his voice. Nova shoots him a sad look and shakes her head.

"No. I wish they did," she says quietly.

"Where the fuck is she?" Vox questions aloud. "I would know if something happened to her, I'd feel it or I would just know or something! She's fucking alive!" he roars. Nova abandons the papers and rushes to him, straddles his lap and cups his face between her hands, forcing him to meet her eyes.

"She's out there, we just need to find her. She is way too fucking smart to die. Thomas is missing as well. So are a few other high ranking members of the Saints." Vox grips her waist. Nova stills and that's when we know she is hiding something. Her eyes keep darting between us as if she has just realized she's said too much.

"How do you know that?" Vox's voice is thick with accusation but there's also heat.

"I-I mean..."

"What the fuck do you know, sister?" Ez snaps. Vox peers around his girl and shoots Ezekiel a scowl which he ignores. Nova twists on Vox's lap and looks at her brother.

"I hired Vance, Terry and Phil to help us. I know they are just lawyers but given that they will have access to the upcoming cases, I thought they would be able to help. Plus, Alexander is bringing in more people to help us look for her." At the mention of her and Alexander being on speaking terms, Vox's face turns a shade of red. His eyes are spitting fire and promise punishment, Nova is going to get her ass spanked for that revelation. Vox ignores all our protests for more information when he grips her waist and turns her so she is facing him.

He may be a sinister motherfucker and can kill a man with his bare hands, but Nova is his kryptonite. To hurt her would be to hurt himself, which is why Ez will never try to keep his best friend away from his sister, we all know Vox will die for Nova without batting an eye. He showed us how much she means to him when he went after her and left us to go after Vivian.

"Witch." He purrs her name but everyone knows he is using the allure of sex to get her to talk. "You've been keeping secrets from me and talking to guys behind my back, you know how I feel about that shit, don't you?" The fact he is remaining calm and not fucking the answers out of her shows me he has matured and is finally learning how to use his words. I will admit though, the raw sexual tension wafting off them like a perfume has me wishing my girl was here and sitting on my lap like that.

"Vox..."

"Shhh, witch, unless you plan to share your secrets with the rest of the class, your mouth will be used for something else." The innuendo is clear.

"I'll fucking knock your ass out, Hatchett," Ezekiel seethes but the couple just ignore his threat.

Nova squirms in his lap and it's obvious she is close to breaking, Vox just needs to push a bit harder. We're all waiting with bated breath for her to give us something, just a fucking crumb of information.

I need hope.

I never thought I would be the guy that chases a girl but Vivian isn't just any girl, she's the *one*. She is my ending, she's my cure to an addiction I didn't know I had.

"Alex thinks he knows where she is," she blurts out. Unlike the movies, no one begins shouting or demanding answers, we all remain still and silent waiting for her to continue. "Halo hacked into the Pentagon and I also asked Dawson if he could get his aunt Katie to help hack the FBI and CIA database to see if there was any record of her."

"And what did they find?" Vox's tone betrays his calm exterior, he's hanging onto his patience by a thread like the three of us.

"They think she is being held at a black sight but the problem is, there is no location for any of the black sights, so Halo and Katie are running a tracking program to sift through the agencies."

"What will that do, Nova?" Hayze asks.

"We're hoping one of them will lead us to Vivian," she answers.

"So, the feds have her?" I breathe out, feeling an intense sensation wash over me. I've seen enough movies to know that those black sites don't operate within the law. They could be doing anything to her and there is not a fucking thing we can do about it.

We're useless to her.

"We don't know that for sure. There is no arrest record for her, Thomas or any of the other members that have gone missing," she says with a hint of guilt in her tone.

"What about Tate?" Ez asks. "She was with Vivi, we all saw her in the photo."

Nova purses her lips and thinks for a second before shaking her head. "I don't know, I'll ask Halo to look into it."

"You and that fucker buddies now, huh?" Vox grits out.

"Halo is nice, it isn't like that, dick bag. Him and his boss are trying to help me find my best friend. I won't lose someone else I care about, Vox, I can't." Vox wraps his arms around her and pulls her flush against him.

"We have to tell my mom, witch. She has been going

through hell trying to find my sister." Nova melts at his words and nods.

"I didn't want to say anything and give you all false hope. I'm sorry." A whoosh of air escapes me at her declaration. I get her reasoning, I do, but it doesn't make it any easier to swallow the bitter fucking pill.

"I want in on the search," I announce.

"Me too," Hayze says.

"We're all going to help The Butcher and his crew. That's our girl and I'll be damned if I sit back and wait for someone else to fucking find her," Ez declares.

"We'll all help," Vox states. "Call him, witch."

CHAPTER THIRTY-SEVEN

Vivian

The weather has turned and now the sun hardly chases the chill from my bones. I've been here for ten weeks. Christmas is in four days and it fucking hurts to know that I won't be there to spend it with my guys or my family. Fiona is a fucking bitch and refuses to allow me to leave even though I have told her everything. Thomas squealed weeks ago, the second they started interrogating him he folded so he wouldn't get the death penalty. Unlike the other members, he isn't being sent to a prison where he'll get visitors, he's going to Panama where he'll spend the rest of his life rotting in a prison that is ruled by the inmates. Fiona says the guards are only there to make sure the inmates don't escape, other than that they never enter the prison they just stand outside and shoot whoever tries to escape.

Have I been treated badly while I've been here? No.

Do I have freedom to roam the halls? No.

What they have done though means a lot, they brought me a cream colored urn that contains David—Tracer's ashes. Fiona said he didn't have any family and she thought he would want me to be the one to have them. I suddenly realize how Nova feels now, the person you cared for so much is nothing but a jar. This is what their life has amounted to, being burnt to a crisp and stuffed into a jar that will rest on a mantle.

Mike, one of the guys who first came to me with Fiona when I got here, has been giving me updates on my family and the guys. They are all at CHU, playing football and going to class like regular college students. Mike said there has been no sign of them wearing the masks which is good. I'll miss the masks but their freedom means so much more. Mike managed to sneak me some photos of Ez, Hayze and Arch and I sleep with them under my pillow every night. It's not the same as feeling their skin on mine but at least I have something to look at while I'm stuck in this prison cell every day.

The door opens but I don't look up from my journal, Fiona brought it to me a few days after I woke. When I'm not doing physio on my leg, I write all day long. I've managed to formulate a code for bookkeeping, it needs more tweaks but I think this thing would help a lot of businesses to keep track of their expenses and profits.

"Your friends don't quit, do they?" I ignore Fiona as I continue to work on my code. She likes to come here every day and taunt me. I know she doesn't believe me when I tell her I have no idea where all the money went. "Did you know they hacked into the CIA's server trying to find you?" I bite the inside of my cheek to keep from smiling, they didn't give up on me. "Thomas was transported to Panama last night."

"Good," I bite out.

"He wasn't alone." I lift my gaze to her finally. She leans against the wall next to the open door which is odd in itself.

She always closes it behind herself when she comes in. Her arms are crossed over her chest. I raise my brow prompting her to continue. "Drew, Paul, Smith, Enders, Toby and Wayde will keep him company." My brows hit my hairline in surprise.

"What did the six others do?" I rasp out.

Her face hardens. "They helped track down the other members that Thomas had planted, there were a lot more than we thought." Her tone is ominous. "They had Saints planted in the fucking King's guard! Those bastards were planning..." She clamps her mouth closed and shakes her head, clearly she has said too much and honestly, the less I know the better so I keep my curiosity in check and remain silent. "You ever gonna tell me what happened to the money?" She tries to sound casual but fails.

"I thought you said David listed everything in his report?" I know she only said that to scare me but if it was true, I would have been in handcuffs and sent to prison for embezzlement weeks ago.

A small smile tugs at the corner of her mouth. "You're not what meets the eye, are you, Vivian?" Surprise thrums inside me, that's the closest thing she has ever said to a compliment.

"I wish I could say the same about you but that would be a lie. You look like a bitch and your personality matches it." Instead of storming out of here like she normally does, she actually smiles, like a real one and nods her head in approval which just floors me.

"I didn't get to where I am by sucking dick. In an industry dominated by men I had to become this bitch so I could rise. I admire you, Vivian." I splutter and gape at her.

"You what?" I squeak out.

"I admire you."

"Why?"

"You did what you had to in order to save the ones you love.

You became the first lordess in the history of the Haven Saints. You did what no other woman has ever done, you led a brotherhood and took them down from the inside. I may not be able to prove that you were the one to bankrupt them and clearly Tracer knew the truth and still wouldn't give you up. It's because of the respect I had for Tracer Adams that I am going to trust his judgment of you and close this case."

I leap off my bed and stand. I stare at her with my heart pounding inside my chest. I try to keep hope from rising inside me but it's futile. "What are you saying, Fiona?"

"You will have a tail on you, we'll always be watching you, Vivian. If you so much as steal a candy bar I'll cuff your ass so fucking fast your head will spin."

"Are you letting me go?" I say barely above a whisper.

She purses her lips. "Stay away from any ex-members of the Saints. If you ever try to reconstruct the Saints, I will push for the death penalty."

"Fuck the Saints, they can all rot in hell," I snarl.

"Good answer, now get your shit together. You leave in twenty minutes." She turns ready to leave but pauses in the doorway. She looks back at me over her shoulder. "You know what Tracer said in his report?"

I shake my head. "No."

"He admitted that he might be compromised because he loves the Lordess of the Haven Saints like a daughter and didn't think he could slap the cuffs on you when the time came." Tears gather in my eyes. "Tracer Adams was one of the coldest sons of bitches I have ever known and never cared for anyone or anything except for his job. You gave him a chance to experience what it's like to love and for that you should be proud. Have a good life, Vivian. I hope I never see you again."

I snort. "The feeling is mutual, Fiona, trust me," I call after her, the fact she has left the door open has tears spilling, I'm free. The only thing I am taking with me is my urn filled with Tracer's ashes.

I'm going home!

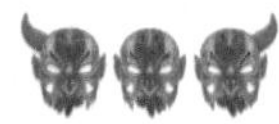

I'VE BEEN BLINDFOLDED since the moment Mike came to get me and escort me out of wherever the hell I have been staying. The entire car ride I wasn't allowed to look, even when I was led onto the plane. So I've kept my eyes closed and tried to quiet the war inside me.

Will they be happy to see me?

Will they be mad?

What if they don't feel the same?

All those types of thoughts have been plaguing me and I can't stop the fucking nerves from taking control. My palms are sweaty and my knees are weak, my leg is aching from not being able to move around but the pain is nothing like what it was when I first started healing. The doctor Fiona had, told me that it will take a while before I don't walk with a limp which makes me feel insecure. I know it's stupid and will go away after some time, but it is what it is.

Another thing that has been bothering me is knowing that the guys would have been served the papers about Ezy A. They know the truth now. Will they hate me for what I did? I really fucking hope not because I only wanted to help them and with everything I managed to do while I was leading the Saints, it would set them all up for life.

I hope they will let me be a part of that life.

"You can take it off," Mike says as the plane touches down. I push the blindfold up and slowly blink my eyes open, adjusting to the sudden blindness from the light. I press my face against the window and gasp at the sight of the airport.

"Holy shit, you brought me here?" I breathe out.

"Their last game is tonight before they all go on break for Christmas. I thought you would want to be there." I turn away from the window and shoot Mike a grateful smile. Having him with me made being stuck there for months bearable. He has been a friend to me and I hope he knows that I will always be grateful for the care and compassion he showed me.

When we disembark there is a car waiting for us. I take a step toward it but freeze at Mike's words. "Stay out of trouble, girl." I turn away and frown at him, he's still standing on the stairs of the plane.

"You're not coming with me, are you?" I ask.

He smiles sadly and shakes his head. "This is the end of the road for me, kid. That car will take you to CHU." I race back up the stairs and throw my arms around Mike. He stands there stiff for a second, then finally gives in and returns my hug.

"Thank you, Mike," I whisper.

"Get out of here, kid," he says. I pull back and smile up at him one last time, then race down the stairs toward the car.

The entire car ride I can't seem to control my excitement or my freaking libido, the thought of seeing them again and being able to touch them, hold them and just breathe them in is exhilarating! I know I should probably stop and buy a phone to call my mom, but my need to see my guys is so overpowering that I know I won't be able to do anything until I set my eyes on them. The drive takes longer than I wanted, thanks to an accident on the freeway. When the driver finally pulls into the parking lot, I shout my thanks, then jump out. The place is packed and I can hear the roar of the crowd. I curse beneath my breath, there's only like five minutes left of the game. I take off toward the entrance and run through ignoring the girl shouting out that I need to pay.

I don't stop until I'm gripping the railing. I can see the

teams on the field. I scan my gaze over the CHU team, trying to spot my guys. I lean over the railing to try to get a look at the bench but I don't see them, panic begins to build inside me.

"Vivian?" I whirl around and come face to face with Dawson.

"Hey," I rush out then turn back toward the game. The QB snatches the pass, then that's when it hits me, Dawson is the QB and so is Vox. But, if he is here and that guy isn't my brother, where the fuck are they? I whirl around to face Dawson who is smiling wide.

"Looking for three specific guys?"

I chuckle and nod. "Yeah. Why aren't you out on the field and who is the new QB?"

Dawson grins. "Technically, he's the old QB."

I cock my head to the side in confusion. "Huh?"

"Your guys and your brother aren't here."

"Oh my God, did they get dropped from the team?"

He shakes his head. "No, this game is to... settle old scores, so to speak. The Quarterback out there is my Uncle Corvin, my dad and other uncles are out there as well."

I jerk back in surprise. "Why?"

He sighs and scrubs a hand down his face like this isn't something new for him. "My Uncle Saint likes to run his mouth and then settle the score on the field. Knowing him, my uncles and Dad can shut down any other team. This game is for their pride, nothing more." I roll my lips over my teeth to keep from smiling. Dawson rolls his eyes.

"Any chance you know where my guys are?" I hedge.

He smiles and nods. "Come on, I'll give you a ride."

"Oh, you don't have to—"

He cuts me off before I can finish. "Trust me, you are saving me from having to listen to my dad and uncles talking shit about how they could beat me and my team's ass." This time I can't help but laugh. Dawson playfully glares, then leads me out of there with a hand on my back. Neither of us speak until we climb inside his car. I don't realize I'm shivering until he turns the heat on.

"Thank you," I force out, trying not to let my nerves overcome me.

"Don't be nervous."

"I'm not," I fire back.

He gives me the side eye as he drives. "You're bouncing in your seat."

I instantly stop and tuck my hands between my legs to keep from fidgeting. "Where are they?"

"Packing," he answers.

"For what?" I push.

"Your guys and your brother and Nova are coming up to my family's cabin for Christmas. I believe your mom and the guys' families are coming as well."

"Oh," is all I can manage to say, I have no right to feel left out.

"They didn't want to go, Vivian. I practically forced them and blackmailed them by telling them that your guys' families needed to take their mind off everything. They relented."

"Okay," I mutter.

"We're all heading there tomorrow." I smile and nod, unable to form words. They were going to leave me behind. "No they weren't."

I snap my head toward him. "Huh?"

"You said that out loud."

"Oh."

"They made sure that my Aunt Katie would be taking her laptop and that the search for you wouldn't stop while we were all away. I may have also used the excuse of them being able to watch Aunt Katie work to twist their arms into coming as well."

"Why are you doing all of this?" I ask as he pulls his car over to the curb, just outside the guy's house.

"Because my family went through something similar, different circumstances but still the same. I get what it feels like to feel trapped and I wanted to help. Plus, I actually like them."

"You mean, you like them because they want nothing from you and you think you may have finally found some friends that won't use you for your last name?" His face loses all trace of humor.

"Yeah, it's nice to know that not everyone wants to know me because my last name is Dawson." I reach across and place my hand on his, giving it a gentle squeeze.

"Thank you, Dawson, I'm happy I get to call you a friend."

"Me too, Vivian. Now, get out of here before those three realize you're out front and beat the snot out of me for you being in my car." I can't help the laughter that bubbles out of me. Dawson has helped lighten some of the tension coursing through me without even knowing it.

Ready or not, here I come.

CHAPTER THIRTY-EIGHT

Ezekiel

Hayze and Archer are sprawled out on the sofa watching the game, CHU Elite against the Sharks. I shake my head when Corvin Williams throws a long ball to Darius Lockhart who scores the touchdown. The Sharks team is out of breath and practically dying. The CHU team has run over them with ease. I flip the steaks in the skillet just as there is a knock at the door.

"One of you two idiots gonna get that?" I snap. Both of them shoot me the bird over their heads, fucking dicks. I turn the pan off and stomp toward the door. Who the fuck would come here, Vox and Nova wouldn't knock. Which leaves Dawson but I know he's at the game so... who the fuck is it?

I yank the door open ready to tell whoever it is to fuck off but the words die in my throat when I see who it is. Her black hair is loose and frames her angelic face, her blue eyes stare up at me with unshed tears in them. The big coat she wears hides her luscious curves from me. I just stand here staring at her at a loss for words and praying to fucking God this isn't some sort of sick dream and I'll wake up feeling empty inside like I do every day.

"Hi," she says quietly. The sound of her timid voice spears me, her bottom lip begins to tremble when I say nothing. "Forgive me—" I launch forward, grab her face between my hands and smash my lips to hers, swallowing her moans as she grips my wrists, clinging to me like she is as afraid as I am that she will disappear. Our tongues tangle, her taste invades my senses and I groan at the familiarity of it.

"Dude, what the actual fuck!" Hayze roars from behind me. I pull back and stare down at her, my body is shielding her from his eyesight.

"I'll break your fucking jaw for hurting Vivian," Archer vows. I smile down at her, she beams back at me and gives me a slight nod to step aside but I don't move even when I hear those fuckers charging toward us. Just before they reach us she speaks, forcing them to a standstill.

"I'd be hurt if he didn't kiss me." It takes them a fraction of a second before they are shoving me out of the way and standing in front of her, both with looks of awe and wonder. I get it, they are trying to convince themselves this isn't a dream like me and she is really here. I help them out by slipping in behind her and wrapping my arms around her. She melts against me.

"Bet you wished you fuckers answered the door now, huh?" I tease. Hayze is the first to snap out of it. He reaches out, grabs the back of her head, and then leans down, resting his forehead against hers. She cups his face between her tiny hands. Tears scale down her cheeks and its only now I realize that this must have been just as hard for her as it was for us.

"I love you, Vivi baby," Hayze whispers.

"I love you too," she chokes out, then seals her lips to his.

The sight brings a smile to my face. Before Hayze has a chance to deepen the kiss, Archer shoulders him out of the way, drawing a gasp from Vivian. Archer just stands there breathing hard as he looks at her. I feel her stiffen and tighten my hold, reminding her that I am right here and she isn't alone.

"You never, and I mean fucking never, sacrifice yourself for us again, am I clear?" he growls. Hayze shoots him a scathing look, telling him to reign in his temper, but Archer ignores him.

"No." My eyes widen at her reply. "I'll do it all over a-fuck-ing-gain if it means the three of you get to be free. Now, am I clear?" I bite my bottom lip to keep from smiling, our baby has claws and I fucking love when she uses them. "Are you going to kiss me or just stand there brooding?" Archer doesn't need to be told twice, in an instant he has lips sealed to hers. I cut a glance to Hayze to gauge his reaction and find him smiling. It brings us all happiness to see her happy but not only that, just knowing that we are all in love with her and will do anything to protect her makes everything work.

"Okay, fucker, let's take this inside because my balls are freezing," Hayze bites out. Vivi breaks the kiss then turns to Hayze.

"I can help warm them." The three of us practically fall over our own fucking feet like idiots as we shove her inside the house, lock the door and then Archer is dragging her into the living room. She pulls free of his hold for a second and pulls... an urn out of her pocket and places it on the counter. Hayze switches the TV off and I draw the blinds closed, while Archer drags her the remainder of the way, choosing not to ask about the urn and forces her to her knees. Hayze and I both come to stand beside Archer. Vivian looks at each of us with a hungry look in those beautiful blue eyes.

"You're about to get punished. Choose a safe word, baby,

because you're gonna need it." Her eyes widen to the size of dinner plates at Archer's decree.

"Hospital?" she says, the three of us nod, that one works.

"Mouth open," Hayze barks.

"Hands behind your back.," I order. She does as she is told. The three of us push our pants down our legs and it's no fucking surprise that we are all hard, it's been fucking months since we have been inside of her and I know none of us will last long. She runs her eyes over all our cocks, then swallows audibly.

"Suck them," Archer demands.

"Can I use my hands?" she asks.

"Fuck, yes," Hayze answers. She doesn't tease or try to make any of us beg, she needs this as much as we all do. Her lips wrap around Archer's cock while her hands grip mine and Hayze's, then begin pumping. My head falls back as a groan escapes me.

"Fuck!" Archer shouts. Vivian alternates between sucking each of us off and fuck me the feeling of her hot wet mouth wrapped around me is a feeling I will never be able to replicate. The sound of her slurping and gagging around each of us is euphoric and has me getting fucking hot.

I need to taste her.

I tangle my fingers in her hair and yank her head back. She whimpers from the loss of my dick in her mouth. I gently tug her to her feet by her hair, then release her as Archer and Hayze both take over and undress her. Arch drops to his knees in front of her as Hayze gets rid of the coat and peels her long-sleeve top over her head. Fuck, I can see her nipples poking through her pink bra. Archer peels her jeans down her legs to display a matching pink thong. The fact she is wearing a matching set tells us all she was the one who decided she was getting fucked tonight, not us.

My eyes glide down her perfect body as Hayze starts licking and sucking on her neck, drawing a moan from her. Archer tosses her jeans to the side and sees the same thing I do, the pink scar on her leg from where that cunt broke it.

"Hey?' she says, pulling both mine and Archer's attention to her. Hayze unclasps her bra and lets her tits free. "I'm okay," she says, trying to reassure us. Archer shakes his head trying to shake away the evil thoughts. She can see we both aren't relaxing so she grips the waistband of her thong and pushes it down her legs, instantly we're both distracted from our dark thoughts at the sight of her perfect pink pussy that is already glistening with need.

"You're beautiful," Arch rasps out. A shy smile crests her face. Hayze steps behind her, then reaches around and cups her full tits in his hands, twirling her nipples. She flings her head back against his chest and cries out.

"She's perfect," Hayze agrees.

"She was made for us," I add just as Archer swipes his tongue through her folds. Vivian jerks in Hayze's hold. I grip my dick and pump slowly, watching my girl as Archer eats her cunt. Her cries grow louder and louder until she is screaming out her release, clearly we aren't the only ones who can't last tonight.

"I need you all," she breathes out. Hayze releases her and takes off down the hallway to get the lube no doubt. I shift around them and sit down on the sofa.

"Sit on my cock, baby," I order. Vivian's pupils dilate, then eagerly does as I instruct and climbs onto my lap. I line myself up with her entrance and then she slowly slides down onto me. Both of us moan—fuck, I can feel my balls already tightening and the instant I'm balls deep in her she flops forward.

"Fuck, you feel so good inside me," she purrs as Hayze comes up behind her, squirting lube onto his dick. I twist so I am lying flat on my back with her on top of me to give Hayze room. He rubs the globes of her ass causing her to jerk, which sends shockwaves of pleasure through me. When he parts her cheeks and begins lubing her up, Archer moves to the top of our heads. Vivian shifts forward and opens her mouth, ready to take him. Archer wastes no time in fucking her mouth. Hayze shifts into position and I wait for him to get situated. I feel it the second he pushes through her tight muscle wall, her pussy clamps down on my cock and she moans on Archer's cock.

"Good girl, baby, take their cocks like that while you choke on mine." Either it's Hayze's dick in her ass or Archer's words that turn her on more because I can feel her growing slicker. I reach up between us and twist her nipples. She bucks and cries out. Hayze practically fucking roars when he gets inside her. Vivian begins moaning and taking control from all of us. She has her hand wrapped around Archer's cock pumping him in time with her thrusts.

Fuck, we're all here for the ride now.

"Shit, Vivi baby, like that," Hayze praises when she slams down onto us.

"Oh my God, I love your cocks," she moans.

"Get your fucking mouth back on my dick, I want to come down your throat," Archer demands. Vivian obeys without complaint as Hayze and I back off slightly, letting her do her thing. Her head bobs up and down faster, trying to keep up with Archer's thrusts. "Fuck, swallow every drop, baby," Archer grits out a second before he's coming with her name being shouted. Vivian swallows every last drop of his cum before she releases him. Arch bends down and kisses her, then steps back. Unable to remain still any longer, I push her back so she is flush against Hayze who wraps an arm around her middle, securing her to him as I thrust up inside her.

A scream tears from her as I continue to fuck her. "You like that, baby?" Hayze forces out through clenched teeth as he matches the intensity of my pace, Vivian's eyes are glazed over. I can feel her pussy clamping down on my dick and know she is nearly ready to come again. "Yes, like that, baby, I'm gonna fill this pussy with my cum."

"Oh my God, yes. Please, don't stop!"

I grind my teeth and stave off my pending orgasm, needing to feel her come before I empty myself inside her.

"Vivian!" Hayze roars as he comes.

"Fuck yes!" Vivian screams as her own orgasm tears through her. I fall over the cliff with her, fucking stars dance in my eyes as I empty everything I have inside her, marking her as mine. Knowing that the three of us have filled every hole has me wanting to beat my fists against my chest and tell the whole fucking world that Vivian Tempest is ours.

She is ours, now and forever.

"Oh my God, that was fucking amazing," she pants out. Hayze smiles and places a kiss on her cheek.

"That was just round one, baby," he purrs.

Her eyes widen as she looks down at me. I shoot her a wink and nod. "I hope you slept on the way here, baby," I coo.

"Get over here, head down ass up, baby. My turn to fill that pussy up," Archer orders from his spot on the rug beside us. Vivian can try as she might to look like she doesn't want to move and obey Arch but her pussy betrays her, I can feel her pulsing and clamping down on me trying to milk my cock for another orgasm.

"Go please your man, baby," I say. Her eyes blaze with lust and that one look has my dick growing hard inside her again.

CHAPTER THIRTY-NINE

I've slept most of the drive to Dawson's family cabin. Archer sat in the back with me and told me to lay my head on his lap and sleep, so I did. I barely got a wink of shut eye last night. Just when I thought they were finally done with me, one of them would want to fuck again which just forced the other two to match his stamina. The sweetest moments were when the three of them would fuck me hard and rough but whisper words of admiration and love in my ear. I can still feel the ghost of each of them inside me. It's been a long time since I have felt this content and I'll be damned if I ever let anything get in the way of me being with them ever again.

They made me promise to never push them away again last night and I wept. I swore that there is nothing on this earth that would ever take me away from them again. I could tell that my words eased some of their worries, but I know it will take time for them to believe me fully, which is fine. I plan to spend every day of the rest of my life showing them how fucking much I love them and that I'm not going anywhere. I told them about the urn and how it contains David's ashes. I expected them to tease me or something but all they did was say how sorry they are for my loss and placed the urn on the mantle in the living room.

"Holy shit, Dawson is loaded," Hayze mutters. I sit up and try to shift toward the other side of the car but Archer wraps an arm around my waist and tucks me into his side. I sigh, trying to act bothered but the deadpan look he gives me tells me he knows I'm full of shit. I chuckle and snuggle into his side as I stare out his window.

My jaw unhinges!

When Dawson said cabin, I pictured a small, weathered log cabin in the mountains with barely any space, but what I see before us is a fucking lodge. The place is huge! Like I mean it has huge A-frame windows, allowing you to see the beautiful mountains that surround you. Downstairs all you see are windows allowing the natural sunlight to beam in daily, with shrubs planted around the house, a swing hangs on the front porch. There are other smaller cabins that surround the master-piece in the center, this palace is stunning. Even with the windows up I can smell the pine trees. I smile unable to stop the feeling of happiness radiating through me.

This feeling is everything I have always craved and dreamed of. Being here with my guys so madly in love and happy is everything. I couldn't ask for a better Christmas gift than this, everything I will ever need or want is in this car.

"You ready to face your mother?" Archer asks quietly.

"Forget Jane, Vox is going to lose his shit when he sees her," Hayze adds, making me cringe.

"If he has an issue with her coming to us first, he can fucking take that shit up with me," Ez bites out as he puts the car in park. I look out the window just in time to see the front door open to reveal Nova standing there in a hideous Christmas sweater. The sight of my best friend has tears of gratefulness surging inside me but the second the looming presence behind her steps onto the porch, my eyes widen and laughter catches in my throat at the sight of my twin standing there, looking like he hates life as he wears a bright green Grinch sweater.

"Oh shit, maybe we should hide her until later," Hayze mutters.

"Why?" I ask.

"He hasn't seen her yet, the tints on the windows are too dark," Archer mumbles.

"Huh?" I hedge.

"Fucking Nova is going to get us all killed," Ezekiel mutters bitterly.

"What's going on?" I snap.

"Your brother is clearly being forced to wear that fucking ugly thing by Nova, which means he is already in a bad mood." I roll my eyes at Hayze, and before they can stop me, I scoot away from Archer and push my door open, ignoring their protests as I run around the car and stand at the edge of the walkway facing my brother. Instantly his face blanks of emotion. Nova stumbles forward and grabs his arm for support as she peers down at me from the porch. I feel my guys slide up behind me and flank me on either side.

"What are you two doing out here—" My mom appears at Nova's side and clamps her mouth closed, unable to finish when she spots me. It takes her a split second before a sob claws its way out of her. Then she is racing down the stairs to me. I run to her and we both clash together, crying as we hold each other tight. "Oh my God, my baby," she cries.

"I'm here, Mom," I choke out through my tears as I hold her close, never wanting to let go.

"Vivian, I have missed you so much. I thought I lost you." Her sobs grow and I begin to worry about her, then her legs give out. Before she drops to the ground, a hulking form appears and wraps his arms around both of us holding us close and tight.

"I got you both, always." I pull one of my arms free from my mom and wrap it around my brother who buries his face in the top of my head. "I love you, Vi."

"I... love you... too," I cry as I grip him tight. Vox's breaths are coming in fast rapid pants as he tries to reign in his emotions. Mom pulls back, breaking our three way hug to grab my face. She stands there with tears trailing down her cheeks, looking at me. As if my twin can sense I need him he stands beside me and wraps an arm around my shoulders, anchoring me.

"Don't ever do that to me again, okay?" I nod.

"I won't," I promise.

"I thought I had lost my baby," she chokes out—guilt churns inside me.

"She's too annoying to die, Mom. I told you that." I scoff and elbow my brother in his ribs, which just earns me getting my hair ruffled by him.

"Let me go tell the other's, they are going to be so happy you're okay." I nod and watch as she rushes back inside. Vox shifts to stand in front of me. The mood instantly shifts from happy to ominous. My guys push forward to stand at my back, showing Vox that they will shut him down if he plans to go off on me.

"Thank you, Little Sister." I reel back and smack into Hayze.

"W-what?" I stutter.

Vox smiles. "You saved all of us. I guess it turns out I didn't need to protect you, you did that all on your own." My bottom lip trembles as warmth spreads through me.

"From the womb to the tomb, Brother," I whisper.

"Okay, I waited long enough, my turn." Nova shoves Vox aside and then she is wrapping me up in a bone crushing hug that robs me of air. "I missed you."

I melt into her. "I missed you too."

"We never gave up, Vivi. We searched for you."

"I know, thank you for trusting me," I say low enough for only her to hear.

"Always." We pull apart and smile at each other.

"We don't have to wear one of those as well, do we?" Hayze asks as he wraps an arm around my waist. My brother narrows his eyes but says nothing.

"Actually, yes. You all have one each. Don't fucking deny Jane, it made her so happy to see Vox wearing his." All the guys start laughing at my brother's expense. Vox shoots them all glares before storming back into the house. "He is such a Grinch."

My eyes widen. "You helped my mom choose his sweater, didn't you?" I ask.

Nova pushes her tongue into her cheek and shrugs. "I may have made a suggestion." The five of us all laugh at my poor twin's expense.

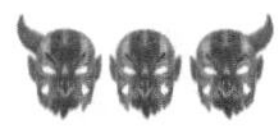

I CAN'T KEEP the smile off my face. Mom, Lilly, Olivia and Mary made all the boys wear their Christmas sweaters and they even made them take a group photo that Nova and I forced them to send us, and you best believe that photo of them grinning like they were in pain is our phones' wallpapers. Dawson's family has been nothing but welcoming and so nice. I was nervous to meet Leah, Alex, Katie and Val considering I hacked into their husband's computers but none of them held it against me. I was so shocked to see Katie with Crue and Saint, their marriage may not be legal but to them it is. Both guys are so in love with her and dote on the children. Henry and Shane have been grilling Corvin, Crue, Saint, Beckett and Darius about the teams they used to play for.

Everyone has been so happy and kind that it makes my heart swell inside my chest. "I wish my mom was here to see this," Nova says sadly from beside me. Pain blooms inside me.

I turn to face her. "I'm so sorry, Nova. I know Ez promised you Thomas's head on a silver platter but I wish I could take it all back—"

"It's not your fault, Vivian," she says as she slowly turns to me. I see nothing but understanding in her eyes. "My mom was fucking incredible and she loved you. She wouldn't have wanted you to blame yourself for what happened. I just miss her and Waylen so fucking much, ya know?"

I nod. "Actually, I do. I have an urn of my own now." I explain to her about what happened to David and being the freaking amazing person that she is she offers me her support and tells me she is here for me always.

"You answering questions?" Vox asks as he suddenly appears behind us on the porch, scaring the fucking shit out of us.

"Seriously? That isn't funny," Nova scolds, earning a dry stare from my brother.

"What questions do you have?" I ask.

"A lot," Archer says as he, Ez and Hayze join us on the porch. I nod and motion for them to follow me. We make our way around the wrap around porch. I claim the swing and Nova joins me, leaving the four guys to stand. I can hardly take any of them seriously wearing those fucking sweaters. They may be hard and ruthless but none of them are willing to insight their mother's wrath by taking them off. My mom was even considerate enough to buy one for Dawson, who unlike these four actually seems happy to wear his.

"Ask me whatever you want to know," I say.

"Why did you make a company in our name when we..." Ez lets his sentence trail off so I finish it for him.

"When we weren't even a thing?" He purses his lips and nods. "Honestly, I don't know. I think a part of me always wished what we are now would be a possibility, but I never wanted to hope. Plus, the name seemed to fit."

"How so?" Hayze pushes.

"The letter *A* was used as a scarlet letter to mark women who were viewed as promiscuous. I felt it fitting since I had planned to take over a male dominated society and rule them," I answer.

"Fuck yes, get it girl," Nova praises. The guys all snicker at her remark which has me scowling at them.

"Look, I know you guys are still salty about what I did and how I did it, but this was the only way I knew I could end them once and for all and give our families freedom. Your fathers will never have to answer another call from the Saints, our mother's will never have to bury another loved one. You guys can go to the school you want to and not the one they chose for you. I won't be forced to marry someone I don't love—"

"Damn fucking right," Ez adds, cutting me off. I shoot him a wink.

"Ezy A was my way of making sure they would never be able to rebuild and hurt anyone else."

"How did you do it?" Archer asks. I can hear the curiosity in his voice.

"Dawson's family dealt with a similar situation. I had a

meeting with them and they helped me. Because of them I was able to funnel the money from the Saints into an offshore account that can't be traced, then I funneled it back into Ezy A to fund the builds for the hotels like Lividica. Ezy A is also funding the build for the expansion of the high school and the build of the college in Hollow Hills. Because of Ezy A, we are able to offer kids an education. We didn't have a local college but we will. These hotels will give thousands of people jobs. A shitty start because of the Saints, but it will end with a happy ending because of Ezy A." I implore them to understand my reasoning.

"But you aren't even listed as an owner, why?" I look at my brother and smile.

"I knew the feds would come knocking on my door as the lordess and I couldn't have anything traced back to me and risk them shutting down everything I built. So I knew the only way to do what I did was to banish all of you."

"Because you banished them, the feds would never look to them for anything because they were never involved. I'll say it again, you are an evil genius." I preen and smile at Nova's compliment.

"Vivian, we can't accept this, you worked so hard for this, not us," Ezekiel argues.

I shrug my shoulders. "Too bad. I'll help you all from behind the scenes but I can never be the face of Ezy A."

"Why?" Archer pushes.

"Because the CIA is watching me. They can't prove I'm the one who stole the money and they won't stop hunting. I didn't just take a few hundred thousand," I admit.

"How much did you take?" Hayze asks skeptically.

"Three hundred million," I mumble. All of them begin sputtering and choking on their own spit.

"Are you fucking crazy!" Vox shouts.

"Don't fucking yell at her, asshole," Hayze warns, earning a glare from my brother.

"Wait, how much is Ezy A worth with all the hotel builds and everything now?" Nova asks.

"It's now a billion dollar company." All five of them stand there with their mouths open in stupor. I nibble on my bottom lip nervously, but the second my guys drop their eyes to my mouth, I see desire lurking in their gazes so I release it quickly. Getting horny in front of my brother is a sure fire way to get all three of them digging their own graves and I personally don't need another death on my hands.

"Who else knows what you did?"

I look to Ez as I answer his question. "David knew but he's obviously not here anymore which just leaves... Tate." I suddenly feel like a real piece of shit, I haven't thought about her until now.

"What happened to her?" Nova rasps out.

"Believe it or not, just before the guys arrived Nexus did." Every single one of them wear varying looks of shock, surprise and disbelief.

"Nexus? As in Nexus care for no one but himself Nexus?" Hayze blurts out.

I nod. "Yeah. He got Tate out before the lights came back on."

"Where is Thomas, Vi?" Ezekiel just asked the million dollar question that I have been waiting for.

"He and six others will spend the rest of their lives in a prison in Panama. Their existence will be wiped from records and the CIA will make it look like they never existed." Hatred laces my tone.

"He'll never get out, right?"

I turn to Nova and clasp her hand in mine, meeting her

gaze. "I promise you, where he is going is worse than hell. He will suffer every day for the rest of his miserable fucking life."

"Tate deserved a better father and brother," she mutters.

"Tate deserved more than what she got, that's for sure," I agree.

"Do you trust her?" Vox asks in an unyielding tone.

I debate his question for a minute before I nod. "Yeah, I do."

"You know if she is with Nexus, she'll be hunted by Alexander. He won't stop until Nexus pays for what he did to his sister." Nova's admission has my stomach cramping with worry for my friend.

"Alex won't hurt her," I say, hoping that I'm not grasping at straws and that Tate will be safe.

EPILOGUE

Vivian

Six months later…

It's summer break and the four of us are all heading back to Hollow Hills for the first time to check on the rebuild of the school and the college. It finished a couple of weeks ago but the guys had exams they couldn't miss, so we pushed our trip back. I'm starting at CHU in the fall and I can't fucking wait. I am so excited to go to college with my guys, Nova and my brother. Speaking of my brother, I hear the roar of his car pulling into our driveway.

"Vox is here!" I call out.

"Fuck him," Hayze shouts from outside the door, bringing a smile to my face. The three of them were supposed to be packing our bags in our car, but the second they heard me turn the shower on they all came running down the hallway. I slammed the bathroom and locked it or else we would be late.

"Just unlock the door, baby. We'll be fast, I swear," Archer pleads.

"You're a liar, you three wouldn't know what a quickie is if it kicked you in the dick."

"Vivian, do you want to spend the entire drive sucking our dicks as punishment?" Ezekiel claps back.

His threat doesn't have the effect he's hoping for, my mouth waters at the thought of tasting them all. My pussy pulses and I know that whoever is sitting in the backseat with me will give in and weaken to my pleas, ultimately ending in me getting the orgasm I now crave.

"Who wants to go first?" I call back. I laugh when I hear the three of them cursing, they act like we don't fuck every single day. They all race home after practice and refuse to take one car because they race each other on the way back. Apparently they have a deal, whoever wins the race gets me to themselves, then the others have to wait. I always act like it's annoying but in truth, I fucking love that they all still can't get enough of me.

"Are you fuckers ready?" I hear my brother yell.

"Yeah, we're coming, asshole," Archer snaps back, clearly annoyed he didn't get to fuck me.

"Hurry up, I want to beat the traffic," Vox volleys back.

"He said we're coming, dick!" Ez snaps. I wait till I hear their footsteps leaving the room before I unlock the door. Before I have a chance to open the fucking thing it swings open and Hayze is pushing his way inside.

"Oh my God, get out," I say. He just wags his brows and flicks the lock.

"Baby, shut the fuck up and bend over the counter. We have three minutes tops for me to make you come before they realize what we're doing."

I'm fucking weak!

I obey him like a puppet, my pussy is pulsing with need and who am I to deny her what she wants?

HAYZE and I got caught by Archer who is now refusing to speak to Hayze, even when we were speaking to the contractors at the school, he was being an asshole. When we were taken on a tour of the college, Archer dragged me into an empty classroom and fucked me on the desk. Jesus Christ it felt so naughty, but oh so right. The second we caught up with the others, Ez shot me a knowing look and I know without a doubt, I'm going to be getting fucked somewhere and soon from the lustful look in his eyes.

Turns out, to pay the other two back for leaving him out, my darling husband ravaged my greedy cunt in the backseat of the car while Archer drove us to our hotel. Yes, we are staying at Lividica. The entire elevator ride up to the penthouse, Vox has refused to look at any of us and won't say a word. I look at Nova in question. She just laughs and shakes her head.

"Why is Vox in a mood?" I ask when we all step out of the elevator and the guys carry our bags inside.

Nova beans at me and shakes her head. "Babe, when the car stopped at the lights we could see it rocking and it took me pulling your brother's dick out to stop him from smashing the windows of your car." My jaw slackens, Nova throws her head back and laughs. "You are going to drive him mad."

"Too late, he's already nuts," I mutter, making her laugh harder. We spend the next couple of hours relaxing and getting ready to visit Lividica. I haven't been back here in months and I'll admit I'm chomping at the bit to get downstairs and see the state it's in. Since Tate isn't running things, Andre has taken over. Don't get me wrong, he's great but Tate was just... perfection.

"Baby, you look fucking edible," Archer says as he enters the bathroom. His gaze rakes down my body, sending a shiver through me. I decided to go with an all-black silk dress with spaghetti straps. The front has a plunging neckline and stops just above my belly button, displaying the swell of my tits.

I take in the sight of him in the mirror and practically salivate at the sight of him in a suit. "You look fucking amazing."

Arch shoots me a wink then places a kiss on my cheek. "Just wait till you take it all off of me later." I groan, earning a chuckle from him. "Come on, sexy, we have to go." I let him lead me out and down the stairs. I smile at the sight of Ezekiel and Hayze on the sofas talking to Nova, who looks fucking stunning in a yellow strapless dress that hugs her body like a glove. The instant they sense my presence, both their heads snap up to me and their eyes darken.

"Fuck," Hayze breathes out.

"I vote we send Vox and Nova in our place and we stay here," Ez says, making me laugh.

"Eww, no," Nova admonishes and shoots her brother a grossed out look.

"Shut up, brat, as if I don't know what you and that dick do," Ez fires back.

"Yeah, I don't need that mental picture of my twin," I say, cutting off their bickering.

"Thank fuck you don't look like him or have the same body parts," Hayze tacks on.

"We have the same eyes, dick, so every time you look at her, it's like looking at me." All three of my guys groan and mumble curses at my brother's statement.

The six of us make our way downstairs and I hate to admit it, but I feel so nervous. I know it's stupid and that it's just a club, but this place was my baby and my first big venture in taking down the Saints. This place holds a special place in my heart. The guys have been trying to reassure me that everything is fine and I have nothing to worry about, but I won't relax until I see it for myself. The red doors are opened for us. Archer and Ez flank me while Hayze and Vox flank Nova. Vox tried to assert himself and tell me and Nova we weren't allowed to come here but we both squashed that shit.

My breath hitches as we walk through and I see everything has changed, it's now decked out in shades of purple and black which has an alluring effect. When I finally make it into the heart of the place, I gasp. Everything is fine, nothing is broken or messed up, the place has changed though. The tables are now black with matching chairs but they are those medieval looking chairs with the cushions on them. Men sit around the tables drinking and laughing, some of the girls are standing around them but the biggest shock is seeing the black jack table.

"We thought we would add some things that we know guys like," Ez whispers, then points out another table where they are playing Texas Hold 'em. I marvel at the sight—I'm rendered speechless.

"We would never let your baby fall, we know how much this place means to you," Archer says. Words fail me so all I can do is nod.

"Come with us," Hayze says. Vox tries to nix the plan but we all ignore him. Hayze leads us down the hallway toward the back, where the girls locker room is. I purse my lips not liking the idea of them going in there, but when he veers left and punches a code into the door, I start to think they have hired a room for us. I follow him inside only to come to a halt. It's not a room, it's an office. "We can't take credit for all of this though, baby."

I look up at him and frown. "Huh?"

"We had help," Archer says as he comes to stand beside Hayze.

"We knew you only trusted one person with this place," Ez adds as he joins the guys.

"I'm not following," I admit.

"Figures." I whirl around at the sound of her voice, my eyes are wide and my mouth is ajar. "Hello, Vivian."

"Tate," I breathe out.

She smiles and nods. "Surprised?"

I scoff. "Ya think? What are you doing here?"

She shrugs. "They offered me my job back and I took it under a few conditions." I peer over my shoulder at my guys, the three of them smile encouragingly and nod.

"What conditions?" I ask Tate.

"I can never stay in one place for more than two weeks. They can never ask me questions about my brother and if The Butcher ever asks about me, you tell him you don't know where I am." I gasp.

"Alex is hunting you?"

Her eyes darken and her fists clench at her sides. "Something like that. Now you know their secret and not that it wasn't good to see you and all but I have a lot of work to do before I fly out in the morning, so can you all get out of my office?" Laughter erupts from me. I dart forward and wrap my arms around her, shocking the shit out of her.

"Thank you, Tate." She softens and returns my embrace.

"Thank you for trusting me. I mean it, Vivian." I pull back and stare at her.

"I know. I just hope you have a great fake ID." I try to sound stern but fail.

"Yeah, your boys hooked me up so don't worry." The guys usher me out of there and we join Nova and Vox at one of the tables. The waiter brings us a round of drinks and before any of them can take a sip, I raise my glass.

"To new beginnings and living our lives on our terms," I say. All of them cheer and smile as they take a drink. I look around at each of them and my heart swells inside me. I fucking did it. I shutdown the Saints and still got my guys. I fucking won and no one will ever be able to take that away from me because miracles happen every once in a while and I got mine. My best friend is happy, my brother is safe and in love. My mom is happy living in Washington with the others. But me, I got the guys and I couldn't be more fucking grateful for how things turned out because nothing will bring me down from this high.

I don't need wings to help me fly because these guys will always make me soar just from loving me like they do.

This is my first solo why-choose and I hope I didn't disappoint you with this one. I just knew from the moment I started writing Vox and Nova's story that Vivi would have to have all three of them!

I hope you enjoyed Ezekiel, Hayze, Archer and Vivian's story as much as I did writing it.

Want to know more about Crue, Saint, Beckett, Corvin and Darius? They have their own series and it is complete now, check out the Playing For Keeps series on kindle.

Don't worry, Alexander 'The Butcher' Denver will be getting his own book, *Filthiest Of Them All*.

ACKNOWLEDGMENTS

Marky Beez, my love, it has been my greatest pleasure and honor to have you by my side as I trialed three peens at once. Thank you for being so understanding and knowing that I needed to do that for work purposes of course.

My children, my vagina destroyers. I love you both beyond words and would commit homicide for you both.

Leah, there are no words to describe how much I love you and how grateful I am for you and all that you do for me.

Jaye Pratt, thank you! There ya go, I said something nice. No, seriously though, thank you for helping me with this book.

Sarah, thank you for being the greatest PA I could have asked for and always allowing me to vent my annoyance when I'm writing, it means more than you know, my love. But, most importantly, thank you for being such an amazing friend.

Debbie, you drive me insane with how fast you read and catch me no matter how far in front I am! I love you boo. Thank you for always sticking with me.

Clare Bear, thank you for being on this crazy ride with me for as long as you have been. I always love your edits and feedback with each of these books. I love you so much xxx

Erin, babe, you are the missing piece to our foursome and I am so grateful that you decided to join us. You keep me on my toes as I write and I love you for it.

My beta babes, Taay, Amber, Amanda, Nicole, Samantha, Patti, Morgan & Rizzo, I fucking love you crazy ladies. Truly, you are the best fucking hype team and I love that you never spare my feelings in your edits. It's because of that why these books are what they are.

My ARC army girls, thank you beautiful souls so fucking much for always sticking by me and trusting me to mend those hearts that I break. You ladies have been with me since day one pretty much and I will always be so eternally grateful for each and every one of you!

Lizz, you are worth your weight in fucking gold, my friend. I truly can't thank you enough for all that you do for me and these books. They wouldn't be what they are without you!

My darling dark delicious readers, thank you again for following me and reading each of these books. I know I break your hearts and leave you mad when I end a book on a cliffy but I love that you trust me enough to heal those hearts and come back for more, I love you.

Sam xxx

ALSO BY SAMANTHA BARRETT

ALSO BY SAMANTHA BARRETT

Mafia Romance

Murdoch Mafia Series

Played By The Bishop

Tormented By The King

Tortured By The Knight

Tempted By The Queen

Turned By The Pawn

Ruined By The Rook

Murdoch Mafia Novella

Stalemate

Memento Mori Series

Reign Of Royal

Broken By Sin

In Havoc Lays Chaos

Godfathers of the night

London has Fallen

Damned By His Angel

Re Della Strada

Shattered Soul

Fractured Heart

Tainted Essence

A Beautiful Nightmare

Redemption

Anarchy

<u>Brutal Savages</u>

Savage Lies

Brutal Truth

Savage Beast

Brutal Beauty

ABOUT THE AUTHOR

Samantha Barrett is originally from Auckland, New Zealand but now lives in Brisbane, Australia.

Sam writes all things dirty dark and delicious with a side of twisted mind fuck.

She is a lover of all things red flags and an anti-hero is a must.